# HOME SWEET CHRISTMAS

# HOME SWEET
# CHRISTMAS

## SUSAN MALLERY

**WHEELER PUBLISHING**
A part of Gale, a Cengage Company

LIBRARY OF CONGRESS CIP DATA ON FILE.
CATALOGUING IN PUBLICATION FOR THIS BOOK
IS AVAILABLE FROM THE LIBRARY OF CONGRESS.

ISBN-13: 979-8-8857-8263-0 (hardcover alk. paper)

Published in 2022 by arrangement with Harlequin Enterprises ULC.

Printed in Mexico
Print Number : 1     Print Year : 2023

Tiffany — A thousand thanks
for suggesting the trees of Christmas
Past, Present and Future
for the town of Wishing Tree. They were
the perfect addition.
You're the best! This one is for you.

# ONE

"Your teeth are lovely, Camryn. Did you wear braces as a child?"

Camryn Neff reminded herself that not only was the woman sitting across from her a very wealthy potential client, but also that her mother had raised her to be polite to her elders. Still, it took serious effort to keep from falling out of her chair at the weirdness of the question.

"No. This is how they grew."

Hmm, that didn't sound right, although to be honest, she didn't have a lot of experience when a conversation turned dental.

She refocused her mind to the meeting at hand. Not that she knew for sure why Helen Crane, leader of Wishing Tree society, such as it was, and sole owner of the very impressive Crane hotel empire, wanted to meet with her. The summons had come in the form of a handwritten note, inviting her to the large, sprawling estate on Grey Wolf

7

Lake. Today at two.

So here Camryn was, wearing a business suit that had been hanging in her closet for over a year. The dress code for Wishing Tree retail and the dress code for the job in finance she'd left back in Chicago were very different. While it had been fun to dust off her gorgeous boots and a silk blouse, and discover her skirts still fit, she was ready to get to the point of the invitation.

"How can I help you, Mrs. Crane?" she asked.

"Helen, please."

Camryn smiled. "Helen. I'm happy to host a wrapping party, either here or at the store. Or if you'd prefer, I can simply collect all your holiday gifts and wrap them for you." She casually glanced around at the high ceilings of the sitting room. There was a massive fireplace, intricate molding and a view of the lake that, even with two feet of snow on the ground, was spectacular. And while there were lovely fall floral displays on several surfaces, there wasn't a hint of Christmas to be found. Not in Wishing Tree, the week before Thanksgiving. Those decorations didn't appear until the Friday after.

"I have some samples for custom wrapping paper," she said, pulling out several sheets of paper from her leather briefcase. "The designs can be adjusted and the colors coordinated with what you have planned for this holiday season. Wrapped presents under a tree are such an elegant touch."

"You're very thorough," Helen murmured. "Impressive." She made a note on a pad. "Are you married, dear?"

"What?" Camryn clutched the wrapping paper samples. "No."

Helen nodded. "Your mother passed away last year, didn't she?"

A fist wrapped around Camryn's heart. "Yes. In late October."

"I remember her. She was a lovely woman. You and your sisters must have been devastated."

That was one word for it, Camryn thought grimly, remembering how her life had been shattered by the loss. In the space of a few weeks, she'd gone from being a relatively carefree, engaged, happy junior executive in Chicago to the sole guardian for her twin sisters, all the while dealing with trying to keep Wrap Around the Clock, the family business, afloat. The first few months after her mother's death were still a blur. She barely remembered anything about the holidays last year, save an unrelenting sadness.

"This year the season will be so much happier," Helen said firmly. "Victoria and Lily are thriving at school. Of course they still miss their mother, but they're happy, healthy young adults." The older woman smiled. "I know the teen years can be trying but I confess I quite enjoyed them with Jake."

Camryn frowned slightly. "How do you know about the twins?" she asked.

Helen's smile never faded. "It's Wishing Tree, my dear. Everyone knows more than everyone else thinks. Now, you're probably wondering why I invited you over today."

"To discuss wrapping paper?" Although even as Camryn voiced the question, she knew instinctively that was not the real reason.

Helen Crane was close to sixty, with perfect posture and short, dark hair. Her gaze was direct, her clothes stylish. She looked as if she'd never wanted for anything and was very used to getting her way.

"Of course you'll take care of all my wrapping needs," Helen said easily. "And I do like your idea of custom paper for faux presents under the tree. I'll have my holiday decorator get in touch with you so you two can coordinate the design. But the real

10

reason I asked you here is to talk about Jake."

Camryn was having a little trouble keeping up. The order for wrapping and the custom paper was great news, but why would Helen want to discuss her son?

She knew who Jake was — everyone in town did. He was the handsome, successful heir to the Crane hotel fortune. He'd been the football captain in high school, had gone to Stanford. After learning the hotel business at the smaller Crane hotels, he was back in Wishing Tree, promoted to general manager of the largest, most luxurious of the properties.

They'd never run in the same circles back when they'd been kids, in part because she was a few years younger. She'd been a lowly freshman while he'd been a popular senior. Her only real connection with Jake was the fact that he'd once been engaged to her friend Reggie.

Helen sighed. "I've come to the conclusion that left to his own devices, Jake is never going to give me grandchildren. I lost my husband eighteen months ago, which has been very hard for me. It's time for my son to get on with finding someone, getting married and having the grandchildren I deserve."

Well, that put the whole "did you wear braces" conversational gambit in perspective, Camryn thought, not sure if she should laugh or just plain feel sorry for Jake. His mother was a powerful woman. Camryn sure wouldn't want to cross her.

"I'm not sure what that has to do with me," she admitted.

Helen tapped her pad of paper. "I've come up with a plan. I'm calling it Project: Jake's Bride. I'm going to find my son a wife and you're a potential candidate."

Camryn heard all the words. Taken individually, she knew what Helen was saying. But when put together, in that exact way, the meaning completely escaped her.

"I'm sorry, what?"

"You're pretty, you're smart. You've done well at Wrap Around the Clock. You're nurturing — look how you've cared for your baby sisters." Helen smiled again. "I confess I do like the idea of instant grandchildren, so that's a plus for you. There are other candidates, of course, but you're definitely near the top of the list. All I need is confirmation from your gynecologist that you're likely to be fertile and then we can get on with the business of you and Jake falling in love."

"You want to know if I'm fertile?"

Camryn shoved the samples back in her briefcase and stood. "Mrs. Crane, I don't know what century you think we're living in, but this isn't a conversation I'm going to have with you. My fertility is none of your business. Nor is my love life. If your plan is genuine, you need to rethink it. And while you're doing that, you might want to make an appointment with your own doctor, because there's absolutely something wrong with you."

Helen looked surprisingly unconcerned. "You're right, Camryn. I apologize. Mentioning fertility was going a bit too far. You're the first candidate I've spoken to, so I'm still finding my way through all this." She wrote on her pad. "I won't bring that up again. But as to the rest of it, seriously, what are your thoughts?"

Camryn sank back on her chair. "Don't do it. Meddling is one thing, but you're talking about an actual campaign to find your son a bride. No. Just no. It's likely to annoy him, and any woman who would participate in something like this isn't anyone you want in your family."

Helen nodded slowly. "An interesting point. It's just they make it look so easy on those reality shows."

"Nothing is real on those shows. The

relationships don't last. Jake's going to find someone. Give him time."

"I've given him two years. I'm not getting younger, you know." Her expression turned wistful. "And I do want grandchildren."

"Ask me on the right day and you can have the twins."

Helen laughed. "I wish that were true." Her humor faded. "Do you know my son?"

"Not really."

"We could start with a coffee date."

Camryn sighed. "Helen, seriously. This isn't going to work. Let him get his own girl."

"He's not. That's the problem. All right, I can see I'm not going to convince you to be a willing participant. I appreciate your time." She rose. "I meant what I said about the wrapping. I'll arrange to have all my gifts taken to your store. And my holiday decorator will be in touch about the custom paper."

"Is the holiday decorator different from the regular decorator?" Camryn asked before she could stop herself.

Helen chuckled. "Yes, she is. My regular decorator is temperamental and shudders at the thought of all that cheer and tradition. He came over close to Christmas a few years ago and nearly fainted when he saw the tree in the family room."

She leaned close and her voice dropped to a conspiratorial whisper. "It's devoted to all the ornaments Jake made for me when he was little. There are plaster handprints and little stars made out of Popsicle sticks. My favorite is a tuna can with a tiny baby Jesus in the manger tucked inside. There's bits of straw and a star." She pressed both hands to her heart. "I tear up thinking about it."

Baby Jesus in a tuna can? Helen was one strange woman.

Camryn collected her briefcase and followed Helen to the front door. Helen opened it, then looked at her.

"You're sure about not being a part of Project: Jake's Bride?"

"Yes. Very." Camryn kept her tone firm, so there would be no misunderstanding.

"A pity, but I respect your honesty."

Camryn walked to her SUV and put her briefcase in the backseat. Once she was behind the wheel, she glanced at the three-story house rising tall and proud against the snow and gray sky.

The rich really were different, she told herself as she circled the driveway and headed for the main road. Different in a cray-cray kind of way.

She turned left on North Ribbon Road.

When she reached Cypress Highway, she started to turn right — the shortest way back to town. At the last minute, she went straight. Even as she drove north, she told herself it wasn't her business. Maybe Jake knew about his mother's plans. Maybe he supported them.

Okay, not that, she thought, passing the outlet mall, then turning on Red Cedar Highway and heading up the mountain. She might not know Jake very well, but Reggie had dated him for months. Reggie was a sweetie who would never go out with a jerk. So Jake had to be a regular kind of guy, and regular guys didn't approve of their mothers finding them wives.

Besides, she doubted Jake needed any help in that department. He was tall, good-looking and really fit. She'd caught sight of him jogging past her store more than once and was willing to admit she'd stopped what she was doing to admire the view. He was also wealthy. Men like that didn't need help getting dates.

The sign for the resort came into view. She slowed for a second, then groaned as she drove up to the valet. Maybe she was making a mistake, but there was no way she couldn't tell Jake what had just happened. It felt too much like not mentioning toilet

16

paper stuck to someone's shoe.

If he already knew, then it would be a short conversation. If he didn't care, then she would quietly think less of him and leave. If he was as horrified as she thought he might be, then she'd done her good deed for the week and yay her. Whatever the outcome, she would have done the right thing, which meant she would be able to sleep that night. Some days that was as good as it was going to get.

Jake Crane stood at his office window, gazing out at the mountain. The air was still, the sky gray. About six inches of fresh powder had fallen overnight. His two o'clock meeting had been moved to next week and sunset wasn't for two and a half hours. There was no reason he couldn't grab his gear and get in an hour or so of snowboarding, then return to work later and finish up. One of the advantages of his position was the ability to adjust his hours, if he wanted. Except, he didn't want to go snowboarding.

Oh, he loved the sport, the rush of speed, the trick of staying balanced, testing himself on the mountain. He enjoyed the cold, the sounds, the sense of achievement as he mastered a difficult run. He was a typical

17

guy who enjoyed being outdoors. Just not by himself.

He had friends he could call. Dylan had the kind of job where he, too, could take off if he wanted and make up the time later, and Dylan was always up for snowboarding. Only that wasn't the kind of company he was looking for. He missed having a woman in his life.

He'd been avoiding that truth for a while now. Given his incredibly disastrous track record, he'd sworn off getting involved. As he saw it, the only way to keep from screwing up in the romance department was to not get romantically entangled. An easy, sensible solution. What he hadn't counted on was being . . . lonely.

Sex was easy. He could head to Seattle or Portland, meet someone, have a great weekend with her, then head home. No commitment, no risks of breaking her heart, no getting it wrong. Except he'd discovered he didn't enjoy those kinds of relationships. He wanted more. He wanted to get to know someone and have her get to know him. He wanted shared experiences, laughter and, worst of all, commitment. He wanted what other people made look easy.

But if he got involved, he would completely mess up. Or he could turn into his

18

father, and he refused to do that. So he did nothing. A solution that was no longer working for him, which left him where he'd started. Staring at the mountain with no idea what to do with his personal life.

The phone on his desk buzzed.

"Jake, there's a Camryn Neff here to see you. She doesn't have an appointment, but says it's about something personal."

Camryn Neff? The business community in Wishing Tree was small enough that he knew who she was. She owned Wrap Around the Clock — a store that sold wrapping paper, and wrapped and shipped gifts for people. The hotel referred guests to her when they wanted items they'd bought sent to friends and family or simply shipped home.

He knew her well enough to say hello at a business council meeting, but little else. He thought she might have younger sisters.

He pushed a button on his phone. "I'll be right there."

He crossed the length of his large office and stepped out into the foyer of the executive offices. Camryn, an attractive redhead with a cloud of curls and big, brown eyes, stood by Margie's desk.

Wishing Tree was a casual kind of place, so he was surprised to see her wearing an

19

expensive-looking suit and leather boots with three-inch heels. Her posture was stiff, her expression bordered on defensive. Camryn hadn't stopped by to sell him wrapping paper, he thought, wondering what was wrong and how he'd gotten involved.

"Hello, Camryn," he said easily.

"Jake." She seemed to force herself to smile. "Thanks for seeing me on such short notice. I wasn't sure I should come, but then I couldn't not talk to you and . . ." She pressed her lips together. "Can we go into your office?"

"Of course." He motioned to show her the way, then followed her inside. He pointed to the corner seating area, where the couch and chairs offered a more informal setting.

"Can I get you something to drink?" he asked. "Coffee? Water? Bourbon?"

At the last one, she managed a sincere smile. "I wish, but it's a little early in the day for me. Plus, I'm not a bourbon kind of woman. Brown liquor isn't my thing."

"We have a nice selection of vodkas in the main bar."

Camryn chuckled and relaxed a little in her chair. "Tempting, but no."

Jake had taken a seat on the sofa. He leaned toward her and asked, "How can I help you today?"

Her body instantly tensed and the smile faded. She crossed and uncrossed her legs. "Yes, well, I wanted to tell you something. It's not my business, really." She paused and met his gaze. "It would have been if I'd said yes, but I didn't. I want to be clear about that."

"Please don't take this the wrong way, but so far you haven't been clear about anything." He smiled. "Except not liking brown liquor."

"I know. I'm sorry. I'm trying to find the words. I should just say it. Blurt it out."

He considered himself a relatively easygoing guy who could handle any crisis, but she was starting to make him uncomfortable. What could she possibly want to tell him? Not that she was pregnant — they'd never been on a date, let alone slept together. He doubted she needed money. The store was successful and if she did need a loan, why would she come to him? While they knew a lot of the same people, they didn't hang out together, so an issue with a mutual friend seemed unlikely.

"I saw your mother today."

Jake held in a groan. Those five words always meant trouble and mostly for him.

Camryn met his gaze, her brown eyes

21

filled with sympathy and concern. "She invited me to the house. I didn't know why but hoped it was to buy custom wrapping paper. We can design nearly anything and have it printed. In fact, I have some ideas for custom paper for the resort. I've been playing with the logo and there are —"

"Camryn?"

She blinked. "Yes?"

"My mother."

"Oh, right. That." She swallowed and looked at him. "She wants to find you a wife. She had a plan. It's called Project: Jake's Bride. She's interviewing women as potential candidates. Apparently, she's done waiting for you to find someone on your own."

He stood, then wasn't sure what to do. Pace? Run? Shout? His mother had always been a meddler, but this was bad, even for her. Project: Jake's Bride? Seriously? *Seriously?*

"She wants grandchildren," Camryn added helpfully.

He sank back on the sofa and resisted the urge to rest his head in his hands. "She's losing her mind."

"I don't think so. She's very lucid and completely in control. I wasn't sure if you knew."

22

He stared at her. "I didn't know."

"Yeah, I can tell by the look on your face."

"Horror and murderous rage?"

She smiled. "You're not mad. Resigned, maybe. You love your mom, so you can't hate her. But I get this isn't ideal."

Jake collapsed back against the sofa. "The woman is trying to find me a wife, Camryn. I think *not ideal* undersells the moment."

He swore silently as he realized he had no idea what he was going to do about the problem. Telling his mother to back off was the equivalent of looking at the sky and discussing the weather. The exchange was frequently unsatisfying and ultimately futile.

"I'm shipping her off to Bali. She enjoys tropical weather. I'll buy her a nice condo, supply a staff. She can take up painting. Like that painter." He paused. "What's his name? Oh, Paul Gauguin. But that was Tahiti, not Bali. Which is fine. They're both beautiful this time of year."

"What makes you think she'd agree to go?" Camryn asked. "Your mother seems highly invested in your personal life."

"I'll trick her. I could do that." He would tell her he was eloping and wanted her there for the wedding. Then he would lock her in the newly bought condo and —

He looked at Camryn. "Why did she tell

23

you all this?"

She ducked her head, but not before he saw color flare on her cheeks. "She, ah, thought I would be a good candidate."

Jake hadn't realized the situation could get worse, which he should have. When it came to Helen Crane, that was always a possibility.

"My mother invited you to her house to discuss the possibility of us marrying?"

Camryn nodded slowly. "Although she did say she thought we should start dating first. Get to know each other."

"You're defending her?"

"No, it's just she was impressive, and talking about it like this makes her sound . . ."

"Outrageous? Impossible?"

"A little. I understand why you're upset. She actually wanted me to provide proof of fertility, which is what set me off."

Proof of — He stood again, only to realize there still wasn't anywhere to go.

"I'm sorry about all of this," he said stiffly. "That she butted into your life and dragged you into one of her crazy schemes. I'll make this go away."

Somehow. There had to be a way to get her to stop what she was doing.

Camryn rose. "There are other candidates. I don't know who they are, but she men-

24

tioned them. Some might have kids. She said my younger sisters were a plus. She called them instant grandchildren."

He held in a groan. Other candidates? Unsuspecting women who were going to be approached by his mother?

She looked at him. "She's lonely, Jake. She lost her husband less than two years ago and she's by herself in that huge house. I know she has friends and a life, but it's not like having a husband around. Wanting grandchildren is pretty common at her stage of life." She held up a hand. "Still not defending her. It's just, I get what she's doing and when you think about it, she's really very sweet."

"Then we'll let her find you a husband. See how sweet she seems then."

Camryn laughed. "Point taken. Anyway, I wanted you to know."

"I appreciate you coming here and warning me. I owe you."

Her eyes brightened. "Really? Because I could bring some custom wrapping paper samples by for you. They'd look lovely under the dozens of trees I know you'll be putting up."

"Sure. Make an appointment with Margie and bring them by. We support local whenever we can."

"Then I'll see you again, soon. Samples in hand."

"I look forward to it."

He escorted her out of his office. Once she'd left, he turned off his computer, grabbed his coat and then headed for the door. He paused by his assistant's desk. "I'm going to be gone a couple of hours. Text me if there's an emergency. Otherwise, I'll be back around four."

Margie, a forty-something brunette with three teenaged sons and a husband who adored her, frowned. "You okay, boss? You look, I don't know, stressed maybe."

"I'm fine," he lied. "I'm going to stop by and see my mother, then I'll be back."

Margie sighed. "I hope when my boys are grown, they're as good to me as you are to her."

Jake only nodded, because he couldn't say what he was thinking. That the whole Bali/Tahiti plan made the most sense, but if she wouldn't agree, he was going to hire some kind of keeper. And take all her electronics away. And possibly her car. He understood she was missing his father and he wanted to be there for her, but there was no way in hell he was letting her move forward with Project: Jake's Bride. Not now. Not ever. No. Just no.

# TWO

Jake let himself into the house where he'd grown up. After tossing his coat across the entry table, he walked through the large, two-story foyer and down the hall. This time of day he knew his mother could be found in her sitting room. Unless she was interviewing yet another potential bride, he thought grimly. His only hope was that one candidate per day was her limit.

The journey was a familiar one. When he'd gotten home from school, he'd always made his way here. The same when he'd returned from college. The large room with big windows and a view of the lake was where he'd talked about his day, lamented his schoolboy problems and been told everything would be fine. His father's office was where discipline was meted out, but his mother's sitting room was only about the love.

He paused in the open doorway. His

27

mother was on the phone, taking notes as she listened.

"Yes, that sounds like an excellent suggestion for the menu. Perfect. Everyone will enjoy the meal."

He studied her, pleased to find her looking as she always did. Capable, intelligent and still beautiful, even at sixty. He knew one day he would walk into this room and realize his mother had gotten old but thankfully, this wasn't that day.

She looked up and saw him. Her instant smile welcomed, as always. She motioned him inside, then finished her call and rose, her arms open wide.

"This is a surprise," she said, sounding delighted. "Was I expecting you?"

"You weren't."

He hugged her, then kissed her cheek. Together they moved to the comfortable sofa in front of the window and took their usual places.

"Shouldn't you be at work?" she asked, her voice teasing. "You are still running the hotel."

"I'll go back to the office after we talk."

"All right. What are we talking about?"

He looked at her. "Really, Mom? You have to ask?" He shook his head. "Project: Jake's Bride? What were you thinking?"

28

Instead of looking chagrined, his mother beamed with delight. "She told you. I wondered if she would." She pressed her hands together. "This speaks very well of her character and moves her to the top of the list!"

"No," he said, thinking Tahiti might not be far enough away. "Mom, stop. You can't do this. You can't find me a bride."

"I don't know why not. One of us has to and you're not dating. You've been back in town a year and as far as I can tell, you haven't been out with anyone. In fact, I don't think you've had a girlfriend since you and Reggie broke up."

She was right — he hadn't. There were the weekends in Portland and Seattle, but he wasn't going to discuss those with his mother. Plus, they weren't about dating as she understood the term. They were for sex and nothing else.

"You never should have let Reggie go," she said firmly. "You should have tried to win her back."

"There wasn't any winning. Besides, she and I got over each other way too quickly for us to have been as in love as we thought. She's happily married and I wish her only the best."

"If she wasn't your one true love, why

29

aren't you dating? I need grandchildren, Jake. I don't just want them, I need them in my life."

"Then adopt some."

Her gaze turned steely. "Trust me when I say this isn't a subject I find funny."

"You don't scare me. Besides, you're the one messing in my life. Stop it right now. No more interviewing women. Who does that?"

"I'm being proactive."

"This is bad, even for you," he told her. "You've always been a meddler, but never like this. Stop it right now. I'm not kidding. Don't mess in my life."

She sighed. "I can't help it. I love you." Her expression softened. "I want you to be happy. A good marriage is wonderful."

So she'd been telling him, all his life. Only he'd discovered that her marriage to his father hadn't been as perfect as she'd claimed. A shock that had stayed with him. The fault hadn't been hers. Instead, his father had been to blame.

"You're wrong," she told him. "I know what you're thinking. He was a good man and I loved him with all my heart. He made me happy."

"Except for the cheating."

His mother turned away. "I prefer not to

think about that. No one is perfect."

"There's a difference between a personality quirk and running around on you, Mom. Maybe what he did is okay with you but it's not okay with me."

Her gaze turned knowing. "But that isn't the problem, is it?"

She knew him too well — she always had. He would guess it was a mom thing. Yes, he was angry that his father had turned out to be less than he had always assumed, but the bigger issue was his not wanting to be like his old man. He'd never cheated, but he'd sure messed up a bunch. It was the main reason his mother didn't have the grandchildren she wanted so desperately.

He rose and kissed her cheek again. "I love you. Stay out of my life."

His mother smiled. "We both know that will never happen. Now, about Camryn. Didn't you think she was pretty?"

"Not listening," he said as he walked to the door. "Not hearing a word you're saying."

Camryn's very strange day calmed down after her trip to the resort. Jake's outrage made her feel a whole lot better about the Project: Jake's Bride situation. Okay, not better for him, but happier that he hadn't

31

known. She had no idea how he was going to stop his very determined mother but that was on him, not her. The bright spot of meeting his mother and talking to him was the promise of holiday wrapping orders and the possibility that the resort would order custom paper from her. If she could get them to stock it in their gift shop, that would be amazing.

A little before five in the afternoon, Camryn had finished ordering what she needed for the following week. She waved at Wendy, who would close up at seven, and headed to her SUV.

The gray skies had cleared and stars twinkled overhead. This time of year, sunset was around four-thirty. The temperature was in the low twenties. Camryn breathed in the chilly air, enjoying the faint scent of wood smoke from a family's fireplace.

Once behind the wheel, she started the engine, then gave her vehicle a few seconds to warm up. The drive home would take less than ten minutes. Nothing was very far in Wishing Tree. Her move to Chicago, after college, had been a shock to her system. Not only the millions of people, but also how far things could be. She'd had friends who commuted an hour a day.

That didn't happen here, she thought as

she backed out of her space and drove onto the street. There also weren't traffic jams or crowded streets or crime waves. Wishing Tree was the kind of place where neighbors knew each other and tourists provided plenty of revenue, especially this time of year.

While she'd enjoyed growing up here, she hadn't planned on coming back. She'd loved her life in Chicago — her friends, her work, her gorgeous condo. But her mother's illness and subsequent death had changed everything. Camryn had returned to raise her sisters. Lily and Victoria were fifteen — sophomores in high school. They were finally happy again, back to their regular selves after a year of trying to accept the horrific loss of their mom.

Camryn knew she was healing, as well. The pain wasn't as sharp, the missing not as devastating. She would always regret not having her mother around, but now she could think of her without the breath-stealing sorrow.

She pulled into the familiar driveway and pushed the button to open the garage door. While she waited, she glanced to her left and grinned when she saw the neighbor boys had built a huge snow fort on the front lawn. The massive structure leaned a little to one side, but there were walls and a few colorful flags fluttering in the night.

She walked in through the mudroom and into the kitchen. From upstairs came the sound of "Silent Night" played by a flute, and from the family room she heard laughter and conversation. The house was warm, the lights all on. Dishes from the twins' after-school snack were stacked in the sink.

Normal, Camryn thought happily. And normal was the best.

"I'm home," she called, walking into the family room.

Victoria lay on the floor, her feet up on the sofa. She saw Camryn, smiled and sat up.

"She's home. I gotta go. Uh-huh. See you in homeroom."

She dropped her cell phone on the carpet and stood, then hurried to hug her sister.

"Angie thinks Braydon smiled at her, but we all know he didn't, so there's that. And Lily's been playing 'Silent Night' for like two hours. Can you please make her stop?"

Camryn grinned. "I'm fine. Thanks for asking. How was your day?"

Victoria laughed. "Sorry. Hi. I'm glad you're home. Can you please make Lily stop playing that song?"

Lily ran into the room. "I have a solo at

the holiday concert. I have to practice. This isn't news."

"I know but it's starting to get to me."

Lily stuck out her tongue, then hugged Camryn. "She's just jealous of my fame."

"Fame?" Victoria asked with a snort. "You're in a high school concert. It's not like you're on TV or anything."

Camryn put her arms around the twins. "Victoria, is this where I remind you what you were like at the art exhibition last spring? You got a little out of control when you won the watercolor prize. We all get a turn to shine."

"Oh, I don't care if she shines. I care if she plays 'Silent Night' forty-seven bazillion times a day."

But the words were said with a smile.

The three of them walked into the kitchen. Lily, barely five-three with long, straight, flame-red hair, went to the sink and started loading the dishwasher. Victoria, five-seven with auburn curls like Camryn's, opened the refrigerator to take out ingredients for dinner.

"Did you tell her about Angie and Braydon?" Lily asked. "As if."

"I know, right?" Victoria set down a large sealed plastic bag of vegetables. "He would never go for her."

35

"Why is everyone so obsessed with Braydon?" Camryn asked as she washed her hands.

"Because he's the guy." Lily looked at her pityingly. "Didn't you have a guy when you were in high school? Someone everybody had a crush on? You know, handsome and older." She sighed. "I love him so much."

"You love who you think he is," Victoria pointed out. "Same as me. We don't actually *know* him."

Camryn emptied the bag of vegetables onto a baking sheet. Before leaving for work, she'd cut them up and seasoned them with olive oil, salt and pepper so they'd be ready for roasting when she got home from work. She'd also assembled the chicken and tortellini bake so it was ready to pop into the oven.

The first few months after their mom's passing, the three of them had lived on casseroles brought by friends and neighbors, and takeout. But Camryn had quickly realized she was going to have to figure out a way to run Wrap Around the Clock, take care of her sisters and put dinner on the table every night. She'd made a list of dishes she and her sisters all liked then had gone online to find easy recipes.

"So was there?" Victoria asked her. "A guy

36

like Braydon?"

Camryn laughed. "I'm sure every class has a Braydon. Ours was Jake Crane. And yes, he was older than me." He'd been very swoon-worthy back in high school. Come to think of it, he'd been a little swoon-worthy today.

"Why do I know that name?" Lily asked.

"His family owns the big resort."

"So he's rich." Victoria looked thoughtful. "Braydon isn't rich, so does that mean we're more evolved than you were?"

"Would you love Braydon less if he were rich?"

Lily and Victoria looked at each other and grinned.

"No," Victoria admitted. "I'd love him more."

Camryn grinned. "Then you are no more evolved, my sweet. I'm sorry to disappoint you."

"I can live with being shallow," Victoria told her. "I'm only fifteen. I'll get more emotionally deep as I mature."

"You're never going to be mature," Lily told her. "I'm the mature one."

"Are not."

"Am, too."

Camryn listened to their good-natured teasing, pleased they were loud, demanding

37

and occasionally self-centered. In a word —
teenagers. This time last year they'd been
too quiet, but they were in a better place
now, she thought. All three of them. The
holiday season was starting and she was
determined this one would be full of laughter and happiness. They would make good
memories, she vowed. After what they'd
been through, they needed that.

"This is a mistake," Dylan Tucker said casually as he tapped on the folder in front of
him.

Helen smiled at him from across the
kitchen island. "Isn't the word *mistake* a
little strong?"

"How about disaster? Is that better?"

Helen laughed, then reached over to pat
his hand. "You're looking out for me. I appreciate that, but I know what I'm doing."

"Want to bet on that?"

Helen had been in his life since the first
day of first grade, when he and her son Jake
had met and become best friends. She'd
always looked out for him, had been a sur-
rogate mother when his own had been
unavailable, or indifferent. She was the
person he most looked to for advice and
sometimes, annoyingly enough, she was the
voice in his head.

But she was also a meddler who believed she knew best, and sometimes that quirk of character was a pain in the butt for everyone around her. An example of that was the folder in front of him. Inside was a detailed plan, complete with lists, names and strategies.

"Project: Jake's Bride?" he asked, his tone dry. "Is that really how you want to get your only son married?"

"Someone has to take charge. Jake certainly isn't doing anything about his single state. I'll tell you what I told him yesterday — I've waited patiently for him to find the right woman and settle down, but he's been back in town a year and he hasn't even been on a date."

She paused expectantly, as if waiting for Dylan to fill in the missing information. Not going there, he thought humorously. He and Jake never tattled on each other.

"So you're going to find him a wife?" Dylan asked. "What makes you think he'd cooperate?"

"He loves me," Helen said firmly. "I'm his mother. He really doesn't have a choice. He's not happy right now, but he'll come around." The smile returned. "I've actually become very good at guilting both of you. It's a gift."

"You're sly."

"I can be, yes." She picked up her cup of coffee. "Did you decide on your charity project for the season?"

"Books," he said. "I'm going to give every child in Wishing Tree a book."

"That's wonderful. What a perfect idea. You'll want to order them from Yule Read Books in town, of course. Oh, I know. You can hire Camryn from Wrap Around the Clock to wrap them for you. I met her yesterday and she's a lovely young woman."

There was something in Helen's tone. A knowing or a certainty.

"How did you meet her?"

"I had her stop by so we could chat."

His gaze fell on the folder. "Is she a candidate?"

"I think she might be."

He didn't know if he should be impressed or run for cover. Either way, he was going to have a long talk with Jake, later. There was nothing his friend could do to stop his mother, but better for Jake to know what was happening so he could . . . Well . . . Honest to God, Dylan had no idea how Jake was going to protect himself from the force of nature that was Helen.

"Did you tell her about Project: Jake's Bride?"

40

Helen's blue eyes widened. "Of course. I wouldn't lie."

"That would have been an interesting conversation to listen to. How did she take the news?"

"I'm not sure she believed me."

Dylan thought that Camryn should enjoy her ignorance while it lasted because Helen rarely rested until she got what she wanted. Not that he knew Camryn well enough to warn her. He knew her to say hello, but they'd never run in the same circles. She was a few years younger and if he remembered correctly, had moved away for a few years, after college.

"I assume you have other candidates," he said.

"Several. Some local, some from out of town. I'll be hiring a computer expert to do deep background investigations on all of them. It's all very high tech."

Dylan did his best to hide his smile. "You go, girl."

"I will." Her gaze turned speculative. "Are you seeing anyone?"

"No way. We're not talking about my personal life. You have your hands full with manipulating Jake into marrying the woman of your dreams. Leave me out of it."

"Don't you want to find someone special

41

and settle down?"

She knew he did. Willingness was not the problem. It was finding a woman he could fall for that seemed to be getting in the way.

"Helen, I love you dearly, so I say this with great affection. Stay out of my personal life."

"But not Jake's."

"You should stay out of his, too, but he's your kid, so you have more power there."

She picked up the glass-and-silver carafe of coffee and refilled each of their cups. "I was excited to hear the town is reviving the tradition of Snow King and Snow Queen this year."

"Are they? It's been a while." He vaguely recalled there being a Snow King and Queen when he'd been growing up. They showed up at events around town and did things.

"Five years. The rules have changed, thank goodness. Having just anyone throw their name in the hat, so to speak, wasn't working at all. That last year the Snow King was a six-year-old boy and the Snow Queen was Mrs. Percy." Helen sighed. "She was eighty-seven."

"I'm sure she was a lovely Snow Queen."

Helen shook her head. "It was an impossible situation. She fell at the Holiday Ball and we were all terrified she'd broken a hip.

Thankfully, she was fine."

"I don't remember any of this."

"You've never been political, darling."

He chuckled. "The Snow King and Queen are political?"

"Of course not. I was being funny. You were in your early twenties. What did you care about town traditions? My point is, they've updated the rules. Now those who enter must be single and between the ages of twenty-one and thirty-five. I'm quite looking forward to seeing how it all unfolds. They'll be together at the start of the Advent Calendar. By the way, this year the big town event is a scavenger hunt."

"How do you know that?"

"I have my ways."

"You are terrifying."

Helen preened. "Yes, I know. Isn't it lovely? Oh, and the Snow King and Queen will be judging Cookie Tuesdays. It's three Tuesdays this year. Would you like me to tell you the cookie categories?"

Was it just him or was she looking at him the way a spring robin looked at a juicy worm? "Helen, what's going on? Are you arranging for Jake to be the Snow King?"

"Why would I do that?" She motioned to the folder. "I already have a plan for him. I did make a sizeable donation to the town

43

building fund. They were very grateful."

A prickling sensation trickled down the back of his neck. No, he told himself firmly. Helen loved him. She would never . . .

"It's you, Dylan," Helen told him sweetly. "I've arranged for you to be the next Snow King. Technically, there's a drawing on Saturday, so I would appreciate you acting surprised."

"What?" He stood. "No. Absolutely not. Helen, I'm not going to do it."

Her smile never wavered. "Did I mention there's a crown? You're going to look so handsome."

# THREE

River Best had picked a bad day to give up diet soda. She missed the fizz, the faint chemical aftertaste, the clink of the ice in a glass. She'd been up for over twenty-four hours, she had a headache and she really, really wanted to pop the top of a chilled can of diet anything. Just to get her through.

"Focus," she told herself, typing furiously and ignoring the steady throbbing in her back. The scumbag piece of dirt she'd been tracking for the past fourteen hours had to have left a clue somewhere. She'd accessed his computer remotely and had gone digging. She'd broken into his bank accounts, his email and traced his very gross browsing history. She'd learned a lot about the piece of human lint, but she hadn't yet found him.

She spun in her chair and studied the giant map of the United States pinned to the wall. Next to it was her dry-erase board, covered with handwritten notes. Devon

Greene, age five, had been taken by her uncle. Ian Greene, a loan shark with suspected mob connections and a couple of murder charges he'd managed to beat, had kidnapped his niece to convince his brother not to testify against him. The pair had been missing twenty-six hours. Twelve hours in, the authorities had run out of leads and contacted her to work some computer magic.

River stood, then groaned as her back locked up. She breathed through the pain before limping over to the map and tracing the pushpins she'd used to mark all the places Ian had visited — at least according to the past five years of credit card records. He operated out of Chicago, for the most part. He visited Las Vegas regularly, had gone to Florida twice. He was a city kind of guy who flew rather than drove to his destinations.

So why were there two gas station charges in Sioux Falls, South Dakota, two weeks apart?

She traced a line from Chicago to Sioux Falls. Interstate 90 was the most obvious route, but to where? The highway ended in Seattle, but Ian had never gone there. He really wasn't a Montana kind of guy and Idaho was —

River hurried back to her computer and scanned the credit card receipts again. She'd seen something, back about four years, something that hadn't been like all the rest. An entrance pass to Yellowstone National Park.

A quick internet search told her that most of the park's roads closed in early November. Today was the sixteenth but *closed* didn't mean *impassable.*

She grabbed her cell phone and dialed.

"Tell me you have something," Sergeant Griffin said, his voice thick with tension. "Anything."

"Yellowstone National Park. He went there four years ago."

"Greene? He doesn't do nature."

"Credit card records don't lie. He got gas in Sioux Falls right around the time he went to the park."

"That's thousands of square acres to cover."

And they were short on time, she thought grimly. "You said he's not a nature guy, so he's not going to camp. Not with a kid. So look for a cabin with smoke coming out of the chimney. You need a drone with thermal imaging."

"Keep looking for another location," Griffin said. "I'll be in touch."

47

The call ended before she could respond.

River returned her attention to the screen. Greene didn't have a social media presence, but there were other ways to leave a digital trace and she was going to find every one of them.

Six hours later her phone rang.

"We got her," Griffin said. "Cabin in Yellowstone. Just like you said."

River sagged back in her chair. "She's okay?"

"Hungry, wants her mom and dad, but yeah, she's good. We owe you."

Relief settled on her like a blanket. "I'll send a bill."

Griffin chuckled. "I have no doubt. The team says thanks."

"Tell the team they're welcome."

She hung up and dropped her phone onto her desk. Exhaustion descended and with it came awareness of the agony from sitting for twenty-plus hours. She turned off her computer, then slowly stood.

Her back was a mess. Dr. Chi, her orthopedic surgeon, would be furious if he knew how long she'd been sitting without stretching. He would point out he hadn't done three surgeries just to have her squander his hard work, then he would want to know if she was all right.

"Not this second," she whispered as fiery pain ripped through her.

She hobbled over to the wall and leaned against it, slowing her breathing. After several minutes her muscles began to un-lock, easing some of the pain. She began the familiar stretching routine she'd ne-glected for the past two days, moving slowly, being careful as she changed positions. After about twenty minutes she was able to stand fully upright and nearly square her shoul-ders without having to clench her teeth against the discomfort. She would stretch again when she got home, then take a hot bath. It would take a few days for her muscles to settle down, but finding Devon was worth it.

Telling herself the victory should be celebrated, she walked over to the small beverage refrigerator in the corner and pulled out a can of diet cola. She opened it and took a long, slow drink. The cool fizz of familiar, happy flavor filled her mouth.

"You're going to kill me, but I'll die happy," she said aloud before setting down the can to collect the takeout containers she'd accumulated over the past two days.

She'd ordered taco salad from Navidad Mexican Café. She'd left the lettuce, but had devoured everything else, including all the chips and salsa. There were a few wrappers from Judy's Hand Pies. They didn't, as a rule, deliver, but Shaye was a friend and had dropped off a half dozen pies on her way home from work. There were coffee containers from Jingle Coffee and three empty water bottles. A person accumulated a serious amount of trash doing her job.

River separated the recycling from the regular garbage and put them in their respective bins. She unlocked her small attic office and stepped onto the landing before heading down the stairs to empty the bins.

The shock of entering the real world hit her. First of all, sunlight poured in through large windows. Sure, her head knew it was the middle of the day but her sleep-deprived body had assumed it was still nighttime. Second, the store — Wrap Around the Clock — was crowded with customers buying wrapping paper in anticipation of the upcoming holidays. The happy chatter, the bursts of laughter, the general bustle, made her want to duck back into the quiet and safety of her workspace.

Trash and recycling, she told herself. After that she would get her things and head home for her bath, before sleeping for fifteen or twenty hours. Then she would be ready to reenter the normal world.

She stepped out back and was hit by a blast of cold air. Despite the bright blue skies, the temperature was well below freezing, as all the snow on the ground attested.

"So unnatural," River murmured. She'd grown up in a suburb of Los Angeles and had moved to Wishing Tree about six months ago. Seasons were still confusing and she'd yet to emotionally accept the reality of snow. It was pretty enough but the cold was a constant shock.

River scurried back into the store only to be confronted by Camryn — owner of Wrap Around the Clock, and River's friend and office landlord.

"Have you been up for two days?" Camryn demanded, her hands on her hips.

"I've been working."

"For two days?"

River thought about the frightened five-year-old, taken by someone she thought she could trust.

"I had a rush job."

Her friend's brown eyes darkened with emotion. "Am I going to hear about what you did on the news?"

"Possibly but they won't use my name."

"I worry about you. Did you get any sleep at all?"

"Not since getting the job. I'm going home now."

"Still up for lunch tomorrow?"

River fought through her exhaustion to process the question. She and Camryn, along with a few other women in town, were getting together for lunch on Thursday. She'd been in her office since early Tuesday morning, making this Wednesday afternoon.

"Of course, I'll be there."

"If you're too tired . . ." Camryn began.

River cut her off with a quick shake of her head. "I want to be there," she said quickly.

Lunch with her friends was one of the highlights of her week. She might still be wrestling with the concept of snow, but she was all in when it came to her new friends. After being an outsider for most of her life, she was thrilled to be part of a group. Sure, she needed sleep, but she needed her friends just as much.

"Then we'll see you at Blitzen's Pub at noon." Her smile widened. "We'll have a great time and catch up on all the gossip."

"I know we will," River said cheerfully before waving and heading for the stairs.

She took them slowly, her body protesting the effort. But her office space was worth it. Not only was she the only one on the floor, she could also come and go as she pleased.

Being close to all the store's activity without having to actually be a part of it was an added bonus. She could engage on her own terms and retreat when things got to be too much for her.

She walked into her office and began the process of layering for her walk home. Sweater, coat, scarf, hat. She waited to slip on the gloves until after she'd slung her backpack over her shoulder and carefully locked her attic office door. Only then did she put on the lined gloves before heading downstairs.

She went out the back way, circled around the building, then crossed The Wreath on her way to her street. The air was unbelievably cold. She could see her breath. If the clouds came in later, as the weather had predicted, there would be more snow.

Everything about Wishing Tree was strange to her. She was used to the anonymity of a big city, driving everywhere rather than walking. Back in LA she could slip in and out of a grocery store without running into three people she knew. No one talked to her before. Now she had dozens of conversations a day. Wishing Tree was her home and she was making a place for herself here.

This was what she'd wanted, she reminded

herself, making her way up Mittens Avenue. Familiarity. Belonging. Moving to Wishing Tree had given her the chance to make a big change in how she lived her life, and she was determined to take advantage of that. She was tired of being lonely. Which meant that after sleeping for the next twenty or so hours, she would shower, dress and put on her best smile before joining her new friends for lunch. Because they were her last, best hope at figuring out how to be like everyone else, and she wanted that more than anything in the world.

"There's something wrong with your mother," Dylan announced as he stalked into Jake's office.

"You're just now getting that?" Jake asked. "I know what she's done to me, but what's your beef with her?"

Dylan walked over to the corner seating and threw himself on the big leather sofa. He'd spent plenty of time here, hanging out with his friend. The office was large, with wide windows and a view of the mountain. He was less impressed by the trappings of wealth than by the fact that from Jake's office, you could see several of the ski runs.

"She wants me to be the Snow King," he said as Jake settled in a chair. "No, she says

I'm *going* to be the Snow King. According to her, it's all arranged."

Jake grinned. "I'm ready to mock you, but I don't know what a Snow King is."

"I didn't, either. Not exactly. So I went online." He drew in a breath. "It used to be a thing, like years ago. Every year, the Saturday before Thanksgiving, people put their names in a hat. A Snow King and Snow Queen were drawn at random. They're basically the hosts to all the events around town. They show up at the Lighting of the Trees, Cookie Tuesdays, are there on December first when the town Advent Calendar begins. Their reign ends the night of the Holiday Ball, when the Snow King and Queen dance the first dance together."

He sat up and glared at Jake. "I don't want to be the Snow King."

"Why not? Judging a cookie contest isn't exactly hard duty. Who's the Snow Queen?"

"I have no idea. The rules have been changed to require candidates be single and under thirty-five or something." He'd been less concerned about that part. "There was something about an old lady falling at the ball a few years ago."

Jake frowned. "Was she all right?"

"Helen said she was fine." He sat up. "Why does your mother do this to me? She loves me. I'm her favorite."

Jake snorted. "I doubt you're her favorite."

"I'm better-looking. I'm better educated."

"I went to Stanford."

"I'm a graduate of the school of life, my friend." His humor faded. "I don't get it for real. She's never done anything like this before."

"Meddled?" Jake asked drily. "She's always been an involved parent."

"Not like this. Not with me."

Jake didn't look sympathetic. "Is this where I remind you about all the times you've complained about not having a woman in your life? How you're looking for someone special but can't find her?"

Dylan groaned. "I might have mentioned it once or twice."

"Or weekly. You can't say stuff like that in front of my mom. She wants us happy. It's her way. You presented her with a problem and now she's solving it."

"What are the odds of me liking whoever is chosen as Snow Queen?"

"That's not the point. She's getting you out there, forcing you to meet people."

"I have no problem meeting people."

Jake stared at him without speaking.

"I do fine," Dylan said, but with a little less force, because the truth was the only people he was meeting these days were clients, and very few single women came to him for custom cabinetry. His customers were mostly well-off couples living in Seattle or Boise.

As for the possibilities closer to home, so far he hadn't met anyone who made him think about a second date, let alone forever. Wishing Tree wasn't exactly overflowing with possibilities. It was the kind of town where you settled down, not found the love of your life.

"I should move," he grumbled.

"Just to avoid being Snow King?" Jake asked. "That sounds extreme."

"No, to meet someone. It's not going to happen here."

"You'd hate living anywhere else."

That was true, Dylan thought. He'd been born here and planned on living out his days here. The town suited him. He liked the quirks, the people, the traditions. He had a great house with a couple of acres and a workshop he'd built exactly how he wanted it. No way he'd find that somewhere else. Plus, his family was here. Jake and Helen were all he had.

"Maybe I should try online dating," he said doubtfully. "You ever done that?"

"No." Jake's mouth twitched. "You know

there's a website for farmers looking for love. Maybe there's one for semisuccessful craftsmen."

"Why do I bother with you?"

Jake grinned, obviously undeterred. "I'll help you write the profile. I'm not sure how we'll handle your trust issues, though. Maybe a woman is too much for you. Maybe you should start with a dog and work your way up."

Dylan did his best not to laugh. "I'm ignoring you."

Jake nodded. "I've got it. 'Aging woodworker seeks single woman for sex and babies.' "

"Aging? We're both thirty-three."

"You look older."

"You're so full of crap. You're the suit guy. I'm ruggedly handsome."

"You smell like pine."

"Some women like that."

"They'd probably prefer a guy who doesn't smell."

They both laughed.

Dylan leaned back on the sofa again. "I'm screwed."

"It's three weeks of Christmas cheer. You'll meet a nice woman, eat some cookies and dance at the ball. It's no big deal. Hey, maybe you'll get lucky and she'll be everything you've been looking for."

"Maybe," Dylan said, hearing the doubt in his voice. While he would very much like Jake to be predicting his future, what were the odds? "I can't believe Helen did this to me."

"She'd tell you it was a sign of love."

"I think it has more to do with her needing a hobby." He glanced at his friend. "Could be worse. I could be you."

Jake wondered if his mother had shared the news of her latest project.

"She told you?" he asked.

"Oh, yeah. Project: Jake's Bride. She always does the unexpected."

Jake still hadn't figured out what he was going to do about his mother. Talking to her wouldn't be enough — she had no reason to listen. Once she decided she was right about something, her opinion was unchangeable.

"She wants grandchildren," he grumbled.

"Not a surprise. It's a mom thing. She should have had more kids. Then there wouldn't be so much attention on you."

"I would have liked that, but it's a little late now."

Dylan frowned. "I wonder why you were an only."

Jake looked at his friend. "My dad. He

got a vasectomy when I was five or six."

Dylan's eyes widened. "What? How do you know that? What kid knows that?"

"He told me later — when I confronted him about the affairs."

Jake had been devastated to discover his father with another woman. Oh, he hadn't walked in on him in bed, but he'd seen him at a swanky hotel restaurant. He'd been flying in to meet his father in Los Angeles and had impulsively come in a day early — just to get some beach time. While sitting at the bar, enjoying a quiet drink, he'd seen his father walk into the restaurant, a beautiful, younger woman clinging to him.

Jake had followed the couple inside and had watched as they were seated. He hadn't known what to think, what to say. He'd been too caught up in rage and disappointment. His entire life his mother had talked about their glorious marriage and how happy they were together. In that moment he'd realized it was all a lie.

Jake returned his attention to his friend. "I wanted to know what kids he might have left along the way and he told me about the vasectomy. To this day I don't know if my mom knows and I'm sure not going to tell her."

Helen had been hurt enough by the man

she'd loved her whole life. Jake wasn't going to contribute to the problem by blurting out something that painful.

"You're not him," Dylan said quietly. "You've never been like him."

"You sure?" Jake asked. "I look like him, I'm good at the business like him. We had the same sense of humor, the same smile."

"You'd never cheat. You never have."

"No, but I wondered."

Dylan exhaled sharply. "That's not what happened. Iona showed up and said she regretted letting you go. She said she was still in love with you. It was a shock and for one second, just one, you wondered if you were still in love with her. That's not cheating. That's asking the right question."

"I didn't know what I was feeling," Jake said. "In that moment I was confused and pissed and a dozen other emotions. I'd just asked Reggie to marry me. We'd had our engagement party the night before, then Sunday morning Iona turns up on my doorstep."

He remembered looking at her in disbelief, wondering why this day of all days had to be the one she picked. She'd begged him to take her back, telling him she was still desperately in love with him. He hadn't known what to say and she'd taken his silence as interest.

She'd reminded him of how good they'd been together, of all they'd meant to each other. And for one second, one flicker of time, he'd wondered if he was still in love with her.

He'd immediately told himself he wasn't, that Reggie was the woman he wanted to be with, but the asking had rattled him. It had made him question himself and his commitment to his future wife. What if not being sure meant he was like his father?

Not knowing what to do or how to fix a problem he couldn't define, he'd thrown out Iona, then had abruptly broken up with Reggie — a truly dickish move that had shattered both their hearts. He'd relocated to the family resort in Aspen to give himself some time to think.

Iona had followed. At first, he'd ignored her, but one night he'd given in to all she'd offered. Afterward, lying in her bed, he wondered if he was one step closer to being like his dad.

"I screwed up," he said bluntly. "I had dozens of opportunities to make a good decision and at every single turn, I picked poorly. I hurt Reggie, I ended up hurting Iona and I hurt myself. I'm tired of getting it wrong." He glanced at Dylan. "It's easier to be alone."

"But not much fun."

"No."

"Want to be Snow King? I hear there's cookies."

Jake managed a chuckle. "Thanks but *I* hear they already have their man."

"I wouldn't mind if you took my place."

"I have my own problems. Or have you forgotten about Project: Jake's Bride?"

Dylan grinned. "I'm never going to forget that. So Camryn Neff is the first victim. Do you know her?"

"We met yesterday when she came here to tell me about my mother's plan. She wanted to make sure I knew."

"Good for her. What did she say?"

"She explained about her meeting with my mother and what it all meant for me."

She'd been a little shell-shocked, so they'd had that in common.

"Got to admire her honesty," Dylan pointed out.

Jake narrowed his gaze. "No. Don't even joke about that. I get enough matchmaking from my mother."

Dylan's grin was unrepentant. "She's pretty, right? I know who she is. Curly red hair." He paused. "You like women with curly hair."

63

"Shut up."

"She has sisters, doesn't she? Younger, I think. Different father."

"You're like an old woman with all the gossip. And yes, there are younger sisters, or as my mother calls them, instant grandchildren."

"You should ask her out."

Jake rose and pointed to the door. "Get out. Now. Leave and never come back."

Dylan laughed as he stood. "It's supposed to snow tonight, then be clear tomorrow. I can move some things around if you want to go snowboarding."

"Sure. I'll look at my schedule and text you a few times."

Dylan waved and walked out of the office. Jake started for his desk, then circled around to stand in front of the window and look at the mountain.

Yes, Camryn had been pretty, he admitted, if only to himself. And he'd appreciated her honesty and straightforward attitude. But that was as far as things were going to go. He knew his limitations — he didn't like them, but he respected them. No way was he screwing up, yet again, and breaking hearts in the process. Not just because he didn't want to hurt anyone but also because he was tired of getting burned himself.

# FOUR

River slept fourteen hours straight and woke up feeling human again. After doing her morning stretches and taking a quick shower, she checked her work emails before going downstairs into her big, bright kitchen. Her two-story townhouse was relatively new, with an open concept living area downstairs and two bedrooms and bathrooms on the second floor. It was bigger than she needed, but she'd fallen in love with the miles of quartz countertop and the double ovens. Plus, her address was on Mittens Avenue. How was she supposed to resist that?

It was only a little after seven in the morning when she turned on both ovens. After her intense all-nighter, she was due for a little playtime and for as long as she could remember, baking had been her go-to way to have fun without involving a computer. She pulled ingredients out of the pantry and placed them by her stand mixer.

She would start on the cheesecake-stuffed red velvet cookies first, then make eggnog meltaways. If her timing was right, everything would be baked and cooled so she could take them to lunch with her friends. She'd bought small, holiday-themed tins that would each hold about eight or nine cookies.

River worked methodically, occasionally glancing at the recipes she nearly knew by heart. Soon the smell of baking cookies filled her kitchen. She measured bourbon and rum into the meltaway dough and started the mixer.

At exactly eleven forty-five, she placed four tins in a small tote bag, then began the laborious process of dressing to face the cold. First, she replaced her slipper socks with lined boots. She had a heavy down coat, a scarf, a hat and gloves. The restaurant was close enough for her to walk, so after collecting her purse and the tote, she mentally braced herself for impact before stepping out onto her small porch.

The cold nearly made her stagger. Seriously, what was with the sharp jab of it filling her lungs as she breathed? Why had people decided living somewhere so far north was a good idea? River shuddered, then made sure her front door was locked before bravely heading out in the certain death trap that was a nineteen-degree day.

It had snowed during the night, but the sidewalks were already shoveled. As she headed toward The Wreath — Wishing Tree's answer to the traditional town square — she told herself she would survive the ten-minute walk there and back, despite how her teeth were chattering.

She did her best to distract herself by admiring the yard decorations on nearly every lawn and porch. There were stacks of gourds, festive fall-colored garlands and snowmen. Lots and lots of snowmen.

River had discovered there was a town rule that no snowmen could be displayed until the first snowfall. She'd heard that last year the snow had been incredibly late — well into December. Unfortunately for her, this year the first snowfall had been in October. She'd admired the flakes falling from the sky, excited to see snow in the wild for the first time in her life. The thrill had quickly died when she'd actually stepped outside and had discovered with snow came a drop in temperature.

"I was meant to live in warmer weather," she murmured to herself. But instead of settling on one of the Hawaiian islands, she'd fallen for this particular town and now she was stuck. "In a frozen wonderland," she said as she walked between a couple of shops and entered The Wreath.

The large open circle hosted all kinds of events. Free concerts, the weekly farmers' market, although that was a spring-to-fall thing. From what she'd read on the town's website, there would be several activities over the holidays, including a tree lighting and a town Advent Calendar.

She made her way to the far side. She was meeting her friends at Blitzen's Pub. During the day the restaurant was like any other, hosting families and tourists, offering a variety of takes on traditional pub fare. Promptly at four in the afternoon, the clientele changed to younger and rowdier. Blitzen's Pub was where you went in the evening if you wanted a loud, happy crowd. River reached the front door, eager to head inside. Not only to get warm, but also to see her friends.

Back in LA she'd never had a group of girlfriends. She'd had her computer friends, but they were mostly guys and scattered around the world. Growing up she'd been too quiet and shy to fit in. The scoliosis hadn't helped. Her form, rare and aggressive, had meant a huge body brace that had caused a lot of the other kids to pick on her. Then the surgeries had started, causing her to miss weeks of school. Fitting in hadn't been an option for her.

Her work was solitary, her nature, reclusive. Making friends had been difficult and she'd found it easier to simply retreat into her own private world. Over time she'd figured out that what was easy wasn't necessarily healthy. When she and her sister Kelsey had first seen Wishing Tree, they'd immediately recognized the potential of the town.

River had met Camryn and rented space from her, then had gotten to know Camryn's circle of friends. She liked those women and she knew they liked her.

She pulled open the heavy door and stepped into the warm pub. The decor was faux English with wood paneling and heavy beams overhead. Most of the tables were filled, as were the seats at the bar. The scent of French fries mingled with the aroma of hot chocolate.

She looked around and spotted Paisley Lovell waving frantically. The gorgeous blonde motioned her over. As she approached, River saw Shaye and Reggie were also in the large corner booth they'd claimed.

69

"You made it," Paisley said, sliding out to give her a hug. "I was worried. It's freezing out there and I know you don't love the cold."

Reggie and Shaye hugged her, as well. River had never had friends who were so physically affectionate. At first, she'd found the greetings uncomfortable, but now she looked forward to those few seconds of welcoming contact.

Reggie, a brunette with an easy smile, laughed. "You'll acclimate. Five years from now you won't even bother with a coat until it's below forty."

"I can't imagine that," River admitted, just as Camryn walked into the pub.

There was another round of huggy greetings, then she and Camryn hung their coats and scarves on the hooks by the booth and everyone slid into place. River handed out the tins of cookies.

Camryn laughed as she took hers. "I'll admit that when your job went past ten hours, I knew there would be baking to follow. The twins and I thank you."

Shaye opened the tin and sighed. "These look amazing. You're such a good baker. I can cook, but the mysteries of dough elude me."

Paisley leaned over and took a deep

breath. "They smell delicious and fattening. I'm going to need more treadmill time, but it will be worth it."

Their server came over and took their orders. River tried to be strong, but ended up asking for a diet soda along with fish and chips. When the server left, Reggie spoke.

"So what's everyone doing for Thanksgiving?"

Paisley wrinkled her nose. "I'll be visiting the folks. As will all my brothers. All. Of. Them." She sighed. "They'll grill me about my lack of love life and flaunt their happily married status in my face."

"But they love you," Shaye pointed out. "That's something."

"It is. What about you?"

Shaye's smile grew brighter. "Lawson and I will be hanging out with his family, as per usual."

Reggie grinned. "I adore Toby's grandmother, so I get wanting to hang with the in-laws, but you love yours more than anyone I know."

"I do," Shaye admitted with a laugh. "I can't help it. We'll be in town for the long weekend."

"I'm staying in town, too," Reggie said. "The usual crowd. Dena, Micah and little

71

April. Belle and Burt."

River laughed. "You include the dogs in the guest list?"

Reggie grinned. "Burt and Belle are family."

"Belle's better dressed than all of us," Camryn added. "She's a big girl, but she has style."

Camryn was right, River thought. Reggie custom-made clothes for her Great Dane, including coats and sweaters to keep her warm in winter.

"The twins and I will be having a nice Thanksgiving at home," Camryn said. "I'm working on the menu. Family favorites and a few new things."

Reggie nudged Camryn with her shoulder. "This year will be better. It won't be the first Thanksgiving without your mom."

"I'm counting on that," Camryn admitted. She turned to River. "What about you? Aren't your sister and her fiancé going away for the holiday?"

"Yes, they're visiting Xavier's family in upstate New York. My mom's coming to stay with me for the long weekend."

Something she was looking forward to very much. The only downside of moving to Wishing Tree — aside from the cold — was missing her mom.

"Just the two of you?" Camryn leaned toward her. "Want to have Thanksgiving dinner with me and the twins? We could split the cooking duties and share a turkey."

The invitation was unexpected, but nice. "That would be great. Thanks for suggesting it."

Camryn smiled. "I think we'll have fun. I'll get with you in a few days so we can coordinate what we're having." Her smile broadened. "And I assume you'll do some baking?"

River laughed. "I promise. As will my mom. She taught me everything I know."

Camryn pretended to swoon. "I genuinely can't wait."

The server returned with their drinks. Paisley waited until she left to say, "So the box is up for Snow King and Snow Queen, everyone. Are we all putting in our names?" She paused. "Okay, not Reggie and Shaye because you have to be single. But Camryn and River, you totally should do it."

"I don't know what a Snow Queen is," River said.

"Do we still have those?" Camryn asked. "I thought the town had done away with the tradition."

"It's back," Paisley told her. "Okay, so on Saturday the Snow King and Snow Queen will be chosen. I think they're literally drawing their names out of a hat. If you're chosen, you're kind of a holiday ambassador. You turn on the lights for the tree lighting, you're part of the first night of the Advent Calendar, you judge Cookie Tuesday."

It sounded like a lot, River thought. "What's Cookie Tuesday?"

Everyone turned to Camryn.

"You haven't told her?" Shaye asked. "She's the best baker we know." Shaye looked at River. "Every Tuesday between Thanksgiving and Christmas is a cookie contest. They have different cookies on different Tuesdays. Like sugar cookies one Tuesday and gingerbread cookies the next."

"You'd totally kick butt," Reggie said firmly. "On the first Cookie Tuesday, the cookies are auctioned off for charity. The sophomores at the high school are running the auction for their holiday charity project." She smiled. "My mother told me all about it. She keeps up on town gossip."

"Apparently," Camryn said with a laugh. "And she's right. It is the sophomores. The twins have mentioned it eight or nine times already. They're very excited."

Paisley nodded. "It's up at the resort. River, you have to enter."

"She can't," Camryn said primly. "She's going to be Snow Queen."

"What?" Reggie, Shaye and Paisley said together.

River opened her mouth, then closed it. "Excuse me?" Snow Queen? She couldn't. "I can't be. I'm too shy and not very good with people."

Paisley waved a hand. "You're fine with people." She looked at Camryn. "How can you know she's going to be Snow Queen?"

"Because we're all going to nominate her. We each get a vote, right? Shaye and Reggie can't enter themselves, so they have to enter someone else. Let's put in River's name."

"Let's not," River said weakly. "I'd have to do scary things, like stand in front of a crowd." That was so far out of her sad little comfort zone as to be unfathomable.

"You're the one who told me you wanted to find a way to be part of everything happening in town," Camryn reminded her. "This is the perfect solution. It's for a limited period of time, you'll do a bunch of fun stuff and you'll meet people. Being Snow Queen would be good for you."

Paisley nodded slowly. "I can see it. So if we all nominate River, that's five of us."

"I'm not nominating myself," River said quickly, thinking maybe she shouldn't have told Camryn how much she wanted to fit in with the town.

Paisley waved away that comment. "We can talk to everyone we know and have them put in her name."

Was it just her, or was it getting warm in here? She tugged at the neckline of her sweater. "Seriously, this is a bad idea. I'm not Snow Queen material."

She couldn't stand in front of a crowd. What if they wanted her to speak? She'd faint. Or vomit. Both were very, very bad.

But her friends were on a roll. By the time their lunches arrived, the four of them had a plan.

"If you're serious about this, I'll be forced to hack into the city government and change the votes so someone else wins."

Camryn and Paisley looked at each other, then at her.

"Sorry to say this," Paisley said, not sounding sorry at all. "We're an old-fashioned kind of town. We write a name on paper. Now statistically, I suppose someone else could win, but we'll do our best to make it you."

"I thought you were my friends," River whispered, not sure how things had gotten so out of control so quickly.

"We are," Camryn said, patting her shoulder. "And that's why we're going to make this happen."

After lunch Camryn and River left the restaurant together to walk back to Wrap Around the Clock. Camryn was pleasantly full from her Scotch egg spinach salad, and happy from spending time in the company of her friends. One of the nice parts of moving back to Wishing Tree had been reconnecting with the women she'd known since childhood, she thought. She liked their shared past.

She also liked her new friends, she thought, glancing at River.

"Did I push too hard about you being Snow Queen?" she asked. "You talk about wanting to fit in with the town and it's a really good way to do that. But if it's too much, I'll tell Paisley we need to back off."

River glanced at her. "I want to say I can't do it, but honestly, I think it would be good for me to put myself out there." She worried her lower lip. "Is there any public speaking?"

"No. You just have to go to different events and be pretty." Camryn frowned. "Wow, did that sound sexist. But you know what I mean. The duties are ceremonial. Plus, there's a good chance that our plan will fail and someone else's name will be drawn."

River exhaled. "I'm going to let you go ahead and I guess we'll see what happens."

"You're being very brave."

"I'm trying."

An effort Camryn admired. Not everyone was willing to face their fears and concerns so directly. People should go after what they wanted.

"Moving here when you and your sister didn't know anyone was the hard thing," she said. "Snow Queen will be a lot easier than that."

"I hope so," River told her with a laugh.

"I've become the meddling friend," Camryn said as they walked into the store. "It must be the season. First Helen Crane, then Paisley and me."

"Who's Helen Crane?" River asked they shrugged out of their coats.

"The Cranes own Mistletoe Mountain Resort. They're the rich family in town. Helen Crane asked to see me on Monday." Camryn pulled River into the back room and lowered her voice. "Jake Crane is her son. You must have seen him around town. He's good-looking, successful and single."

"I'm not sure I have."

Camryn thought about the many times she'd noticed Jake jogging past her store.

"He's worth a second look. Anyway, Helen lost her husband a couple of years ago and she's lonely and ready for grandchildren. Apparently, Jake isn't dating enough to satisfy her so she's decided to find him a wife on her own."

River's green eyes widened. "How?"

"Project: Jake's Bride. She's going to come up with a list of suitable women then somehow get them together with Jake." Camryn paused. "Now that we're talking about it, I'm not sure of the details."

"You're a candidate?"

"No. I mean, she wanted me to be, but I said that wasn't happening. Then I went and told him what was going on. He was a little stunned and said he'd take care it."

"I wonder if she's using a dating profile app to match him up with different women. There are some good ones available."

Camryn smiled at her friend. "No. Don't help. She's a menace."

"Maybe you'd like being married to Jake," River teased.

"Yeah, that would be a firm no."

Camryn wasn't interested in finding love right now. She was planning to leave Wishing Tree as soon as her sisters graduated from high school. Better to wait until she went back to Chicago, where she planned to settle permanently and resume the life she'd left behind. Not that she didn't love her hometown — she did. But this wasn't what she'd planned for herself. Instead, losing her mom had changed everything. At least until Camryn could get things back on track.

"Poor Jake," River said as she walked toward the stairs that would take her to her office. "What his mother's doing puts mothers everywhere in perspective. I know I won't be complaining about mine anytime soon."

"I know what you mean," Camryn said. "Project: Jake's Bride. What was she thinking?"

River pushed aside the black dancing bunny sculpture on the coffee table and set down her mug of tea. Despite the fire in the stone fireplace, she just couldn't get warm.

"Is the heat on?" she asked.

Kelsey, her sister, grinned at her. "It's set at sixty-eight, there's a fire and you're wearing a thick sweater."

"I still have thin Southern California blood. I get cold if it's below seventy."

"Then it's going to be a long winter."

"Tell me about it." River sighed. "How did you adjust so fast? You should have the

80

same thin blood."

"Just lucky, I guess."

"Or it's the power of love," River teased. "You need to adjust because of Xavier."

"Then we need to find someone for you so you're not so cold."

"I'm in," River said lightly.

The high-pitched sound of ten-year-old girls laughing drifted up from the basement. Kelsey glanced toward the basement stairs, her expression relaxed and happy.

"Brooklyn has friends," River said quietly. "She's fitting in."

"I know and I'm so grateful. I was worried about her being the new girl, but everyone has been so welcoming." Kelsey chuckled. "I got an email from her teacher saying she was talking a little too much in class and needed to pay attention." She pressed a hand to her chest. "My daughter, who used to never talk to anyone if she didn't have to. I was thrilled."

"Did you say that to her teacher?"

"No. I said I would discuss the problem with Brooklyn."

"The diplomatic answer."

Kelsey picked up her own mug of tea and took a sip. "Moving here was the best decision I ever made."

"And the most impulsive."

Seven months ago Kelsey had been contacted by a lawyer, who had informed her of an unexpected inheritance. Her paternal grandfather had died, leaving her a house in Wishing Tree. Kelsey hadn't heard of the man or the town but she'd dutifully flown up to meet with the lawyer and see her inheritance. She'd returned to Los Angeles and had announced she and Brooklyn were moving.

River, worried that Kelsey was making a mistake, had insisted on coming with her. Some to help with the logistics but mostly to keep an eye on what was happening. But Kelsey and Brooklyn had both settled in immediately. Brooklyn had started making friends, while Kelsey had met and fallen in love with Xavier Lauris, a local doctor.

Come September, River had been scheduled to return to Southern California, but Wishing Tree had worked its magic on her and she'd decided to stay, as well.

"Sometimes you just know when something's right," Kelsey said.

River raised her eyebrows. "Are we still talking about your move or have we shifted to your handsome fiancé?"

"Possibly both." Kelsey's humor faded. "I don't want you to be alone for Thanksgiving. I shouldn't have agreed to go back east with Xavier."

River collapsed on the sofa and buried her face in a pillow. "Stop! I won't be alone." She straightened. "Mom's coming up and we've been invited to join Camryn and her sisters."

Kelsey looked doubtful. "You're really going to go?"

"Yes. We're sharing cooking duties. We haven't worked out the details yet, but we will and I'll be fine. Don't worry about me."

"I can't help it. Worrying is part of being an older sister."

River knew that was true. Kelsey had always looked out for her.

"I'm better here," she said. "Like your daughter, I've discovered that people are nice and they help me fit in."

Kelsey looked at her. "I want you to be happy."

"I am."

Her sister continued to watch her. River sighed.

"I'm fine. Why won't you believe me?"

"Because I know being quote-unquote normal, as you call it, isn't easy for you and that the only reason you came to Wishing Tree in the first place is because of me. I want to be sure you're staying because it's what you want and not to keep an eye on me."

"I'm here for me," River said firmly, wanting to convince her sister of her okay-ness. She searched for some way to explain that while she wasn't the most outgoing person in the world, she was making progress. She was —

She sat up straight and grinned. "I'm going to be the Snow Queen."

Kelsey stared at her. "Excuse me?"

"Snow Queen. The Snow King and Queen are ceremonial hosts for the Wishing Tree holiday events. All my friends are putting my name in to be chosen and I'll be doing the same later today. You should nominate me, too."

She immediately wanted to call back that suggestion. Every time her name was put in the box, she had one more chance to win. If someone would give her the total number of entries, she could calculate exact odds, but as it was, she'd be forced to estimate.

Kelsey put down her tea. "You'd really do it? You'd be the Snow Queen?"

No. No way and not even for money. Uh-uh. Only saying that would make Kelsey worry more and River didn't want that. Plus, she knew in her gut that while she would be nervous every second she was

Snow Queen, the act of following through with all the required duties really would be good for her. She would meet people, she would be forced out of her quiet, shy comfort zone.

"There's a cookie contest," she said by way of answering. "I worry about judging other people's baking. But other than that, I'm okay with what I have to do."

"I'm impressed," her sister admitted. "When's the crowning?"

River winced. "There isn't a crown."

"How do you know?" Kelsey grinned. "Maybe it's a really big one with glitter and shiny ornaments."

"No one puts ornaments on a crown."

"If anyone did, they'd live here."

A crown? River didn't want to think about that. "The drawing is tomorrow. At The Wreath."

"Xavier has to work but Brooklyn and I will be there to cheer you on." She sighed dramatically. "My sister, the Snow Queen."

River glared at her. "You can be so annoying."

"Then my work here is done."

# FIVE

"How's this?" Victoria asked, showing Camryn a design on her tablet. Stylized initials created individual yellow and blue flowers scattered across a pearlized background.

"That's beautiful. I like the iridescence. I wouldn't have thought of that. Let's see how it looks on paper."

Victoria flashed her a smile before heading over to the custom racks on the back wall. Hundreds of different wrapping papers hung from rods. They were grouped by category — weddings, birthdays, holiday — and then by color. There were also plain sheets in a rainbow of colors. Victoria perused the various shades of white, picking three different options and carrying them back to Camryn. Together they studied the choices.

Camryn placed the tablet on the least pearlized paper. "I know this is subtle, but the pattern will be more visible. If it comes out as well as I think it will, I have some ideas for the ribbons we could use."

Victoria nodded. "Less might really be more in this case. Let's see how it looks."

While she uploaded her design, Camryn loaded the blank wrapping paper into the inkjet printer. Moments later the first sample came out. A second quickly followed.

Wrap Around the Clock offered custom wrapping paper options. Customers could design their own and upload it to one of the store's wide-format printers, or they could commission a design. In this case Shelley, the maid of honor, wanted to surprise the bride with custom-wrapped wedding gifts. She planned to secretly email all the guests and have them send their presents to Wrap Around the Clock. Camryn would then wrap and decorate them all, creating a beautiful display. She'd come up with a few designs of her own, but Victoria had been the one to suggest using the bride and groom's initials to create a stylized floral motif.

Victoria joined her at one of the big wrapping tables. She placed a small, empty box in the center of the paper and began to wrap it. Camryn perused the selection of ribbons and trims. She found an iridescent blue and a pale yellow, along with a pretty lace. After layering them, she tied them on the package.

"That's beautiful," Victoria said, touching the bow.

"It is. I'm really happy with it. I'll take pictures of the package and email them to Shelley, along with pictures of the paper and pricing." She smiled at her sister. "I'm thinking of putting this design in our custom catalog. What do you think?"

Victoria's eyes brightened. "You'd do that? I could use other initials in different colors to show how it would look."

"That would be great."

Victoria went to work on her tablet, using her stylus to draw different initials.

Camryn watched her for a second, thinking her sister's talent must have come from her father. Camryn and her mom had been able to do basic design work, but nothing like Victoria could create. The twins each worked a few hours a week in the store. They both wrapped packages and handled shipping. Lily sometimes manned the cash register, while Victoria spent a couple of hours a week working on new designs.

Except for her time away at college and the five years she'd spent in Chicago, Camryn had always had a connection to the store. She remembered using leftover scraps to make clothes for her paper dolls. She'd started coming up with different ways to decorate packages when she'd been ten or eleven. Her mom had always had a "Package of the Week" display, showing how to use little extras to make the gift presentation special. Lily and Victoria had grown up the same way. Wrap Around the Clock was a part of their lives and she supposed it always would be.

River did her best not to think about the ceremony that was getting closer by the minute, instead focusing on the routine background checks she'd been hired to do. The first two had gone well, but the third one was heading in an awkward direction, she thought as she stared at her computer screen.

"Future nannies shouldn't trash their ex-boyfriends on Facebook," she murmured, copying several fairly hostile posts. "And wishing his dick falls off is never a good look."

She went to Instagram and dug around. There were a half dozen photos of the candidate with different guys that bordered on pornography, and lots of pictures of her obviously drunk.

"The internet is forever," she murmured, copying the least objectionable of them into her file. "Why don't people get that?"

She poked around various online sites for another hour before typing up her report. Between the woman's really bad credit score and her questionable social media posts, she wasn't anyone River would hire to look after a kid. But that wasn't her decision to make — her job was to provide a detailed background report for her client. She'd just finished sending off the material when Camryn knocked on her half-open door.

"I brought you coffee and your empty plate," her friend said with a grin and she put an oversize serving plate on River's desk. "The coffee cakes were a big hit with the customers and the twins. You're very sweet to them."

River laughed. "I like baking and they're always appreciative. I think it's a good partnership."

Camryn handed her a mug of coffee, then took a seat in one of the visitor chairs. "It is for them. And I'm happy to have less guilt about not giving them homemade treats. How are you feeling?"

The change in topic caught River off guard for a second, then she remembered what was happening in a few hours. "I'm fine."

"Nervous?"

"Some, but I keep telling myself that I might not be chosen. The random nature of the drawing gives every name entered an equal chance. Depending on the number of entries and how many times my name was put in, I figure the odds of me being picked are less than one in six. Maybe one in five."

"You did the math to get to that conclusion?"

"I always liked statistics. Knowing the numbers comforts me."

Camryn looked slightly confused by that confession, but River was used to people not understanding how numerical details could make an uncomfortable situation tolerable. She could trust numbers to behave in certain ways — they were constant and dependable. They never misunderstood or thought she was strange. They just were.

"I can't decide if I should wish for you to be Snow Queen or if I shouldn't," Camryn admitted. "Which do you want?"

"You know that your wishing won't change the outcome."

Camryn grinned. "You're saying I don't have magical powers? Come on, be more supportive than that."

"I want to be picked and not be picked equally."

Camryn nodded. "That makes total sense. For what it's worth, if you are chosen, you'll be an adorable Snow Queen. You're so petite, with delicate features. Maybe a little more princess-looking than queen, but I have faith in your ability to pull it off. And I'm sorry if we shouldn't have gotten involved."

"It's okay. I know you were doing what I said I wanted." River picked up her coffee. "Which is nice to think about."

"Thank you for saying that. I mean, it could be worse. Your mother could have launched Project: River's Husband."

"My mom isn't really the type to mess with my life. Unlike Jake's mother. Have you heard any more on that?"

"No. I told Helen I wasn't interested and I'm sure she's taken me off the list." Camryn paused. "Okay, I hope she has. I'm pretty sure."

"You don't sound sure at all," River teased. "You said before you barely knew Jake. Do you want to be that quick to reject the possibility? What if he's the one?"

"He's not. Besides, I'm not interested in finding someone now. This is a temporary gig for me."

"I don't understand," River admitted. "What does that mean?"

"When the twins graduate from high school, I'm going back to Chicago. It's where I lived before my mom got sick and I moved back home. I had a whole life there that I loved and while Wishing Tree is great, I miss what I had. When Mom died, I knew I couldn't uproot the twins, so I stayed, but it was never going to be permanent."

"They're only sophomores, so you have nearly three years before they graduate."

"I know."

"That's a long time to put your life on hold."

Camryn gave her a look that had River worrying she'd said the wrong thing.

"My life isn't on hold," Camryn murmured then paused. "No, you're right, it is." She sighed. "I love my sisters and the store and the town, but it doesn't exactly feel like my life. Does that make sense?"

River nodded. "You stepped in to take over for your mom, both with your sisters and Wrap Around the Clock."

Camryn relaxed. "Exactly. I had a career I loved, friends and it all changed with no warning."

"You're going back to . . ."

"Chicago. That's the plan. Which means I

93

can't fall in love with someone so completely tied to Wishing Tree."

River understood the problem. "Three years is a long time to wait to find the right person. Plus, you have to put off starting a family." She paused, not sure if she'd said the wrong thing. "Not that everyone wants to be married and have kids."

"I do want that. Just not here."

"Makes sense. What about the business?" she asked. "Are you going to sell it?"

Camryn shook her head. "No. I'll keep it for the twins. I'll hire a manager to run things." Her expression turned wistful. "My grandmother started this business, then left it to my mom and she left it to the twins and me. It's a family thing. It should stay that way."

"Traditions are nice."

"I agree." Camryn rose. "Okay, smart friend, I'll leave you to work. Want to meet downstairs at quarter to three? We can walk over together. Oh, just so you know, the twins really want you to be the Snow Queen."

"I appreciate the moral support. Yes, I'll come downstairs to walk over with you."

At two forty-two, River locked up her office. She'd put on an extra sweater and had warmer gloves than usual. The drawing was outside, in The Wreath, and she didn't know how long it would last. Staying warm, or at least not freezing, was a priority.

Wrap Around the Clock was bustling on a Saturday afternoon. There were wrapping parties in each of the private rooms customers could rent out, and over a dozen shoppers examined paper and ribbon. She spotted Camryn standing with her sisters and walked toward them. Victoria saw her first and waved.

"We're so excited," the teen said with a grin. "We've never known a Snow Queen before. They haven't done it in like four or five years and I honestly don't think we cared when we were ten."

"We didn't," Lily said firmly, holding out a small circle made of lace and ribbon. "We thought you should have a crown, whether you're picked as Snow Queen or not."

The unexpected and sweet gesture made River's chest tighten. She touched a curve of lace, momentarily at a loss for words. "I've never had a crown before," she whispered at last, setting it on her head. "Does it fit?"

"Perfectly." Victoria linked arms with her. "You look very royal. I like it." She reached over and fluffed a bit of River's short, spiky hair.

Camryn and Lily nodded approvingly.

"All right, let's head out before The Wreath gets too crowded," Camryn said. "We want to be able to see everything."

They collected coats and hats. River reluctantly took off the crown to pull on a wool beanie, then carefully tucked it into her cross-body bag. She looped a long scarf around her neck three times before pulling on gloves.

Lily grinned. "You really don't like the cold, do you?"

"It's not my favorite."

"Maybe you should have thought that through before putting your name in for *Snow* Queen."

River laughed. "An excellent point."

They stepped out into the sunny, freezing afternoon. Wrap Around the Clock opened directly onto The Wreath. River could see a large crowd of people in front of what looked like a small stage. To the left was a stack of resin gourds, each about four feet across. To the right was a giant Pilgrim hat. The recent snow had been cleared and various vendors had set up kiosks, selling things like hot chocolate and roasted chestnuts.

The scene was idyllic, River thought, in an "I'm not sure this is real" kind of way. She'd grown up in Van Nuys — in the center of the San Fernando Valley — where the local farmers' market had seemed much less magical than this. She'd known a few of the neighbors, but not many. Of course she'd always been more interested in being on her computer than going outside and talking to actual people.

But life was different here, she thought as the four of them joined the throngs of people making their way to the stage. People knew each other's names and called out greetings. Going to the grocery store was as much social as it was shopping.

Victoria pointed and waved. "Look! It's Brooklyn and Kelsey."

River saw her sister and niece, who immediately hurried toward them. Kelsey grinned as she approached.

"I'm so excited to be related to royalty," she teased.

"Oh, we're not sure River is going to win," Camryn told her with a laugh. "Last I heard, the odds are one in five."

"I was hoping for at least one in four," Kelsey said, hugging River. "I voted for you and so did Xavier. And he told everyone at the hospital to vote for you."

River's stomach sank. "That would change the numbers."

She distracted herself by pulling the

97

ribbon-and-lace crown out of her bag. "Victoria and Lily made this for me," she said, putting it on her niece's head. "What do you think?"

Brooklyn smiled. "I can wear it?"

Victoria eyed her critically, then nodded. "It looks amazing on you. Lil, we should all wear crowns. It could be our thing."

Lily looked doubtful. "You think?"

"Yes. We'll be delightful."

"Or weird."

Shaye and her husband, Lawson, stopped to say hello. While they were all chatting, River felt a tap on her shoulder. She turned and saw Howard Troll, owner of Holiday Spirits, one of the businesses that edged The Wreath.

Howard motioned for her to follow him. He stopped a few feet away from her group of friends.

"I still owe you a drink," he said earnestly. "You need to come by so I can repay you."

"You don't owe me anything," River told him. "Howard, I billed you for my time and you paid the bill. We're even."

Two months ago Howard had shown up at her office, frantic and terrified. His computer had been infected with ransomware and the hackers were demanding five thousand dollars to release the machine.

River had fixed the problem in less than an hour and had installed a better firewall.

"You saved me," Howard told her. "Come have a drink."

"Now?"

He chuckled. "No. Another time. Bring a friend."

With that he left. River rejoined everyone, not sure why Howard felt the need to do more than pay his bill. While he'd been concerned about the hack, it hadn't been an especially difficult job. Still, he'd mentioned her dropping by more than once and she'd learned that when people repeated something, they were often trying to send a message about the importance of what they were saying.

Interactions were complicated, she thought. Unlike numbers or computers.

"It's nearly time," Brooklyn said, grabbing her hand. "Aunt River, I really want you to be the Snow Queen. Aren't you excited?"

"I am," River told her, because telling a ten-year-old she was terrified and filled with dread didn't seem to fit the spirit of the moment.

"Big crowd," Jake said, sounding far more cheerful than the moment required.

"Shut up," Dylan muttered.

His friend looked at him with feigned surprise. "You're not happy about the good citizens of Wishing Tree showing up to see you crowned as the next Snow King?"

"You know I'm not. Maybe your mother changed her mind."

Jake laughed. "You've met my mother. You know that doesn't happen."

"Is this where I bring up Project: Jake's Bride?"

Jake's humor faded instantly. "Way to bring down the room."

"We'll suffer together."

"What suffering? You're going to show up at Cookie Tuesday and light some trees. My mother is looking to find me a wife. These two things are not equal."

Dylan knew Jake was right. Snow King was a short-term gig but a wife was forever. At least that was how he'd always seen it. A lifetime commitment, and one he wanted to make. If only he could find the right woman.

"Did you hear anything about who's going to be the Snow Queen?" he asked.

Jake shook his head. "No. I think she's going to be chosen the old-fashioned way — with a random drawing. Unlike your reign, which is steeped in corruption before it even begins."

"You're right. I should be disqualified."

100

"Your luck isn't that good."

Camryn clapped with everyone as the recorded music started and several town officials stepped onto the stage. Geri Rodden, the city manager, walked to the microphone.

"This is the five-minute warning," she said. "We'll choose the Snow King and Queen in five minutes."

Camryn glanced at River, who was talking to Paisley and Shaye. River looked more nervous than happy. Maybe putting her name in so many times had been a mistake, she thought. Even though River talked about wanting to get more involved with the town, she might not enjoy being Snow Queen. Although it was probably too late to take back all the votes.

She was going to learn a lesson from this experience, she told herself. No more messing in people's lives. An easy promise to keep seeing as this was her first real attempt. Unlike Helen Crane, she thought, and her ridiculous attempt to get her son married.

Thinking about Helen caused her to think about Jake. And as if thinking about him conjured him, she spotted him talking to his friend Dylan.

He really was good-looking. Tall and broad-shouldered, with that dark, curly hair.

Despite the casual setting, he still had an air of confidence about him — as if no situation would ever be too much for him to handle.

A few seconds later Camryn realized she was staring and told herself to look away, only before she could, Jake glanced in her direction, spotted her and smiled. Still holding her gaze, he said something to Dylan, then started walking toward her.

Awareness immediately engulfed her, which was a ridiculous reaction considering she didn't know the man beyond saying hello. Yes, they'd had a rather strange and intimate conversation about Project: Jake's Bride, but otherwise, they weren't even acquaintances, so feeling something very close to nerves in her tummy didn't make sense at all.

"Here for the crowning?" he asked as he reached her.

"Of course. I've heard this is the first one in several years. It's an event."

He glanced around at her group of friends, then pointed to her sisters. "The potential grandchildren?" he asked, his voice teasing.

She grinned. "That would be them. Victoria and Lily." She lowered her voice. "I haven't told them how they would have helped me in the competition. Your mother was impressed with my smile, plus the twins. Lucky for you I wasn't interested — otherwise, I would have shot to the top of the list."

Jake returned his attention to her. "You say that as if I'd mind."

She knew he was both teasing and being nice, but neither explained her sudden urge to toss her hair. "I stand by my original premise that you're not interested in your mother finding you a wife."

He shuddered. "You're right. I'm not." He leaned close. "I told her to back off, by the way. So you shouldn't be hearing from her again."

"You don't think it's going to be that easy to get her to stop, do you? I barely know the woman and I'm convinced she's difficult to distract once she's made up her mind."

His brows rose slightly. "Dylan and I were just discussing the same thing." He shook his head. "You're right. I'm going to have to have another conversation with her about butting out of my personal life. Or send her to that island."

"You can't deport your mother."

"No, but I can dream about it."

## SIX

Dylan stood waiting while the ceremony began. Everyone around him talked and laughed in the chilly afternoon, as if excited about what was going to happen. He tried to tell himself that maybe Helen hadn't been able to convince whomever was in charge to have him win, although he knew that was wishful thinking on his part.

Right on time, Geri returned to the microphone and announced she would be drawing the Snow King first, then reached into an actual black top hat to draw out a name.

"Dylan Tucker," she said, looking out into the crowd. "Dylan, are you here?"

He heard hoots and cheers as he walked up three steps where yes, a plastic crown was placed on his head. Geri winked at him.

"You know, not every man could carry off a crown like that. You look good."

"Thanks."

Geri was still chuckling when she reached

into a second black hat and pulled out a small white card. She glanced at the name.

"River Best."

Dylan thought he knew most of the women around his age in town, but he'd never heard of River Best. He searched the crowd until he saw a petite woman walking toward the stage. Her head was down, her gait hesitant.

Without thinking, he crossed to the end of the stage. River paused at the bottom of the stairs and looked up at him. Her big green eyes were wide and filled with apprehension. She looked nervous and unsure, as if she wanted to be anywhere but here.

"It's okay," he said quietly. "You'll be fine."

"I didn't think I'd have to stand in front of a crowd."

"You don't think the plastic crown is going to make up for that?"

Her gaze shot up to his head and for a second, the corners of her mouth twitched, as if she was going to smile.

"Not really," she murmured.

"It'll be okay. I'm right here."

He held out his hand. She hesitated for a moment, before putting her gloved fingers on his bare palm. Despite the thick material, he felt the contact, along with a sizeable jolt right in the chest.

She climbed the three stairs, then clutched his hand tightly.

"I can't do this," she told him. "It's terrifying."

"I'm right here." He reached up his free hand and pulled off her beanie, revealing short, spiky, dark hair. "You'll be fine."

She stared at him. "You don't know that. I could be very un-fine. I could be a disaster. Maybe I'll be the worst Snow Queen ever." She paused. "Not that I want to be bad at the job. It's just the crowd."

"I know. I'm still right here."

She nodded, then faced Geri. He could feel her shaking as the crown was settled on her head. She made two attempts to smile before getting it right.

"We're going to wave at the little people now," he told her, raising his hand.

She flashed him a grateful look, then waved.

"You're very kind," she told him. "Thank you."

"We're a team. Plus, you know, the only royals in town. We have to stick together."

The smile turned genuine and at the sight of it, he felt his breath hitch. She was stunning — all big eyes and the kind of mouth a man only dreamed about. He didn't know anything about River Best but every fiber of his being hoped she was single, straight and desperate to fall for a master cabinetmaker.

River had known a lot of people had shown up to watch the ceremony but she hadn't realized how big the crowd was until she saw it from the stage. Everywhere she looked were people staring back. Families and groups and couples. Dozens of faces. Hundreds. She'd never been comfortable being the center of attention and this was that times a million. The only solid point in an otherwise spinning world was the man standing next to her.

Dylan, she thought. The new Snow King. He was nice, she thought gratefully. And funny.

"Thank you all for coming today," the official said. "The Snow King and Queen activities will be listed on the town website, www.WishingTreeWashington.com. We spell out Washington, people. And remember that registration for Cookie Tuesday opens Monday and the second Cookie Tuesday is the gingerbread competition, for those of you who want to plan your calendar. Next Friday is the tree lighting and I hope to see everyone back here for that."

With that, she turned off the microphone.

Immediately, the music started up again. The woman turned toward them and smiled.

"River, I'm Geri Rodden, the town manager. Nice to meet you."

It was only when she held out her hand that River realized she was still holding Dylan's in a death grip. She released it and shook hands with Geri.

"Nice to meet you," she managed. "I'm a little nervous."

"You did fine. Now, the duties are fairly simple and ceremonial." She handed them each a business card. "Email me your contact information later today and I'll get you the official schedule. It will tell you when and where to be. The first event is the tree lighting, of course, followed by the Advent Calendar launching on the first. Once we get into December, we'll need you two to three times a week, culminating with the Holiday Ball Christmas Eve." She paused. "Do you two know each other?"

"We don't," Dylan said easily.

"You might want to get acquainted. You're going to be spending a lot of time together. All right, I think that's everything," she said. "You know how to reach me if you have any questions. Oh." She plucked the crowns off their heads. "I'll be keeping these. They're only to use for official duties."

She nodded at them and walked off the stage. River watched her go, a whole lot less concerned about the crown than the actual duties. As soon as she got home, she would email Geri and wait for the list. She wanted to know what was expected. Maybe the information would make the job seem less daunting, although she had her doubts.

"I wanted to keep the crown," Dylan said with a heavy sigh. "You know, wear it at work to impress the guys."

River stared at him, knowing he was kidding. Because for him, this wasn't a big deal. He could probably speak in public, too, if he had to.

He smiled at her. "You okay?"

She was better enough to notice he had a nice smile, and she liked the way his blue eyes crinkled at the corners. "I've stopped shaking but that's probably because no one's staring at me anymore. This was a bad idea."

"Why? You'll be a great Snow Queen."

"You don't know that."

"You were hoping not to be a bad one before. The fact that you're worried about doing a good job means you'll be great."

"I'd like to think that's true, but I think there are a few flaws in your logic."

109

"We haven't been officially introduced. I'm Dylan."

"River."

"I've lived here all my life and we've never met before. When did you move to town?"

"About six months ago. It's nice here. I like it. I have an office above Wrap Around the Clock." She worried her lower lip, not sure how much to say. "I told my friends that I wanted to get more involved in things and meet people. I'm in computer security, so it's just me alone all day at work. I mean, if you want me to investigate someone digitally, I'm who you call, but the rest of it, the social stuff, it's hard. I'm an introvert and well, shy. My friends nominated me. I mean, all my friends and their friends, so here I am, but maybe it was a mistake."

His steady gaze never left her face. "You left out *honest.*"

"What?"

"You're honest." He pulled her beanie out of his pocket and slid it on her head. "Like I said, I grew up here and I know all the traditions. You're not doing this alone. I'm your Snow King and you can count on me. We'll get through this together and I think we're going to have a lot of fun."

"Thank you. That makes me feel better."

"Good."

They started for the stairs. Dylan went down first, then held out his hand to her. She took his until she reached the ground, then released his fingers.

Before she could think of what she was supposed to say next, a well-dressed older woman walked up to them.

"Dylan, you were a charming Snow King. I look forward to seeing you at the tree lighting." The woman turned to River. "Hello, my dear. I'm Helen Crane. Nice to meet you."

"Hello."

Helen Crane? The mastermind of Project: Jake's Bride? River took a step back.

"I would like to make an appointment with you. Three o'clock on Monday at my house. Does that work?"

An appointment? For what? River wanted to blurt out that she would be a terrible candidate, but wasn't sure that was appropriate.

"I'm free at that time," she said instead.

"Excellent. I've been to your website and saw you have a contact form there. I'll email you my address. I look forward to us doing business together. I'll see you Monday."

"Yes, ma'am."

Helen patted Dylan's arm and walked away.

Dylan watched her leave. "I was hoping she was going to let it go," he said, then returned his attention to River. "My guess is she's going to hire you to do some background checks."

"You know her?"

His smile returned. "Yeah. Jake and I have been best friends since the first grade. I practically grew up at their house. Helen's been like a mother to me for years."

"And the background checks?" she asked.

He hesitated. "I should probably let her explain it."

"I know about Project: Jake's Bride," she blurted. "My friend Camryn is a candidate. Or she was. She talked to Jake and I guess they worked it out. I'm fine with Helen hiring me, but I don't want to be, you know, considered."

She paused, aware she might have said the wrong thing. "Not that I think Helen would pick me. I'm not special or anything. I'm not saying I'm not a good person, but I just don't think I'd be on her radar and that's better for everyone."

*Stop talking!*

She screamed the instruction silently, knowing that if her lips kept moving things were going to get worse. She ducked her head, wishing the human act of conversation and communication wasn't so fraught.

"River?"

She raised her head and looked into his kind blue eyes. "Yes?"

"You're charming and I look forward to us getting to know each other."

"You do?"

"Very much."

He thought she was charming? No one had ever said that about her before. Ever.

"Me, too," she admitted. "Thanks for helping me get through the ceremony."

"Anytime."

"So I'll see you at the tree lighting."

One corner of his mouth turned up. "I think you're going to see me before that."

"We'll be home by nine," Lily said as the Snow King and Queen crowning wrapped up.

Victoria nodded earnestly before adding, "Even though it's not a school night."

Camryn held in a smile. "You're being very responsible," she said. "Go have fun."

The twins flashed her smiles before running off to join their friends for dinner and a streaming movie at Angie's house.

"They grow up so fast," Jake said, his voice teasing. "One second they want you around for everything. The next they're abandoning you to be with their friends."

Camryn laughed. "I'm fine being abandoned. I like that they're happy." She glanced toward the stage where River was talking with Dylan.

"You know Dylan, right?" she asked.

"Sure. We've been best friends since we were kids. He's practically my brother."

"I only know him to say hi." She stared into his hazel eyes. "Tell me he's a good guy."

Jake looked momentarily confused. "You're interested in him?"

"What? No. It's River. I feel responsible for her being chosen as Snow Queen and I want to make sure she's going to be hanging out with someone nice." She hesitated, not sure how much to say. "She's a little shy and not always comfortable with people."

"Then don't worry. Dylan's one of the good ones and he'll take care of her."

"Thanks. I feel slightly less guilty now."

"How about I buy you a non-brown liquor drink at Holiday Spirits? We'll celebrate a successful Snow King and Queen crowning."

The invitation was a surprise. She barely knew Jake. Not that she minded. So far he was easy to talk to and she didn't have many

114

handsome men asking her out for drinks.

"That sounds nice. Thank you."

They made their way across The Wreath and walked into the bar. Only a few of the booths were taken. Jake motioned to one in the back. She nodded and led the way, pausing to hang her coat and scarf, then slid onto the smooth, padded seat. Jake settled across from her.

"My mother set up Dylan," he said.

"Excuse me?"

"She arranged for him to be Snow King."

Information Camryn hadn't known. "How does he feel about that?"

"Resigned mostly."

"Remind me never to capture your mother's attention."

Humor brightened his hazel eyes. "She is a force to be reckoned with."

"Which means you're probably going to have to deal with the consequences of Project: Jake's Bride."

"Yeah, I kind of figured that."

Howard walked over to their table. His plaid shirt was accented with a pumpkin print bow tie. "Specials are on the board. My niece is in town and she's going to culinary school, so we're offering an appetizer plate with every drink." He glowered at them. "Don't get used to it."

"We won't," Jake said solemnly, even as he winked at Camryn. "I'll have a Scotch, no ice."

Camryn glanced at the chalkboard. "A Cranberry Martini, please."

Howard wrote down their orders. "I'll be back in a few."

Camryn waited until he'd left to lean forward and whisper, "Food at Holiday Spirits. It's so unlike Howard."

The bar was true to its name. Hard liquor was served and that was what customers were expected to order. While beer and wine were on the menu, they were actively discouraged, and except for the occasional cocktail-tasting dinner, food wasn't readily available.

"You notice he didn't tell us what the food was," Jake pointed out.

She grinned. "I think we're just expected to like it."

She glanced around at the paneled walls and the turkey-centric decorations.

"I can't believe it's Thanksgiving next week," she said. "I really need to get my act together on planning a menu."

"Do you have family other than your sisters?" he asked.

"No. It's just us. I've invited River and her mom over for dinner, so there will be five of us. That should be fun."

He studied her. "Your sisters are a lot younger than you."

"You mean the potential grandchildren?"

He flashed her a smile that made her insides get fluttery — a sensation she ignored.

"I mean them, yes."

"My mom remarried. The twins and I have different fathers." She thought about her stepfather. "Their dad was a great guy. A talented painter who could never get his art career off the ground." She wrinkled her nose. "So he painted houses. It was such a waste of so much ability. I think that's where Victoria gets her mad skills. I sure don't have them."

"What happened to him?"

"He died of a heart attack. There was no warning. One second he was working and the next he was gone." She still remembered the shock. "It was my senior year of high school. We were all devastated."

He reached across the table and lightly touched her hand. "That must have been tough on the family."

"It was. I couldn't get into all the things you're supposed to do that last year, like prom. I was sad and lost. I almost didn't go away to college, but my mom insisted." She looked at him. "The twins still needed her and I think that helped her a lot."

Howard returned with their drinks and a large glass of water for each of them. He set three plates between them.

"Toasted ravioli, pizza-stuffed mushrooms and fruit skewers with a balsamic glaze."

Camryn's stomach immediately growled. "Sounds delicious. Thank you, Howard."

"Like I said, don't expect this all the time. It's not happening."

He stalked away. Jake reached for a ravioli. "What about your biological father?"

"I don't remember him. He took off when I was a baby. For a long time it was just Mom and me." She took a stuffed mushroom. "I was happy when she remarried and got pregnant, but none of us were expecting twins."

She took a bite. The tangy pizza sauce and cheese blended perfectly with the earthy mushroom.

"You lost your mom last year?" he asked.

Camryn nodded. "She called to say she was sick, so I came home to see her. Only she wasn't sick. She was dying. She'd kept her illness from me because she didn't want to interrupt my life."

His hazel gaze was steady, his expression sympathetic. "That's a lot. You had to move

118

back to take care of the twins."

"I couldn't ask them to move back to Chicago with me. Not when they were already going through so much. We were all in shock. To be honest, the last three months of the year are a blur."

"I know the feeling. I lost my dad about eighteen months ago. It was hard."

"How are you doing now?"

"It's easier. I still miss him."

There was something in his voice — regret, maybe. With a hint of anger. Camryn wondered if the emotions were about his father or something else. Not that she would ask — they weren't that close.

"It's been hard on my mom," he added. "She's alone in that big house with not enough to do."

"Leaving her plenty of time to plot ways to get you married."

One eyebrow rose. "Could we not talk about that?"

"You have to give her credit for being creative."

"No, I don't."

They smiled at each other.

"The potential grandchildren seemed to have a good time at the crowning," he said.

"They did and I'm glad. I want this to be a great holiday season for them with lots of fun things for them to do. After last year, we need new memories."

"And a really big Christmas tree."

She laughed. "Yes, definitely one of those."

"Do you miss Chicago?"

"Yes, but less than I did last year. It's very different there, but I still have ties. A condo, for one thing. When I realized I was going to have to stay here for the twins, I leased it out, so it's waiting for me when I go back."

He looked at her in surprise. "You're leaving Wishing Tree?"

"Uh-huh. After the twins graduate high school, I'm going to move back to Chicago. It's always been my plan. I liked living in the city. I had a lot of friends and there was always something to do."

"What about the business?"

"I'll hire a manager so it stays in the family." She smiled. "Although Wrap Around the Clock is nothing on the scale of your family business."

"The concept is the same. We both have ties to the community and family expectations. Did your mom want you to stay around to run the store?"

"No. She wanted me to go do whatever made me happy. What about you?"

"I always knew I'd end up in the family

business. Hotel management is in my blood."

"And you like it?"

"I do. My father was the type to insist I start at the bottom and work my way up. From the time I was fifteen, I worked at the resort every summer. I was a bellman, a server." The killer smile returned. "I spent six weeks as a housekeeper."

She hadn't known. "You cleaned hotel rooms?"

"Five days a week. I complained at the time, but it was a good experience for me. I have great respect for our housekeeping staff."

"Do you clean your own place or do you have people in?"

He sipped his drink. "I've hired a service."

"You're such a guy."

"I know how to clean my condo. I simply choose not to."

Camryn and Jake finished the appetizers and ordered a second round of drinks. It was almost six when they left Holiday Spirits. The sun had set nearly two hours before and stars dotted the night sky.

"My head is spinning a little," she said, breathing in the cold air. It was the second cocktail, she thought. She didn't usually indulge. "But in a good way."

Jake put his hand on the small of her back. "You're a lightweight."

"It's because I don't drink brown liquor."

"Probably. Come on. I'll walk you home. I want to make sure you get there."

She glanced up at him. "It's six blocks. I'll be fine."

"I'm still walking you home."

He was smiling as he spoke, his gaze locked with hers. She found herself swaying toward him, thinking he had a really nice mouth and it had been a long time since anyone had kissed her. She could use a man kiss, and while she was on the subject, she could use a little man touching, as well.

"What are you thinking?" Jake asked. "You have an interesting expression."

No way she was sharing her thoughts with him. "Just stuff. Girl stuff. You don't want to know."

"I'm not sure I believe you, but I'll stop asking. Can you walk? Should I get my car?"

"I'm fine."

She took a couple of steps to prove her point, then nearly slipped on a patch of ice. Jake was instantly at her side, wrapping his arm around her waist to hold her upright. Somehow she ended up with her hand on his shoulder and his face close to hers.

"You're really good-looking," she murmured.

He grinned. "Thank you. I think you're good-looking, too."

She waved her free hand. "You don't. You're just saying that because of what I said. Plus, the hair."

He raised his gaze slightly. "What about your hair?"

"It's red and it's curly. Some guys don't like that. I went out with this one guy who ended things after two dates. He said he couldn't get past the curly hair. That I always looked messy, like I wasn't even trying. He was a jerk."

"Yes, he was, and dumb and rude and an idiot. I apologize on his behalf."

"You don't have to but it's nice that you did." She drew in another breath. "Okay, I can walk now."

"You sure?"

She was, but walking wasn't actually her activity of choice. She would prefer kissing. Jake kissing, to be specific. Funny how a few days ago she hadn't even known him at all and now she was thinking about a little lip-on-lip action. Not that she was going to say that to him. It would take way more than two cocktails for her to blurt out that piece of information.

She patted his shoulder before stepping back. This time she stayed fully upright.

"See?"

He watched her for a second, then took her gloved hand in his. "Just to keep you steady."

They headed toward Gingerbread Lane.

"We're supposed to get more snow next week," she said. "We really enjoyed the first snow this year. Last year it was so late and the twins and I weren't paying attention. But this year we went to The Wreath and drank hot chocolate with everyone. It was great."

"The three of you are going to have a good holiday this year. It's going to help the healing process."

"I hope so. My sisters are only fifteen. They've been through so much already."

"You've been through a lot, too."

"But I'm older. I can handle it."

"Being older doesn't make it hurt less."

She blinked at him. "That's deep. You're deep."

He chuckled. "Thank you."

They continued the few blocks to her house. She liked how he kept hold of her hand. Sure, it was just for safety reasons, but it still felt nice.

They reached her house. Jake waited while

she dug out her keys and opened the front door.

"This was fun," she said, wishing there was a reason to invite him inside. You know, to kiss and stuff.

Stuff? Was she thinking sex with Jake?

"It was," he said. "Plus, food at Holiday Spirits. That makes it extra special."

She forced her slightly liquored brain to focus on the conversation.

"I liked the pizza-stuffed mushrooms."

"Me, too." He smiled at her. "You need to drink a couple of glasses of water and maybe take an ibuprofen."

"For what?"

"The headache you're going to have in the morning."

"You're sweet to worry, but I'm okay."

"I hope so." He studied her for a second. "You going to be all right by yourself?"

"I'm fine. Totally."

She would drink the water, as he'd suggested, then try to figure out where the idea of having sex with Jake had come from.

He hesitated for a second, then leaned close and lightly kissed her cheek. "I like the curls. They're sexy and they suit you."

With that, he turned and walked away.

Camryn stepped inside and closed the door behind her. While she appreciated the compliment, she couldn't help wondering why he hadn't kissed her on the mouth. Because a real kiss from Jake would be better than even pizza-stuffed mushrooms — of that she was sure.

# SEVEN

Dylan sanded the last corner of the fiber-board inlay, then blew off the dust. He ran his finger around the intricate design to check for any rough edges, then walked to the cabinet door and lowered the decoration into place. For most projects he didn't bother with practice pieces, but these doors had a complicated design that would twist and turn. Each swirl was only three-eighths of an inch wide and done in ebony. Working out the kinks in fiberboard would save him a lot of hassle later.

Once the faux inlay fit perfectly, he would move on to the next piece, until he'd completed one door's design. The built-in cabinets were for a large house in Seattle. They stretched the full twenty-two feet of the dining room and would be topped with Italian marble.

As he worked, his mind returned to the topic that had captured his attention two days ago. No, not topic. Person. He'd been unable to get River out of his mind.

Everything about her appealed to him. She'd been direct, honest and guileless. Okay, he thought, holding in a grin, pretty and oddly sexy in her thick coat and unflattering beanie. He'd liked her smile and the way she'd pushed past her fear. Oh, and she had friends who looked out for her, so that meant something. He'd spent most of Sunday trying to come up with an excuse to get in touch with her, only to realize that while he knew people who knew her, he wasn't close enough with them to ask for a phone number. He'd regrouped and come up with a plan for today, which explained why he was watching the clock, waiting for it to be close enough to lunch that he could make his move.

At eleven-fifteen, he made a few notes with his red Sharpie, then washed his hands and grabbed his coat. He drove the three miles from the cabinet shop to The Wreath and parked. From there it was a short walk to Wrap Around the Clock. He would make arrangements with Camryn, then head upstairs to River's office.

Despite the fact that it was a Monday morning, Wrap Around the Clock was busy. Several customers perused wrapping paper selections, and a young mom with a baby in a stroller stood in front of a large-format printer. He glanced around until he spotted Camryn, then crossed to her.

"You have a minute?" he asked.

She smiled. "Sure. Are you here on official Snow King business?"

"No, this is personal." He glanced around at all the customers, then looked back at her. "Can we talk somewhere private?"

"Of course."

She led the way to a good-size room with rectangular tables pushed together in the center. A dozen or so chairs were in place around the table, and on the walls were posters showing different ways to wrap a package.

"What happens here?" he asked, not clear on why anyone would want to layer ribbon and lace, then hang a sparkly tag from a package. Not that he'd wrapped much himself. Like most people in town, he dropped his gifts off here and picked them up later, when they were nicely decorated. He supposed it was possible he'd given ribbon-and lace-bedecked packages and had never noticed.

Camryn moved an empty wrapping paper tube to the end of the table, pulled out one of the chairs for him and took a second for herself.

"We have wrapping parties here. Friends bring in their gifts and wrap them together."

"That's a thing?"

She grinned. "It can be. We offer catering from local restaurants. Holiday Spirits can bring in drinks. It's a fun evening." She pointed to the posters. "Depending on what kind of party it is, we'll offer suggestions on how to wrap the gifts. We'll put out a selection of paper and trimmings and give advice on how to make each gift special."

Was it a woman thing? He only ever asked for the present to look nice.

Humor brightened her brown eyes. "You don't have to understand it, Dylan. Just bring your gifts here and we'll do a good job without ever discussing the details."

"Good. Thanks." He paused. "That's what I want to talk to you about. Doing some wrapping." And after they had that conversation, he was going to head upstairs to see River.

Anticipation quickened his heartbeat.

She pulled a small tablet out of her work apron pocket. "I'm impressed you're getting such an early start on your holiday shopping. Most people wait until we're well into December."

"These aren't gifts for friends," he said, still thinking of River. "I'm having seventeen hundred books shipped here. I ordered them from Yule Read Books and . . ."

Two sentences too late, he realized what he'd said. He swore silently, knowing he only had himself to blame — he should have thought through what he was going to say. He always did, every single time, until now.

Camryn stared at him blankly. "I'm sorry, did you say seventeen hundred books?"

"Yes."

"You bought seventeen hundred books and you want them wrapped?"

He knew there was no way to fix this. "I'm giving them to the elementary school-aged children in town. The exact number is one thousand six hundred and eighty-seven, so I guess thirteen of them don't need to be wrapped. They'll go to the library."

She opened her mouth, then closed it. "I don't understand. Even if they're only five or six dollars each that would be close to ten thousand dollars. Plus the cost of wrapping. And shipping them to the store. And sales tax."

She stood and stared at him. "You're the town's Secret Santa. You're the one who fixed those roofs in October when we had that big windstorm. The families didn't have

131

insurance because they couldn't afford it and someone paid for the roofs."

She paced to the door, then turned. "You did the summer camp scholarships. There were twenty. No one knows where the money came from."

She returned to the table and sat down. "I don't understand. How can you do all this? You make cabinets, right? They're nice and all but how can you afford . . ."

She pressed her lips together. "I'm sorry. That's not my business. Let me work up some options for the books. I'm assuming you won't want name tags, so we can do a simple kid-friendly wrapping paper and a bit of ribbon. That'll keep the costs down."

She'd gone from shocked to professional in a very short period of time, he thought, impressed by her quick journey. "I appreciate that. You should have my email address on file."

She typed on the tablet, then nodded. "I do. You're right here. I'll have a bid to you by the end of the day."

He waited for her to say more, but that seemed to be it.

"I don't want anyone to know it's me," he said quietly.

"I won't say anything."

He knew he had no choice but to trust

her to keep her word. "Thanks." He rose. "Is River in her office? She said she works upstairs. I thought we should get to know each other a little before starting our reign."

Camryn stood. "She's there." She walked to the door, then turned back. "Dylan, River's a little shy, so it would be great if you were a nice guy."

He liked that Camryn was protective. "That's always my goal."

"Good." She waved her tablet. "I have a lot of questions, but I'm not going to ask any of them. Or say anything to anyone." She smiled. "The kids are going to love the books."

"I hope so."

They walked into the store. Camryn went to help a customer while he went to the back and took the stairs two at a time, then knocked on the closed door.

He had no idea if whatever he'd felt Saturday had been a trick of the moment or if his attraction had been real. He supposed he was about to find out.

The door opened. River looked at him in surprise. "Dylan, um, hi."

It was the first time he'd seen her without a huge down coat covering her from shoulders to knees. She was gorgeous. Spiky, dark hair, big eyes and a tentative smile tugging

133

at her perfect mouth. She was small and slight, but with just enough curves to give a man ideas.

He wanted to haul her against him and kiss her until they were both breathless. He wanted to do a lot of things that were inappropriate, but fun to dream about. Only right now he didn't have to dream — he had her right in front of him.

"River," he said, giving her his best smile. "I thought, seeing as we're going to be spending time together as Snow King and Queen, it would help if we got to know each other. Can you take a break and join me for lunch?"

Her eyes widened in surprise and her lips parted slightly. Maybe it was him, but it seemed she kind of retreated into herself for a second. He braced himself for her to say no, then she drew in a breath and said, "I'd like that. I read over the list of duties and there are more than I thought. You're right, we are going to be spending a lot of time together, so being comfortable around each other makes a lot of sense."

He relaxed and leaned against the door frame. "The special over at Joy's Diner is Monte Cristo sandwiches and they make the best ones. Interested?"

Her smile turned genuine and kicked him

right in the middle of his chest. All the air rushed out, leaving him trying not to gasp. Jeez — how did she do that?

"I like Joy's Diner a lot and I've never had a Monte Cristo sandwich."

"Then let me introduce you. I think you're going to be amazed."

She laughed softly. "Give me a second to save my work."

She pushed the door open wider, in obvious invitation. He stepped inside and glanced around. The space was bigger than he would have thought, with several windows facing The Wreath. River had a large L-shaped desk with three computer screens and an ergonomic keyboard. There was a map of the United States on one wall and a big dry-erase board. To the left was a sitting area and a few floating shelves where she displayed several books and a snow globe. He took a step closer and saw a happy bee inside.

"I'm ready," she said.

He turned as she crossed to a coat rack. She kicked off clogs, exposing thick, rainbow-colored socks, then stepped into snow boots. She shrugged into her massive coat, wrapped a scarf around her neck and pulled on her beanie.

He held in a smile. "We're going about

half a block."

"It's cold outside. Unnaturally cold."

"I think the temperatures are pretty normal."

The smile returned, offering another body blow. "I meant for me. I grew up in Los Angeles. I shiver when it's below seventy."

They went out onto the landing. River locked the door, then led the way downstairs. As soon as they stepped outside, she pulled gloves from her pockets and put them on, then looked at him.

"You don't wear gloves?"

"It's not that cold and I keep losing them. I'm fine."

"But it's like twenty degrees. Won't you get frostbite?"

"Not in half a block."

"You don't even have on a hat."

He chuckled. "I'm acclimated. Talk to me when it's fifteen below. Now, that's cold."

She visibly shivered. "If it's ever that cold, I'm never leaving my townhouse."

They walked the short distance to Joy's Diner. As they stepped up onto a curb, she seemed to lurch a little, but before he could ask if she was all right, she was striding toward the diner. Once they were inside, Dylan spotted a booth on the back wall and pointed to it.

"How about there?"

She nodded and walked toward it, pausing to unwind her scarf and pull off her hat. Once their coats were hung, they slid in across from each other.

Dylan told himself to play it cool — that no woman liked a guy who was too eager.

River glanced around at the diner. "I like it here. The atmosphere is so friendly and welcoming. I guess all the restaurants are like that in town. It's nice."

"You said Saturday you've only been in town for about six months and today you said you're from LA. How did you get here?"

Their server came up to the table and put down glasses of water and menus.

"Hi, you two. The special today is Monte Cristo sandwiches. They're really good. We serve them with a side salad. You'll probably want to get fries for the table, too. Now, what can I get you to drink?"

He motioned for River to go first. She glanced at the menu, then back at the server. "I'll have a diet cola, please."

"Coffee," Dylan said. "Black is fine."

"You got it."

Their server left. River pushed away her menu.

"I'm going to try the special."

"Me, too. Want fries?"

The smile returned. This time he was a little more used to the kick and managed to keep breathing.

"Fries would be great."

"Then we'll get them. So you were going to tell me how you ended up in Wishing Tree. There has to be a story. Wishing Tree isn't exactly a place a lot of people in California have heard of."

She laughed. "That's true. I sure hadn't. My sister Kelsey unexpectedly inherited a house in town from her grandfather. She wanted to make a change in her life, so she decided to move here with her daughter, Brooklyn."

"Wait, your sister inherited from your grandfather, but you didn't?" That wasn't right.

"It's complicated," she murmured, picking at her paper napkin.

"We have the whole lunch to talk about it. Unless the topic makes you uncomfortable."

"It doesn't." She drew in a breath. "Kelsey and I are adopted. We share a mother, but have different fathers. The inheritance came from Kelsey's paternal grandfather. In the will he said he'd known about her his whole life, but hadn't had the courage to reach out to her. As he got older, he regretted that, so he left her his house. She didn't know anything about the town or the condition of his place, but she came to see it and knew she wanted to move here."

River looked at him. "I couldn't let her move over a thousand miles away by herself. She's my sister! What if something happened? So I came with her. I was only going to stay a few weeks, but then I realized I liked the town and thought maybe I could fit in here. Plus, I can work from anywhere."

Their server returned with their drinks. Dylan ordered for both of them. When they were alone he said, "Are you glad you moved to Wishing Tree?"

"I am. The weather's tough for me, but other than that, I like my life here. I walk to and from work. I'm making lots of friends, which is great. People seem more friendly here, or maybe it's me. Maybe I'm more open."

"Did you leave family in LA?"

"Our mom." River unwrapped her paper straw and dropped it into her soda. "It wasn't easy to leave, but it was the right decision. Brooklyn, Kelsey's daughter, was having trouble in school. She's really smart and quiet and she got bullied a lot and she was having trouble making friends."

She paused as if she was going to add

something, then continued. "Kelsey had already moved her to a different school twice, but with social media and kids being kids, it didn't help. She's doing really well here. She loves her teacher and has a group of girlfriends." She smiled. "She's thriving. Kelsey and I talk about it all the time. It's such a relief."

She was incredibly open, he thought. Just laying it all out there — which took a certain level of courage.

"You're close to your sister and niece," he said.

"I am. They're my family."

"Did you leave anyone special behind?" he asked. "A boyfriend? A husband?"

Shock widened her eyes. "I'm not married and there's no boyfriend."

"Huh," he said, picking up his coffee to keep from clapping. "I would have thought men in Los Angeles were smarter than that."

A blush stained her cheeks. "I don't know what to say to that."

"I think something along the lines of 'Thank you, Your Majesty' would be fitting."

She laughed, a light, happy sound that was just as killer as the smile.

"Thank you, Your Majesty," she said, still laughing. "No, wait. I can't say it and mean it. I just can't."

"Another hope dashed. So your mom's the only family left in LA?"

"She is."

"And she was okay with both her daughters leaving?" he asked before realizing that might be a difficult subject.

"She wanted Brooklyn to be happy and knew moving was the best option and she agreed that Kelsey shouldn't go alone." River sipped her soda. "My mom is a librarian. She's very social and has tons of friends, so we don't worry about her very much. She can take care of herself."

She paused. "But I miss her. There's just the four of us and we've always been so tight. It's hard not having her close. I'm trying not to bug her about moving up here, but I do mention it more than I should."

She shook her head. "Okay, I have to stop talking so much. Tell me about yourself."

"Why do you think you're talking too much?"

"Because I am." She glanced at him, then back at the table. "You're easy to be around. You make me feel comfortable."

He tried not to read too much into that comment, or cheer. Cheering would definitely frighten her and that was the last thing he wanted.

"I like you talking," he said. "I think the

141

reason we're comfortable with each other is we're the only two royals in town. Who else are we going to hang out with?"

She laughed, as he'd hoped she would.

"Wow, you're starting to get serious about the royal thing," she said, her voice teasing. "If this keeps on, I'm going to have to talk to someone in health services and I'm not sure I'm equipped or trained for that kind of encounter."

He grinned. "You don't have to worry. I'm mentally sound."

He leaned toward her and lightly touched her hand. Just a brief second of contact with his fingers grazing her knuckles. There was heat and an embarrassing spark, at least on his end, but more important, she didn't pull back.

"I've never known anyone who was adopted," he said. "Did you and Kelsey stay in touch with your birth mom?"

"No. She was a distant cousin of our mom's, really young and couldn't handle two kids. Kelsey was three when she gave us up, but I was still an infant. I have no memories, which is okay. She gave us to our real mom and we never saw her again."

"Are you okay with that?"

"It's what I know. I don't really think about her. We were loved and that's what matters."

"Did you always know you were adopted?"

"No. If Kelsey knew there'd been someone else raising her, she forgot pretty fast. When I was fourteen, our mom sat us down and told us what had happened. At that point in her life, our mom had realized she probably wasn't going to get married and have kids of her own, so she thought of us as a gift and a blessing."

She smiled softly. "It's kind of nice being thought of as a gift."

Dylan took in the information, doing his best not to react in any way. On the inside he was having trouble grasping what that conversation must have been like.

"You didn't have any hints that she wasn't your biological mom?" he asked. "I'm sure she was careful with the telling, but what a way to change everything about your life."

She nodded. "We were both surprised. She explained that when she adopted us, everyone told her to keep the news quiet until we were considered old enough to process it. Now the thinking is different. Doctors and psychologists agree it's best to have a child grow up with the information. Otherwise, their sense of self can be shattered."

She hesitated. "Kelsey and I were upset

143

for a while. It was a lot to take in. I was slower to get over it. For a while I wondered if I could ever trust her again. But after a couple of months, I realized she loved me and had always been there for me."

He couldn't imagine finding out at fourteen that he wasn't who he thought he was. "You were brave."

The smile returned. "Thank you. I'm not sure I was, but it's nice of you to say." She paused. "Once we'd processed the information Mom asked if she should get in touch with our birth mom and we agreed she shouldn't. We were happy, we were a family. That was all we needed."

Their sandwiches arrived. River cut her two halves into quarters and then drizzled dressing onto the salad. Dylan again marveled at her ability to be so open with someone she barely knew. Before he could consider his words, he found himself saying, "I never knew my dad. My mom got pregnant in high school and while she'd wanted to give me up for adoption, she decided to keep me."

River stared at him. "For real? She told you that?"

He nodded. "She wasn't a bad parent, but she wasn't really interested in me. She made it clear that as soon as I was eighteen, she was leaving Wishing Tree, so I'd better be ready to be on my own."

Her green eyes widened. "That's so hurtful. I'm sorry."

"Don't be. I was fine."

She looked doubtful. He would guess her concern was in part because she was a compassionate person and because she'd grown up being told she was a gift.

He took a bite of his sandwich. When he'd chewed and swallowed, he said, "I met Jake the first day of first grade. We were instant friends and spent all our time together. We've never talked about it, but I'm sure Helen quickly realized my home situation wasn't ideal. I ended up spending more time at Jake's house than at my own. Every September she would take me shopping for clothes and shoes, along with new school supplies." He smiled. "Helen took care of me."

"She sounds really nice."

"She is. Oh, she can be a pain every now and then, but basically, she's my family."

"Did your biological mother leave town?"

"Yes." He looked at her. "The summer I turned sixteen, Helen suggested she sign my guardianship over to Helen and her husband and let me move in with them. They would be responsible for my last two years of high school and getting me settled into the adult world."

"She agreed?"

He remembered her giddy relief. "She was gone by the end of the week." He shrugged. "I hear from her every couple of years. She's living in Miami. I don't know much beyond that."

River studied him. "Do you miss her?"

"Not really. We weren't close. Helen is much more my mother. She's the one who worries about me and more often than not, she's the voice in my head."

River put down her half-eaten sandwich. "So we both come from unconventional families."

"We do."

"This is nice," she told him. "Getting to know you. I really like how everyone here is so open. People share things and get involved. It wasn't like that for me back in LA. Some of that could have been me, I guess. I feel more comfortable here."

"It's a small-town thing," he told her. "We're each other's entertainment."

That made her laugh. "Sadly, I'm not very funny."

"I'm not sure I agree, and you're very charming."

She ducked her head. "Thank you. So are you."

He did his best not to jump to his feet and announce to the other customers that she thought he was charming. They were off to a great start. He couldn't believe his luck — he'd been dreading being Snow King and because of Helen's meddling, he was having lunch with a beautiful, interesting, sweet woman who got his attention in a way he hadn't experienced in what felt like a long time.

He told himself he needed to go slow and think before he acted. That River was special and he didn't want to mess up or scare her off. Which meant there were a few things about himself he couldn't reveal. No, he amended. Not a few — just the one. Until he knew her better, until he was sure, he had to keep the truth to himself and hope for the best when she finally found out.

# EIGHT

Jake liked to think he had the best job in the world. Running the family's resort could be challenging at times, but it was always interesting and he looked forward to getting to work every day. So sitting at his desk and watching the clock wasn't like him, yet here he was, checking the time. Again. Three whole minutes had passed since the last time he'd looked — a dumbass state of being, he told himself. She would get here when she got here and her meeting wasn't even with him, so why did he care?

Only he knew the answer to that question. He'd enjoyed spending time with Camryn and wouldn't mind seeing her again. The only potential problems he could see were first, that his mother had chosen Camryn for her Project: Jake's Bride debacle, and he didn't want to do anything to encourage his mother into thinking he was following her plan. Second, Camryn herself. She'd made it clear she wasn't interested in a relationship — at least not now and not in Wishing Tree. Her "real" life was waiting for her, back in Chicago. Which meant asking her out would be a waste of time for both of them. So he wouldn't. Only he wanted to see her again and she had a meeting with Lucia, his fifty-something-year-old decorator, this afternoon, which was why he was checking the time every fifteen seconds.

He knew Lucia would handle the meeting just fine, but was it wrong for him to pop in and say hello? Wasn't that the polite thing to do? After all, he and Camryn were friends. Sort of. They'd gone out for a drink and they'd both had a good time. At least he had and she'd seemed to. She'd been charming and delightful. If she hadn't just announced she wasn't interested in a man while in Wishing Tree and been a little unsteady from the cocktails, he would have wanted to kiss her when they got back to her house. Seriously kiss her. But he hadn't and that was probably for the best.

He faked working for the better part of an hour, then gave up and left his office. He went downstairs and into the larger of the ballrooms where he found Lucia showing Camryn the hotel's main level floor plan, marked up with the Christmas trees and holiday displays.

They both looked up as he walked into the room and while they both smiled at him, he had to admit he was a lot more interested in Camryn's than Lucia's.

"How's it going?" he asked as he approached the table where Lucia had spread out her plans.

Camryn shook her head. "I'm overwhelmed," she admitted. "The level of detail in every display is astonishing. You have an excellent team."

"I do," he said, winking at Lucia, who laughed.

"I've been decorating Mistletoe Mountain Resort for over twenty years," Lucia said. "Every season we update a few things, try a few trends and generally do our best to give the guests a memorable experience."

Camryn traced the row of Christmas trees in the lobby. "It's a lot of work. I don't know how you get it done in time." She looked at him. "Did you know there are forty-five trees scattered throughout the resort? Forty-five."

"Which is why we can't wait until the Friday after Thanksgiving to start decorating," Lucia said. "The team is getting started today."

Camryn feigned shock, pressing her hand

to her chest. "Does the city council know? Did you have to get a waiver?"

"Lucia takes care of the permitting," he said conspiratorially.

She laughed. "Of course she does." She picked up a roll of wrapping paper and spread it out on the table. "This is what we're talking about. Do you like it?"

While he didn't take a personal interest in the decor for the hotel, he'd been in on a few planning meetings and had been the one to approve this year's color scheme, which was mostly red and burgundy with pops of silver. Camryn's wrapping paper had a swirly red-and-burgundy background with silver ornaments in different shapes and sizes scattered across the paper. There was a second sheet that was the opposite. A swirling silver background with red and burgundy ornaments. Two wrapped and beribboned packages sat on a nearby chair. The finished product, he would guess.

"We hadn't planned on having packages beneath the trees, but it's a fabulous idea," Lucia told Jake as he pulled up a chair. She turned to Camryn. "Unfortunately, for it to work, we're going to be pushed for time. I'd need the bid by first thing tomorrow and the packages no later than Saturday."

"Of course," Camryn said easily. "I'll put

151

together the bid as soon as I get back to my office. For small custom projects, I print the paper myself, but for something this big, I'll have it done at the graphics shop. I've already reserved time, so they can have the paper to me by three tomorrow. The boxes will arrive overnight, so I'll have them tomorrow, as well. I'll deliver the wrapped presents first thing Saturday."

"How many packages are we talking about?" he asked casually.

"Five hundred and fifty," Lucia said, making notes on her tablet.

He hadn't been expecting the number to be that large. "By Saturday?" How was that possible? Thursday was Thanksgiving, so she'd lose a whole day.

"Uh-huh." Camryn patted his arm. "Don't worry. I can do it. I have employees and for projects like this, I call in the potential grandchildren and a few of their friends. They work for cheap and they're surprisingly good at wrapping packages."

Lucia mentioned a few more specifics, then rose. "I was going to walk Camryn around the property so she could see where the trees were going to be."

Jake picked up one of the tablets. "It's all in here, right? Under the decorating tab?"

Lucia frowned. "It is. Why? Do you want

a copy of the plan?"

"I know you have forty-four more trees to put up. You go ahead. I'll give Camryn the tour." He smiled. "Don't worry, Lucia. Camryn and I go way back. We were in high school together."

"Oh, of course, I keep forgetting everyone knows everyone else in this town. Thanks, Jake. I do need to get back to putting up trees."

She shook hands with Camryn and excused herself. Jake motioned to the large room.

"This is the ballroom," he said. "It's big."

Camryn laughed. "Yes, I can see that." She pointed to the far end. "The poinsettia tree is going there, right?"

"Yes, we do that every year. It's lit with small twinkle lights and is fairly dramatic when it's finished. The guests love it. We didn't put it up one year and we received multiple complaints. We're not making that mistake again."

She tucked her notes into her briefcase and rolled up the wrapping paper. "You were right about me having a headache after those two drinks. Thanks for the advice."

"You're not much of a drinker, I take it."

She grinned. "Apparently not. I will say I hadn't eaten since breakfast, so there's that, but the truth is I only go out with my friends, and I rarely have that second cocktail. I hope I didn't say anything inappropriate."

"You were charming."

She laughed. "I doubt that, but thank you for saying it."

She looked good, he thought. Black pants and a pretty orange-and-green sweater. Her makeup was light and her hair just brushed her shoulders. The curls looked soft and for a second he wanted to bury his hands in them.

"Shall we?" he asked, pointing to the hallway. "The majority of the trees are in the lobby, with a few in the main hallway."

She picked up her briefcase, while he took the rolls of paper. They walked to the front of the hotel. A pair of fifteen-foot trees stood by the main entrance. Three decorators manned each one, carefully putting on ornaments. Two additional workers were covering the large fireplace mantel with garland.

"It's going to be beautiful," she said, pulling a sheet of paper out of her briefcase. "Okay, so Lucia said two fifteen-foot trees, twenty twelve-foot ones, twenty-three ten-footers. I think bigger packages will look more impressive than small ones. I'll use

154

both papers and the same ribbon combination to tie everything together." She looked at him. "I'm excited about the challenge."

"You're going to be wrapping twenty-four hours a day."

"Not even close. Trust me, I have a good team and we can pull together something like this."

"Was it difficult to step into running the store?" he asked. "After you lost your mom?"

"A little," she admitted. "I took over while she was still alive. She was sick, but could still answer questions. Then she was gone and it was all on me." Her mouth twisted. "I have a degree in finance and while I know a lot of theories, very little prepared me for being responsible for my employees' paychecks." She grinned. "On the bright side, I always know what everyone's getting for their birthday or Christmas, so that's fun."

He showed her the lounge, where one of the ten-foot trees would go.

"You must have found it difficult to leave all your friends behind," he said. "Do you stay in touch?"

She nodded. "With several of them. It's not like it was, but we keep current on each other's lives. Sometimes they tell me things I don't care about. Like Greyson getting engaged."

"Who?"

"Oh, right. Why would you know?" She looked away, then back at him. "I was engaged when I came home. At first I thought my mom was just sick and would be getting better but I quickly figured out her cancer was terminal. That's when I knew I had to move here to take care of her and my sisters. I quit my job, packed up my condo and leased it out. There really wasn't anything here for Greyson. He was an account executive at a large bank — not a job that relocated easily. Especially to a small town. And he said long-distance relationships didn't work, so we ended things."

Jake stared at her. "Your ex-fiancé wasn't willing to give you a break when your mother was dying of cancer? He couldn't wait a few months to see how things would go?"

"You make him sound awful."

"That's one word for what he did. He was a jerk and an idiot."

There were a lot of other words to describe the man, but Jake kept them to himself. Camryn was the kind of woman a guy moved mountains to be with, and her fiancé had simply walked away?

"You're sweet to defend me," she told him.

"I'm stating the obvious." He paused to do the math in his head. "Wait a minute. Within the space of two or three months you lost your home in Chicago, a job you loved, your friends, your fiancé and your mom? And at the same time you had to take over the family business and become legal guardian to your twin sisters?"

She winced. "When you put it like that, you make it sound like a lot."

"It was a lot. I'm impressed you're still standing. But you're doing better than that. You're thriving."

She flushed. "I'm not all that."

"Yeah, you are. And between now and Saturday you're going to wrap over five hundred packages and run your business. Tell me how that happens?"

"I put on my Wonder Woman costume and get to work," she said, her voice teasing.

"Any chance I can see you in your Wonder Woman costume?"

She laughed. "Sure. Just let me know a good time." She glanced at the decorating plan. "All right. Somewhere around here is a very long, very wide hallway."

"Right this way."

As he showed her where twelve of the trees would line the hall, he thought about all she'd told him. Now he understood why

Camryn was wary about committing herself to a man — the last one had let her down and broken her heart. Knowing that made him wonder if her reluctance to get involved came from wanting to return to Chicago or from not being willing to trust someone again. And even though it shouldn't, he thought maybe the answer to that question was going to be a big deal to him.

Under normal circumstances River would have been nervous about her meeting with Helen Crane, but her brain could only process one crisis at a time and it was currently busy worrying about her lunch with Dylan.

Not specifically about him — he'd been great. Funny, attentive, easy to be with. No, her greater concern was how she'd simply blurted out so much about her past and her life. Where was her edit button? Not that she usually needed it. In most social situations, she was quiet, but when she was around Dylan, she just talked and talked.

He'd seemed okay with their time together, she told herself. He'd listened and laughed and the meal had rushed by. So maybe he hadn't been put off by her info dump. Or maybe he was just extra nice, so his boredom didn't show.

Before she could decide, she drove through the open gates and saw a beautiful three-story house, no doubt on the huge lake she'd driven by on her way in from town. The Crane family had some serious money, she thought as she parked. Being rich wasn't her thing, but she knew it mattered to some people.

She got out and walked to the beautiful carved double doors, where she rang the bell. A few minutes later Helen let her in.

"Right on time," the older woman said, leading her through the house. "We'll go to my office, if that's all right."

"Of course," River said as she caught glimpses of exquisitely furnished rooms, a kitchen larger than her entire townhouse and views of the lake.

Helen's office was a welcoming space done in blues and yellows. The older woman motioned to a comfortable-looking sofa and took a seat opposite. She poured them each a cup of tea and pushed a plate of frosted cookies toward River.

"How was the drive?" Helen asked.

"Easy. The town keeps the roads very clear. I'm still not comfortable driving in snow, so I appreciate that." River sipped her tea. "I have studded tires. I'd never heard of them, but Xavier, my sister's fiancé, suggested I get them. They make a big difference for me."

"They're a smart accessory," Helen told her. "Especially for the winter novice."

Jake's mother was well-dressed, in a knit twinset and dark pants. Her makeup was subtle, her jewelry low-key but obviously expensive. She still wore her wedding set.

River's gaze settled on the large diamond. Seeing it made her think of weddings, which reminded her of why she was here.

"I won't be a good candidate," she blurted. "No offense, but it's not going to happen. I don't do well under emotional and social pressure, and this lifestyle isn't one I'd be good at."

Helen smiled. "Ah, so you know about Project: Jake's Bride?"

"Camryn told me."

"That's right. Your office is above her store so you've become friends. It's good to have people you can depend on in your life." Helen picked up her tea. "Don't worry, River. I'm interested in you because of your computer skills. While you're a charming young woman, I don't think you'd be right for Jake. But what I would like is for you to perform background checks on the contenders. I would like to know all about their online life and anything else you can find out."

She handed River a list of names. River scanned them, visually stumbling at one halfway down.

"Camryn's name is on here."

Helen nodded. "Yes, I know."

"I'm not investigating Camryn without telling her first."

"Interesting, but I understand your concern. Feel free to speak to her."

River didn't know anyone else on the list. She explained about the various levels of investigation and her fee schedule.

"Excellent," Helen said. "Let's do a deep dive on everyone. Send me a contract or however you authorize work and you can get started right away. Are you enjoying your reign as Snow Queen?"

The change in subject surprised River. "I don't know," she admitted. "I haven't had any duties yet. The first event is the tree lighting on Friday."

"It is. You're new to town, aren't you? Let me see. I believe you moved here with your sister."

"Yes. Over the summer."

"Do you like Wishing Tree?" Helen's voice was kind as she asked the question.

"I do. The people are friendly." River worried her lower lip. "Sometimes I do better with computers than with people," she admitted. "I'm more comfortable here. Everyone is very welcoming."

"We do try to show the world our better angels. What are your plans for Thanksgiving?"

"Oh, um, Kelsey and Brooklyn are going back east with Xavier to meet his family. My mom's coming to visit me. We're going over to Camryn's to have dinner with her and her sisters. We haven't worked out the menu yet, but we're going to share cooking duties."

"Camryn's not going to have much time to cook," Helen said. "She has a new wrapping project that's going to keep her busy through the holiday." Her smile turned sly. "Don't tell Jake, but I have a few spies at the hotel. They keep me up-to-date on things."

River had no idea what to say to that. "My mom and I can do the cooking."

"Nonsense. You'll come here. There's plenty of room and so much food, it's embarrassing. I'm having only close friends and Jake, of course. I'll call Camryn and invite her and the girls, as well. Oh, and Dylan, because he's family. Your mother and I must be close in age. I'd very much like to

162

meet her. Why don't you come by around noon? We don't eat until three, but it will be nice to get to know everyone."

"I, ah . . ."

Helen rose. "Excellent. I'm looking forward to the day, aren't you? I'll call Camryn in the morning and confirm everything. All right, my dear, I'll let you get back to work. Send me that contract so you can get going on your investigations. I do hope all the women pass your test, but if they don't, then they're not going to make the final cut. I'm firm on that."

Before she knew what was happening, River found herself standing by her car with a sense of having been managed by an expert. She was happy to take the job, but the Thanksgiving invitation had been a surprise. She wasn't entirely sure she'd agreed to it but had no doubt Helen expected her and her mother to be prompt.

Maybe a big group would be fun, she thought as she drove back to town. Her mother would enjoy meeting her friends, and if Camryn did have a new job, then having someone else doing the cooking might be a help. Plus, Dylan would be there and to be honest, she wouldn't mind spending more time with him. And this time, she promised herself, she would let him do all the talking.

# NINE

Five hundred and fifty boxes took up a lot of space, Camryn thought early Tuesday morning as she stacked them by size. The wrapping paper was confirmed for early that afternoon, and per her latest update, the ribbons and lace were out for delivery today. She had the signed contract, made a couple of posters detailing how to get the look the resort was paying for and later that very day, a team of twelve fifteen- and sixteen-year-old girls would arrive at four to wrap until eight. She was ordering in pizza and sodas and, in a perfect world, would have close to two hundred packages wrapped by the time they were done.

The Wednesday before Thanksgiving was only a half day at school, so most of the teens would return for a shorter session that afternoon. Camryn knew between herself and her employees, they could wrap at least a hundred and fifty boxes on Wednesday, leaving around a hundred or so to be completed on Friday. The teens would return the first week of December to wrap the books Dylan had bought. Those packages were less fancy and easier to wrap, so they'd go more quickly.

"Things are going to be busy around here," she murmured to herself, double-checking she had enough tape on hand to secure the paper. But busy was good. She would make a nice profit on both big projects.

She heard the back door open. Seconds later River walked in.

"Morning," her friend said, beginning the process of unwinding her long scarf and shrugging out of her thick, warm coat. "You're here early."

"I'm starting a big wrapping project for the resort. Just a heads-up. I have a group of teenage girls showing up later. They're good workers, but they can be shrill. Plus, I put on music for them. You'll want to keep your door closed so the sound won't bother you."

River laughed as she put her coat, scarf and hat on the worktable. "Thanks for the warning. That kind of noise doesn't affect my ability to concentrate." She pulled off her knit cap and fluffed her hair. "I saw

Helen Crane yesterday."

"Jake's mom?" Camryn wasn't sure whether to laugh or hug River in sympathy. "She talked to you about Project: Jake's Bride?"

Not that River wasn't pretty and smart, but somehow Camryn couldn't see her with Jake.

"I was afraid it was that, but luckily she's only interested in my computer skills. She's hiring me to investigate the candidates."

"Seriously?" Camryn shook her head. "I both admire and fear her. She's really making a run at finding him a bride. Poor guy."

Honestly, she didn't understand why Jake was single. He was gorgeous, funny, easy to talk to and a lot of fun. She'd enjoyed all her encounters with him. Under different circumstances, she wouldn't mind getting to know him better. And while she was making those confessions, she would admit — if only to herself — that she wouldn't say no to being invited into his bed.

"You're on the list," River said.

Camryn took a second to understand what that meant. "What?" she asked, her voice a shriek. "After she and I talked about this? I'm on the list? Me?"

River shrank back a little. "I'm sorry."

Camryn groaned. "No, don't be. I didn't

mean to shout. This isn't about you. I thought Helen and I had reached an understanding. Apparently, she wasn't listening. Wow. Okay, then."

River continued to watch her.

"It's okay," Camryn told her. "You can investigate me all you want. I have nothing to hide." She thought for a second. "Can I have a copy of what you find? I'm curious about what information is out there."

"Helen's paying for the report. I'll have to get her permission."

"That makes sense." Camryn laughed. "Your job is more complicated than I would have thought. You have to deal with investigating your friends, with crazy mothers, and then me wanting to know what you turn up."

River relaxed. "It's okay. I'm sure she'll say you can see the report." She pointed to the boxes. "Is that for the big resort job?"

"Uh-huh. They need five hundred and fifty wrapped packages by Saturday."

"That's a lot." Tension returned to River's slim shoulders. "When I saw Helen yesterday, she asked what I was doing for Thanksgiving. I told her my mom was coming to town and that we were having dinner with you and the twins and that we were sharing the menu."

"Yikes. You're right — we are, and I've been a total slacker on that. This new job has pushed everything out of my brain. We need to make decisions."

River's hands fluttered. "Yes, well, Helen invited us to dinner at her place. She said you'd be too busy to cook and she has extra food and she wants to meet my mom. She said she'll have a few friends in, plus, you know, Jake. I didn't say yes, but somehow she thinks we're going there on Thursday. All of us. She's going to call you later to talk about it."

"I'm sorry, what?" Have Thanksgiving with Helen and her family, which pretty much meant Jake? "We can't do that. I barely know the woman."

"That's what I thought, too, only she overwhelmed me and then it was done and I was standing outside by my car and I don't know how it happened."

Which sounded very Helen-like, Camryn thought. That woman could move mountains.

"Do you want to have dinner with Helen and whomever else is there?"

"I don't know," River admitted. "It sounds fun and scary at the same time. But you've said you want to make sure the twins have a nice Thanksgiving to start to build new memories. I'm happy to have it just be the five of us, but if you want to go to Helen's, my mom and I can do that, too."

Given how much work she had to do, not cooking would be great, but going to Helen's? Wasn't that kind of strange?

"Let me talk to her," Camryn said. "If she means the invitation, we'll go. If it seems she's regretting asking us, we'll get together this afternoon and figure out the menu. Yikes, and get a turkey so it can start thawing. Does that work?"

"Yes. I'll wait to hear from you." River picked up her coat, then paused. "I had lunch with Dylan yesterday."

"Your Snow King. Yes, he stopped in for some wrapping and then mentioned he was going to go upstairs and see you. Did you have fun?"

River's mouth curved into a smile. "I did. He's nice and easy to be with."

"You have a tone," Camryn teased. "You like him."

River blushed. "Maybe. A little. Relationships are tough for me. I never know how much to say or what guys expect."

"You mean except for sex."

River laughed. "Yes, I'm clear on the sex thing. In a way, that's easier for me. I understand what they want and how to act.

It's the regular stuff that's more difficult."

"I don't know him well," Camryn said. "He was a few years ahead of me in high school. He's lived here his whole life and I've never heard anyone say anything bad about him. Jake says he's a good guy. I guess they're pretty tight."

"That's what Dylan said, too."

"You'll be hanging out, doing Snow King and Queen stuff. That should give you the chance to get to know him in a more casual and organic way. Maybe it will be less stressful than dating."

"You're right," River said. "The lunch was good." She sighed. "I talked too much, but he didn't seem to mind."

"For what it's worth, you'd be a cute couple."

"Thanks. It's been a long time since I had a guy in my life." River's tone was wistful. "I wouldn't mind finding someone special."

She gathered the rest of her outerwear and started for the stairs. Camryn returned to her boxes, telling herself to focus on work and deal with the slightly odd, slightly unsettling, Thanksgiving invitation later.

A little before ten that morning, her cell rang. She glanced at the unfamiliar number before answering.

"Hello?"

"It's Helen Crane, Camryn. Is this a good time?"

"Sure." She walked into her small office and closed the door.

"Has River mentioned my Thanksgiving invitation? I'm hoping you and the twins can join us. There's lots of food and good conversation. We'll be a relatively small group, but mighty in spirit." Helen paused. "I'd enjoy meeting your sisters."

"I thought we'd agreed you'd be taking me off the candidate list for Project: Jake's Bride."

"We discussed it," Helen hedged.

"It's not happening. I'm not participating and you shouldn't be hiring River to investigate the other women. In fact, you need to let the whole idea go."

"What I need is grandchildren, but that's neither here nor there. My request that you join us for Thanksgiving is about enjoying your company, nothing else. I promise not to whisper a word about you marrying my son."

Camryn hesitated. She wouldn't mind skipping the cooking this year, while still giving her sisters a fun day, but it wasn't as if she and Helen were friends.

"I know River is having a little trouble fitting in," Helen added. "And meeting people.

I'm sure her mother worries about her. Having Thanksgiving at my house will let her mother see she has a circle of friends and a social life. Plus, I'm very good with teenagers, so I'm sure your sisters will have a lovely time."

"You forgot to mention how you excel at making people feel guilty," Camryn said drily.

Helen chuckled. "There is that, isn't there? So you'll come over? Let's say around noon? We can all spend time together before we eat at three. If you want to bring something, how about a nice salad? You and the twins can put it together that morning. It will be an easy dish and you'll carry on the tradition of cooking together."

"How did you know we always cooked together on Thanksgiving?"

Helen's voice turned kind. "Because that's what families do. I'll see you Thursday. Goodbye."

She hung up, leaving Camryn standing in her office, feeling like she'd just been managed.

"Mad skills," she murmured. "The woman has mad skills."

She was about to return to the store when she realized there was a big problem with Thanksgiving at Helen's house. A six-foot-two-inch problem who might not want to see her or her sisters across from him at dinner.

"Crap," she whispered. "Double crap."

She glanced at her phone only to realize she didn't have Jake's phone number. Why would she? After hesitating for a second, she looked up the resort and called, then asked the operator to put her through to Jake.

She went to a secretary first, because sure, why not, before he picked up.

"Jake Crane."

"Hi, it's Camryn."

There was a brief pause before he said, "Hey, you're calling me on my work number."

"That's the only way I know to get in touch with you. So I have to tell you something and I want you to be completely honest when you say what you think. If it's too weird or you're uncomfortable, just say the word and I'll totally drop it. It's your thing and if this messes with that, then I want to know."

"You realize I have no idea what you're talking about, right?"

She heard the humor in his voice and hoped he was just as amused when she was done.

174

"Yes, well, okay. So through a series of circumstances that aren't that important, your mother invited me and the twins to Thanksgiving. I would have said no right off, only she invited River and *her* mother, and the five of us were going to have dinner together, so it would be weird for me to refuse. Plus, you know, last year was so awful for the twins and I want them to have a good Thanksgiving and going somewhere else would be a complete change, so there's that, but if it's a problem, then of course we won't go. And it's totally not a Project: Jake's Bride thing, although I should probably warn you that your mother hasn't let that go at all." She paused for breath. "Are you mad?"

"Give me your phone number."

"What?"

"Give me your phone number."

She did. Seconds later her phone chimed with an incoming text.

"I just sent you my contact info," he said. "Now you can call me directly. As to Thanksgiving, you should definitely come. My mom's surprisingly good with teenagers."

"That's what she said."

"The twins will have a good time. I get you accepting the invitation had nothing to

175

do with wanting to marry me. I'll deal with my mother on that directly. Come. We'll have a good day."

"Thanks. I feel better. Also, for the record, your mother has amazing powers of persuasion. I wasn't sure I'd ever said yes, but there we were, agreeing we'd see each other Thursday."

"That sounds like her." He chuckled. "So we're good?"

"We are."

"Then, like my mother, I'll see you Thursday."

"Absolutely. Bye, Jake."

"Bye."

She hung up and slipped the phone into her pocket, happy he'd been so great about the situation. And if she was being honest with herself, she would admit she really was looking forward to seeing him again. A lot.

"I could have driven into Seattle," River said for the third time in the past twenty minutes. "It's not that far, Mom."

Elizabeth, her mother, patted her on the arm. "The shuttle was more convenient and very comfortable. It's a drive to and from the Seattle airport and there's a mountain pass. When you have a little more experience driving in the snow, you can come get me at the airport. Until then, I'll take the shuttle."

Her mother had flown from Los Angeles to Seattle, then had gotten on the Wishing Tree shuttle into town.

"I'm glad it was still daylight when I came over the mountain," her mother added. "Everything was so beautiful with the trees and the snow."

"Plus, you made three friends on the drive," River teased. Her mother was the most social person she knew. Oh, to be like her, she thought wistfully.

"I did. I met a very nice lady who manages a place called Joy's Diner. Do you know it?"

"Yes. It's in the center of town, in The Wreath."

"The town square," her mother said. "I remember when I visited over Labor Day. It's so interesting that it's round, although that must be why it's called The Wreath." She laughed. "I'm looking forward to seeing it all decorated for the holidays. And your townhouse. You hadn't moved in yet when I was here before. Oh, and the office, of course. Last time I was here, you'd just signed the lease. Now you're settled."

River had spent the morning tidying so her workspace was mother-viewing ready.

She generally kept her house pretty clean, but her office could get messy with to-go containers and notes.

"You'll see all of it," River said happily. "We'll have a good time. Are you sure you're all right with our Thanksgiving plans?"

"I'm excited to meet your friends and see the house you described. It sounds wonderful."

"Good. I think we'll have fun. Oh, I've bought everything we'll need to bake pies. We can start tonight and finish in the morning."

Her mother smiled at her. "Sounds like a perfect plan." Her stomach growled. "But first, maybe some dinner."

River laughed. "Absolutely. I thought we'd go have dinner at the local Mexican restaurant. Navidad Mexican Café. I know enchiladas are your favorite and theirs are really good."

"That sounds nice. Do all the businesses have a Christmas-themed name?"

"Most of the ones in The Wreath. Judy's Hand Pies doesn't and there's a store called Nothing to Do With Christmas, which doesn't carry any holiday items but still has the word Christmas in their name."

Her mother laughed. "The town is as charming as I remember."

River turned onto her street and pulled into her two-car garage. She got out and lifted her mother's suitcase from the trunk, then led the way inside. She'd left lights on, knowing it would be dark by the time they arrived. Her mother stepped into the living room and looked around.

"It's lovely, River. This place suits you. Are you happy?"

River hugged her mom. "I am. Very."

"Good."

She hung her coat and then her mom's. After setting her mother's suitcase at the bottom of the stairs, she gave her a brief tour.

"This is the main living level. The bedrooms are upstairs. There's a small half bath tucked under the stairs."

"The kitchen is a good size."

"I know — it's the main reason I chose this place. That and the name of the street."

She tried to see her townhouse as her mother would. The furnishings were the same ones she'd had in her apartment in Los Angeles. She had a comfortable sofa with an ottoman, and two club chairs. Her small dinette set fit in the eating area, with room to spare.

Her mother crossed to the small fireplace and touched the Galileo thermometer on the mantel.

"I see this survived the move," she said with a smile. "I'm glad."

"Me, too." River had found the thermometers fascinating when she'd been a kid, and her grandfather had given her this one when she'd graduated from high school.

She carried her mother's suitcase upstairs and showed her the guest room and bath.

"It's so comfortable," her mother said. "You've done a good job making a home."

River smiled. "Thanks. Why don't you unpack and get settled, then we'll go get dinner? After that, pies."

"Sounds like a plan."

River went downstairs where she busied herself checking to make sure she had all the ingredients they would need to make pies. She got out flour and cans of pumpkin, along with a couple of pie dishes, then heard footsteps on the stairs. Her mother walked to the kitchen and pulled out one of the stools at the counter.

"River, before we go to dinner, I'd like to talk to you."

Her stomach dropped. "Okay. Is everything all right?"

She wanted to add, "Don't tell me anything bad" but knew that wasn't fair.

Her mother, a pretty brunette with large

blue eyes, looked at her. "I'm fine, but I worry about you. How are you doing, really? You're always so cheerful when we talk and text, but I worry about you settling in."

Relief eased her tension. "Mom, I'm good."

Her mother's worried expression didn't change. "I just want to be sure you're happy and that you have friends. That was the main reason for you moving here. To find a place where you could be comfortable enough to belong."

River walked around the counter and hugged her mom. "I'm doing great. Seriously, you have to believe me. I really do have friends. I'm not that bullied little girl in a back brace anymore."

"You broke my heart with your pain," her mother admitted. "It was so hard to see you suffer physically and then be tortured by the kids at school." Tears filled her eyes. "Girls you thought were your friends turned on you. I was so worried you'd lost your ability to trust anyone. Then I hurt you and Kelsey so much when I told you about being adopted."

She brushed her cheeks. "I was so wrong in how I handled that. I should have told you from the beginning. But I didn't and that gave you one more reason not to trust."

River rushed to her mother and held her. "No. Don't say that. It's not your fault. You did exactly what our pediatrician told you to do. The advice was the same in all those psychology books you read on adopting a child. It's what they believed when we were little."

Her mother looked at her. "I destroyed your world."

"You didn't." River remembered the shock and pain of not knowing who she was. But eventually, she and Kelsey had figured out Elizabeth loved them with all her heart and had only done what she thought was right.

"Mom, we're both doing well. I promise. Kelsey has Xavier and I have friends and a good life here."

"I want you to be happy."

"I am."

"You promise?"

River squeezed her hands. "Yes." She took the seat next to her. "Sometimes it's hard for me to be in social situations and I can still get lost in my work, but less than I used to." She smiled. "Plus, I'm the next Snow Queen."

"I was so excited when you told me about that. I love that your friends all put your name in. They care about you."

"They do. You'll be at the first event. It's

Friday. The tree lighting." River had received her instructions that morning. They were fairly simple. Show up on time and turn on the lights. She was pretty sure she could do both and not mess up.

"I'm getting a life here," River added. "I go out and do things. And hey, Thanksgiving at someone's house. That should impress you."

Her mother smiled. "It does. I'm glad you're developing a network of people you can count on."

River shook her head. "I hear a *but* coming."

Her mother smiled. "You're right. There is one. But you're not dating. Kelsey found Xavier. Now it's your time to fall in love."

"I want that," she admitted. "I'm just . . . wary. Men are complicated and unpredictable. Emotionally, I mean. I'm never sure where I stand and trusting them is hard."

"More bad experiences from your past," her mother said with a sigh. "Part of your reluctance is my fault."

"What? You weren't the really bad boyfriend, Mom."

"No, but by the time I adopted you and your sister, I'd given up on love. I had two wonderful girls, my friends, my career. I didn't bother with a romantic life, so you never saw a functional romantic relationship."

"I don't think you should have gotten married to be a role model. Not everyone needs to pair up. You're proof of that."

"I know and now that I'm getting older, I wonder if I should have tried harder. It would be nice to have someone special in my life." Her mother looked at her. "I don't want you having my regrets."

"I appreciate that and I do want to have what Kelsey has." A man who loved her whom she could give her heart to. Was that possible for her? She just wasn't sure. "I'm terrified of picking wrong, but open to the possibility. How's that?"

"It's a start. Have you met anyone interesting?"

River immediately thought of Dylan. He'd been so great when they'd been chosen and at lunch.

Her mother laughed. "You have! I can see it in your eyes. Tell me everything. Who is he?"

"His name is Dylan and he's the Snow King. We've just met, but he was nice."

"Handsome?" her mother asked, her voice teasing.

River smiled. "Yes, very. Dark blond hair and blue eyes. He's a cabinetmaker and he seems, I don't know, solid, maybe. If that makes sense. Maybe *unflappable* is a better word. Like he can deal with stuff. You'll meet him tomorrow at Thanksgiving."

"I can't wait."

"Don't go planning the wedding. I really did just meet him."

"I won't mention anything about bridesmaids, I promise. But I'll keep my fingers crossed."

River grabbed her mom's hand. "I'm so happy you're here."

"Me, too. I'm excited about the snow."

River straightened and wrinkled her nose. "It comes with really cold weather. I have extra scarves and gloves for you. We'll be walking nearly everywhere and it's freezing out there. I don't like that part."

"You'll adjust. The town is so pretty."

"You should move here," River said, laughing. "I know I promised not to mention it every fifteen minutes, but Mom, you so should. Then you'd be close to both of us."

She expected her mom to dismiss her idea, but instead, she glanced down and then back at her. "I'll admit I've been thinking about it. Only a little, but maybe."

"You mean that? You've thought about relocating to Wishing Tree? What about your job and your friends?" River tried to tamp down her excitement. "I know thinking isn't doing, but I'm thrilled you've gone that far with the idea."

"I've worked at the library nearly thirty years. I'm vested in my pension. I'll be sixty-two next year, so I could take early retirement." Her smile was rueful. "The house is empty with Kelsey and Brooklyn gone, and I miss all my girls. I think real estate prices are much higher in Los Angeles and there's no mortgage on the house, so I could use the proceeds to buy something here and still have money to put aside for my old age."

River did her best to keep from squealing. "This is the best news, Mom. I won't push, but I'm really happy." She stood and hugged her mom. "I think you'd like living here." She stepped back and smiled. "When the pies are baking, I'll go online and see if there are any open houses this weekend. You know, just to get an idea of what's available."

"That sounds like fun. But we're just looking. I'm not ready to buy."

"I know. We'll explore the Wishing Tree real estate market so when you *are* ready, you'll find the perfect home."

# TEN

Dylan arrived at Helen's house a little after noon on Thanksgiving. There were already several cars in the circular driveway. He knew that some friends of Helen's would be joining her for dinner. Jake, too, of course, and per the text he'd received yesterday from his friend, Camryn and her sisters.

"Helen isn't even subtle," he said, walking toward the front door. He knocked once and let himself inside, then followed the sound of conversation to the family room.

"Hello," he said as he entered.

Helen, always the center of attention, rose and crossed to him, taking both his hands in hers.

"My darling boy. You made it."

Over her shoulder he saw Jake grinning as he mouthed "Darling boy?" Dylan knew there would be hell to pay later for that.

He kissed both her cheeks. "Thank you for having me," he said.

"Always. And the flowers you sent are lovely." She motioned to the eight or nine people in the room. "You know everyone, I believe."

He nodded and went around greeting everyone. Jake slapped him on the back.

"Suck-up," he said in a low voice. "You're trying to make me look bad by sending flowers."

Dylan grinned. "I was raised to treat people right. We can't help that you're a loser."

Camryn walked into the room then and smiled at him.

"Hi, Dylan. I was checking on my sisters. They're upstairs in the media room, watching a replay of the Macy's parade. Have you seen that giant screen on the wall? It's the size of a movie theater."

Jake moved next to her. "We come here to watch football games every Sunday," he said. "You're welcome to join us."

She smiled at him. "I do enjoy the game, but I can't say the same about the twins."

"Then come by yourself."

Dylan watched the brief exchange with interest. According to Jake, his mother had backed off on her Project: Jake's Bride plan and had given up on Camryn as a potential candidate. Dylan had his doubts about both

188

assumptions. He would say that Camryn's presence here indicated the opposite. He would also guess that Jake was interested in Camryn, which was going to make for an entertaining afternoon.

The doorbell rang. Helen looked at him. "Dylan, be a dear and get that for me."

"Sure."

He walked to the front of the house and opened the door, only to find River and an older woman standing on the porch. They each held a wire rack that held two freshly baked pies.

"River?"

She gave him a tentative smile. "Hi. Helen invited me and my mom for Thanksgiving." The smile faded. "Is that all right?"

"More than all right," he said, holding the door open wide. "It's great. Come in."

He ushered them inside, then carefully took the pie racks and set them on the large entry table.

"I'm Dylan Tucker," he said, helping her mother with her coat.

"Elizabeth Best." River's mother smiled at him. "You're the Snow King."

"I am." He winked. "But we're an informal crowd. You can just call me Dylan."

Elizabeth laughed. "You're so gracious. Thank you for that."

189

He turned to River. "Hi. I didn't know you were going to be here. You're a really terrific surprise."

She ducked her head, then looked back at him. "Thank you."

"It's a fun group," he said, picking up one of the pie holders. She took the other. "You know Jake and Camryn and her sisters. Helen also has a few friends she's known for years. There's tons of food. A catering service delivers the meal in the morning and Helen finishes it all here. About a half hour before we eat, it's all-hands-on-deck with the prep but until then, it's just easy."

He led the way into the family room. Helen rose and greeted River and her mother, then introduced them around. Dylan delivered the pies to the kitchen. River followed a few minutes later.

"Do these need any special treatment?" he asked.

She shook her head. "We made the pumpkin pies last night, so they're completely cool. They're fine at room temperature. The other two are spiced apple and mincemeat. We made them this morning, so they're still warm. Sitting out will be good for them."

She was so beautiful, he thought, staring into her green eyes. Earnest and sweet and she smelled like cinnamon and vanilla. How was he supposed to resist that?

"You made four pies in two days?"

The smile returned and so did his reaction to it.

"I like to bake. Once you get the crust down, pies are pretty easy, but it was still fun to make them with my mom."

"You're having fun with your mom?"

"I am." She pressed her hands together. "She's thinking of moving here in a year or so, to be close to Kelsey, Brooklyn and me. I hope she decides to relocate."

"Me, too. We have the tree lighting tomorrow."

"I know. I got the email." Her eyes brightened with amusement. "The instructions were fairly simple. Show up on time and throw a switch."

"It might be snowing."

She sighed. "I saw that. I get the snow will make things pretty, but it usually gets colder when it snows."

"Poor River, done in by the weather."

"I looked online. It's seventy-eight right now in Los Angeles. That seems much more normal to me than snow."

He groaned. "Seventy-eight? That's just plain wrong. You want snow for the holidays. That's why there are so many songs about Christmas and snow."

"That's just people making the best of a bad situation."

He laughed. "You can't believe that."

"You know I'm right."

He chuckled, more than pleased that she was obviously getting more comfortable around him.

"What can I get you to drink?" he asked. "There's red and white wine along with soft drinks and beer."

"I'll wait for dinner to have wine," she said. "I'll take anything diet."

He filled a glass with ice and found a can of diet cola. After she was set, he went into the family room to take Elizabeth's drink order. He poured her a glass of white wine and took it to her.

Jake followed him back to the kitchen. "Trying to make me look bad?"

"You're busy with Camryn," Dylan told him, then added, "You like her."

"Maybe. Not that it matters. She doesn't plan to settle in Wishing Tree. Once the twins are out of high school, she's moving back to Chicago."

"Maybe not," Dylan told him. "She's already been here what? A year? Plus three more, and it's not like she'll leave the minute the twins graduate, so after four or five years she'll go back? Does she have family there or even friends?"

"She seemed determined."

"You could try to change her mind."

Jake grinned. "You in league with my mother?"

"I don't have to be. You haven't been interested in someone in a while."

"Yeah, and there's a reason."

Dylan looked at his friend. "You're not your dad."

"You don't know that."

"I do. You're a good guy, Jake. You're not going to screw up that way." Dylan glanced toward the family room. "I'm just saying, you're interested and I don't see her backing away. See where it goes."

Jake followed his gaze. "Maybe. What about you and River?"

"I'm all in and ready to mention having babies."

Jake shook his head. "We both know that's cheap talk."

"Okay, yeah, but she's intriguing and I want to get to know her."

"You might want to wait to tell my mom that," Jake suggested. "She already meddles too much. If she finds out she was right to make you Snow King, she'll try for something even more dramatic."

"I find it humorous that you're afraid of

your own mother."

"Like you're not," Jake said.

"Never. Now, if you'll excuse me, I'm going to sit next to River and tell her funny stories about when we were kids."

"Let me guess," Jake said. "You'll be the hero of every one of them."

"Absolutely."

Camryn split the last of the bottle of Painted Moon Winery red wine between her glass and Jake's.

"The advantage of doing cleanup," she joked. "First pick of the leftovers."

He touched his glass to hers. "I like how you think, but if you're worried about missing out on leftovers, don't be. My mom will send you home with as much as you can carry."

"I won't say no to it. Leftovers mean no cooking tomorrow."

She looked around the huge kitchen. There were miles of counter space and nearly every surface was covered with serving bowls and platters and dirty dishes.

"Okay, we're going to need a divide-and-conquer strategy here," she said.

He nudged her toward the table by the window. "Or we could sit here until we finish our wine and *then* figure out a strategy.

194

To ease your mind about our task, my mother keeps a stack of to-go containers in the pantry, so dividing up the food between everyone who wants it will be easy."

"She thinks of everything."

"Sometimes she thinks of too much."

She sat in one of the chairs. She was too full — which was how Thanksgivings were supposed to end — and very happy. Despite being around a bunch of adults, the twins had had a good time. Everyone had paid attention to them, and Dylan and Jake had kept the teens laughing throughout the meal.

"My sisters had a wonderful time today," she told him. "I'm grateful so I refuse to say anything bad about your mom."

"I respect that. I'll grumble for both of us."

"Or maybe you can surrender to the inevitable and accept that she just might find you your one true love."

His hazel gaze settled on her face. "Really? What are the odds of that?"

"Probably small, but depending on the size of the field, it could happen." She sipped her wine and hoped he couldn't tell she was smiling.

"Is the thought of my mother's matchmaking still funny when I point out that for all we know, you're still on the list?"

"I am still on the list," she said smugly. "She asked River to investigate me. Well, not just me, but all the candidates. Apparently, there are several."

He groaned. "Tell me you're kidding."

"Oh, Jake, we both know I'm not."

He sighed heavily. "What am I going to do with her?"

"Endure."

She studied the man across from her, thinking that while a serious relationship was off the table for an assortment of reasons, she wouldn't say no to something less . . . traditional. Jake was a handsome, confident guy who'd been involved with a lot of women. She would guess he knew what he was doing in bed and wouldn't that be nice? A practiced seduction with an attractive man whose company she also enjoyed sounded like the perfect from-her-to-her holiday gift.

Her gaze dropped to his hands and for a second, she fantasized about how they would feel on her body. If only there was a way to casually ask if he was interested in a little no-strings sex.

"Have you and the twins talked about your mom today?"

The contrast between what she was thinking and what he'd asked was startling.

"How did you know?"

"It's Thanksgiving. You lost your mom, what, in October? You'd talked about how last year the holidays were a blur of sadness."

The combination of kindness and concern in his voice made her want to fling herself at him — and not for anything naughty. Instead, she had the strangest urge for a body-engulfing Jake hug. One that made her feel warm and safe and protected.

"We did," she said, putting down her wine. "In fact, we spent the morning going through some boxes we'd put in the garage last year. Her clothes and jewelry and a few mementos."

She looked at him. "We're going to donate her clothes and we decided who got which pieces of jewelry." She smiled sadly. "There wasn't much, of course. I'll be putting everything into the safety-deposit box next week. We were sad, but I think we also healed a little."

She leaned toward him. "Sometimes I feel like I'm living her life rather than mine. The store, raising the kids, that kind of thing. But then something happens and I realize I choose to be here because it's the right thing to do."

197

"For you and the twins, or just for them?"

"I think for all of us. As much as they've needed me to help them heal, I've needed them, too. I decided to have us go through everything today because I knew coming here would be a distraction."

"I get it. This is our second Thanksgiving without my dad. He's been on my mind and I know Mom's been thinking about him a lot."

There was something in the way he spoke. The tone, maybe? Or something else. She wasn't sure.

"You miss him, too, don't you?"

"Sure," Jake said, avoiding her gaze. "He was my father. It's different for her. He was a bigger part of her life."

She supposed that made sense. A parent was different than a life partner.

The twins ran into the kitchen.

"Helen said we need to go see the lake," Victoria said eagerly. "Her friends went home so it's just us now. There's a full moon and she said it's really beautiful and spooky at the same time."

"You can't beat spooky," Jake told them, then looked at Camryn. "Any interest?"

She looked out the window and saw only a reflection of the kitchen. "At the risk of sounding like River, it's maybe twenty degrees outside and I'm not in the mood to be that cold." She smiled at him. "You can go with them. I'll start the cleanup."

"I've seen the full moon before."

Lily sighed. "When I'm almost thirty, I'm going to do everything."

"Still not getting out of this chair," Camryn said with a laugh. "But you have fun."

The teens ran out.

"I thought sure the guilt would work," Jake said.

"It does, but it has to be more significant than going outside when I'm perfectly comfortable sipping my wine and enjoying good company. Although I'm sure the moon looks beautiful on the lake. Ask me back when it's mid-July and I'll be a firm yes."

"It's a date."

Their eyes met. Camryn felt a distant kind of emotional and physical *ping* somewhere deep inside her chest. Interesting, she thought, wondering if he shared her reaction or if she was having a little fantasy all on her own.

Somewhere at the other end of the house, a door slammed. Camryn used the distraction to look away.

"The twins are excited about the tree lighting tomorrow," she said. "I'm glad it's late enough that I'll be done with work."

"Will you have a big crowd for Black Friday?"

"Not until the afternoon. People go shopping, then drop off what they've bought." She smiled. "I'll have the morning to finish wrapping packages for the resort."

"How's that going?"

"Nearly five hundred are done."

"Already?"

"I told you I had it covered. Yes, four hundred and eighty-seven packages are beautifully finished. I'm going to rent a van to get them up to the resort in a few trips."

"Don't do that," he told her. "We have a couple of vans. Tell me a good time and I'll send them down to the store."

"Are you sure?" she asked, thinking that would save her at least a hundred dollars on a rental. "I have a van reserved."

"Cancel it. We can —"

A sharp scream came from outside. Camryn and Jake were instantly on their feet and moving toward the French doors off the family room. Dylan already had it open and was heading outside, River and her mom right behind him.

The twins came running to the house, Lily holding something in her arms.

"She's dead!" the fifteen-year-old cried. "Camryn, she's dead!"

200

Victoria was at her heels, with Helen right next to her.

"We don't know that," Jake's mom said firmly. "Let's get her inside and see."

Camryn had no idea what they were talking about. As Lily rushed into the family room, Camryn saw she was carrying a small dog. The animal had ice- and snow-coated fur and its tiny eyes were closed.

"Dylan, go get towels from the linen closet," Jake said calmly. "Mom, go with him and bring me a couple. Dylan, put the rest of them in the dryer. We want them warm."

Dylan disappeared down the hall, Helen and Elizabeth following. Jake took the impossibly small dog from Lily.

"River, take the girls upstairs to the media room."

"What are you going to do?" Victoria asked, her voice a wail. "Is she dead?"

"I don't know. She might just be very cold. We're going to find out." He looked at them. "If she's not all right, I'd rather you weren't here, okay?"

The twins looked at each other and nodded slowly. River stepped between them and guided them toward the stairs. Camryn looked at the tiny, still dog in Jake's arms, not sure how something that small could survive in the cold.

Helen and Elizabeth returned with several towels. Jake wrapped one around the dog and began brushing off the snow and ice. He rubbed her gently, trying to get blood circulating. He stopped for a second and stared at the dog, as if willing her to move. There was nothing.

Camryn pressed her lips together, trying not to cry. Who would have left a tiny dog like that out in the snow? Its coat wasn't much protection and it could easily have been eaten by a wolf.

Jake continued rubbing the dog until Dylan returned with a warm towel. He wrapped it around the dog and moved to the sofa where he sat with her cradled in his lap.

"Come on, little girl," he said quietly, stroking her face.

A paw moved.

"Jake," Camryn said eagerly. "Did you see that?"

She settled next to him, watching the dog intently. The dog's body shuddered, then she started shaking.

"More warm towels," Jake said to his mother. Helen raced to get them.

When she returned with two, Camryn put them on her lap. Jake shifted the dog to her and she quickly wrapped her up in the toasty fabric. The little dog barely weighed anything and Camryn could feel her ribs through her coat.

"It's all right, baby girl," Camryn murmured softly. "You're okay. We're warming you up."

The little dog opened her eyes and stared at them. She looked confused and fearful.

"You're safe, sweetie," Helen cooed, sitting on Jake's other side. "Poor little dear. How on earth did she get outside, so far from everything?"

"I have no idea," Jake said, eyeing her.

Camryn continued to rub the dog through the towel. The dog eventually raised her head a little, then looked around. The trembling subsided.

She tried to sit up, but couldn't.

"She's probably starving," Camryn said. "And thirsty."

"Let's take her in the kitchen and get her water and plain turkey breast," Jake said. "Just a small amount. If she's been starving, she'll need a few days to adjust to eating again."

"How do you know all this?" Camryn asked as she rose, the dog in her arms.

"I run a resort in the mountains," he said easily. "Cold weather rescue comes with the terrain. We have a rescue team based near the resort, but I've taken a few courses myself, so I'll know what's going on."

"Show-off," Dylan grumbled good-naturedly. "I'll go upstairs and let River and the twins know the dog's okay." He paused. "What kind is it?"

"A long-haired Chihuahua," Elizabeth told them.

"If you say so."

Helen put several towels on the large kitchen table. Camryn sat in a chair and set the wrapped dog on the towel, careful to move slowly.

"How are you doing?" she asked softly. "You scared us. Yes, you did."

Jake brought over a small bowl of water. The dog lapped several times before lying back down and closing her eyes.

"She's exhausted," Camryn said, stroking her soft fur. The dog had a white head, tail and front legs, and was light brown everywhere else.

Helen cut a few slivers of turkey breast and handed them to Camryn. She offered them to the dog who gulped them down.

"Is she okay?" Victoria asked as she and Lily raced into the room, Dylan and River just behind them.

"Indoor voices," Camryn said mildly.

"She's got to be scared, so let's talk softly." She fed the dog more turkey.

The twins hovered near the table, watching the little dog.

"She's so small," Lily whispered. "I don't know how we found her. I saw something out of the corner of my eye and we went to look."

They inched toward the table. Lily held out her hand to the dog, who sniffed her fingers, then gave her a tentative lick. The teens sat at the table and took turns petting her. After a few more bites of turkey, the little dog lay back on the towels and closed her eyes.

Camryn agreed with Lily — finding this little creature had been a miracle. And how had she been left in the snow? She was too small and too unsuited for the climate.

"I wonder if she got away from some vacationers," she said.

"There aren't any cabins around here." Helen pressed her lips together. "The house sits on five acres, so we're on our own out here. No one has ever dumped a dog by us before. I don't know what to think."

"Someone dumped her?" Victoria asked, tears filling her eyes. "So she'd die?"

"We don't know what happened," Jake said calmly. "But we found her now and she

205

seems to be doing better. The question is what do we do with her?"

The twins immediately turned to Camryn.

"We can take care of her," they said, speaking as one. "She's so small — she wouldn't get in the way."

"She's not our dog," Camryn pointed out. "She could be lost. We have to find out if she has a family who's missing her."

"Not very much if they left her alone in the snow," Helen said.

"Mom." Jake shook his head. "Let's be helpful. We need to get her to the vet to see if she has a microchip that will tell us who she belongs to. We also need to get her checked out medically."

He was right, Camryn thought. "I can't do that," she told the girls. "I have to wrap presents in the morning, then the store will be busy in the afternoon, and the day after is Small Business Saturday." Helen seemed the obvious choice to keep the dog, but Camryn wasn't comfortable volunteering her.

"But she needs us," Lily said earnestly. "Camryn, please. She's so small and alone. We'll totally take care of her until we can find her family."

"And if she doesn't have one," Victoria

started, only to be nudged into silence by her sister.

"I can't get away from the store," Camryn repeated. The dog probably wasn't going to be that much work, but she had to be seen by a vet. And weren't there authorities that needed to know about her?

"If you're okay keeping the dog," Jake said, "I can take her and the twins to the vet tomorrow. The hotel is quiet, so I can get away whenever we can make an appointment."

"That's an excellent idea," Helen said firmly. "So it's settled. Camryn and her sisters will take care of the little dog and Jake will get her checked out. In the meantime, the twins can go online and figure out what we're supposed to do when we find a lost dog in Wishing Tree. Girls, you stay with her while the rest of us divide up the food and clean the kitchen. You'll want to get her home and settled as soon as possible."

In less time than she would have thought, Camryn was carrying two bags of leftovers to the car. The twins both sat in back, the tiny dog bundled between them.

Jake helped her load the food in the front seat, then walked her around to her side.

"I'm going to be home," he said. "If you

207

need anything, feel free to call."

She nodded, glanced at her sisters, then back at him. "We have a dog. I mean, just for the weekend, probably, but still. How did it happen?"

"I have no idea. She seems to be doing better. Just remember — small meals."

"Of chicken and rice. Yes, I remember. So when I get home, I'm cooking for one."

He lightly touched her cheek. "You're a really good sister."

"You're a really good rescuer. Amazing skills in the cold dog resuscitation department."

He smiled a slow, sexy smile that had her wishing they were alone and she'd had maybe one more glass of wine so she could suggest they try a little kissing and if that went well, take things to the next level. But they weren't and she hadn't.

"Please thank your mother again," she said. "We all had a great time."

"Plus the bonus dog."

She laughed. "Yes, there's that."

"I'll be in touch with the twins after I call the vet."

"You're a good man, Jake Crane."

"You say that to all the guys you know."

"Actually, you're the only one I've called Jake Crane."

# ELEVEN

First thing Friday morning, Jake called the Wishing Tree Animal Shelter and explained what had happened. The volunteer who answered the phone quickly checked for a report of a lost dog.

"A Chihuahua, you say?" the woman said, sounding doubtful. "We don't get many of those up here. Sounds like maybe a vacationer lost their dog."

"That's what we thought."

She checked the database. "No reports of a lost Chihuahua. We have access to a statewide reporting system for lost dogs and I don't see anything within a hundred miles of Wishing Tree. I'd say she was dumped but that doesn't happen much in this part of the state."

At least that was something, he thought, hoping no one had been so cruel to the tiny dog.

"We're taking her to the vet this morning," he said. "To have her checked out medically and to find out if she has a microchip. What's the next step if she doesn't?"

"Bring her by the shelter. We'll take pictures and get information out on social media. We have room for her. There's a two-week waiting period, in case her owners show up. After that, we'll put her up for adoption. If she's as cute as you say, she'll go quickly."

Jake had a feeling the twins wouldn't like the idea of the little dog going into the shelter for two weeks or someone else adopting her.

"Can she stay where she is for the waiting period?" he asked.

"You mean be fostered? Sure. It's always better for the animal to be in a regular home than in a shelter. They're less stressed and happier. We can talk about that when you bring her in."

"Will do. Thank you. We'll be by around one-thirty."

He hung up and made a few notes. The morning had been a busy one. He'd arranged for the resort vans to swing by Wrap Around the Clock at four to pick up wrapped packages for the decor. The lost dog had a vet appointment at noon and they would head to the shelter right after that.

He texted Camryn what he'd learned from the volunteer at the shelter and confirmed he would pick up the twins at eleven-thirty, then turned his attention back to work.

A little after eleven he headed into town. When he reached Camryn's house, the twins were waiting for him. Victoria held the dog, who was wrapped in a warm blanket.

"Thanks for helping us," she said formally.

Lily nodded earnestly. "Yes, Jake. We know you're busy and have a very important job. You're very kind to take so much of your day on our behalf and we're grateful."

He smiled at the teens. "Did your sister make you practice that more than once?"

They looked at each other, then back at him.

"She did," Victoria told him. "But we totally mean it and appreciate it a lot. So does Tinsel."

"Tinsel?"

"Our dog. Oh, and she's a girl."

Lily nudged her. "We're not allowed to say she's our dog. What if she has a chip?" She looked at him. "We went on the shelter website so we know what's going to happen. Camryn says we can foster her but we have to realize her owners are going to come get her. So we're not supposed to get attached."

Too late for that, he thought as he held open the back door of his SUV.

The twins clung to each other as the veterinarian ran the scanner over Tinsel's tiny body. Seconds later he shook his head.

"No chip."

The sisters hugged each other, then jumped in place. The vet looked at Jake.

"Happy news, I take it?"

"I think they're hoping to adopt her. We're heading over to the shelter when we're done here so she can be put in the database."

"If her owners do come to claim her, someone should have a talk with them. No dog should be left alone in the cold, but especially not one like this."

He examined her carefully. "She's about three or four years old. In good health, considering all she's been through. But she's severely underweight. I'd say she needs to gain a pound or a pound and a half."

"We know about giving her small meals," Lily told him. "Our sister Camryn made boiled chicken and rice last night and we've been giving her that every three hours. Just a couple of tablespoons."

"That's a good start. I'll get you the name

of a high-protein canned food that will help her put on weight. She'll be on that, along with kibble, for about three weeks. Then you can transition her to regular dog food, but do it slowly."

He gave them a couple of sheets of paper that listed instructions, along with recommended brands.

The vet eyed the dog. "I don't usually say this, but you might want to get her a sweater for inside the house and a jacket when you take her out. She can't tolerate cold the way a bigger dog can."

Lily and Victoria looked at each other. "We'll talk to Camryn when we get home," Victoria said. "We can walk to the pet store, but she'll have to call them with her credit card so we can buy what we need."

"I'll take you," Jake said easily. "We'll go to the shelter and register Tinsel, before dropping her off at home. We'll grab lunch, then hit the pet store and get all the supplies Tinsel will need."

The twins looked at each other, then surprised him by rushing forward and hugging him.

"Thanks, Jake," Lily said earnestly. "You're the best."

"You are," Victoria echoed.

He hugged them back thinking, not for

the first time, he would have liked a couple of siblings in his life.

While Lily and Victoria got Tinsel settled at the house, Jake texted Camryn the afternoon plans. When she didn't answer right away, he figured she was with customers or wrapping the last few packages. Probably for the best, he thought with a grin. That way she couldn't tell him he was doing too much.

He took the twins to the burger place out by the skating rink, then they drove to the large pet store across from the outlet mall. The twins had measured Tinsel to make sure they got the right size jacket and harness for her. Jake pushed the cart as they filled it with food and beds, a very pink leash, and two tiny Christmas dog sweaters.

"Reggie makes clothes for her dog," Lily told him. "Belle's a Great Dane, so she's hard to shop for. I wonder if she could teach us to make clothes for Tinsel."

"Not your dog," he said for possibly the fourteenth time in the past couple of hours.

"But she *could* be," Victoria pointed out. "If nobody claims her and we convince Camryn we really, really will do *everything* for her."

"We love her already," Lily added. "We have our own rooms but last night we stayed

214

in mine so Tinsel could sleep with us and feel safe."

"Sacrifice," he murmured, thinking Camryn was in deep trouble when it came to that little dog. Or the teens would get their hearts broken when her owner turned up and claimed her.

"We need toys," Lily said, pointing to a display of doggy tennis balls.

"Belle size." Victoria held up a huge ten-inch tennis ball.

They laughed, then Lily picked up a package of the smallest yellow balls. "These are perfect."

"She'll want something that squeaks," Jake told them. "And something she can chew."

As the twins studied the selection of dog toys and discussed their options, Jake glanced at his phone and saw Camryn had texted him back.

You're doing too much. Stop! Please! I'm going to owe you forever as it is.

He smiled, thinking he kind of liked the idea of her being in his debt. Under other circumstances, he could think of really interesting ways for her to make things even. But she'd made it clear she wasn't looking for a relationship, and he didn't see her being the casual-sex type, which left him wondering why he always managed to end up on the short end of the relationship stick. He supposed this time he could absolutely say his disappointment wasn't his own fault. So maybe that was an improvement.

Still, given the choice, he'd much rather have Camryn than a life lesson — if only that was an option.

"Are you going to be all right on your own?" River asked as she and her mom walked toward The Wreath where the tree lighting ceremony would take place.

Her mother laughed. "I'll be fine. I'm meeting Helen, and she's going to introduce me to a few of her friends. After the ceremony we're having dinner. I have a key to the front door and I know my way home. You don't have to worry about me."

Apparently not, River thought, more than a little envious of her mother's ability to connect with people so easily. She'd only met Helen the day before, but they had hit it off and would probably become lifelong friends. River knew, relationship-wise, she moved at a much slower pace.

Not a bad thing, she told herself. As long as she kept looking to get involved and connect. She was doing better than she had been and she needed to celebrate her forward progress.

The night was cold and cloudy. Snow had fallen earlier in the day, but wasn't expected again until the morning. As they approached The Wreath, she saw more and more people. The open space was already filling up as people came to participate in the first event of the Christmas season.

Once they entered The Wreath, they could hear the Christmas music. All the stores circling the area had been decorated with twinkle lights, and three large trees stood by the stage.

"River!"

She turned and saw Dena, her husband, Micah, and their baby daughter.

"Are you excited about the tree lighting?" Dena, a pretty brunette, asked.

"I am," River said, thinking she was telling the truth. Sort of. She was nervous about standing in front of so many people, but she was happy to be seeing Dylan again. She'd enjoyed his company at dinner yesterday.

She introduced her mother, then spotted Camryn and her sisters and waved them over.

"How are you?" River asked. "What happened with the dog?"

"Tinsel," Lily said, hugging her. "We named her Tinsel."

"She's so sweet," Victoria added. "She doesn't have a microchip, so we took her to the shelter and they put her in the database, so now we have to wait for two weeks to see if her owners claim her."

Lily nodded. "And Jake took us to the pet store and we bought her tons of stuff and we hope we see Reggie because we want to ask her to teach us to make dog clothes."

Camryn looked at River. "Hi. We're good and living a dog-centric life. Obviously, we'll be fostering Tinsel until her owners are found."

"If they're looking for her," Victoria muttered.

Camryn sighed. "They're bonding, and telling them not to doesn't seem to be helping."

"What do *you* think of Tinsel?" River asked.

Camryn smiled. "She's kind of sweet, but still a dog, so a lot of responsibility. We'll figure it out."

Helen joined their group and asked about Tinsel. Paisley walked over and was told about the lost dog, then Reggie, Toby, Toby's son Harrison and Belle, the Great Dane, arrived.

As everyone talked and laughed, River realized that over the past six months, she'd actually made friends with a lot of people in town, which was kind of a big deal. This was what it felt like to belong, she thought happily.

Paisley tapped her shoulder. "All right, Snow Queen. It's time."

River glanced toward the stage and saw that Geri, the city manager, was up there next to the three huge trees.

River looked at her mom. "You'll be all right with Helen?"

Helen linked arms with Elizabeth. "Don't you worry. We have a fun evening planned. I'll have her home by midnight."

"Enjoy yourselves," River said, then started for the stage.

The closer she got, the more her sense of happy belonging seemed to fade until she was a mass of nerves and regrets. Why had she agreed to do this? She wasn't very good at —

"Hi."

She turned and saw Dylan walking toward her. Instantly, her stomach calmed, even as her breathing quickened. He looked good. Strong and handsome, with an easy smile that let her know he would make sure she got through the evening.

"Hi, Dylan." She glanced at his hands and saw they were bare. "It's freezing. You should have gloves."

"Naw. I'm fine."

"You'll get frostbite." She hesitated a second before pulling a pair of men's gloves out of her coat pocket. "Here. My mom and I went shopping today and I saw these and I thought of how you said you're always losing them." Her voice trailed off.

He stared at her without speaking and she had no idea what he was thinking. Oh, no — had she messed up? Was he upset? Annoyed? Did he think she was weird or awkward or —

The smile returned. "You bought me gloves? For real?"

Relief replaced worry. "You don't want to get frostbite. It's bad."

"I've heard that." He pulled on the gloves and flexed his hands. "Perfect. Thank you. That was very thoughtful."

"You're welcome."

They continued toward the stage. As they got closer, River realized the trees were taller than she'd first thought and each was decorated differently.

"The trees of Christmas Past, Present and Future," Dylan told her. They stopped in front of the one on the right. It was covered with beautiful, old-fashioned ornaments made of wood or mercury glass or porcelain. Each had a small tag attached.

"They're beautiful," she murmured, touching a tiny ballerina.

"This is the tree of Christmas Past. Local families donate a special ornament for the tree lighting," he told her. "Some of these have been passed down for generations. They're labeled so the right family gets theirs back tomorrow."

He moved to the middle tree that was decorated with handmade ornaments. There were snowmen made out of Ping-Pong balls, painted wooden beads in the form of stars, and glitter-covered snowflakes.

"The tree of Christmas Present. A couple of weeks ago all the kids in town made an ornament for the tree. The schools co-ordinate an afternoon dedicated to making the ornaments. Local businesses donate the supplies."

She smiled at him. "Makes me wish I'd grown up here."

"I wish you had. I would have met you sooner." He moved to the last tree.

"Let me guess," she said with a smile. "The tree of Christmas Future." She looked at the simple paper ornaments. There were circles and squares, all tied to the tree with yarn. "What are these?"

"Wishes," he told her. "This is the wishing tree. People write up their wishes and put them on the tree, hoping they'll come true."

She turned over a cutout heart. "I wish there was no more hunger," she read aloud, then glanced at him. "So not a wish anyone can make happen in an afternoon."

"Some of them are aspirational, but some are more practical." He turned over a square. "I want basketball shoes. Size 5." He pointed to a three-digit number on the bottom. "That's the reference number. If someone wants to donate a pair of size 5 basketball shoes, they would take the wish and put it, with the shoes, in a collection bin at any of the fire stations. A few days before Christmas the gifts are wrapped and delivered."

"I've seen trees like this before. We had one at the mall where you could buy toys for kids. I always got a couple of things, but somehow this feels more personal. So anyone can make wishes come true?"

He smiled at her. "Absolutely." He pointed to the stage. "Shall we?"

He took her hand and together they walked up onto the stage. Geri was already there, paperwork in hand.

"You made it. Good. Tonight is simple. I'll say a few words, everyone will count down from ten, then you'll pull the lever." She pointed to a large pole with a knob at the end. "Please wait until everyone says one. Two years ago the lights went on at three. It was very disappointing."

She handed them their crowns. "You'll want these."

"Not really," Dylan whispered in River's ear.

She laughed and pulled off her hat, then set the crown in place. Geri removed a remote from her pocket and pushed the button. The music was cut off mid-note. She moved to the microphone.

"Good evening, everyone. I'm Geri Rodden, your city manager."

"We know this part," someone yelled.

Geri smiled. "I just like to be sure. Tonight is the official town Lighting of the Trees. If you loaned us an ornament for the tree of Christmas Past, it will be available for pickup tomorrow morning at City Hall. Wishes from the tree of Christmas Future can be taken tonight. But please remember — if you take a wish, you're committing to fulfill it." Her expression turned stern. "We don't want any disappointed children on Christmas morning."

"She's a little intimidating," River murmured.

"You'll do fine."

"How can you know that?"

"You're a rule follower."

"Mostly."

At least these days, River thought. There had been a time when she'd been comfortable hacking into companies and government systems with no regard for the laws she might be breaking. She'd ended up paying a price for that.

Geri started the countdown. When everyone shouted "One!" she and Dylan pulled the lever and all three trees lit up. The trees of past and future had white lights that twinkled while the present tree was covered in multicolored lights. The music came back on and the crowd began to sing along with "I'll Be Home For Christmas."

Geri nodded approvingly. "Right on time. I've scheduled twenty minutes for pictures. Go stand in front of the trees. Once you're done, I want the crowns back. Don't think you can wear them home. They're city property."

"Pictures?" River asked faintly.

"You don't have to do anything but stand there and look pretty," Dylan said, his voice teasing. "You'll be good at that."

His compliment warmed her from the inside.

Sure enough, for the next twenty-plus minutes, there was a line of people wanting to have pictures taken with the Snow King and Queen. River held babies and hugged grandparents and smiled until her face hurt. Once they'd worked through the line, Geri appeared to collect their crowns.

"You're off duty," she said, putting the crowns into a large tote bag. "You have a bit of a break until next Thursday. That's the first of December and the beginning of Advent. I'll email you the particulars but I won't tell you the town event until the day of. That way I don't have to worry if you've kept the secret or not."

Dylan chuckled. "You're not a very trusting person, are you?"

"I've learned to be cautious." Geri nodded at them. "Have a good night."

She turned and disappeared into the crowd.

Dylan turned to River. "Do you have time for me to buy you a hot chocolate?"

Anticipation fluttered in her stomach. "I'd like that."

# TWELVE

River and Dylan made their way across The Wreath to Jingle Coffee. There was a line, but it moved quickly. Just as they were placing their orders, a table in the corner opened up.

"Want to grab that?" Dylan asked, pointing. "I'll bring the hot chocolate."

River nodded and claimed the table. While she waited, she pulled off her hat, then unwound her scarf. She hung both on a hook on the wall, then placed her coat on top, before sinking into a chair.

Her back hurt, probably because she'd been neglecting her stretching what with all the busyness of the holiday weekend. Tonight, she promised herself. She would spend a full half hour stretching before taking a hot bath.

As she waited for Dylan, she glanced around. She'd been in Jingle Coffee on Tuesday morning, on her way to work. Like

226

the rest of the town, the store had been decorated to celebrate Thanksgiving. But now, one day after that holiday, it was all about the December holidays. Beautiful menorahs sat on shelves right next to small Christmas trees. There were stuffed reindeer, penguins with hats and a Christmas mouse. Wreaths hung on the walls, and garland decorated the door frame.

Dylan walked over, a hot chocolate in each hand. He smiled as he approached the table and she felt her lips curve in return.

"I asked for extra marshmallows," he teased as he set down their drinks.

"You're spoiling me."

He pulled off his outerwear, then sat across from her. "Feeling better about your Snow Queen duties?" he asked.

"A little. If they're all like tonight." She grinned. "With Geri in charge, I'll always know exactly what's expected of me. I find that comforting."

She sipped her drink. "There's something really satisfying about how connected the town is. Like the wishing tree. We had something similar back home, but here I feel like if I buy those basketball shoes, I might actually see the kid wearing them, which would be great." She paused. "I'm not making sense."

"You are. You want to be generous, but it's nice to see that generosity in action."

"That's exactly right."

She looked around at the crowd in the coffee shop. She didn't know that many people by name, but their faces were familiar.

"Back in LA it was my mom, my sister and my grandfather. He lived with us until he died. I liked having him around. He never understood what I did with computers, but he respected my passion." She smiled at the memories. "His thing was antique pocket watches. He learned to repair them when he was a boy. For a while, he didn't have many customers because only a few collectors cared about them, but they had a resurgence of popularity in the 1980s. He taught Kelsey everything he knew and she repairs them now."

She glanced at him. "There are collectors all over the world. They ship their watches to Kelsey and she repairs them. She has vendors who replicate the parts using the same techniques that were used hundreds of years ago. It's all custom work. Obviously, most of the watches are owned by wealthy people although she does get the occasional client who inherited a watch and wants it to work again."

Dylan frowned slightly. "Jake's father had a pocket watch. At least I think he did. I'll have to ask him."

"It must have been hard on you when he died. He was like a father to you, as well, wasn't he?"

"Yeah. He and Helen were good to me from the first day Jake and I met. Knowing Helen the way I do now, I'm sure she quickly realized how difficult things were for me at home. She always went out of her way to make sure I had whatever I needed. New clothes and school supplies in September, presents for the holidays." He cupped his drink. "My birthday's in the summer and they always planned a family trip over the date and invited me along. I owe them a lot."

"They sound nice."

"They were." He looked at her, his expression intense. "I know this sounds strange, but sometimes I feel I have to protect them — especially now that it's just Jake and Helen."

"Protect them? In what way?"

"They have a lot of money and people assume things when you're rich. I saw how other kids sometimes treated Jake differently than they treated me. If he was having a party or going to a theme park, they would try to get me to ask him to invite them. As I got older, the dynamic played out in different ways, but it was always there. There's a kind of respect that isn't earned but is instead assumed."

"I never thought about something like that happening, but it makes sense that it does," she said. "I have wealthy clients, but all our interactions are through emails and maybe a few phone calls. I don't have any personal contact with them." She smiled. "And what with not being rich myself, I'm pretty safe."

"Better that way," he teased. "You can know who your real friends are."

"Information that's important," she murmured. She was always careful about who she trusted, but once that trust was earned, she was an all-in kind of friend.

"Helen's house is huge," she said. "It must be hard on her, living out there by herself."

"I'm sure she's lonely. My guess is she would rather live in town, but she doesn't want to sell the house and Jake has no interest in it. I think she's hoping he'll get married and then want to move into it with his new family."

"Too bad he and Camryn aren't a thing," she joked. "The twins would love living on the lake."

"Plus, there would be plenty of room for the new addition."

"Tinsel?"

"Is that what they're calling the dog?"

"Uh-huh. You know they're only fostering."

Dylan's gaze met hers. "Two teenage girls and one small, cute dog. Does anyone think that's only temporary?"

"Camryn's probably hoping."

"I doubt that's going to end well for her."

River laughed. "I know, but I don't want to point that out to her."

They talked for another half hour, then put their empty mugs on the tray in the corner and collected their coats.

"Thanks again for my gloves," Dylan told her.

"You're welcome." She wrapped her scarf around her neck. "I fully expect you to lose them, so don't feel guilty when that happens."

He studied her for a second. "You won't be mad? I mean, I'll try not to, but it could happen."

"They're a gift. Once you accept them, they're yours. I have no ownership. I'm glad you like them but if they get lost, I'm not going to read anything into it."

Nuance wasn't her strong suit. She'd

learned a long time ago her life was easier if she simply accepted things at face value. She wasn't always right but at least she was consistent.

They stepped out into the cold. River took a second for her lungs to adjust to the frosty air.

"I can't wait for summer," she murmured as they walked through The Wreath.

"Technically, it's not winter yet."

"I know. January and February are going to be long."

"Maybe we should plan a trip to Hawaii and break up the stretch."

"Don't tease me about warm weather," she told him. "I miss my seventy-degree days."

"Poor River. Unsuited for snow and cold."

"I'm like a hothouse orchid. Slightly odd and unable to survive outside."

He looked at her. "You left out *beautiful*. Hothouse orchids are beautiful." His voice was soft, almost tender.

Oh. Was he saying she was, too? Was he flirting? She hoped he was, just as she hoped he hadn't been completely kidding about going to Hawaii. Okay, she barely knew him, but she liked what she'd seen so far.

They turned on Mittens Avenue and walked toward her townhouse. In too short a time, they were standing on her front porch.

"The lights are off," she said, staring at the windows. "I'm both impressed and shamed."

"Because you didn't leave the lights on?"

She laughed. "No, because my mother has been in town all of forty-eight hours and already has a more exciting social life than I do. She's always had the ability to make friends easily. I am, as always, impressed."

"You do okay."

"Thanks. I had fun tonight," she added, hoping he was going to kiss her.

But instead of leaning close, Dylan took a step back. "I did, too. I'm excited to find out what we're doing for the first day of the Advent Calendar. Dress in layers. We might be outside."

"Then you should try not to lose your gloves."

"I'll do my best."

He waited until she'd opened the door, then walked to the sidewalk.

" 'Night," he called, before heading back toward The Wreath.

" 'Night."

She went inside and closed the door behind her, then turned on the lights. As she took off her coat and hung it, along with her hat and scarf, then stepped out of her boots, she wondered if Dylan was interested in her. Sometimes she was sure he was and others she wasn't. Like tonight. He'd been so warm and friendly at Jingle Coffee, but then hadn't kissed her when he'd walked her home. Was he being polite? Was she reading too much into what he considered a friendship?

"Relationships are hard," she murmured, going upstairs.

There was an open area on the big landing where she had a small desk and a laptop. She never worked at home, but sometimes she wanted to check email or do a little shopping. She started to open her computer, then stopped herself.

No, she thought, stepping back. She wasn't going to investigate Dylan. She didn't do that anymore — not personally. People deserved privacy and she had to learn to trust them to tell her what she needed to know. Dylan wasn't the kind of guy to have secrets. Not everyone did. At least that was what she tried to tell herself.

"Is that a Christmas sweater?" Camryn asked, more than a little overwhelmed by the amount of stuff a five-pound dog had accumulated in a day. There were dog toys scattered across the rug in the family room and a dog bed by the fireplace. On the kitchen counter were cans of dog food and a bag of kibble.

"The vet said she should wear a sweater indoors and a coat when she goes outside," Lily said while Victoria nodded. "She's underweight by over a pound, which doesn't sound like much but she's only five pounds so that's like twenty percent of her body weight."

"We have a feeding schedule for her," Victoria added. "We made a chart and everything. We're taking good care of her and she's really good about letting us know when she needs to go potty. She stomps her front feet." Victoria smiled. "It's super cute. Oh, and we shoveled a path on the back porch and a bit of the lawn because the snow was higher than her when she needed to go to the bathroom."

"You've been busy," Camryn murmured.

"Fostering is important," Lily told her. "We've been reading about it online. Dogs get really stressed in shelters, so it's better if they can be in a family where they feel safe and remember what it's like to be part of a social group. So if her family is found, she'll be ready for them."

The twins exchanged a look.

"If they aren't," Victoria began, only to be nudged by her twin.

"Let's assume they will be," Camryn said, pulling out her phone. "You said Jake paid for all this?"

"Uh-huh." Victoria picked up Tinsel and snuggled her close. "He was great. Really patient and he picked out two of the dog beds."

"There's more than one dog bed?"

The twins shared another look. Victoria petted Tinsel.

"The family room, the kitchen and one in all three of our bedrooms."

"Five beds?" Camryn repeated faintly, wondering how much Jake had spent on her behalf and how much that amount was going to mess with her monthly budget.

"She has to sleep somewhere," Lily pointed out.

Camryn assumed saying "the floor" was not a good move.

It wasn't that she minded the little dog, it was more how fast things had happened along with the uncertainty of their situation. The twins were obviously bonding with Tinsel and would be heartbroken if her family was found. If they weren't, well, Camryn didn't want to think about that.

"I'm going to talk to Jake," she said, waving her phone. "I need to get him a check to repay him for all this."

"The beds were on sale," Victoria told her. "We made sure of that. I think the special dog food was expensive. And, you know, the vet bill."

Right — the vet bill. She had a feeling this month she wasn't going to be putting her usual amount into her savings account.

"After dinner we need to go back to school," Lily said. "To make decorations for the cookie auction. We can walk there, but maybe you can come get us when we're done at eight?"

Of course — the class charity project this year. The sophomores were in charge of the cookie auction for the first Cookie Tuesday. Once the cookies were judged, they were sold off and the proceeds went to a local charity. The teens would run the auction and decorate for the event, which was being held up at the resort.

Was it just her, or did her life suddenly seem to be spiraling out of control?

"I'll come get you," she said. "Let me call Jake, then we'll start on dinner."

She retreated to the rarely used living room and plopped on a sofa, then pushed a few buttons on her phone. It was only as the call connected that she thought she should have texted rather than risk interrupting him. Only there was so much to say and sometimes texting didn't get it done.

"Too much pink?" Jake said by way of greeting. "I tried to steer them in a different direction, but they insisted."

His teasing voice and words had her smiling. "I have no idea what you're talking about."

"Then you haven't seen the dog beds. I personally think the unicorn one was a little over the top, but I'm sure Tinsel looks cute in it."

"You bought her a unicorn bed?"

"No, your sisters did. I was just the vessel."

She thought about all the time he'd taken with her sisters and a stray dog.

"You were amazing today," she said. "I can't begin to thank you, but I'm going to try."

"No thanks necessary. I had fun. Your sisters spilled all kinds of secrets about you, by the way."

Camryn laughed. "I doubt they talked about anything but Tinsel. Besides, I don't have any secrets. My life isn't interesting enough."

"So they were lying about the tattoo?"

She smiled. "Yes, they were. Seriously,

Jake. The twins are happy and excited and you bought so much stuff. Tell me the amount and I'll get you a check first thing in the morning."

"Not necessary. It was my treat."

Her eyes widened slightly as she thought about all the toys and beds and food, not to mention the vet bill.

"You can't pay for it. She's not your dog."

"She's not yours, either."

"I know, but we're apparently fostering her, so I have a responsibility to take care of her." And if things went how the twins wanted, in two weeks they were going to have a serious discussion about their wanting to adopt her, after which Camryn would be faced with the unpleasant task of telling them no. And if she wasn't willing to break their hearts, then she was going to have to get used to the idea of having a dog.

"Jake, you can't pay for it all."

"Too late." His tone was light. "She was found on my mom's property so the way I see it, we're joint owners here. You take care of Tinsel and I provide child support. So to speak."

"You're being too generous."

"How about this? The next time I piss you off, you have to give me a pass."

She smiled. "You've never pissed me off."

"Then I have that going for me. I was happy to help. I enjoyed spending time with Victoria and Lily. They remind me of you."

She had no idea what that statement meant. Reminded him how?

"In a good way," he added, his voice teasing. "They're very intelligent, caring young women with big hearts. You and your mom should be really proud of them."

Unexpected tears burned in her eyes. "She would be happy to hear you say that."

"You doing okay?"

"Why do you ask?"

"You have a lot going on. Work, the project for the resort, Tinsel. The packages look great, by the way. Guests are impressed."

"I'm glad you're happy," she said, blinking back tears. Crying? She didn't have time. "Think of me for all your wrapping needs."

"You know I will."

There was something in his tone. Something low and sexy that made her insides get a little squishy. She had the thought that she would rather he was in front of her, instead of at the other end of town. While she was wishing for things, she wouldn't mind having Jake in her life — in a romantic kind of way. Not only for the sex, and she was totally on board for sex, but for a little hugging and having someone to lean on, even temporarily. She'd been dealing with a lot for over a year now and every now and then, she wanted to share the load.

"I have to go make dinner," she said reluctantly. "The twins have to work on decorations for the cookie auction. Victoria's on the committee and Lily goes along to help." She drew in a breath. "Thanks again for everything. You were amazing. I owe you."

"I was happy to help. If you need anything else, you know where to find me."

"Thanks, Jake."

"Anytime."

She hung up and thought longingly about finding him in her bed. She allowed herself a three-second fantasy, then stood and walked back into the chaos that was her life.

The early-morning crowd at Joy's Diner was mostly people heading off to work. There were a couple of tables of construction guys, a half dozen office workers and an intense group from the hospital. Dylan arrived first and claimed a table by the window. He drank coffee while he waited for Jake.

He was tired and cranky, and he had no one to blame but himself. He'd blown it with River. He'd made a rookie mistake and now he worried it was unrecoverable. The last thing he wanted was for her to put him in the "friend" column. Once a guy found himself there, it was over. Women were funny that way. One wrong move and a man was punished for life.

"You look grim," Jake said as he walked up to the table and took a seat.

Their server, a plump woman in her fifties, instantly appeared with coffee.

"Morning, Grace. A number five for me."

"I'll take the same," Dylan told her. "Thanks."

Jake raised his eyebrows. "The vegetable omelet?" he asked. "You eat pancakes for breakfast."

"I'm changing things up."

"Yeah, you're punishing yourself for something." Jake picked up his coffee. "What is it?"

Dylan leaned back in his chair, then shifted forward and lowered his voice. "I screwed up with River."

"When?"

"At the Lighting of the Trees ceremony."

"How? I heard it went great. It's not like you pushed her off the stage or anything." He paused. "Did you push her off the stage?"

"Of course not. I told her about the trees

and we got hot chocolate afterward and talked, then I walked her home."

Jake held in a smile. "Are you thinking you were too boring?"

"You're not helping," Dylan pointed out.

"Wasn't trying to. So what's the issue?"

Dylan held in a groan. Such a rookie move, he thought grimly. "We were standing there on her porch and I didn't kiss her. It was a moment. A lost opportunity and now I can't get it back. She's going to put me in the friend zone and you know that's unrecoverable."

"I've heard that's true."

Dylan glared at him. "Don't pretend you've never been put in the friend zone. Every guy has. It's death."

"I've been told friend-zone sex always has a pity aspect," Jake said conversationally.

Dylan pointed to his coat hanging on a hook by the table. "She bought me gloves."

Jake's brows drew together. "Excuse me?"

"I told her I was always losing mine and she bought me gloves. She bakes. She's so damned beautiful and she gets shy and scared around people and I think she likes me and I didn't kiss her."

"So kiss her next time." Jake shook his head. "You're in a bad way, Dylan. It's embarrassing. Pull yourself together. So you didn't kiss her. You've learned your lesson. If she bought you gloves, you're not in the friend zone — at least not yet. You obviously like her, so start acting like it. Tell her she's pretty. Ask her out." One corner of his mouth twitched. "Compliment her on her shoes."

"You're a jerk, you know that?"

"The first two suggestions were good ones. If you like River, do something about it."

Dylan knew his friend was right. And he did like River. She was sweet and beautiful and unexpectedly fun. Smart, too. Probably smarter than he was.

"What if she —" he began.

Jake shook his head. "No. Don't go there. She's not going to care about the money."

"You don't know that."

"I know she doesn't know about it and she doesn't need to know for a while, so just pretend to be normal and ask her out." Jake drank more coffee. "You're wrong about the money thing. You take it too seriously."

"You don't take it seriously enough."

Grace appeared and put a plate down in front of each of them. Dylan stared at the egg white omelet. Vegetables filled the center. Just vegetables. Not meat or cheese.

There was also a side of whole wheat toast and orange slices.

"This is disgusting," he said, wondering why he hadn't ordered his usual blueberry pancakes with a side of sausage. He had a physical job — he needed to fuel up to start the day.

"It's healthy. If you eat the whole thing, you'll have had two servings of vegetables and one of fruit and it's not even seven in the morning. It's how adults eat. You eat like a seventeen-year-old boy."

"A happy seventeen-year-old boy," he said, taking a bite of the omelet and trying not to gag. "I'll ask her out. You're right — I can't get the lost opportunity back, so I need to not screw up again." He paused. "I do like her."

"Huh. I wouldn't have noticed."

"Shut up."

Dylan took another bite, then pushed his plate away. "I can't eat that."

Jake grinned. "I'm not even surprised. Nor is Grace."

Sure enough their server appeared with a large plate of blueberry pancakes and a side of sausage. She took away the omelet and put the pancakes in their place.

"I knew you couldn't do it," she told him. "And don't for a minute think I'm not charging you for both breakfasts."

"I'll get the bill," Jake told her with a wink. "Dylan has a thing for a girl who just put him in the friend zone. He needs comforting."

"Men are idiots," Grace muttered as she walked away.

"I'm going to kiss her," Dylan said when she'd left. "Next time I see her. I've learned my lesson. No more missed opportunities for me. She bought me gloves. You think that means she likes me?"

"I think it means she wanted you to kiss her."

# THIRTEEN

Camryn was surprised to find that Tinsel was actually a pretty decent work companion. She was polite to customers, quiet, clear on when she needed to go out to use the bathroom and loved to dive into the piles of paper scraps that seemed to accumulate every day. Seeing as Tinsel slept with the twins, Camryn had brought in the dog bed from her room so the Chihuahua had a place to sleep in her office. Her sisters had made sure to dress Tinsel in one of her holiday sweaters and had sent along a little red cow toy that crinkled. Tinsel frequently carried it around in her tiny mouth, making her even more cute.

"You're going to be a problem," Camryn told the sleeping dog. Tinsel dozed through the statement, not a huge surprise considering she'd already acted as host at two wrapping parties that afternoon.

Camryn knew her sisters would be devastated if the dog's family was found. So far no one had been in touch with the shelter or responded on social media. There was well over a week to go. Of course if her family wasn't found, then it was up to Camryn to decide her fate. Was she willing to take on a dog and the responsibility that went with it? Yes, the twins would help but in the end, she would be Tinsel's mom.

"You're really not that much trouble," she said softly.

Again, Tinsel didn't stir.

She returned to her billing, which she did weekly. She'd already sent her invoice to the resort, but still had one to prepare for Helen Crane and the packages her holiday decorator had ordered. Helen had taken a selection of boxes, which Camryn appreciated. Nothing like the resort's order, of course, but who could compete with that?

She'd hoped to see Jake at the Lighting of the Trees last Friday, but hadn't been able to find him in the crowd. Not for any reason other than to thank him for helping out her sisters with Tinsel. And except for the call she'd made later, they hadn't spoken. Not that they usually did. They barely knew each other. But for some reason he'd been on her mind lately and she wouldn't have minded spending some time in his company, which was strange. Why should she want that when they weren't really friends and they certainly weren't dating and it wasn't as if she was looking to have a man in her life at all? Only if she was, she would probably pick him. But she wasn't, so she hadn't and —

"Hi."

She looked up and saw the origin of her confusion standing in the doorway to her office. He was tall, holding a coat over one arm and smiling at her in a way that had her tummy wishing it knew a few dance moves.

"Hi."

Tinsel opened her eyes, spotted Jake and flung herself out of her bed and toward him. The tiny Chihuahua danced on her back feet, scratching at his knee, begging to be picked up, all the while giving little yips of pleasure.

"Hey, pretty girl," he said, lifting her into his arms and snuggling her close. Her long tail whipped back and forth as she kissed his chin and cheek.

He grinned at Camryn. "This girl knows how to make a man feel special."

"I'd take lessons, but I think me dancing like that would only be frightening."

"Oh, I don't know. I might enjoy it."

His smile was easy, his posture confident. Jake was a man who knew his place in the world and was comfortable with where he belonged. Must be nice, she thought, knowing she was still figuring things out in her life. Probably because so much had changed so fast — all without her input or consent.

He lowered Tinsel to the floor. The Chihuahua gave herself a little shake before returning to her bed and curling up.

"How's she working out?" he asked. "Can she wrap packages yet?"

"Her ribbon skills need work, but she's great with customers." She motioned to the chair on the other side of her desk. "Have a seat."

He shook his head. "I'm only going to stay a second. I wanted to stop by and ask if you'd like to have dinner with me."

She waited for the rest of the sentence. "Because I have a work project I want to ask you about." Or "My personal wrapping needs have gotten out of hand." Only he didn't say anything else. He just stood there, looking very handsome with a half smile tugging at his mouth.

"You're asking me out to dinner?" she confirmed.

"Yes. Oh, this has nothing to do with my mother's project."

Dinner? As in . . . dinner? "Like a date?"

The smile widened. "Yes."

He was asking her out. On a date.

Her whole body went into tingle mode. Funny how she'd just been sitting here, thinking about him, wishing she could have seen him and here he was.

"That would be nice," she said, smiling back at him.

"Great. Let's say Friday. I know you'll be busy Thursday, taking the twins to Advent."

"Sounds good."

"I'll pick you up at six-thirty, then."

"I'll be ready."

"I look forward to it."

With that, he turned and left. It was only after he was gone that she remembered she wasn't getting involved with anyone while she was in Wishing Tree. That she was putting that part of her life on hold until she was settled back in Chicago.

"Oh, it's fine," she told Tinsel. "It's just dinner."

The dog thumped her tail in agreement.

Kelsey flung herself on the sofa. "Tell me everything," she said, sitting back up and grabbing a couple of candied fruit cookies and a peppermint twist Kiss from the plate on the coffee table.

"Okay, now," she said with a laugh. "What did I miss?"

River tucked her feet under her and smiled. "We had the best time. Mom made friends with everyone she met and is even talking about maybe moving here."

"That *is* good news. I'm glad you enjoyed the holiday weekend."

River thought about the tree lighting and subsequent hot chocolate time with Dylan. "I did. Very much."

"How was Thanksgiving with Helen Crane?"

"Good. Easier than I thought. Helen had a few friends in and they were really nice. The next night Helen and Mom went out to dinner after the tree lighting. Oh, and we found an abandoned dog."

River explained about Tinsel and how she was being fostered at Camryn's house. "The twins are totally in love with her and I think even Camryn will be sad if someone comes to claim her, but no one has so far."

She picked up a peppermint twist Kiss and nibbled on the edge. "Tell me about your long weekend. Did Brooklyn do okay? How was Xavier's family?"

Kelsey's expression softened. "We had the best time. The flight was long and crowded, of course, but once we were there, it was wonderful. I adore his parents. Three of his four sisters were home so I got to meet their families." She looked at River. "You know how shy Brooklyn can be."

"Totally." She and her niece had that in common.

"She was more outgoing than I've ever seen her." Tears filled Kelsey's eyes. "She walked up to people and introduced herself. She stayed with us the whole time and talked and laughed."

River remembered how Brooklyn would often retreat into herself when she got into a new situation, much as she had when she'd been her age. "That's amazing. You must be thrilled."

"I am. It was like a miracle. Moving here was the best decision I ever made."

"You liked Xavier's family?"

"I did. They were very sweet to us. His mom kept asking about the wedding plans, but not in an obtrusive way. I can't wait for her to meet our mom. They're going to get along really well."

Kelsey picked up another cookie and eyed her sister. "So . . . how's Dylan?"

River felt herself flush. "I assume he's fine. I haven't seen him since the Lighting of the Trees."

Kelsey's mouth twisted. "Really? I thought

253

sure he'd ask you out or something."

River had been kind of hoping for the same thing. "He's been very sweet at the events we've had so far, explaining the traditions."

"And?"

"And that's all. I thought he was interested, but I guess not."

"You could ask him out."

She stared at her sister. "No, I couldn't. Before you start lecturing me on being brave and all that, let me point out you couldn't have asked out Xavier. I know other women can do that sort of thing, but we can't."

Kelsey nodded. "You're right. I would totally freak and you'd be a puddle. We should work on being braver."

"Right now I'm focused on getting through the Snow Queen duties. I'll be brave in the New Year."

"If Dylan does ask you out, you should say yes. I asked Xavier about him and he said Dylan's a good guy. He's solid and decent and a really talented cabinetmaker."

Which made him sound exactly like someone she would like. Trustworthy was important. But she didn't say that. She knew if she did, Kelsey would point out that not every man was out to scam her. That not everyone had secrets. That she should be more trusting.

All possibly valid points but none that would cause her to be less cautious. She'd been hurt too many times to offer her heart freely. But that didn't mean she wouldn't say yes if he should ask . . . and she was really hoping he would.

The first night of Advent, River arrived at The Wreath twenty minutes early, as per Geri's instructions. She'd been told to dress in layers and assume about an hour of downtime. To that end, she had on two sweaters under her coat, and had brought a backpack with cookies, hot chocolate, slip-on shoes and one of the books she'd checked out from the library. She also had a flashlight, a small first-aid kit and a charger for her phone.

The town Advent Calendar had been set up by the trees and the stage. Boxes numbered from one to twenty-four were stacked in six rows of four. A large screen stood behind the stage. Holiday music played from speakers. She would guess there already were a couple of hundred people gathered, with more arriving.

River made her way to the stage, not sure what to expect from the evening. She'd read up on the history of the Wishing Tree Advent Calendar and knew that the first night's event was always a town activity. Last year a miniature golf course had been set up in The Wreath.

"Hi," Dylan said, falling into step with her. "Excited about tonight?"

"Yes, and nervous. I have no idea what the town event will be, but Geri made it clear we're involved."

He reached for her backpack and slung it over his shoulder. "So you're prepared for anything?"

She wasn't sure if he was teasing or judging. "I have a few supplies."

He grinned. "I can't wait to see what they are."

They paused by the stairs to the stage to wait for Geri. She showed up a couple of minutes later.

"Right on time," she said. "That's what I like to see." She glanced around to make sure no one could hear them. "It's a scavenger hunt," she said in a low voice. "You're the prize."

The prize? River took a step back. "What does that mean?"

"You'll be found," Geri explained. "People will break up into teams of six or eight and follow the clues. The first team to find you wins."

"We don't have to do anything?" Dylan asked. "Just wait to be found?"

"That's it." Geri's expression turned stern. "I didn't bring the crowns because you won't need them. And no telling anyone where you are. Can I trust you?"

"I won't say a word," River promised.

"Me, either."

Geri's expression stayed skeptical, but she nodded. "I suppose you have to know." She leaned close and lowered her voice. "You're going to wait in the Christmas Museum. In the Forest of Lights, to be specific." She paused. "I wonder if I should confiscate your cell phones."

Dylan moved close to River and put his arm around her. "Geri, why would we want to ruin anyone's fun by telling them where we are?"

Geri's expression of suspicion relaxed. "That's an excellent point. All right, off you go. And be casual about leaving. Check that you're not followed."

"Will do," Dylan said easily, then turned to River. "You ready?"

"To casually but stealthily make our way to the museum? Sure."

Geri sighed. "All I ask is that you cooperate." She walked up onto the stage.

With Dylan's arm around her, River was less concerned about Geri's attitude. She liked how he pulled her close and that there was a protective quality to his touch. She didn't feel he was taking charge — instead, it felt like he understood she was nervous and was prepared to get between her and whatever scared her.

Or maybe she was reading a little too much into what could be described as little more than a hug.

Dylan dropped his arm. "Ready to slink away?"

"Yes. I've never been to the Christmas Museum before. Kelsey, Brooklyn and I tried to go in late September, but it was closed for remodeling."

"They shut down for a couple of weeks every fall to put up new displays. About three-quarters of the museum stays the same, year after year, but there are parts that change. According to Geri's timetable, we'll have an hour to explore." He smiled at her. "When I was a kid, Helen took Jake and me every year. It was a whole tradition. We went to the museum, had lunch at Joy's Diner and then went shopping. She always helped me pick out a present for my mom. Now that I think about it, she paid for the

258

present, as well. We would drop off whatever it was at Wrap Around the Clock, then go to the movies. Afterward, we'd pick up the wrapped gift and she'd take me home."

"Helen was good to you."

"She was. In a lot of ways, she's my real mom. She's the one I used to talk to when I had a problem at school."

"Or with a girl," River teased.

His smile turned wry. "Yeah, that."

"What kind of troubles did you have with girls? I can't imagine you weren't popular in high school."

He was the type to play sports and make friends easily, she thought. He would always know what to say and how to make people want to spend time with him.

"It wasn't getting the girl so much as keeping the girl," he admitted. "Being a good boyfriend is a learned skill." He leaned close and lowered his voice. "I'm much better at it now, in case you were wondering."

"Good to know," she murmured, as little zips of hope and anticipation whipped through her entire body.

Victoria and Lily jumped up and down as the big screen lit up with big letters. *Advent — Day One!*

"What do you think it is?" Lily asked,

grabbing Camryn's arm. "Parker says it's going to be a charity project, but that's never on the first night. It's always something like ice skating."

"I don't know what it was last year," Victoria said. "Did we go?"

"I don't think so," Camryn told her. "But tonight we're all in."

"Not you," Victoria teased. "You're going home."

"My feet hurt."

"You're so old," Lily pointed out with a grin.

"Hey, I had a long day at the store. We're getting into our busy season."

She'd been on her feet since eight that morning, which wasn't all that unusual, but in addition to her usual running around, she'd made a big dent in wrapping the hundreds of books that Dylan wanted wrapped.

Not that she was complaining. She loved that Wrap Around the Clock was successful. Between the steady income from the store and the nest egg of her mom's insurance policy, money wasn't a huge issue for her. She had a savings account from when she was working in Chicago and the small college fund her mother had left for her sisters. If all went well, the insurance money wouldn't be needed at all. Her plan was to split it among the three of them once the twins were out of college. They could put it away or use it for the down payment on a house or a condo.

Several of her sisters' friends ran up and joined them. They all counted down to the big reveal. The screen flashed the numbers until one, then lit up with *Town Scavenger Hunt!*

"I want to do that," Lily shouted.

"Me, too."

"Me, three."

The teens jumped up and down, screaming loudly. Camryn held in a wince.

Geri walked up onto the stage and spoke into the microphone.

"Hello, everyone and welcome to the first night of Advent. You'll be breaking up into teams of six to eight people. I have the clues here. You'll be searching for the Snow King and Queen."

"That's so fun," Lily said. "Camryn, you're missing out."

Camryn laughed. "I'll survive. I'm going to go home, put on my animal-print bathrobe and snuggle with Tinsel while you two have a good time."

As she spoke, she casually glanced around The Wreath, hoping to spot Jake. Not that she needed to see him. She would be going out with him tomorrow, an interesting and unexpected turn of events. But still, it would have been nice to run into him, even for a few minutes. Only he didn't appear to have shown up for the event.

She stayed long enough to make sure the twins were on a team with their friends and understood the rules of the scavenger hunt, then reminded them to be home by nine and made her way through the crowd. She'd nearly cleared The Wreath when Jake appeared at her side.

"Not interested in finding the Snow King and Queen?" he asked.

She grinned. "Not especially. It's been a long day. I thought I'd enjoy some quiet time at home."

"You just want Tinsel all to yourself," he teased.

"She is easy to be around. What about you? No team of guys ready to hunt down Dylan and River?"

"Not tonight. I'll walk you home instead."

She thought about pointing out she knew the way and as this was Wishing Tree, she was perfectly safe, but she enjoyed Jake's company. Plus, the whole going on a date with him tomorrow. Why would she refuse?

"How's Tinsel settling in?" he asked as

they left The Wreath.

"Really well. She comes with me to work every day and fits in so much better than I'd hoped. She's good with the customers, is really quiet and always lets me know when she needs to go potty."

Jake chuckled. "Does she say *potty*?"

"Not in words, but she does this little dance, so I know."

"She has you trained already."

Camryn realized that was true. "Impressive on her part. The twins love her — no surprise. I'm worried about how they'll handle it if her family is found."

"And how you'll deal if they're not."

There was that, she thought. "They're going to want to adopt her," she admitted.

"Are you going to say no?"

"Probably not, but we'll have a serious conversation about them needing to take some of the responsibility."

"At least until they go off to college. Then she's all yours."

"I know, but I'm getting okay with that."

They turned at the corner and she saw her house up ahead. So . . . once they got to her door, she needed a plan. Did she simply say good-night and walk in by herself? Did she invite him in for a few minutes? Was inviting him in too pushy? Would he think she wanted to have sex with him? Which she kind of did, but not tonight when the twins could come home at any moment. Plus, going from "we've never kissed" to "let's do it now" seemed a little awkward, at least for her. Maybe if she invited him in, he would kiss her and wouldn't that be nice?

They walked up the front steps. She got out her key, then looked up at him.

"Want to come in for a glass of wine?" she asked.

His hazel eyes brightened as the corners of his mouth turned up. "I'd like that."

He followed her into the house. Tinsel jumped out of her bed and raced toward them, barking happily. She danced around both of them, trying to greet them and give kisses.

"Okay, okay," Jake said, shrugging out of his coat, then dropping to the floor. "I can't resist a pretty girl like you, can I?"

Tinsel threw herself at him, climbing onto his lap and putting her front paws on his chest before licking his chin. He stroked her from shoulder to butt.

"Hey, you," he said quietly. "You settling in all right? You've got a good family here."

Tinsel's tail wagged in agreement.

"You do have a way with the ladies," Camryn teased, hanging her coat on the rack and putting his next to hers. She unwound her scarf and stepped out of her boots. "Years of practice?"

"Tinsel's an easy audience."

"I don't think you've had a lot of trouble getting women."

He stood and scooped up Tinsel, holding her against his chest. "Are you asking why I'm single?"

She hadn't been, but suddenly she wanted to know. "Why aren't you married? You're a good-looking guy who's smart, capable and so far I haven't noticed any obvious deal-breaker flaws."

He followed her into the kitchen. "You make me sound god-like," he joked.

"Yeah, not that." She pulled a bottle of white wine out of the refrigerator and got two glasses from the cupboard. As she poured, she added, "Look at you with Tinsel. She's not exactly a masculine dog, but you don't have any trouble with her."

"I'm not threatened by holding a Chihuahua."

"That's kind of my point. So, Jake Crane, what's the problem?"

They went into the living room and sat on the sofa. Tinsel raced over to Camryn's lap and curled up facing Jake. He sipped his wine before setting the glass on the coffee table.

"I'm not a good bet romantically. I screw up relationships."

The flat statement surprised her. "What does that mean?"

"The reason I'm not married with a couple of kids is I get in my own way and screw up a perfectly good thing by doing something dumb." He angled toward her. "Five or six years ago I met a woman named Iona. She was beautiful and vivacious and compelling and I couldn't get enough of her."

Not exactly information she'd been seeking, she thought ruefully. "She sounds amazing." Which was a better response than what she was actually thinking, which was more along the lines of "I feel desperately inadequate."

"She was my world," he admitted. "If it were up to me, I would have proposed that first night."

Wow. Double wow. "That's fast."

"I was in love."

"You were infatuated. You can't love someone you don't know."

"You're right," he said easily. "The love came later. We dated, we moved in together, she said I was the one."

"So you proposed."

"I was about to when she told me we were done. That she'd fallen out of love with me and wanted to move on. I didn't see it coming and her leaving hit me hard."

She sipped her wine. "I get all that, but you didn't mess up. She did."

"There's more."

"Ah, okay. Continue."

"It took me more than a year to get over her. One day I ran into Reggie, literally. Coffee went flying, we were both drenched, then she smiled and I smiled."

Right, they'd been engaged. She'd briefly forgotten. She was also regretting asking why he wasn't married. Hearing about other women he'd loved wasn't the thrill she'd thought it would be.

"We started dating and you know the rest."

"I know you got engaged and then broke up."

He frowned, then nodded. "You weren't here. You were still in Chicago. I proposed on the Friday after Thanksgiving, Paisley threw us an engagement party on Saturday, and Sunday morning I broke up with her, without telling her why."

"What?"

Camryn's voice was loud enough to cause

Tinsel to raise her head.

"Sorry," she murmured, stroking the dog, before looking at Jake. "What?" she asked in a more normal tone. "You broke up with Reggie two days after you proposed?"

"Told you."

"No. You have to say more than that. You're not a jerk kind of guy. What happened?"

His hazel gaze was steady. "Iona showed up Sunday morning. The day after the engagement party. She said she'd made a mistake and wanted us to get back together."

"That is sucky timing."

"Tell me about it. I told her I was in love with someone else and had no interest in her. She left." He paused. "But once she was gone, I couldn't stop thinking about her."

"Of course you couldn't. She'd been important to you. You would have been wondering why that exact moment. Had she known about the engagement? Did she just want to mess with you or were her feelings sincere? And what did she expect you to do with that information after so long?"

"Good guess." He picked up his wine. "I worried that my inability to stop thinking about her meant I wasn't as in love with

Reggie as I thought."

"You freaked."

"I overreacted."

"Same difference."

He surprised her by smiling. "You sound like your sisters."

"I think we all have a little fifteen-year-old girl in us."

"No way I'd admit to that," he said. "I broke up with Reggie and made a bad situation worse by not telling her why at the time. She knows now," he added.

"Just like that." Camryn didn't know what to say. "What happened with Iona?"

"She showed up again and asked for a second chance."

"You gave it to her."

"I did. Four months later I realized I'd made a huge mistake, both in dumping Reggie and getting back with Iona."

Ugh — the conversation was getting less pleasant by the second. "You regret letting Reggie go? Are you still in love with her?"

"No." His smile was gentle. "We both got over each other too quickly for a marriage to have ever lasted. I'm sorry that I was such an idiot. I screwed up and hurt us both. I should have talked to her. I should have handled everything differently. I messed up."

"One time." She thought for a second.

"Okay, maybe three times, but that doesn't mean you're not going to be successful at love."

"I'm careful," he said.

She sensed there was more than he was telling her, but didn't ask what. While she was attracted to him, she didn't know him well enough to pry into something that personal. If he wanted her to know, then he would tell her.

"I was engaged when my mom got sick," she said. "If my ex ever came crawling back, I would tell him no, then back my car over him."

"That's very violent."

She smiled. "Okay, not the car part but I would never trust him again." She thought about what Jake had told her about Iona. "I've never felt that kind of instant attraction to someone. It must have been very powerful."

"It was, but it was also deceptive. Because of how I felt, I believed what I wanted to believe about her. It took me longer than it should have to realize she wasn't as wonderful as I'd assumed."

"Plus the beautiful part. That tends to blind men."

"How many men have you blinded?" he asked, his voice teasing. "Twenty? More?"

"What? Me? I'm not beautiful." Not with her red curly hair. "I'm not saying I'm ugly but I'm not going to turn heads."

"You couldn't be more wrong." He rose as he spoke, waving at her to stay seated. "Don't disturb Tinsel. I know the way out."

Wait, what? He couldn't imply she was, um, well, beautiful, and then just leave.

But it seemed he could. He bent down and lightly kissed her, then walked over to get his coat.

"I'll see you tomorrow," he said. "For dinner."

And then he was gone.

Camryn stayed on the sofa, her thoughts swirling. She wasn't sure what, exactly, had just happened. Jake had shared some personal stuff, casually said he thought she was attractive and then had left. What did that mean?

"Men are so confusing," she told Tinsel. "You should definitely stay single. It's so much easier."

Advice she should take, she thought, even as a little voice in her head whispered that while it was much easier, it wasn't nearly as much fun.

# FOURTEEN

The Christmas Museum was just northeast of The Wreath — a five-minute walk, at best. But River and Dylan took the long way so no one would realize their destination. They circled by Long John's Pajama Shop and The Egg Nog, took Grand Avenue to Jolly Drive, then went up to Noble Street and back down West Mistletoe Way before walking up to the Christmas Museum. Dylan pulled the key from his pocket and unlocked the door. As he pushed it open, he looked to his left and went totally still.

"Over there," he said quietly, pointing.

She turned and saw a moose about twenty feet away. The huge animal sniffed the air, glanced once in their direction, then headed north.

"Are there usually moose in town?" she asked in a whisper, following Dylan into the museum.

"No. This one hangs around the area. He's

spotted a handful of times a year. As a rule, he doesn't bother anyone, but don't think he's friendly. If a moose gets spooked, he'll charge you. He's big and strong, and he can do a lot of damage with those antlers."

She shuddered at the thought. "I'll keep out of his way."

Dylan went to work, turning on lights. As various sections of the space came to life, River realized the museum was much bigger than she would have thought. The entryway held a ticket counter opposite a large stained-glass window depicting the Nativity. Open shelves held dozens of Nativity scenes created in different styles with different mediums. There were the traditional wood and porcelain, but also glass, clay, fabric and what looked like a large LEGO Nativity. Classic carols played from hidden speakers.

Dylan showed her where to leave her coat, scarf, gloves and hat. She unbuttoned one of her sweaters and hung it up, as well, but kept on her boots. He held up the backpack.

"Should we take advantage of your supplies?" he asked.

She laughed. "Probably. I brought hot chocolate and cookies, along with home-made candy." She didn't mention the first-aid kit or the flashlight.

"Dream girl," he said, taking her hand in his. "You're funny, sweet and you make candy. Where's the bad?"

She felt herself blush. "It's not hard to make candy."

"I'll take your word for that." He took a step, then paused. "We go through the Santa room first. It helps to take a couple of deep breaths before entering."

"What do you mean?"

"How much do you like Santa?"

"A lot."

"Good. Then this will make you happy."

She wasn't sure what he meant until they stepped into the next room, which was, quite literally, filled with every kind of Santa imaginable. Dolls and carvings and pictures and plushies. Tall, short, tiny, life-size, round, thin. There were Santa posters and ornaments, Santa wreaths, strings of plastic Santa lights, Grinch Santas and Snoopy Santas and everything in between.

River laughed. "I love it."

"Good. Some people are freaked out by the Santa room."

"Not me. I've been very good this year."

Interest darkened his blue eyes. "Really?"

She told herself to be brave and meet his gaze. "Yes."

"Interesting."

The next room had Victorian villages displayed on tables and shelves. Some were newer but many of them looked old and delicate. Several holiday-themed trains snaked around the villages. Dylan flipped a switch and the trains began to move on their small tracks.

There was a room with Christmas trees decorated with odd ornaments. One tree had only beer ornaments while another was covered with bug and lizard ornaments, along with a few commemorating Covid 19. The shelves on the walls were stacked with sheet music and books of Christmas hymns.

"Okay, next is my favorite room," Dylan said. "Which happens to be where we're supposed to be found."

They went down a short hallway, then turned and entered the largest room she'd seen in the museum. The ceilings were high, there weren't any windows and everywhere she looked, she saw trees made entirely of light. Some twinkled, some were steady. They were all colors and sizes and seemed more than a little magical.

"The Forest of Lights," she breathed. "It's beautiful."

"I like it." His mouth twitched. "I'll admit that when Jake and I came here, we ran around and played army, which wasn't exactly in keeping with the spirit of the room."

"You were a kid having fun. I think it's okay."

He led her through the forest. At the far end were several tables and chairs. They sat down and she opened her backpack.

"You really did bring hot chocolate," he teased.

"Of course. I like to be prepared. Kelsey jokes if there's ever word of an apocalypse, she wants to be near me. She knows I'll have the most supplies."

He chuckled. "How did she and Brooklyn enjoy Thanksgiving?" he asked. "Was there any stress meeting Xavier's family?"

"She had a good time." She passed him a plastic mug. "His parents adored Brooklyn and she loved being spoiled. Kelsey's really happy and looking forward to everyone coming here for the wedding the first weekend in May."

River was looking forward to it, as well. She wanted to see her sister and Xavier start the rest of their lives together.

"I'll stay with Brooklyn while Kelsey and Xavier go on their honeymoon," she added. "We're going to have a good time together."

"You two get along?"

River nodded as she unwrapped the cookies and fudge she'd brought. "I was there when she was born. Kelsey and I learned how to deal with a baby together. Our mom was great about helping."

"What about Brooklyn's dad?"

River thought about Kelsey's broken heart and how instead of wanting to be a father, Brooklyn's dad had simply wanted to avoid the responsibility. "He's not around. It's okay," she added. "We didn't need him and now she'll have Xavier."

"What about you?" he asked lightly. "Any ex-husbands I should worry about?"

"A few bad boyfriends, but I've never been married. What about you?"

"Nope. I was engaged for a few months but it didn't work out."

So at one time he'd planned on spending the rest of his life with someone. She wanted that but so far it had never happened.

He leaned toward her. "Some of the breakup was her fault, but just as much was mine. I let pride get in the way. I made some dumb decisions. Not cheating," he added quickly. "I wouldn't do that."

"Me, either." She nibbled on a ginger-bread cookie. "Relationships are compli-cated. People want different things at differ-ent times. Love means different things to different people."

"You were hurt," he said quietly.

"A few times." She looked at him. "I had scoliosis as a child. A rare form that really twisted my spine. I had to wear a body brace, and eventually, I had several surgeries."

He stared at her. "Are you okay?"

"Now. It was tough in a lot of ways." She tried to tell the story without actually reliving any of the memories. "I got bullied a lot by the other kids. I'm shy by nature and that made things worse. Some girls I thought were my friends turned on me. Then when I had surgery, I would miss school for weeks or months. So I was always the outcast."

He touched her hand. "I'm sorry."

"Thanks. But it made it hard to figure out how to read people, and I think that's part of the reason I don't always get it right. It's hard for me to trust. I don't expect an emotional dump the first time I meet someone but I don't like secrets. They're usually not good."

She wasn't sure, but she thought he might have tensed at her statement. But before she could decide, he smiled and said, "I don't know. Some secrets are kind of fun. What if I told you I'd been regretting the fact that I didn't kiss you that night I walked you home? Good secret or bad?"

Her gaze dropped to his mouth and she suddenly wasn't sure what to do with her hands.

"Good secret," she whispered.

"I think so, too."

He leaned toward her. River knew she could easily shift back and avoid the kiss, only she didn't want to. She liked Dylan and for her, the physical part of a relationship was so much easier to understand. Bodies rarely lied.

She closed the last few inches between them and let her eyes flutter closed. A heartbeat later his mouth brushed against hers — softly at first, but then with a little more intensity. He shifted closer and put a hand on her arm.

She tilted her head slightly, enjoying the feel of his lips claiming hers. Heat radiated from him, along with a clean male scent.

He broke the kiss long enough to stand and pull her to her feet, then into his arms. She went willingly, wanting to press herself against him. His sweater was soft, his chest muscled and broad. She wrapped her arms around his neck and leaned in, letting him take some of her weight. His hands settled on her hips as he kissed her again. She parted and he swept inside.

Wanting came to life, along with the knowledge that she felt safe in his arms. A combination that was tough to find, she acknowledged.

He moved his hands up and down her back, their tongues tangled. In the distance she vaguely heard the sound of voices of laughter. She turned just as Dylan stepped back.

"We've been found," he said ruefully. "I need to talk to them about their timing."

Their eyes met. She saw passion there, and humor. She liked that he wasn't mad. Experience had taught her that a guy who blew up at the little things was a stressful partner in the long-term.

She stepped back just as several teenagers burst into the room.

"You're here!" one of them yelled. "We got 'em. We found the Snow King and Queen."

"Come in."

Hearing the words, Jake pushed open Camryn's front door and stepped inside.

"I'm in the kitchen," she called as Tinsel burst into the living room and headed right for him. She stopped in front of him, doing her stomping, circling dance, her tail whipping with enthusiasm, her eyes bright with

280

excitement and affection.

"Hey, little girl," he said, scooping the tiny dog into his arms.

She wiggled to get closer, all the while drenching him with eager kisses.

"Yes, I missed you, too," he said with a laugh. "You're all I think about."

He walked into the kitchen and found Camryn opening a shipping box. She looked at him and grinned.

"Really? That's my competition? She's younger, blonder and has a better body than me. Am I the pity date?"

He took in her gorgeous hair, the sweater dress that clung to every mouthwatering curve and the high-heeled leather boots that made him think about her wearing them, sexy lingerie and nothing else.

Jake suddenly found it difficult to talk — and to keep his dick under control.

"No pity," he managed to say. "You look incredible."

Her smile turned knowing. "This old thing? You're sweet to notice."

He relaxed. "You know you're stunning."

She laughed. "Not exactly a word I would have used, but every now and then things come together." She glanced around and lowered her voice. "I just need five minutes. These came today and I want to get them

281

unpacked and hidden before the twins get home. They're skating with friends. They'll swing by here, pick up their overnight bags and Tinsel, then head out for a sleepover."

"If they're not here, why are we speaking in whispers?"

She laughed. "Because they always seem to know when I'm unpacking their Christmas presents and show up. It's quite the skill."

She pulled out two smaller boxes and opened one, then held up a . . .

He frowned, not quite able to make it out. "That's a taco holder?" he asked, doubtful, taking in the primary colors and what looked like spines.

"Not *just* a taco holder," she scoffed. "It's a dinosaur taco holder. For their stockings."

"They're teenagers."

"It's silly. They'll love them. Okay, let me go hide these in the back of my file cabinet and I'll be ready to go."

He petted a happy Tinsel while he waited. When Camryn returned, he picked up the shipping box. "I can recycle this for you," he said. "That way there's no evidence."

"Thanks. I appreciate that. Let me get my coat."

He put Tinsel in her bed on the sofa, then helped Camryn with her down coat. She wore heels that brought her closer to his height, which he liked. She also smelled good — some combination of vanilla and temptation.

He escorted her to his SUV. Technically, they could have walked to the restaurant, but given the low temperatures and her heels, driving made more sense.

"I made reservations at Buon Natale," he said as he held open her door.

"I love Italian."

"Good."

He got in and started the engine, then made sure the heat was flowing on her side of the SUV.

"I would have thought you'd take me to the resort," she said, her voice teasing. "There you have total control."

"I thought about it, but I didn't want you to feel pressure." He glanced at her, then back at the road. "It's my turf where, you're right, I have the power. There are also over two hundred hotel rooms. I didn't want to give you the wrong impression."

"That you expected me to sleep with you tonight?"

"Yeah, that."

"Interesting. What if I'd said yes?"

His blood instantly heated as he looked at her, trying to judge the seriousness of her question. "Would you have?"

She sighed heavily. "I guess we'll never know."

"I could be at the resort in fifteen minutes."

"Oh, but we have reservations in town, Jake. We wouldn't want to back out on those."

He eyed her. "You're playing me."

She smiled. "Just a little. Because I can and because you're looking especially handsome tonight."

He chuckled. "You're going to be a challenge, aren't you?"

"Very possibly."

He stopped in front of the valet and handed over his keys, then walked around to help her out of the car. As she rose, he drew her close and whispered, "Fifteen minutes. Twelve if I speed."

She laughed. "Ask me after I've had a glass of wine."

They went inside and were immediately shown to a quiet corner table. Their server took their drink orders, explained about the specials and left. Camryn looked around.

"I haven't been here in forever. It's not the kind of place I come with my friends. When I was younger, it was a special-occasion restaurant. I should start the tradition back up with the twins."

"What about on dates?" he asked, hoping he sounded casual.

She looked startled. "I don't date."

"Because you'll be leaving Wishing Tree in three years?"

"I guess that's a part of it. To be honest, I haven't considered dating since I moved back. At first, I was totally involved with my mom. She went into hospice within a couple of weeks of me coming back. Then my fiancé dumped me. Then I had to take over the business while raising my sisters and dealing with the loss of my mom."

He reached across the table and placed his hand on hers. "I wish I could have helped."

"Thanks. You're the type who would have known what to do." She frowned slightly. "I have no idea why I said that. I mean, I believe it. You're capable and you have a strong moral compass, but we don't really know each other."

The server appeared with their cocktails. Jake waited until she was gone to say, "We were in high school together."

She laughed. "Barely. Don't forget, you were the handsome, worldly senior and I was the fourteen-year-old who couldn't believe how mature all the guys looked and sounded. That's what got to all of us. The low voices. After the squeaky tones of middle school, it was a shock."

"At that age, a few years makes a difference."

She nodded. "Plus, you were popular and I was just regular."

"I don't believe that."

"It's true. I did ordinary stuff. You were a football captain. Plus, your family has money." She paused. "Was that weird for you? Knowing some people were interested because of the wealth?"

"I'm used to it," he admitted. "In a way, the money thing is harder for Dylan than for me. He sees it from a different perspective. Girls would try to get close to him to get close to me. He feels he has to protect me from anyone who wants what I have rather than who I am."

"That's a good quality in a friend."

He sipped his Scotch. "Just so we're clear, if you'd been age appropriate, I would have gone out with you."

Her eyes widened. "Really? That's so nice. Thank you. I would have gone out with you, too." She leaned toward him. "So, Jake Crane, did you have sex with your girlfriends in high school?"

The question surprised him. "A gentleman doesn't kiss and tell."

"Oh, come on. Tell a little. I didn't lose my virginity until the summer after high school. Would we have done the wild thing if we'd been dating back then?"

"Yes."

"Would I have liked it?"

Was it just him or was it hot in here? "You're flirting with me."

"A little. I hope that's okay."

"Very okay. I'm liking it."

They smiled at each other.

"All right," she said. "Let's shift to a safer topic. My flirting skills are a little atrophied and I don't want to push it too much. The twins are having a great holiday season. They're loving all the traditions. They were on one of the first teams to find River and Dylan yesterday and are very proud of that."

"Good for them."

"I know. It's exciting. Oh, speaking of the twins . . ." She fished her phone out of her handbag and glanced at the screen, then smiled. "All is well. They've picked up Tinsel and are at their friend's house." She waved her phone. "I have a text from the mom confirming."

She put her phone away. "So how's *your* mom doing? I know this is only the second Christmas with your dad gone." She paused.

"More important, how are you doing?"

The question surprised him.

"I miss him," he admitted. "I know she does, too."

"They were married a long time."

"Nearly forty years." He glanced at the table, then back at her. He told himself to change the subject, to not blurt out the thought that always came to mind when he thought of his father. Camryn didn't need to know. Only suddenly, it seemed he needed to talk about it, and one thing he knew about her was that she was a good listener.

"He cheated on her," he said bluntly. "More than once. I found out when I was supposed to meet him at a conference. I went in a day early and saw him with another woman. When I confronted him, he said it wasn't a big deal. That sometimes a man had needs."

He shook his head. "Needs? What the hell does that mean? I was furious. He told me to grow up. That my mother knew and was fine with it, so who was I to judge him."

# FIFTEEN

Camryn hadn't seen that confession coming, nor did she know what to say about it.

"I'm sorry," she whispered. "I'm sorry. Helen is wonderful and you should never have been put in that position."

"I was so pissed," he admitted, looking at her. "They'd always talked about how perfect their marriage was. Mom said he was her great love. She told me to make sure I fell in love with someone as wonderful as she had. She told me I was just like him." His mouth twisted. "He's the last person I want to be like."

"She didn't mean it that way. She meant the good parts. You know that. Everyone has a dark side. I'm sorry you had to see his."

Jake's gaze locked with hers. "Later, when we got back from the conference, the three of us talked about his cheating. I know he put her up to it. She was so calm, so understanding. She said it happened every now and then and while she didn't like it, she understood it didn't mean anything."

He grimaced. "You've met my mother. She's a proud, caring woman. I kept thinking how humiliated she had to be, to discuss her husband's cheating with her son. I told them I got it and I left. I'll never forgive him for what he did to her. Not just the screwing around, but making her say it was fine."

Camryn reached across the table and laced her fingers with his. "She loves you, Jake. That's why she said those things. She knew if you hated your father, it would eat you up inside. She wanted you to stay whole. And she loved him. That's obvious."

"She does. Still. And I have no idea why."

Their server appeared to take their order. Camryn quickly ordered a Caesar salad and the evening's featured pasta. Jake asked for the same.

When they were alone, she tried to make sense of what he'd shared with her. She couldn't imagine accepting a husband who cheated. Every marriage was different, but for her that would be crossing a line. And Jake was obviously still furious with his father and determined to be nothing like him. He was —

"That's why you broke up with Reggie," she blurted. "Oh, I'm sorry. I shouldn't have said that."

One eyebrow rose. "You're right. It wasn't Iona showing up so much as me taking a second to wonder if I was making the right decision. I know now that it makes sense to think things through, but in the moment I worried I was like him. That if I was attracted to both of them, then I was a cheating bastard, like my dad. I didn't know how to process what I was feeling, so I did what I thought was the honorable thing. I broke Reggie's heart."

"You said you'd cleared things up with her," Camryn said. "Does she know about . . ."

He shook his head. "I told her about Iona. Dylan's the only other person who knows about my father."

And he'd told her? She wasn't sure what to do with that information. "I won't tell anyone."

"I know."

Despite everything, she smiled. "You can't know that. I could be the biggest blab in the county."

His slow grin had her insides getting squishy. "It's a pretty big county."

"In landmass, not in population. My point

is you're very trusting."

"Only of you."

"Why is that?"

"I have no idea. It's probably because you've been thoroughly vetted. According to my mother, there's even going to be a digital investigation."

Camryn groaned. "That's right. Project: Jake's Bride. River's going to ask her if I can see the digital report on myself. I'm curious about what it says." She picked up her drink. "Tell me about the other candidates."

"There aren't any. I told my mom to back off."

"Didn't we talk about this before? Is there any part of you that believes saying the words will make any difference?"

He chuckled. "No, but at least I tried."

"Tell her you need a break for the holidays."

"That's only a temporary solution." She raised her eyebrows and he groaned. "Yeah, I should take what I can get."

"Exactly."

She looked at him across the table. He was a good guy on the inside, where it really counted, but also sexy and nice to look at on the outside. Too bad he hadn't taken her up to the resort instead of into town.

She would have been seriously tempted by one of those two hundred-plus hotel rooms. Or he could have taken her to his place. That would have been nice. Her house was more of a problem. Yes, the twins were gone but having Jake's car parked out in the driveway overnight would create a bit of a stir in the neighborhood.

Still, it would be worth it, she thought dreamily. To have a little one-on-one time with him. Naked one-on-one time. It had been a very long time and she was confident he knew what he was doing in the bedroom. If only he'd asked . . .

"Camryn? You okay?"

"Hmm? Oh, I'm fine."

"You went somewhere else."

"It wasn't that far."

She told herself she was a self-actualized woman who could ask for what she wanted. Strong women were comfortable with their own sexuality. They put themselves out there. She could do that. She *should* do that, if only to prove to herself that —

"Are you sure you're all right?"

She looked at him. "Would you like to get our meals to go?"

He frowned. "Don't you feel well? Do you want me to take you home?"

She hesitated, not sure why this was so

hard. Indecision swamped her. She nearly said to never mind, only then she would be annoyed at herself all evening.

She gathered her courage in both hands and said, "I thought we could get dinner to go and head to your place."

He looked delightfully confused. "Sure. You'd rather eat there?"

"Eventually."

One beat. Two beats. Three — His eyes widened.

"My place. To eat later," he confirmed.

"Yes." She held in a smile. "Unless you'd rather not."

His arm shot up as he flagged their server. When she walked over, Jake said, "There's been a change of plan. We need our meals to go. We'll take the bottle of wine with us."

There was a flurry of paying the bill and collecting their food, then they were getting into his SUV. Camryn was pleased to still feel relatively calm. There was the requisite growing desire, but she wasn't weirded out about being so forthcoming.

They drove through town and headed out toward the resort where he had a condo.

"I have condoms," he said into the silence.

"Good. I'm on birth control, but I still want you to wear a condom."

"Happy to."

He kept to the speed limit and fifteen minutes later turned into a gated community with houses on one side and condos on the other. He went to the condo side and continued up the hill. His unit was the highest one on the end. He drove into a two-car garage, then collected the food and wine before opening her door.

"Through there," he said.

She stepped inside his place.

Her first impression was of high ceilings and lots of space. He turned on the lights. She saw a massive great room with floor-to-ceiling windows, oversize furniture and what she would guess were views that went on forever. To the left was a dream kitchen with a dining room beyond. A staircase led upstairs to what she would guess were the bedrooms.

"Let me get the food in the refrigerator," he said. "I'll be right back."

She hung up her coat, then sat on the mudroom bench to unzip her boots. As she worked, she mentally checked in to make sure she was all right with her decision. There was no worry, no second thoughts — just anticipation and a serious tingling in her girl parts.

He returned and hung up his own coat then faced her. She read desire in his expression, and something else. Not worry exactly. Concern, she thought. Concern that she was absolutely sure.

Men were so delicate.

She crossed to him, raised herself on tiptoe and brought his head to hers, then she kissed him deeply and thoroughly. He responded instantly, wrapping his arms around her and plunging his tongue into her mouth. Passion ignited, burning hot and bright, promising a glorious night with this man.

She ran her hands up and down his back, settling them on his firm butt and squeezing. He chuckled against her mouth.

"This is an unexpected side of you," he said, tugging her dress up several inches, then lifting her in the air.

She instinctively wrapped her legs around his waist to hang on.

"I know," she said, staring into his hazel eyes. "But I kind of like it."

"Me, too."

He nuzzled her neck before letting her slide to the floor. On the way down, every inch of her rubbed against every inch of him. He was hard and strong and erect, and her insides clenched at the thought of him filling her, pleasing her, pushing her over the edge. She shuddered with need.

As if understanding how she felt, he took her hand in his and led her to the stairs. They walked up together, through open double doors into a huge bedroom with two walls of windows. Jake crossed to the nightstand and picked up a remote. Seconds later heavy drapes began to close. He turned on a lamp, then returned to stand in front of her.

She reached for him just as he pulled her close. His mouth claimed hers, she leaned into him and the dance began.

Two hours and three orgasms later, Camryn served up salad while Jake opened the wine. They'd already put the garlic bread and entrées into the oven to warm, and set the table in the eat-in kitchen. He'd dressed in jeans and a sweater, while she'd borrowed a soft, old sweatshirt and had pulled on a thick pair of his socks.

She felt good. Out of her comfort zone for sure, but in a satisfied, confident kind of way. Yes, there were things they needed to talk about and ground rules to be set, but for the first time in what felt like forever, she was happy and feeling just a little bit wild.

She set down the plates and took her seat across from him.

"Your place is really nice."

"Thanks. The views are good and it's close to work." He smiled at her. "I can't decide which is sexier. Your hair or the fact that you're not wearing a bra."

She shoved a hand through her mussed curls. "Yes, well, the whole writhing in bed as I begged you to never stop did mess with my hair." She took a bite of salad. "You really don't mind the curls?"

"I like them. Why do they bug you?"

"They don't but a lot of guys don't like them."

"Once again, a lot of guys are idiots."

She smiled. "Thank you. I think so, too."

Soft music played in the background and there was a fire in the great-room fireplace.

"You have a good life here," she said. "It's quiet."

"Sometimes too quiet."

She looked at him. "Interesting, but I happen to know your mom is looking to get you married. Maybe you should stop resisting."

"Gee, thanks for the advice. Tell me about tonight. You okay?"

"It was my suggestion, something I'm very proud of, by the way. I'm feeling powerful and in charge."

"Two excellent qualities, but if I remember

298

correctly, you were the one who wasn't interested in a relationship — at least not while you were in Wishing Tree. You're saving that part of your life for when you leave. So how are we defining what happened?"

His tone was curious rather than judgy, which she appreciated, and she knew what he was asking. Going out to dinner was one thing but becoming lovers put a whole new spin on what they were doing. Was it for a single night? One and done, so to speak, or was there more? Was she changing the rules? Did she want a relationship with Jake?

Almost as soon as she asked herself the question, she felt herself immediately backing away. No, not a relationship, she thought firmly. She wasn't interested in a commitment or getting involved in any serious way. She was leaving — what was the point? If things got too serious, one of them would get hurt and she didn't want that. But she also didn't want to have things over — not yet anyway.

"Could we do this through the holidays?" she asked. "Sex and dinners out and fun, without any obligation. Come the New Year, we go back to being friends."

She paused. "Not that we were friends before. I meant we weren't *not* friends, but . . ."

"I know what you mean," he told her, his hazel eyes unreadable. "To clarify — you want us to keep seeing each other sexually, hang out in other ways, with no emotional involvement and the goal of ending things right after New Year's Eve."

She set down her fork, not sure why his words bothered her. He'd repeated what she'd said, which was what she wanted. So why did it sound so empty and sad? Was it the *no emotional involvement* part?

"We'd still like each other," she clarified. "I like you and I assume you like me."

One corner of his mouth turned up. "Yes, Camryn, I like you."

Something quivered deep inside her belly. "What do you want to do?"

He hesitated before saying, "I'm open to your plan. I think there could be complications but I'll give it a try."

"You mean the twins," she said. "They can't know we're seeing each other — you know, that way. They'd start to get attached. I've seen it with Tinsel. If her family shows up, they'll be destroyed."

"You're comparing me to a dog?"

"Not in a bad way."

He chuckled. "The pasta's nearly ready. Eat your salad."

"What about our deal?"

300

He looked at her. "You're on. I'm willing to let you use me for sex and hang out in other ways with the idea the twins will have no idea what's going on."

"Thank you."

"You're welcome."

He got up and pulled their pasta and the bread from the oven. As she watched him, Camryn told herself this had been a good night. She'd spent an amazing couple of hours in Jake's bed and was going to get several repeat performances. Plus, hanging out with him was always fun. It was a total win-win with absolutely no downside at all. She knew what was going on between them and she was strong enough to avoid letting her heart get involved.

Dylan held his end of the cabinets as he and Greg carried them into the house. He told himself to pay attention to what he was doing, otherwise he was going to do something stupid like run into a wall, or trip over a threshold. Not only would that put the custom cabinets at risk, but Greg would also make sure everyone back at the shop knew he'd been a klutz. But concentrating was more difficult than usual this morning. He'd pulled up to the job only to realize the house his clients owned was maybe a quarter block from River's townhouse.

It was still early — barely quarter after seven. The sun wouldn't make an appearance for nearly an hour. No way she would see him if she left her place to walk to work. For all he knew, she was already in her office and he would come and go without her ever realizing he was in the neighborhood.

"I should call her," he muttered to himself.

"What, boss?" Greg asked, walking backward into the kitchen.

"Nothing."

He should call, he thought again, but silently. They'd texted a few times, but he should do more than that. He should ask her out officially. On a date. He liked her, he wanted to spend time with her — when people were in that situation, they dated. Plus, they'd already kissed and that had been amazing.

"Boss, this is heavy. Can we put down the cabinet?"

"What? Yeah. Sure. Let's put it down."

He forced his mind to stay on work. He and Greg got the cabinets into the kitchen, where he would spend the rest of the day installing them. Greg would be back later that day to help with the uppers. He confirmed the time with his helper, then went to his truck and began unloading supplies.

On his last trip outside, he saw River walking toward him.

As always she was bundled up with a thick coat, a scarf, boots, a hat and gloves. She was petite and the outerwear dwarfed her. But her smile was bright and the kick he felt in his gut was real enough.

"Good morning," she said, waving at him. "I saw your truck. Do you have a job here?"

He motioned to the house. "We're remodeling the kitchen. I designed the cabinetry."

"I didn't know you worked in Wishing Tree."

"Most of my jobs are in Seattle. I get a few in Boise and Portland. Every now and then I have one here. Come see what I'm doing."

She followed him inside the house. The freshly installed hardwood floors were covered with paper. The new windows were in and the walls painted.

"There's still a lot of work to do in the primary bath," he said, walking into the kitchen. "I'll get to those cabinets in a couple of weeks, but we're starting here."

She took off her scarf and hat, then began to study the cabinets.

"They're reclaimed wood," he told her. "All from old barns torn down in the Pacific Northwest. It's a challenge to get enough of the same type of wood for a project this big. Then I have to match the colors to create the pattern you see here."

He'd used brown and gray boards to complement the quartz the clients had picked. The backsplash was a simple flat subway tile. The cabinetry would be the real star of the show.

"They're beautiful," River said, pulling out a drawer. "Look how perfectly everything fits."

"Penny's a baker, so I designed several cabinets specifically for her supplies."

He showed her the pullout for a stand mixer, then pointed to an electrical plug on the wall. "This cabinet will go there. She'll be able to plug in her stand mixer once, then the shelf can bring it up to counter height when she needs it and the mixer is already plugged in."

He showed her the custom racks for cookie sheets and cooling trays, and the place where she would store her cake pans.

River studied the stand mixer cabinet. "I have cabinet envy," she admitted with a laugh. "I have a stand mixer but I have to drag it out every time I use it. My kitchen has plenty of counter space, but nowhere near enough storage. All my trays and cookie sheets are stacked in the pantry. I love what you've done here."

"I like designing special pieces for clients," he said. "Sometimes people know what they want, but a lot of times they have a problem they need me to fix. In this case I got to do that and work with the reclaimed wood."

She looked at him. "You're very talented."

The compliment made him want to go slay a dragon. "Thanks. I've been working with wood since high school. I got a part-time job working where I do now." He grinned. "I started by hauling lumber and sweeping floors. I went to full-time after I graduated."

"I'm surprised Helen didn't offer to put you through college."

"She did, but I knew this was what I wanted to do. I've studied with woodworkers all over the country and learned different techniques. What about you? Did you study computer science?"

She took a half step back. "I wasn't that successful at college. I was more interested in hacking than my classes. The other subjects were interesting but when it came to anything to do with computers, my friends and I knew way more than our professors." She shrugged. "It's a changing field and we were on the cutting edge of technology."

She gave him a rueful smile. "At least that's how we saw ourselves."

He wanted to hear more. He wanted to sit across from her somewhere and listen to her talk for hours. Coffee, he told himself. He should invite her to coffee. She was self-employed and could get to work whenever she wanted and he would make up his time by staying late. The house was empty, so the clients wouldn't mind.

The doorbell rang. Dylan glanced toward the front of the house, wondering who could be stopping by. All the neighbors knew the owners had moved into a rental for the remodel.

"I should get that," he said as he walked out of the kitchen.

He opened the front door and found a tall, middle-aged woman on the front porch. He recognized her immediately, even though they'd never met, and swore silently.

"Do you know who I am?" the woman asked, looking both nervous and determined. "I saw the company trailer parked out front, so I thought maybe you were here and I could talk to you for a second."

Dylan heard River walk up behind him. She saw the woman.

"Do you need to help her?" River asked. "I should get to work anyway." She smiled at him. "The cabinets really are beautiful."

And then she was gone. So much for coffee and listening to her forever, he thought glumly before looking at the stranger.

"We don't need to do this," he said.

"We do." Tears filled her eyes as she twisted her hands together. "You saved him. My son. You paid for his braces. He was in pain and was teased all the time at school and now he's going to be like everyone else. I wanted to thank you. Because of you, his life is changed forever. I could never afford the treatment and we didn't have dental insurance and every day he would cry because of how he felt and what the other kids said. That's never going to happen again."

Dylan knew she meant well and that her gratitude was heartfelt, but this moment was the exact reason he did what he did in secret. He didn't want the attention or the thanks. He wanted to fix the problem and escape without anyone knowing who he was.

"No one told me," she added quickly. "At the orthodontist. I just happened to see your information on the computer screen, where they billed you." She pressed her lips together. "I wanted you to know I was so grateful. So appreciative. I'll remember what you did for the rest of my life, as will my son."

"I'm glad I could help," he said gruffly. "If you could maybe not tell anyone it was me?"

"I won't say a word. But I wanted you to know what you did made a difference."

With that, she turned and left. Dylan watched her go, happy things were working out and wishing she'd never found out who he was.

# Sixteen

"Are you all right?" River asked Camryn as they walked the short distance to Navidad Mexican Café to meet their friends for lunch.

Camryn looked at her innocently. "I'm fine. Why would you ask?"

"I don't know. You seem . . . different. Happy, but in a way I haven't seen before."

Camryn raised her eyebrows. "That's so interesting. I have no idea what you mean, but honestly, I'm great. The twins and I decorated the house over the weekend. We'll be getting our tree in a few days. They're doing really well this year. It's so much better than last year when we were all so sad. I love how happy they are. Part of that is Tinsel, of course. She's such a sweetie."

Camryn pointed across The Wreath to the large trees. "Aren't they beautiful? I love our town traditions."

"They're really nice," River murmured,

wondering if it was just her or if Camryn was acting weird. Not that she was the best judge of human behavior. Sometimes she didn't understand it at all.

That morning was a good example, she thought. She'd really enjoyed the unexpected time with Dylan and had wanted to stay longer, but then that woman had shown up. There'd been something about his body language. Almost guilt, which made no sense. She didn't think the two even knew each other, except the woman had wanted to talk to Dylan so there was some connection.

Maybe it was just about work, River told herself. She had a remodel she wanted to discuss. In her next life, she told herself. In her next life she would be intuitive about people.

They reached the restaurant and went inside. Paisley and Shaye were already at a table. They all greeted each other, then River and Camryn took their seats. Camryn eyed Shaye's margarita.

"Day drinking? That's so not like you."

Shaye laughed. "I had my last final this morning and I'm celebrating. I'm out of college until after the first of the year." She held up her drink. "I have the rest of today off, then I'll be working extra hours at

Judy's Hand Pies so the other employees can take some time off."

"You go, girl," Camryn said with a laugh.

"Congratulations," River told her.

"Thanks." Shaye held up crossed fingers. "I think I did well on my finals, but I won't know for sure until my grades are posted."

"You'll do great," Paisley said. "I'm jealous of the day drinking but I have to get back to work. Jake's a great boss but I don't think he'd appreciate me showing up drunk."

"I have to work this afternoon, as well," River said. "I don't think a margarita would help my computer skills."

Camryn gave a mock heavy sigh. "I'm working, too. So you're on your own, Shaye. But let's plan an afternoon off for all of us and have a girls' day celebration. We'll invite all our friends."

"Deal," Paisley said. "So what's new with everyone?"

"Not much," River murmured.

Camryn picked up the menu and studied it. "Same for me. Things are quiet."

"The pre-holiday lull," Shaye said. "Then in a week, we're all scrambling like crazy."

River nodded in agreement. She knew her Snow Queen duties were going to get more frequent. Information that would have worried her last week, but less so now. Dylan would be there with her. Handsome Dylan who kissed like a dream.

Their server came by and took their orders. While Shaye ordered a second margarita, the rest of them settled on sodas and iced tea. They all chose the Monday special — a taco salad — then added a large platter of nachos to share.

When he'd left, Paisley sighed dramatically. "I can't believe we're all so boring right now. Something fun has to be happening to everyone." She turned to River. "I heard people really enjoyed the scavenger hunt."

"I heard the same," River said with a smile. "They were running around in the cold while Dylan and I waited in the museum. We had fun — I've never been and it was wonderful to see all the Santas and the trains and the trees."

"I haven't been this year," Shaye said. "Lawson and I have been making a list of fun things to do once my finals were finished."

"That's a good place to start." Camryn grinned. "Make sure your handsome husband takes you to the Holiday Ball. You could wear a Cinderella dress and everything."

Paisley closed her eyes and sighed. "I'd look good in a Cinderella dress." She opened her eyes and looked at River. "Speaking of dresses, what are you wearing?"

"To what?"

All three of her friends stared at her.

"To the Holiday Ball," Camryn said. "River, you do know it's a dressy event?"

River tried not to flinch. "No. What do you mean? I thought it was just a . . . I don't know . . . something." To be honest, she hadn't much thought about the final night of her reign and she'd just assumed it was called a ball to be playful. A dance?

"It's a formal occasion," Paisley told her. "We're talking long dresses and guys in tuxes. Like prom for grown-ups."

No, River thought frantically. Just no.

"I can't do that. I can't go to a dance. I've never been. I don't know how." Her chest tightened. "No one told me about that."

Her friends looked at each other. Camryn gentled her voice.

"It's okay. You can do this. We'll help. Just breathe."

"I'm breathing." Sort of. "Tell me what happens."

Paisley drew in a breath. "It's been a few years since we had a Holiday Ball, so this

313

one will be a big deal. It's going to be at the resort, in the larger ballroom. You and Dylan will have the first dance, then everyone joins you. I think there's food."

The room spun a couple of times. "I have to dance in front of people?"

"Just the one time."

To think she'd been enjoying her reign as Snow Queen. "I don't know how. I can't do this. I don't own a fancy dress. I've never been to a dance."

"What about high school?" Shaye asked.

"I never went. No one asked me. I was geeky and shy and no guys noticed me." Plus, she'd spent half her high school years recovering from surgery, so had missed weeks and weeks. Not something she needed to get into right now. There were more pressing issues.

"You'll be fine," Camryn said quickly. "It'll be okay."

"It won't!" She had to go find Geri and resign right this minute.

"Okay," Paisley said firmly. "We'll come up with a plan. I'll come over and we'll shop for dresses online. You're really petite so we want to get something that doesn't overwhelm you. So that takes care of one problem. The dance part is easy. Ask Dylan to teach you. He knows how."

Everyone stared at her.

"How can you possibly know that?" Camryn asked.

Paisley's expression turned smug. "Because I was one of the partners. I took dance for a few years. Helen Crane brought in an instructor for Jake and Dylan when they were fifteen." She grinned. "They were not happy, but they couldn't tell her no, so they were stuck. Anyway, a few of us from the dance studio were asked to be partners." She turned to River. "Dylan can totally teach you to do a basic waltz. That's all you'll need to get you through the night."

River still felt sick to her stomach. "I can't ask him to teach me to dance. He'll think I'm pathetic."

"No way," Shaye told her. "He'll think he's lucky to have an excuse to hold you in his arms. I mean, come on. You're all tiny with the spiky hair and that undercover sexuality. It makes guys wild."

River blinked at her. "Excuse me?"

Shaye stared at her glass. "I think I forgot to eat breakfast and that drink went to my head, but you know what I mean."

Camryn nodded. "I agree. You're hot and I'm sure Dylan has a thing for you. He'll probably think you telling him you can't dance is just an excuse for a little snuggling.

How will he resist?"

"No way," River said firmly, remembering their kiss and how much she'd enjoyed it. "I'm not risking Dylan thinking I'm a dork."

"Then we'll ask Jake to teach you," Paisley said.

Camryn drew back. "We will?"

"Why not? He knows the same steps and he's a good guy."

"She's right," Shaye said. "Camryn, you ask him. You have access, what with being a contender for Project: Jake's Bride."

Paisley and Shaye laughed while River managed a fake smile. She was still trying to take in the whole "Holiday Ball" revelation. If she could learn to dance, the night might not be too much of a disaster, she thought. It would be kind of fun to go to a ball with Dylan.

"Do you think Jake would be willing to help?" River asked Camryn. "Could you talk to him about it?"

Camryn hesitated only a second. "Sure. I'll get in touch with him and mention the problem. We can both help you with the dancing and Paisley will find you a dress. You'll see — it will all work out."

"We've come up with a plan," Victoria said

as she tore lettuce for the salad. "About Tinsel."

Camryn continued to chop bell peppers to add to the onion she'd already diced. "The two weeks aren't up until Thursday."

"We know." Lily walked in from the dining room where she'd been setting the table. "We've been checking in with the shelter every day and no one's claimed her yet. So if she doesn't have a family . . ."

The twins looked at each other.

"The adoption fee is two hundred and fifty dollars," Victoria said quickly. "It's a lot, we know."

"We thought we'd each put in seventy-five dollars from our savings," Lily added. "And the rest could be our Christmas present."

Victoria wiped her hands on a towel. "We worked out a schedule. How we'll take care of her as much as we can, you know with school and all. You said she's okay at the store, so if she can go with you during the week, we'll manage the weekends. Plus, we can do more during the summer when we're out of school."

Camryn set down her knife. She'd known this conversation was coming but had thought she would have a couple more days. Not that she was going to say no to her sisters — they'd all fallen for Tinsel.

"College will be a thing," Lily admitted. "I'll be in Seattle at the University of Washington and Victoria wants to go to Cal-Arts in California. But that's three years away and by then Tinsel will be totally comfortable in the house and going to work with you. Plus, we've been talking and maybe our sophomore or junior year one of us could get an apartment off campus and take her or something."

Camryn hadn't thought that far in the future and didn't want them worrying about it, either.

"Let's focus on where we are now," she said firmly. "We've all fallen for Tinsel and I agree if no one shows up to claim her that we'll adopt her."

The twins screamed before rushing to hug her.

"For real? We can keep her?"

"This is so great. We have a dog!"

Camryn held them both. When they stepped back, she said, "I'll pay a hundred and fifty of the adoption fee and you each put in fifty from your savings. We'll keep the Christmas presents out of it."

Victoria twirled in the kitchen. "I talked to Reggie and as soon as the adoption is for sure, she's going to teach me how to make dog clothes. I'm going to make her a whole wardrobe, just like Belle's."

Lily looked doubtful. "I don't think I'll be good at making clothes."

Victoria waved that comment aside. "That's okay. You can write her a song or something."

"No, I want to learn, too."

They rushed out to tell Tinsel the good news. Camryn picked up her phone and typed in a text.

It's official. If no one claims Tinsel, she's going to become one of the Neff girls.

Seconds later Jake answered. She's a lucky dog. She'll look good as a Neff girl. How are you?

She smiled. Good. Busy. I'm having a little trouble figuring out how to get away.

Finding a couple of hours to take advantage of Jake was a priority but with her everyday work, the seventeen hundred books she was wrapping, the holidays in general and the twins, she was a little over-extended.

I know how to be a patient man. My schedule is more flexible than yours. Say the word and I'm there. Tomorrow is the first Cookie Tuesday. Aren't the twins on the decorating committee for the auction?

They are. I'm helping as well. She drew in a breath as she mentally went through the schedule. After the auction they're having dinner with friends, so I could be free from the time the auction ends until maybe eight-thirty.

She paused. Was she being too practical? Suggesting they sneak away for a quick hour of sex might not be Jake's thing. She hesitated another second, then hit Send.

I'm in came the instant reply. She laughed.

Great. Is your place okay? In case they come home early.

Absolutely. I'll put on fresh sheets.

What a guy. I'll wear a thong under my jeans.

You're killing me.

Oh, don't say that. I need you alive for sex.

River did as much research as she could on both the Holiday Ball and Cookie Tuesday. Despite her best efforts, there wasn't much information online, which didn't make her feel better. She was nervous about both events on different levels. The Holiday Ball was obviously fraught — finding the right dress, dancing, having people watch her dance. But from what she'd been able to find out, Cookie Tuesday could be just as dangerous. She and Dylan were expected to judge the cookies. As in say which one was best, second best and so on. Judging hurt people's feelings and River wasn't sure she could do it.

A little after one Dylan texted, asking if she would like him to pick her up on his way to the resort. She quickly said she would. Better to arrive with him than on her own. As the time for the pickup approached, she found herself watching the clock. Anticipation made it difficult to concentrate on work. Now if the Holiday Ball was just her and Dylan, all dressed up, she just might be able to get into it.

Right on time, he walked into her office. She was torn between how good he looked and the lightweight jacket he was wearing.

"That's your coat?" she blurted before she could stop herself. "It's snowing. It's fifteen degrees outside and snowing. You need to bundle."

He chuckled. "I'm fine. It's closer to twenty than fifteen. Practically balmy."

He crossed to her desk and pulled her to

321

her feet, then lightly kissed her. His mouth was cold, but she didn't mind.

"Hi," she said when they parted.

"Hi, yourself." He tugged off his gloves. "Notice that I haven't lost these yet, so there's something to celebrate." He watched her carefully as he spoke. "I brought you something."

Her eyes widened slightly. "I don't understand."

He pulled a box out of his jacket pocket. "You're always giving me things, so I wanted to get you something."

He'd brought her a gift? Her stomach instantly tightened as tension immobilized her. Her instinct was to back away and say she didn't want it, but she knew he wouldn't understand. Worse, her reaction would hurt his feelings. Dylan was a good guy — she had to remember that and act like a normal person.

She took the box and opened it. Inside was a bright pink hippo. Despite her flashback reaction, she smiled as she lifted it out and put it on the palm of her hand.

"Adorable," she said, taking off the small lid on the back of the hippo, not sure what was inside. "Licorice allsorts?" She laughed.

"Do you like them?" he asked anxiously. "I wasn't sure. I thought about chocolate but that seemed too traditional."

"I love them," she said, setting the hippo on her desk and raising herself up on tiptoe. "Thank you."

She couldn't quite stretch enough to kiss him, but he figured out what she was trying to do and bent down. Their mouths touched again, this time with a little more passion than their quick greeting. She rested her hands on his shoulders and closed her eyes.

Dylan quickly shifted from kissee to kisser, pulling her against him and wrapping his arms around her. She sank into him, liking the feel of his body against hers. They would be good together, she thought, liking his combination of desire and restraint. He wanted her, but he wasn't going to push her.

After a few seconds he drew back, his expression regretful. "While I'd like nothing more than to keep kissing you, we have to get going."

"Right. It's Cookie Tuesday." She smiled. "Thank you again for my gift."

"You're welcome." His tone turned teasing. "Now that I know you show your appreciation with kisses, I'm going to be bringing you a lot more gifts."

"I don't need you to bring me anything," she told him. "If you want to kiss me, you should go ahead and do it."

That left him momentarily speechless, which was kind of a good feeling, she thought as she slipped out of her street shoes and stepped into her boots. After putting on her coat, she collected her gloves, scarf and hat.

"I'm ready."

He chuckled. "You know we're only going to be outside to walk to my truck and then walk into the resort."

"It's still going to be freezing. I need my layers."

He waited while she locked her office door behind her. "You really haven't lived anywhere cold."

"I told you — I'm an LA girl at heart. Or at least in body temperature. I went to college at UCLA, so none of this is normal for me, but I'm adjusting. I think next year will be easier for me."

"Or at least less of a shock."

"Exactly."

They went downstairs and through the store. River pulled on her hat and gloves, then wrapped her scarf around her neck before stepping outside.

As always, the chill was like a slap on her face. She shuddered slightly as she hurried along with Dylan toward the parking lot by

The Wreath.

"How's work going?" he asked. "Any fun people to investigate?"

"No, just regular stuff. I do pro bono work looking for deadbeat parents, so I was doing that this morning."

They reached his truck and held open the passenger door.

"What kind of deadbeat parents?" he asked, sliding in on his side.

"The ones who don't pay their child support. It used to just be fathers, but now it's mothers, too." She pulled off her hat. "I don't get it. You had a kid — why wouldn't you want to be financially responsible? But they aren't and I help find them."

He shook his head. "You're impressive, River."

"I'm not. It's usually not that hard to find them. The other thing I was working on is security systems testing, where I try to hack into a system. I have a friend who has contracts with a few big companies. He subcontracts with me every now and then. After we're done with Cookie Tuesday, I'll be working all night, trying to break into their HR system. There's a lot of good information there. Names, birthdates, social security numbers."

"You're going to break into a company's

database and steal people's personal information?"

Yikes — that wasn't what she'd meant. "I won't take anything," she said quickly. "I'll just see if I can get access to it. There's a test file that I have to find and copy as proof of work. It's all legal. Like I said, my friend has a contract and I'm approved to be on the team."

He started the truck. "Today I installed cabinets. Our worlds aren't the same at all. So you're a hacker."

"Not anymore." She pressed her lips together. "But I was."

He glanced at her. "What does that mean? You used to do this stuff illegally?"

She tried not to writhe in her seat. "Yes. In college, which I didn't finish. I should have told you that before, when we were talking about it. I left after two years."

No, not left, she reminded herself, wishing she could lie more easily. "I was expelled after I was arrested by the FBI."

She had to give Dylan credit. Except for a slight tightening of his hands on the wheel, he didn't physically react.

"Go on," he said more calmly than she would have expected.

She held in a sigh. "I was getting into systems because that was what my friends and I did for fun. It was a challenge. I never took anything or did damage, but it was still illegal. Especially, you know, the government computers. And the military."

He swore under his breath. "For real? I thought that just happened in the movies."

"No, it's a thing. We all wanted to be the best. One day there was a knock on my dorm room door and it was the FBI."

She remembered how terrified she'd been. Until that second it hadn't occurred to her she could be caught.

"They arrested me. Kelsey and my mom found me a really good lawyer who helped me make a deal. I told them everything I knew, I showed them what I'd done and how I'd done it, and I went to work for the government for three years. In return, they dropped all charges."

"You did hacking for the government?" he asked.

"No, it was more helping them enhance their security. I was on a team — we worked together. Once I was done there, I started the business I have now. I contract out with different companies to do background checks and sometimes I help law enforcement agencies with stuff. It's all legal. I don't do anything questionable anymore. It's not worth it."

She glanced at him. "I wasn't keeping secrets. But it's hard to know exactly when to say 'hey, I've been arrested by the FBI. How about you?' "

The corners of his mouth turned up. "That would be an awkward conversation to have and you're right. We're just getting to know each other. I will say, as far as secrets go, that's a really good one." The smile faded. "Not all secrets are bad."

"No one's told me any good ones."

For a second she thought he was going to say something. She waited, but he didn't speak.

"So have you been arrested by the FBI?" she asked, hoping to lighten the mood.

He laughed. "I haven't been. To the best of my knowledge, I've never broken the law. Except maybe for speeding tickets."

"Those don't count."

He looked at her, then turned his attention back to the road. "You're a surprise. I knew you were into computers, but I wouldn't have guessed you were a hacker. It's kind of cool. I've never been attracted to a bad girl before."

Her lips twitched. "I'm no one's definition of bad."

"Your life story could be a spy movie. I think that qualifies you."

She relaxed in her seat, grateful he hadn't been repelled by her past. Or judgmental.

"So?" he asked casually. "Tell me about the tattoos. Bad girls always have tattoos."

She laughed. "I don't have any, so I can't be a bad girl."

"Disappointing, but all right. Let me tell you about mine."

# SEVENTEEN

Camryn balanced on the eight-foot ladder, holding the auction banner in place. Victoria stood twenty feet away, her face screwed up in concentration.

"My arm's getting tired," Camryn told her.

"I'm not sure the sign is straight."

Lily, standing at the base of the ladder, groaned. "It's straight enough. Come on, it's a banner for an auction that will be over in two hours. This isn't the Super Bowl."

"A job worth doing is a job worth doing right." Victoria paused. "Or worth doing well. I can never remember. Anyway, it's fine."

Camryn secured the hooks on her end. The maintenance guy helping them did the same at the other end of the banner. She started down the ladder, slightly disappointed that Jake hadn't dropped by. Not that she expected him to help or anything, but they did have a date for after the auction and she'd thought he might want to see her and —

As she reached the last rung, a warm hand settled on her hip.

"Careful," Jake said from behind her. "You looked a little unsteady."

Heat instantly blossomed and it was all she could do not to throw herself into his arms and beg him to find them an empty room right that second. Only there were ten teenage girls in the room and the cookies were due to arrive any second.

She stepped onto the floor and faced him. "You saved me."

"It seemed the heroic thing to do."

Humor brightened his eyes, along with a hint of passion.

Lily moved close and gave him a hug. "Tinsel knew we'd see you at the auction and told us to tell you hi."

"Tell her hi back."

Victoria hurried over and hugged him, as well. Camryn ignored the whisper of jealousy. She would be getting her own Jake hugs later.

"Don't you love the decorations?" Victoria asked. "We're hoping to raise a lot of money for our class Christmas project. We're supporting the hospital. Today is classic sugar cookies. They'll all be decorated and delicious."

"Did you enter anything?" he asked her.

Victoria shook her head. "No. We talked about it but the competition is pretty aggressive and we're all busy with work or school, plus Tinsel and the holidays."

She and Lily walked over to join their friends. Jake looked at Camryn.

"They're doing great," he said. "You must be happy and relieved."

"Yes, to both. We're having a good holiday season. Now we just have to wait for Tinsel's adoption to be finalized." She held up crossed fingers. "Two more days until we can claim her as our own."

"Are you worried her family will show up?"

"A little," she admitted. "I keep telling myself if it was going to happen, it would have by now. I hope I'm telling the truth."

"If not, you'll probably be puppy shopping."

She hadn't thought of that. "I'd rather have Tinsel."

"I know. I'll think good thoughts, too. Are you and the twins going to the Lighted Christmas Parade on Saturday?"

"We are."

"Want company?"

Warmth swept through her. "I would. Very much." She paused. "I assume you mean yourself."

He grinned. "Yeah. Why don't you dress Tinsel in something warm and bring her along?"

"We'll do that."

A dozen or so people carrying large pastry boxes walked into the ballroom. Camryn leaned close.

"Escape while you can. I'll text you when the auction is finished and the twins are getting ready to head off with their friends."

He lowered his voice. "You have until eight-thirty?"

"Yes. The twins are due home at nine. I told them I had errands to run. I fed Tinsel before coming over here and she has a puppy pad in the laundry room, so she's fine."

Camryn told herself to stop babbling. Jake didn't need to know the details of her life. But instead of looking impatient, he smiled.

"You take care of the world," he murmured. "I left a package for you at the front desk. Pick it up on your way out."

"What is it?" she asked, instantly curious. "A French maid outfit?"

"I hadn't thought of that, so no. It's a garage clicker. I'm going to stop and get

Chinese, so you'll get to the condo before me. You can park inside. The door to the unit is unlocked."

"You're letting me in your condo when you're not there?"

He looked confused. "Why wouldn't I?"

"I could snoop."

"You're not the type. Besides, I'm not hiding anything."

His assumption about her character and his thoughtfulness just made her like him more.

"I'm torn," she said softly. "I could be waiting in your bed, but I am wearing the thong I promised. Which would you prefer?"

His pupils dilated slightly. "A bra and the thong."

Anticipation sent warmth down south. "Done. See you then."

"Nothing could keep me away."

"You're too happy," Dylan grumbled as he adjusted the weight on the leg press. "It's barely six in the morning. What's going on?"

They were in the hotel weight room. So far no guests had joined them so they had the place to themselves.

Jake stood in front of the wall of mirrors, doing biceps curls. "Of course I'm happy. I have a good life."

"It's more than that. There's something."

Jake set down the dumbbells on the bench next to him. "Why does there have to be? It's Christmas in Wishing Tree. That's always a good time. I asked my mom to back off on finding me a bride and she has."

"You don't know that."

"No one's shown up, so she listened."

Dylan drew in a breath, then exhaled as he slowly straightened his legs. The weight was a challenge, but he knew he could handle it.

"For now," he said.

"One day at a time, my friend. I'm having dinner with her tonight where I will thank her for agreeing to my wishes."

Dylan wasn't buying that. There was more going on with Jake than he was admitting to. "You're seeing someone."

"Nope."

"You are. I can sense it." But who? Jake had sworn off dating and it wasn't as if someone new had come to town. His friend hadn't traveled anywhere. So who was it?

"Camryn," he said suddenly. "It has to be her. You've hung with her a few times lately. You helped her sisters with that dog."

"Tinsel," Jake said, picking up the dumbbells for his second set of reps.

"You like her. Camryn, not the dog."

Jake avoided his gaze. "Maybe."

"You do. So you're finally going to stop being an ass and get in a relationship."

"It's not like that. What we have is temporary by design."

Temporary? Why would anyone want that? Dylan was looking for something a lot more long-term.

"Temporary is safer for me," Jake added. "Less time for me to mess up. And speaking of women, how are things with River?"

"Confusing."

"I thought you liked her."

"I do." Dylan ignored the burning in his thighs and completed his reps. "She's great, but she's not exactly who I thought."

"In a good way or a bad way?"

Dylan thought about what River had told him — about hacking and being arrested by the FBI. He was still having trouble wrapping his mind around the information. But she'd been so forthcoming, admitting to her mistakes with no excuses. It was like when she'd told him she was socially awkward — she didn't avoid the truth or make herself the hero of every story. Plus, how she'd handled having scoliosis told him she was brave. There was a lot to like.

"A good way," he said, reaching for his water bottle. "She told me some things that change how I look at her. I thought maybe she was the type who needed rescuing, but she's strong, you know? Able to deal with stuff and move on."

"But you like to rescue people."

Dylan started his second set. "That's not true."

"It's exactly true and you know it. Interesting that you're falling for a woman who might not need you to take care of her. That's going to be hard for you."

Something Dylan wouldn't admit was true. "You think you know things but you don't."

"Uh-huh. Sure. So you like her. Does she like you or does she have good taste?"

Dylan ignored the teasing. "She likes me. It's good."

Jake returned the dumbbells to the rack. "But?"

"She doesn't know about the money and I don't know how to tell her. I almost did yesterday, but I couldn't figure out what to say."

"You're an idiot and you worry too much about the money. You're the only one who cares about it."

Dylan shot him a look in the mirror. Jake sat on the bench and picked up his water.

"Okay, so Bobbie cared," Jake admitted.

"A lot." Bobbie's finding out about his lottery winnings and how they'd grown into several million dollars had changed everything.

"She was pissed to find out I'd kept the money a secret and she was even more angry when I wouldn't spend it on her. The money changed everything." It was the reason they'd broken off their engagement. "Money changes people."

"Not everyone," Jake told him. "River's not like Bobbie. She's not going to expect you to move to Seattle and buy a mansion on the water."

"You don't know that."

"No, but you're the one who likes her so you should. Do you really think she's going to freak out?"

Dylan didn't have an answer to that. From what he could see, River was grounded. She was a nurturer who cared about other people and had a realistic view of her place in the world.

"I can't tell her."

"If you keep seeing her, at some point you're going to have to come clean. No one likes being lied to."

"I'm not lying," Dylan said, even as he remembered her saying that she didn't like secrets. "I'm being selective in what I say."

Jake met his gaze in the mirror. "That is so much crap and you know it. Tell her, Dylan. Tell her now. Otherwise, you're going to get more involved and when she finds out she's going to be pissed at you. Worse, you'll have screwed up when you didn't have to."

Dylan understood the advice was sound. He just wasn't sure he was going to take it.

Jake arrived at Buon Natale Italian restaurant exactly at six. As he opened the door he smiled, remembering the last time he'd been here with Camryn. They hadn't made it through dinner — instead, getting their food to go and heading to his place for an incredible evening.

She was amazing, he thought. Beautiful, funny, sexy. The kind of woman whom, under other circumstances, he would find it easy to fall for.

He gave his name to the hostess. "I'm meeting my mom."

The young woman frowned at him. "Your party is already here, but I don't think it's your mother."

That didn't make sense. He followed the hostess back into the restaurant and was led to a table where a pretty, dark-haired woman sat. She smiled and stood as he approached.

"Jake," she said easily. "I'm Nora. So good to meet you. Although I'm pretty sure we've already met. When we were kids. My mom swears I hit you in the head with a sand bucket. If that's true, I apologize."

Wait, what? He glanced from the hostess to Nora and back. The teen shrugged, placed menus on the table, then walked away. Nora sat and Jake found himself doing the same.

"I thought I was meeting my mother," he said, aware he sounded like an idiot. "Who are you?"

The woman smiled. "Nora. Our mothers are friends. Helen set this up, so we could get to know each other. I'm in town visiting a friend from college. When she found out, she suggested we have dinner together." Nora frowned. "She didn't tell you?"

"No. Somehow she forgot to mention it."

He couldn't believe his mother had done this to him. He'd told her to back off and she hadn't listened. Worse, she'd set him up on what he could only assume was a blind date. Project: Jake's Bride strikes again.

"Well, we're here," Nora said with a laugh. "Let's enjoy the evening."

Three weeks ago he probably would have agreed, but that was no longer a possibility.

He couldn't have dinner with Nora while he and Camryn were, um, well, not dating, but something. They were seeing each other sexually and that mattered.

He glanced around, looking for a distraction or an escape, all the while telling himself to act cool and keep it together. He was a man of the world — he should be able to handle the situation without acting like an idiot.

He glanced out the window and saw Camryn on the sidewalk. She had a tote over one shoulder and was carrying what he knew to be a small dog carrier — no doubt on her way home.

"Excuse me for a moment," he said as he bolted from his chair and raced out of the restaurant. He caught up with her at the corner.

"Jake," she said, obviously surprised to see him. "Are you all right? You're not wearing a jacket. It's freezing."

"I was in the restaurant." He grabbed her by her upper arms. "You have to help me. I was supposed to meet my mom for dinner only when I got here, there was a strange woman at the table. Nora. I had no idea. I think she's a candidate for Project: Jake's Bride. I don't know what to say to her or how to handle this. Plus, you know, us."

He held up a hand. "I know it's temporary, but I'm not comfortable having dinner with her while you and I are . . ."

Camryn grinned. "Having sex?"

"Yeah. That." He glanced back at the restaurant. "I'm going to tell her about what my mom's doing. Can you come join me?"

"And everyone thinks men are the stronger gender." She walked into the restaurant. "I have Tinsel with me," she whispered. "I feel like Reese Witherspoon in *Legally Blonde*."

"You're much prettier than her."

Camryn laughed. "Oh, please. Like I believe that. But it's a nice compliment so thank you."

He led the way to the table. Nora looked up when she spotted him but her smile quickly faded when she saw Camryn. Once they arrived at the table, he realized he had no idea how to start the conversation nor what he was supposed to say to explain the situation.

Camryn shot him a "you're such a coward" look before holding out her hand. "Hi, I'm Camryn Neff. Nice to meet you."

"Nora Pineiro." Nora looked at him. "You brought a friend?"

"Not exactly," he said, holding out Camryn's chair, then carefully taking Tinsel's

342

carrier and placing it on the spare seat. She wagged her tail, then quickly settled for a nap.

Camryn looked at him. He shrugged briefly. Honestly, he couldn't think of a single thing to say.

"I'm a candidate, too," Camryn said brightly. "I can't decide if Helen's incredibly sweet or if she should come with a warning label."

"You mean Jake's mother?" Nora asked. "What does she have to do with anything?"

"She wants me to get married and give her grandchildren," Jake told her. "She thinks I'm taking too long to find the one."

Camryn nodded. "She's started something called Project: Jake's Bride. She's collecting candidates for him to consider." The bright smile returned. "I was in shock when she told me. What do you say to an announcement like that?" She laughed. "I admire her fervor, if not her methods. You know we're being investigated. Digitally, I mean. I can't wait to read my report."

Nora looked between them, her expression bewildered. "Wait a minute, this isn't just dinner? I'm a candidate?"

"It looks that way," Camryn admitted. "I don't know how many there are of us but it's definitely a competition."

Jake held in a groan. "It's not a competition. I can get my own girl."

"Despite all evidence to the contrary," Camryn murmured.

He did his best not to smile. "This is you helping?"

"Oh, was I supposed to help?" She turned back to Nora. "We should probably get to know each other. If things work out, you'll be moving here and Wishing Tree is a pretty small town. We could be friends."

Nora stared at her. "I can't decide if you're being nice or if you're a sick and twisted person. Either way, I'm out."

"Oh, don't go," Camryn said, instantly contrite. "I swear I wasn't being mean. Just a little funny and it might have come out wrong."

"Whatever." Nora collected her things. "Don't call me," she told him. "There's something wrong with both of you."

With that, she stalked out of the restaurant. Camryn watched her go.

"Now I feel guilty."

"You didn't do anything wrong," he told her. "This is on my mother, whom I'm going to talk to right now."

"Don't yell," she said as she rose and pulled on her coat. "She's doing what she thinks is best."

"That's what scares me."

Jake had to wait until late Thursday morning to see his mother. He wasn't sure if she was really busy, or if she was avoiding him. Either way, he was determined, so exactly at eleven he showed up at the house where he'd grown up.

Despite the fact that he hadn't lived there full-time in nearly fifteen years, the place still felt like home. He knew every inch of the house. When Dylan had moved in with the family his mom had remodeled the bedroom across the hall so it was an exact duplicate of Jake's. Same size bathroom and closet, same paint color, same linens. She'd wanted to make sure Dylan knew he was welcome and not some charity case she'd taken off the streets.

Back then he'd admired her attention to detail. These days he was thinking it was more of a curse.

He let himself inside and made his way to her office. She was sitting behind her desk, typing on her laptop, her fingers flying over the keyboard. Helen being Helen, she embraced technology. He'd never had to show her how to work her phone or set up her streaming service.

She looked up and smiled. "Right on time.

I'm so proud."

"Mother." He crossed to her and kissed her, then sat next to her desk. "We had a deal."

"I'm sure I have no idea what you're talking about."

"You were going to stop looking for a wife for me."

His mother smiled. "I know I never agreed to that. Why would I? What a ridiculous assumption on your part. Honestly, Jake, when have I not meddled?"

A question he wasn't going to answer.

"The dinner with Nora was a disaster."

"Yes, I heard." Helen eyed him. "Perhaps if you hadn't brought Camryn along, things would have gone better."

"Perhaps if you stopped setting me up, we wouldn't have to have this conversation at all."

"But I was so sure you'd like Nora."

Maybe he would have — under other circumstances. But he was currently otherwise involved. Not that he was going to tell his mother about his arrangement with Camryn. If they were dating, he would tell her that, but he and Camryn weren't exactly following a conventional route.

"You need to stop," he said. "You're messing with people's lives here, Mom."

346

"Which is the point of what I'm doing." She studied him. "Fine. I'll give you a break for the holidays. I know you're busy with work and helping Camryn with Tinsel. They must be getting close to adopting her."

"They'll find out today if they can."

His mother's expression turned speculative. "You're spending a fair amount of time with her."

"No," he said flatly. "No. Camryn isn't interested in anything long-term. We're not involved."

At least not in the way his mother meant.

"She's a lovely young woman."

"She is."

"And her sisters are adorable. Why doesn't she want a serious relationship? Is there someone else?"

"I'm not discussing her personal life with you."

"You're annoyingly discreet."

He smiled. "Thank you."

"And wrong." She patted his arm. "You're worried about the wrong things. You're so determined to not make a mistake that you won't take a chance. What if the love of your life is right there in front of you but you won't risk getting involved?"

"That's hardly subtle."

"Maybe I'm not talking about Camryn."

"Then who?"

She ignored that. "My point is everyone has a story they tell themselves and most of the time that story isn't true. You hold back because you won't be your father. That's your story. But what you refuse to see is you can't be like him. It's not in your nature. But you're afraid of making a mistake, so you refuse to try. Your story gives you a good excuse, by the way. Almost a false sense of security. I have a feeling that Camryn's story is just as much a way to protect herself, as yours is protecting you. Maybe you should test her story a little. Or at least challenge it."

He swore silently, not sure when his mother had picked up that uncomfortable and possibly accurate insight into his character. Bad enough that she meddled but worse that she was able to see past all his emotional barriers.

"You're full of crap," he said lightly, hoping to distract her and change the subject.

"I think we both know I'm not, but we don't have to talk about it if the truth will make you squirm."

"I don't squirm. I'm sitting perfectly still."

"On the outside." Her humor faded. "Jake, I love you more than I love anyone in the world. I mean that literally. I want you to be happy. I want you to find someone to love who will love you back. I want you to know the joy of giving your heart fully. There is no feeling like it."

"I want that, too," he told her.

And he did. But as he stood and pulled her to her feet to hug her, he couldn't help wondering about how she'd felt the first time she'd found out her husband had cheated on her. And the second, and the third. Her love had been tested. It had survived, obviously, but at what price? He'd vowed he would never be like that, never treat his partner that way. All excellent goals. But maybe she was right. Maybe along the way he'd started holding back a little too much. And maybe it was time to expect a little bit more from both himself and those around him.

# Eighteen

River stepped into Yule Read Books, not sure what to expect. Dylan had texted her, asking her to meet him here. She'd been nervous about his reaction to her confession — that she had nearly been a felon — but he didn't seem fazed by the information. He'd been his usual funny, charming self during Cookie Tuesday. Although they'd consulted on which cookies were the best and which should come in second and third, he'd offered to make the actual announcement so she wouldn't have to face disappointing a room full of eager bakers.

The auction had raised a lot of money for the hospital, so that was nice, and she'd even bid on a few lots of cookies, although she hadn't been willing to pay enough to win them. Dylan had taken her to dinner after the event and spent several minutes kissing her good-night at her door.

She'd been tempted to invite him in, she

thought, unwinding her scarf. Once relationships got physical, she was a lot more comfortable. The rules for sex were a whole lot easier for her to understand than the rules about emotions and hearts. But she'd sensed Dylan was the type to want to make the first move, so she'd eventually said good-night and had stepped inside alone.

Now she looked around the bookshop, hoping to catch sight of him. As always the store was crowded with lots of shoppers and enticing displays. There was a whole section of cookbooks and the children's section spilled into the aisle. The gift section was busier than usual, no doubt because it was close to the holidays.

"Hey." Dylan moved next to her and lightly kissed her cheek. "You're here!"

He sounded delighted, which made her relaxed.

"I said I would be."

"I know, but you're a popular woman. You could have had a better offer."

She grinned. "Not likely." She motioned to the customers around them. "They're extra busy today."

"That's because of what's out back."

He took her hand and led her through the store. They exited a rear door and stepped into a large, white tent filled with long tables

351

all covered with books. Piles and piles of books. Signs hanging from the ceiling described the various areas of interest. There were travel books and history books, coffee table books, cookbooks and all kinds of fiction.

"What is this?" she asked. "I come in here all the time and they've never had a tent before."

Dylan wrapped his arm around her. "It's all the books they've bought from estate sales around the country. They buy books in giant lots, then sort through them. The best ones are saved for the holiday book bonanza. You can find anything you're looking for and a lot of things you aren't."

He locked his fingers with hers and they began to walk down the wide aisles.

"My weakness," he said, pointing toward several tables overflowing with comic books. "I loved them when I was a kid. Helen kept me well supplied. Jake never got the appeal, but they were my thing."

"I like graphic novels," she admitted. "The drawings convey so much in just a few frames."

He flipped through comic books while she studied the graphic novels at the next table. After a few minutes he joined her, then reached for one with a cover showing a young woman typing on a computer on one half and wearing a superhero cape on the other.

"Look," he said, his voice teasing. "It's you!"

She laughed. "I'm not a superhero."

"I don't know. You do a lot of good things with your job."

She waited to see if he would say more — maybe comment on her being arrested by the FBI, but he only continued browsing. Okay, she thought in surprise. Apparently, he didn't care about her past.

They spent some time at a table with stacks of travel books before moving to the cookbook section.

"See if you can find any dessert or baking books," she said. "I'm always looking for new recipes."

He held up a spiral-bound book. "How about celebrating with JELL-O?"

"Are you a JELL-O kind of guy?"

"I am. I can make a great marshmallow and apple salad with JELL-O."

"Impressive."

She found a cookie cookbook published in the 1950s and flipped through the recipes. She'd just put it in her "buy" pile when Dylan held up another book.

"Are you a fan?"

She stared at the old-fashioned cover. "Is that for real?" She took the book from him. *"The Nancy Drew Cookbook: Clues to Good Cooking."* She looked at him. "I love it."

"Nancy Drew, huh? I wouldn't have guessed."

"My mom made me read one when I was a kid. It wasn't my thing, but she said I had to at least try them. I was instantly hooked." She flipped through the book, smiling at some of the recipe names. "Detective Burgers" and "Hidden Staircase Biscuits."

"I'm getting this," she said firmly. "I don't care what it costs. I have to have this in my life."

He shook his head. "So now I have Ned for competition."

"How do you know about Ned?"

"My first serious girlfriend had a little sister who was crazy about Nancy Drew. She used to talk to me about whichever one she was reading." He tucked her stack of books under one arm. "So Ned, huh?"

"I never had a thing for Ned."

"You sure? Because I want to know about my competition."

"You're safe from Ned."

They went to the front of the store to pay for the books. Dylan pulled out his wallet, but she insisted she buy her own books. He reluctantly agreed but then bought her a half pound of fudge and a small rainbow pinwheel.

"For your office," he said, taking her bag from her. "Sugar for energy and the pinwheel for when you need to clear your mind to problem-solve."

"Thank you."

Together they walked over to Jingle Coffee. They placed their orders, then claimed a table. Once their coffee had been delivered, River pulled out the fudge and opened the package.

"Hey, that was for later," Dylan told her.

"I can get more. I saw you eyeing it."

"I do like dessert," he admitted, taking a piece.

"So if you ever get mad at me, I can win you back with cookies?"

Something dark and sexy flashed in his eyes. "Cookies could work," he said slowly, as if there were other options.

They were flirting, she thought, hoping she didn't mess up by saying the wrong thing.

"Tell me about your first girlfriend," she said, picking up her mug of coffee.

Instantly, the light died and Dylan drew back a little. Uh-oh — not a happy topic.

He hesitated before saying, "It was a long

time ago. High school. Things didn't work out."

"I kind of figured you weren't still together," she said, hoping to get them back to flirting. "It would make having coffee together awkward."

He grinned at that. "You're right. You're not the type to date a married man." The humor faded. "I don't cheat. I wasn't saying I'd still be here with you if I was with Claire."

"I know." She trusted him to be a good guy. "Tell me about her."

There was a pause, then he sighed. "It's not a story that makes me look good."

"You mean like being arrested by the FBI?"

He relaxed. "Okay, yeah, there's that. So I had a crush on Claire, but I didn't think she was interested in me. She was kind of around a lot, showing up where Jake and I went, but I figured she wanted to date him. I told myself to get over her, but I couldn't, so I came up with a plan. A really dumb one."

"You kidnapped her?"

He laughed. "No. I told her I knew she wanted to go out with Jake and if she'd date me for three months first, I'd put in a good word."

River flinched. "That's a really bad plan."

"I know that now. She looked at me like I was crazy and told me she had no interest in Jake, but if I wanted to ask her out, she would say yes."

"She liked you!"

"I get that now, but at the time I told myself she was embarrassed to admit her crush. Still, I asked her out and she was great. I fell hard. But I couldn't let go of the fact that she had a thing for Jake."

"Wait, she said she wasn't interested in him. Was she lying?"

"No. She was telling the truth. I was the problem. I couldn't believe her." He glanced away. "Or maybe I couldn't believe a girl that great would be interested in me. I kept waiting for her to dump me and go be with Jake."

"He wouldn't do that. Jake's your best friend. He wouldn't go out with your ex-girlfriend."

Dylan nodded. "I agree, but my sixteen-year-old self wasn't that logical or smart. Eventually, Claire dumped me because I couldn't let the Jake thing go."

"You lost her because you couldn't believe in her. Or yourself." She paused, thinking about what he'd said. "Or is it that you couldn't trust her? Trust issues can be a thing. I know because sometimes it's hard for me to trust people. That's on me, not them. I missed so much socially when I was growing up. I don't have all the skills other people take for granted."

His gaze locked with hers. "You're right about not believing in myself. And yes, there are some trust issues. Probably because my mom made it so clear she regretted having me. I like to think these days I'm more willing to give people the benefit of the doubt."

"You didn't judge me," she pointed out. "You could have worried I was a criminal."

He laughed. "You're many things, River, but not a criminal."

"See? You're giving me the benefit of the doubt."

"You're not a criminal," he repeated. "It's not in your nature." The smile returned. "You bought me gloves."

"How does that prove anything?"

"You're the kind of person who gives rather than takes. I like that, and you."

"I like you, too," she said, hoping she wasn't blushing as she spoke.

"No interest in Jake?" he asked, his voice teasing.

"Not even a little."

"That's exactly what I wanted to hear."

■ ■ ■

"Are you seeing anyone else?" Jake asked.

Camryn sat up and stared at him. "What did you just ask me?" She held up a hand to stop him from speaking as she studied his face to see if he was joking or not. He looked amazingly serious.

"You mean like dating?" she asked.

He turned onto his side and looked at her. "Yes. Are you dating anyone?"

She shifted so she was sitting cross-legged, the sheet tucked under her arms, covering her.

"I'm naked. In your bed. And we just had sex. Why would you ask if I was dating anyone? Which I'm not, by the way."

"I wondered." His gaze was steady. "I'd rather you didn't start anything while we're together."

She opened her mouth, then closed it. "I genuinely don't know what to say. Why would I start dating anyone?"

"You're not dating me. You said you wouldn't. You said this was sex until the holidays were over."

She had and while it had been a good idea at the time, she had to admit that maybe she hadn't considered the consequences of her request. She liked being with Jake — in all ways possible — and simply walking away in a few weeks was going to be difficult.

"Jake, there's only you. I only see one guy at a time."

"Me, too." One corner of his mouth turned up. "Women, though."

"Yes, I figured that." She tilted her head. "What brought this up?"

"Nothing."

She waited.

He flopped on his back and stared at the ceiling. "My mother."

"Oh, my. I think I need to be dressed to talk about your mother. What did she say?"

"That I'm not my father and I'm letting my fears get in the way of my happiness."

There was a lot of information in that statement, she thought. She reached for his hand and took it in hers.

"You're not your father," she said firmly. "You're nothing like him."

"Is this where I point out you never knew him?"

"I don't have to have ever met him to know you aren't him. You'd never hurt someone you care about the way he hurt your mom. It's not in your nature."

"You can't be sure."

"I can be and I am."

He looked at her. "My mom said they had the perfect marriage. She lied to me."

"She said what you say to a kid. She said that to make you feel safe and secure. She didn't want you to have any part of her pain. And everyone's different. Maybe she really felt that way."

"Would you?"

"No," she admitted. "If the man I love cheated, I'd be devastated. I'm not sure the relationship could survive."

"I agree."

She smiled. "Which is why you'd never be like him. Tell me a good story about your father."

"We took road trips every summer. Just the two of us." He smiled. "No girls allowed. When Dylan moved in, he joined us. The trips were always different. The Grand Canyon, the Rock and Roll Hall of Fame. Disneyland. You name it, we went. Always by car. We'd be gone two or three weeks, staying at hotels, eating junk food. We went white-water rafting and fishing." The smile broadened. "When I turned eighteen, we went skydiving. My mom doesn't know about that."

"I wouldn't tell her, either," Camryn said, enjoying his memories. "She'd be furious."

"I know. We always had a great time. We'd talk about stuff and listen to the radio. He didn't check in with the office or anything."

"You still love him."

He looked at her. "It's not about what I feel, it's about what he did and who he was."

"He was a good father."

"Not when he cheated on my mom."

Which was true but she couldn't help thinking he was learning the wrong lesson. She leaned toward him. "Jake, I know you worry about your reaction when Iona came back, but you didn't do anything wrong. Asking the question isn't the issue. You're allowed to take five seconds to figure out what's happening. The mistake wasn't worrying — the mistake was not telling Reggie what was happening and letting her help you through the situation."

She paused. "Not that I feel really bad about that, given the circumstances."

He rolled toward her and put his hand on her leg. "I want to believe you."

"Then you should."

"Iona was a mistake. Not the first time, but when she came back."

"She wasn't the one?"

"Not even close." His gaze met hers. "Go out with me."

"On a date?" Weren't they already dating? Sort of?

"Yes, but start seeing me. For real. Exclusive dating. You and me."

Her heart fluttered with two parts anticipation and one part fear. "You mean a relationship."

"Yes. No ending things after Christmas. We go as long as we both want."

Every cell in her body screamed *Yes!* but her brain was less sure. Intrigued, interested, but worried.

"I'm still leaving."

"I know. In three years. A lot can happen between now and then." He smiled. "A month ago you didn't plan on being a pet owner, yet here you are. Tinsel's official mom."

"You're right. We have paperwork and everything."

Start dating Jake — as in they would be a couple and part of each other's lives? She wasn't sure. Oh, she knew she liked spending time with him and the sex was amazing. He was great with the twins and Tinsel. He was strong, funny, easy to talk to and someone she could depend on. Under any other circumstances, she knew he was exactly what she was looking for. Only these weren't *other circumstances.*

"I really do plan to go back to Chicago."

His gaze never wavered. "You've made that clear."

"So this will absolutely end."

"That's the plan."

"But you still want to go out with me?" she clarified. "Exclusively."

"We'd be a thing."

Why? Why would he risk that, knowing there was no happily-ever-after for them? Why would he take the chance?

Before she could figure out the answer, he tugged her toward him. She let herself fall, knowing he would catch her, which he did. His mouth settled on hers and his hands began to move over her body.

When they resurfaced, he lay on his back so she could rest her head on his shoulder. Contentment and the lingering aftereffects of the lovemaking left her weak and incredibly happy. She was still confused about his wanting to date her, but maybe she was making too big a deal of it.

"We're talking girlfriend and boyfriend?" she asked, returning to the topic they'd been discussing.

"Yes. I can dig out my letterman's jacket for you, if you'd like. I'm sure my mom has it up in the attic."

"I was thinking more that I'd for sure have

a date to the Holiday Ball."

He kissed the top of her head. "You absolutely would."

She thought about mentioning she would be careful not to fall in love with him. No way she wanted that kind of pain in her life. But she had a feeling he already knew that part. He was offering her everything she could want, with no real commitment beyond fidelity. What did she have to lose?

"Yes, Jake," she said, tilting her head so she could look into his face. "I'll go out with you."

"I'm glad."

"Me, too." She laughed. "You can tell your mother it's time to end Project: Jake's Bride. You've got yourself a lady friend and Helen now has temporary access to the instant grandchildren."

"You've made her a very happy woman."

# NINETEEN

Paisley wrinkled her nose. "I don't know," she said, walking around River, studying her from every angle. "It's too something."

"Big," Camryn said flatly. "The ruffled skirt is overwhelming."

River stared at her reflection in the large mirror and had to agree with Camryn. Technically, the black gown fit and if she wore heels, the petite length would be perfect. Yet, she was lost in a sea of fabric and that wasn't the look she was going for. She wanted to feel beautiful the night of the Holiday Ball. Elegant and sexy while she watched Dylan's jaw drop when he saw her. It was a lot to ask for a dress, but she was determined to find the right gown.

The three of them were in the bride's room at the Mistletoe Mountain Resort. The raised dais and wall of mirrors made it the perfect place to try on ball gowns.

Paisley walked behind River and gathered

handfuls of fabric from the skirt, attempting to tone down the flouff.

River laughed. "You're not going to be able to follow me around all night, trying to make the skirt less puffy. This one is a definite no."

"You're right," Paisley said as she dropped the fabric. "The top fits perfectly. Even though I'm not a huge fan of the capped sleeves, I see how the designer was going for balance. But this skirt is just too much." She lowered the back zipper before stepping off the dais.

"How many dresses are left?" River asked, holding the front of the dress in place.

"Only one more." Camryn pointed to the three already hanging on the rack against the wall. "The navy one is a maybe. It's pretty, but not a wow. The white one is way too bridal and this one is too overwhelming."

River refused to get discouraged. Camryn was right — the navy one would be acceptable, even if it did lack the jaw-dropping factor she'd been hoping for. If the last one didn't work, she would keep that one and do a little emergency shopping with overnight delivery to find more options. There was still enough time for another round of purchasing and returning.

Paisley shook out a bright red gown. "I have high hopes for this one. Give a shout when you're ready to be zipped up."

They left the room. River quickly let the black gown fall to the floor, then stepped out of it. She only wore a pair of bikini panties and three-inch heels. So far none of the dresses would let her wear a regular bra and she hadn't brought a strapless one with her. Not that there was all that much to hold up, she thought with a chuckle. Just as well — with her slight build, large breasts would make her look unbalanced. She was fine with her modest curves.

She carefully hung the black dress with the others, then took the red one off the hanger. She kicked off her heels, unzipped the back and stepped into the dress.

The crepe fabric was smooth and soft against her skin. As she slipped the spaghetti straps over her shoulders, she saw the neckline was low, but not embarrassingly so. The style suited her and the color was gorgeous. She pulled up the zipper, surprised when it stopped halfway up the small of her back. She turned to look at herself from the rear.

"Oh, my," she murmured.

The dress dipped low, exposing her from shoulders to almost her butt. She faced the mirror and tried to study herself objectively. The red suited her pale skin and made her eyes bigger and darker. The bodice fit like it had been made for her. She slipped on her heels and smiled when she saw the length of the petite dress was perfect.

"I'm ready," she called.

Paisley and Camryn returned to the room.

"Oh, I like the color," Camryn said right away.

"You're gorgeous," Paisley told her. "Stunning enough to be hate-worthy."

River met her gaze in the mirror. "Really? You think I'm hate-worthy?" A heady compliment.

"Totally," Camryn said approvingly.

"No bra for you," Paisley pointed out. "Would you be okay with that?"

"I would." She didn't usually go braless, but she certainly could.

"You look great," Camryn told her. "You're wearing the dress, rather than the other way around. It's elegant and sexy. I like the simple lines and lack of frills. With those shoes, you don't even need to get the dress hemmed."

River swayed back and forth to see how the dress would feel while she was dancing, only to come to a stop when the movement revealed a long slit that ended in the middle of her thigh.

"Did we know about that?" she asked in a high-pitched voice.

She and Camryn turned to look at Paisley, who shrugged.

"I was ordering dresses," Paisley said. "In petite sizes. There weren't a ton of choices. I don't know that I *didn't* know about the slit. I honestly don't remember. Is it a deal breaker?"

River swayed from side to side, then did a slow spin. Yup, the fabric came apart, showing a long length of bare leg. Well, long for her. The flash of skin was unexpected and she had a feeling the first time Dylan saw it, he would find himself experiencing a jaw-dropping moment.

"It's perfect," she breathed, knowing the dress would make her feel sexy and confident. "I'm keeping this one."

Camryn grinned. "If I were you, I'd order one in every color and then figure out where to wear them. It's a stunner and so are you."

"I think I'd look odd wearing this at the grocery store," River pointed out.

"I don't know," Paisley said slowly. "Maybe with the right accessories."

They all laughed, then the two women left River to change back into her regular clothes. When she was dressed, they quickly packed up the three dresses to be returned. They put them in the back of Camryn's SUV. She would take them to Wrap Around the Clock and get them out with the morning shipments. River put the red one in her small SUV.

That done, they walked into the lobby.

"I'm going back to work," Paisley said. "Will you two be all right by yourselves?"

River's stomach dropped. She'd enjoyed the dress shopping but she was less excited about what was to follow.

Camryn pulled out her phone and started texting. "Jake said to let us know when we were ready. We're meeting in the smaller ballroom."

Paisley nodded, then turned to River. "You're going to do great. It's one dance and then you can relax and enjoy the rest of the evening."

River smiled tightly, trying to pretend she wasn't suddenly nauseated.

Paisley retreated to her office while Camryn led the way to the back of the hotel. They followed the signs to the ballroom and stepped inside. Camryn walked to the wall and started turning on lights. Seconds later Jake walked in carrying a small portable speaker in one hand.

"Ladies," he said, smiling at them both.

"Hi," Camryn said.

River started to thank him for helping when she noticed the two of them had locked eyes. There was a very powerful energy flowing between them — two parts sexual and one part something she couldn't define.

Okay, then, she thought, trying not to grin. Things had taken a turn for the interesting between those two. They were obviously lovers, although Camryn hadn't said a word.

River waited until they were able to drag their gazes away from each other.

"River," Jake said, then cleared his throat. He waved the small speaker. "I downloaded a couple of waltzes so we'd have music to practice. At the Holiday Ball, the first song is always a waltz. I confirmed with my mother that's still the case." His smile returned. "She knows things."

"I don't doubt that."

"A waltz is easy. It's a basic box step, with a three-beat rhythm. Up, up, down." He looked at her. "The down is a weight shift."

He put Camryn on his left and River on his right, in a line. "We'll do the lady's steps first. Weight on the left foot, step back with the right, left foot to the side and close. Forward with the left foot, side with the right, close."

He walked forward a couple of steps and demonstrated. "Notice how on the close, you're shifting your weight. That's the down beat as you relax your hip."

He rejoined them. "Weight on your left foot, back with the right, side, then close."

River managed to follow along. The movements felt awkward and unnatural. She had trouble shifting her weight at the right moment and nearly stumbled a couple of times. Jake was patient, showing her over and over again.

"Let's try it with me leading," he said, stepping in front of her and holding out his arms.

"Back, side, close," he said as they moved. Instead of going back, she went forward and stomped on his foot.

"Sorry," she murmured, pulling away. "Why is this so hard?"

"You're getting it," Camryn told her. "Try again."

"Maybe if we showed her," Jake said, turning to Camryn.

Camryn laughed. "I'm just learning this, too. You're the only dance professional in the room."

"I had a few lessons as a kid."

"Uh-huh. You're like a fancy dancer."

Once again, the energy between them was palpable. He held out his arms and she stepped into them. They fit well together, River thought, noticing how Jake pulled her close.

"Back, side, close," he said, his head close to hers. "Forward, side, close."

Their movements were fluid and synchronized. Camryn seemed to melt into him. When their eyes locked, River had a feeling they'd forgotten she was in the room.

Envy gripped her. She wanted that, she realized — that kind of connection. Since moving to Wishing Tree she'd made good on her goal of getting involved in the community. She had friends and a sense of belonging, but at the end of the day, she was still alone. The need to pair bond was biological and powerful in most people. Seeing Camryn and Jake so lost in each other made her want a man of her own. Someone she could love and who would love her back. Someone she could trust to be honest. Someone she could take care of as much as he took care of her.

River grabbed her handbag and walked out of the ballroom. On her way to the cloakroom to claim her jacket, scarf and hat, she paused to pull out her phone. She hesitated only a second before she started typing.

I heard a rumor you know how to dance? Would you have time to teach me to waltz? I'd hate to embarrass the royal family this late in the season.

Three dots appeared almost immediately as Dylan answered.

Anything for my queen. Probably the best place to practice is my workroom. I'm home now, if you're available. His address followed.

I'll be right over.

It took her nearly thirty minutes to get down the mountain, then circle around town. She followed her nav system, heading past the elementary school, then going southeast a few more miles. The houses were older, with large lots and plenty of trees. The streetlights were old-fashioned but lovely.

She pulled into his driveway and parked. Dylan stepped out of the house and started toward her. The second their eyes met, she felt both relief and anticipation — a combination designed to make her happy.

"Hi," he said, opening her door. "You made it okay?"

She nodded. "I used my nav system. I've never been in this part of town. It's nice." She smiled. "So not a fancy condo kind of guy?"

"I wanted a wood shop and there was already a big building for me to upgrade. I like having a little distance between me and my neighbors."

She stepped onto the frozen ground, collected her handbag and tote, then closed her car door behind her. Dylan put his hands on her waist and lightly kissed her.

"I'm happy to see you," he told her.

"Me, too."

He put his arm around her and led her away from the house. They passed a detached three-car garage, then went around back to a large outbuilding. Low lights illuminated a recently shoveled pathway, and she felt sand underfoot.

"Did you clear the walkways just for me?" she asked.

He pulled open the door to his workshop. "I might have given the paths a spruce. You're still not comfortable in the cold."

They walked into the large building. River's first impression was that it was big — with high ceilings and large windows. The temperature was warmer than she'd expected and she wondered if Dylan had come over to crank up the heat so she wouldn't shiver during their lesson.

As she hung her coat and scarf, she watched him watch her. He was a good-looking guy — not that she cared a lot about how someone looked. But it was a nice bonus. He wasn't as tall as Jake, but his shoulders were broader and he was strong.

She had a sudden vision of him carrying her to bed — picking her up as if she weighed nothing and sweeping her away. No one ever had, she thought wistfully. And while the fantasy probably wasn't the most self-actualized ever, she thought maybe every now and then all women needed a good sweeping away in their lives.

Once her outerwear was hung, she pulled a pair of low heels out of her tote and stepped out of her boots. She slid into the shoes and started to say she was ready, only to look past him and gasp.

"You're making rocking chairs."

There were at least a half dozen completed chairs against the back wall and a handful in different stages of assembly. They were all made of different kinds of wood, some simple, some ornate.

Dylan followed to where she ran her hands across the smooth, glossy wood.

"It's more of a hobby," he said. "A few

years back I had a pregnant client who was petite, like you. She complained that all the rocking chairs she tried were too big for her — she couldn't get comfortable. I thought about the problem for a while, then made her a slightly scaled-down version of one she liked. She told a friend and it kind of became a thing."

He shoved his hands into his front pockets. "I have a website. It's not much, but it's how people find me. I only take on two or three commissions at a time. My regular job keeps me busy."

"You have a website? I want to go look."

He winced. "Yeah, don't do that. You won't be impressed. In fact, you'll think a whole lot less of me when you see it."

She smiled at him. "I'm not going to judge you on your website. I think these are beautiful and I'm glad you're making them for people."

"Yeah?"

"Yeah."

They stared at each other. River thought she felt a little tension between them but was afraid that was wishful thinking on her part, especially when instead of stepping closer, Dylan walked to the other side of the large room and turned on a music system. Seconds later the familiar opening notes of "The Blue Danube Waltz" began to play.

"Oh, I'm not ready for music," she said.

He walked toward her. "It's better with music. Trust me."

He showed her the basic steps, repeating what Jake had already demonstrated. This time River found it easier to remember what to do and when he took her in his arms, she managed to take several steps before stumbling over his foot.

She flushed and pulled back. "I'm not very good at this. Sorry."

"You're doing fine. It takes practice."

"Did you really take lessons in high school?"

His blue eyes brightened with amusement. "Jake and I both did. Helen insisted. We were humiliated, but then the dance instructor brought in some very pretty partners, so that helped." He winked at her. "I was very shallow back then and being around a pretty girl always brightened my day."

"You don't like pretty women anymore?" she asked, her voice teasing.

"I do, but I don't talk about it as much."

She smiled at him, then stepped back into his arms. She liked how he held her securely, guiding her by signaling the next move. He pushed back on her hand to remind her to

379

step back and pulled forward when they were supposed to go that way. The waltz started over and they began to dance.

"Back, side, close," he whispered as they moved, just as Jake had. Only when Dylan spoke the words, they felt like a seduction. "Forward, side, close. Keep breathing. Relax. I'm not going to let you fall. Back, side, close. Forward, side, close."

They moved around the workroom. River tried to feel the music and find her way through the steps. After about half an hour, she danced the entire waltz without stepping on his toes even once.

"Great job," Dylan told her. "We should take a break and come back to this in a day or two. By the time the dance gets here, you'll be a pro."

She reluctantly lowered her hands to her sides. "Thank you for helping me. You made it easy and comfortable."

"Happy to help." He turned off the music, then glanced at her. "Here's what I don't understand. How does a beautiful woman like you not know how to waltz?"

She laughed. "I'm not sure where I would have learned. We didn't exactly waltz in high school. I didn't go to any of the dances."

At first, he looked confused but then his expression cleared. "Because you were having surgeries and recovering. You weren't exactly the new kid but you weren't someone they saw every day."

She nodded. "It was tough. I thought of myself as the outsider. I kept up with my studies, but that wasn't really the point."

"It wouldn't have been." His gaze was kind. "After the surgeries, you would have moved slowly, maybe had a limp or stumbled. Plus, you're shy, so that made things complicated."

She took a step back. "That's me," she said lightly. "Flawed."

"No." He moved toward her and touched her face. "Strong. Determined. Brave."

She liked those words, she thought wistfully. Liked the way he was watching her.

"Someone should have seen past that," he said. "Some guy should have noticed the beautiful smile, the pretty eyes. The fact that they didn't means I have to apologize for the stupidity of my sex."

That made her smile. "You don't at all. Besides, it doesn't matter now, but the reality of my situation was that I didn't have my first boyfriend until college and that turned out to be a disaster."

"In what way?"

River hesitated, not sure how much of the story to tell. "He wasn't who I thought."

She grimaced. "He was sweet and kind and thoughtful and I just assumed all that was real. He would bring me gifts. Little things. Colored pens or USB drives. One day he gave me a beautiful necklace. I thought I was so lucky."

Dylan's expression was neutral. "You like giving little gifts so you'd appreciate someone who gave them back."

She nodded. "I was off campus for something and ended up in a cute little gift shop. I was wearing the necklace. The owner saw me and started screaming. She said it had been stolen from the store a week before. She knew it was hers because it was one of a kind. She was so angry. I didn't know what to do, so I ran."

She still remembered how confused and scared she'd been. She'd raced to the dorm and hid in her room for hours.

"I confronted him," she said quietly. "I thought he'd be embarrassed or upset, but he laughed." She looked at Dylan. "He said he was a poor college student, getting by on loans. He didn't have any money. He'd stolen everything he'd given me. He said he did it to make me happy."

Dylan pulled her close. "I'm sorry. He was a jerk and you shouldn't have had to go through that."

River let herself relax in his embrace. Being with him always made her feel good.

"I returned the necklace."

"I know you did."

She looked up at him. "How could you know that?"

"It's who you are."

He lowered his head and kissed her. His mouth was warm and firm, with a hint of restrained passion. His hands settled on her hips. She gave herself over to the kiss, liking how the wanting started low and spread out everywhere. She parted her lips to deepen the kiss and Dylan responded instantly. She settled in to enjoy what they were doing but sooner than she would have liked, he was stepping back.

"Yeah, this isn't a good idea," he said regretfully. "You're too much of a temptation and I don't want things to get out of control, so I'm not going to push anything."

Which was sweet, River thought, both disappointed and understanding.

"It is a little soon to take things to the next level," she agreed, even as she wondered what out of control with Dylan would feel like. Good, she decided. Very, very good.

He waited while she exchanged her shoes for her boots, then helped her into her coat. As he walked her to her SUV, he put his arm around her.

"You okay driving home?" he asked. "I could take you and have Jake help me get your SUV back to you."

"I'm good," she told him. "It's cold but the streets are bare and dry. We're not expecting snow for a couple of days."

"Because you monitor the weather," he teased.

"I didn't used to, but here it seems important."

He opened the driver's-side door. Once she was inside, he kissed her again.

"We'll have another lesson soon," he promised. "You'll do great."

She smiled and started the engine. As she drove to her place she knew that if she was successful on the dance floor, it would be because of Dylan.

Camryn counted out her change for the upcoming day. While most of her customers either had an account or used a credit card, there were still a handful who preferred to pay with cash. She placed the bills in the cash drawer, then carried the extras back to her office to put in the safe.

Business was good, she thought happily, returning to the front of the store and unlocking the front door. She'd had the big project up at the resort and Dylan's book wrap request. She'd finished the latter and he'd picked them up late last night. She had no idea where he'd gotten the money to pay for that many books, nor how he was going to get them delivered to the kids in town and she wasn't going to ask him about either. It was his business.

She briefly wondered if River knew about Dylan being the town's Secret Santa and if she didn't, should Camryn tell her? They were friends and that meant something. But she'd promised not to say anything and it wasn't as if what he was doing was bad. In fact, it spoke well of his character. Still, she didn't like the idea of keeping something from River.

"I hate it when the day starts with a moral dilemma," she murmured. Fortunately, several customers walked in just then, offering the perfect distraction.

A little after eleven Reggie and her Great Dane Belle showed up.

"I figured it was time for the girls to meet," Reggie said with a laugh. "Unless you think Belle is just too much for Tinsel."

Camryn laughed. "I think we should definitely see what happens. Tinsel has some attitude, so I think she'll be fine." She stroked Belle's massive head. "Plus, you're the sweetest girl ever, aren't you?"

Belle wagged her long tail.

They went into the back room. Reggie had Belle sit while Camryn called Tinsel, who was sleeping in her office. The little Chihuahua came trotting out and headed for Camryn, only to stop a few steps away. Her gaze settled on Belle's ankles, then slowly rose. The second their eyes met, Tinsel jumped back as if stunned at Belle's size. Belle stared in equal confusion.

"I think they don't know what the other is," Camryn said quietly, holding in a laugh.

Reggie shook her head. "I barely know what she is." She pulled a small sweater out of her coat pocket and held it up. "I guessed on the size, but this is going to be huge on Tinsel." She eyed the Chihuahua. "I'll try again with much, much smaller needles."

Tinsel cautiously moved toward Belle. The Great Dane flopped down, her huge front paws in front of her. Tinsel got close enough to sniff a toe, then two. Belle lowered her head so they could touch noses.

Tinsel's tail began to wag and she gave a little play bow. Belle was on her feet in a second and racing after her. They ran around the back room before tearing into the store and circling the wrapping tables.

"This isn't going to go well," Reggie said

with a laugh, hurrying after her dog.

Camryn joined her, intercepting the pair and scooping up Tinsel.

"And a friendship is born," she said, kissing the top of the tiny dog's head. "We'll have to plan a playdate."

Reggie gave her a strange look before snapping a leash on Belle's collar. "That's a good idea. Let's do that. And tell your sisters that whenever they want to come over and talk about canine fashion, I'm in."

Camryn knew Reggie had offered to help the twins learn how to make dog clothes. "I know they'll appreciate any pointers. They want her to be super stylish. Are you all right?"

Reggie blinked several times. "I'm fine. Why do you ask?"

"I don't know. You had a strange reaction a second ago. Like I said something to upset you."

"I'm fine." Reggie smiled, then shocked Camryn and possibly herself by starting to cry.

Camryn grabbed her arm and pulled her and Belle into her office. When the two women were seated and the dogs were busy sniffing each other, Camryn pushed a box of tissues close to her friend.

"Talk," she said firmly.

"I'm fine," Reggie told her, wiping her eyes. "Really. I'm so happy. Last year I was scared to come home for the holidays and now I'm living my best life. Everything is perfect." She gave a strangled laugh. "I'm telling the truth."

"So why are you crying?"

"I can't help myself. My hormones are a mess." She sniffed, then looked around the room as if checking to see that they were alone. "You can't talk about this to anyone. You swear?"

Camryn nodded, bracing herself for bad news.

"I'm pregnant."

The unexpected announcement drove Camryn to her feet. Reggie stood as well and they hugged.

"You're pregnant! That's amazing. I'm so happy for you."

"No one else knows," Reggie confessed. "I took the test three days ago. I'm seeing my doctor next week to confirm, but I'm sure. The thing is, I don't want to tell Toby until Christmas Eve. It's silly, but I want to do it. Then I'll tell my family Christmas morning."

"I won't say a word," Camryn promised. "Oh, Reggie, congratulations. You must be thrilled."

"These aren't for you. They're for Tinsel. The adoption's official and for some reason you decided not to have a party. What's with that?"

Reggie nodded from the other side of the table. "Belle loves a party and now that they're friends, I could have brought her. No one has good parties with dogs anymore."

"I want to see Belle and Tinsel playing," Shaye said. "I can't even picture it."

She and River took their seats, then River pulled a wrapped package out of her bag.

"Not you, too!" Camryn said with a laugh. "I'm overwhelmed. The pile of gifts is actually bigger than my dog."

They placed their orders then everyone helped her open the packages. There were Tinsel-size sweaters and coats, little chew toys, organic snacks and a sparkly collar. Once the wrapping paper was cleared away, they all started talking about what was happening in their lives.

Reggie kept looking like she was going to say something, then stopping herself. She met Camryn's gaze and rolled her eyes as if silently admitting keeping her pregnancy a secret was harder than she thought. Paisley talked about the holiday parties up at the resort, telling funny stories about unusual guest requests.

Camryn laughed, enjoying the conversation. This was what she'd been missing, she thought wistfully. Last year when she'd been so sad, the world had simply moved around her. She'd seen what was happening but hadn't been a part of it. Now she'd healed enough to enjoy her life and her friends, to get into the messiness of whatever was happening. She still missed her mother desperately, but it was nice to be able to see the joy in her life.

"I have news," she said, when the food had been delivered and there was a break in the conversation.

Everyone turned to look at her.

"Jake and I are dating. Well, more than dating. We're a thing."

"Since when?"

"OMG! I knew something was going on."

"You and Jake? That's great."

They all spoke at once. Camryn waited for them to quiet before saying, "He's great and we're having fun. The twins like him, as does Tinsel." She thought about mentioning the expiration date, but wasn't sure how to explain that without discussing her plans on leaving. It wasn't a topic she wanted to bring up.

"No wonder he's been so happy lately,"

Paisley said with a grin. "You'll have to give me a heads-up if you ever have a fight so I can stay out of his way."

"Jake wouldn't bring his problems to work," Camryn said. "He's not like that."

Paisley raised her eyebrows. "You're already defending him. It must be serious."

"We're exclusive. It's nice. I like him." She looked at Reggie. "Are you okay with the news?"

Reggie blinked several times, as if holding back tears. "I'm thrilled. He needs someone in his life and you're wonderful and I hope you'll be as happy as Toby and me."

Tears slipped down her cheeks. River and Paisley looked startled. "Are you all right?" River asked in concern.

"She's fine," Camryn said quickly. "She, ah, has her period. We were texting about it earlier. What is it about having your period at the holidays? Sometimes it makes all the emotions run so much hotter."

Reggie shot her a grateful look. Paisley nodded knowingly. "I know. Mother Nature has a cruel sense of humor." She turned to River. "So, Snow Queen. Any action with the Snow King?"

River tensed and blushed at the same time. "What? Me? No, I don't have anything . . . Dylan's nice but we're just . . ."

Reggie pointed at Paisley. "Don't tease her about Dylan. They're still finding their way." She looked at River innocently. "Apparently, he gets lost a lot because he was coming out of your townhouse at seven in the morning the other day."

Camryn's mouth dropped open. "You're sleeping with Dylan? Wow, that's exciting."

River squirmed in her seat. "I wasn't going to say anything because I'm not sure what it means or where we're going."

"To naked town," Shaye murmured happily. "That's so great."

"Everybody's getting some but me," Paisley said with a sigh. "I need a man."

"Say the word," Reggie told her. "We'll put the word out."

"Maybe after the holidays," Paisley said. "Until then, I'll just envy all of you your happiness."

Dylan wasn't sure why Helen had wanted to meet him at Jingle Coffee. Usually, if she wanted to get together, she invited him over to her house, or stopped by his work. He walked into the coffee place to find her waiting outside with two to-go cups.

He crossed to her and kissed her cheek before taking one of the coffees. "We're not going inside?" he asked.

"No. I lured you with a false story. We're going somewhere else."

"All right." He fell into step with her as she started down the sidewalk. "Should I ask where?"

"No. We'll make small talk."

He grinned. "Okay, I'll play along. How are you?"

"Excellent. I do love this time of year. It's been sad recently, but this season is going very well." She looked at him. "How are you and River getting along?"

He thought about the night he'd spent in her bed. No way was he going to talk about that. "Good. She's very sweet and I like her."

"I thought as much. Have you told her about your money?"

The blunt question had him wishing he didn't love her so much. Then he would find it easy to walk away.

"We haven't exactly been talking about that."

Helen's eyes darkened with disappointment. "You're afraid."

"Not afraid." Not exactly. He was . . . cautious.

Helen sighed. "I'm so angry with your mother. And Bobbie. They were both hideous women. There — I've said it. They

417

were awful and selfish and you're paying the price."

The Bobbie reference he got, but his mother? "My mom never knew about my lottery winnings."

"I know and I'm grateful. My point is about how she treated you." Her expression softened. "You were such a sweet little boy. So warm and caring. A good friend to Jake. You tried hard to please everyone, you had lots of friends. But that woman could only see that she'd had to put a few of her dreams on hold. What did she think she was going to do that was so amazing? It's not like you got in the way of her plan to cure cancer."

Helen sniffed. "She was lucky to have you and she never appreciated the gift she'd been given."

He'd heard the rant before. When he'd still been a kid and feeling rejected by his mom, Helen would often go off on her, dissing her in a way a ten- or fourteen-year-old could understand and making him feel loved and welcome.

"I know you were hurt when she allowed me to be your guardian," Helen continued as they turned at the corner, "but I was thrilled. Finally, you could know you were wanted and loved. You had stability. Structure."

He put his arm around her. "You were very good to me. I love you, Helen. You'll always be the mother of my heart."

"And you're as much my son as Jake is. But you're still an idiot."

The shift in topic had him blinking. "Excuse me?"

"An idiot," she repeated. "It's been over a decade, Dylan. In fact, nearly twelve years since you won that money. I've been patient with you. I knew you had to come to terms with being —" she made air quotes "— rich, as you call it. I suppose the problem is you never had a good financial role model. You've seen people try to take advantage of Jake and you've seen your mother want to find a rich man to save her. And then the whole Bobbie fiasco. What you haven't seen is how a sound financial plan can make everything easier."

Her gaze locked with his. "I want that for you."

"A sound financial plan?"

"Yes."

He wasn't sure what, exactly, that meant, nor did he want to ask. Helen seemed to be on a mission and the sooner he let her explain it, the sooner he could make his escape.

"What you're doing now is ridiculous," she added, coming to a stop on the sidewalk. "While giving a book to every child in town is a lovely thought, it's a random act with no real plan. If you want to help children locally, then find out who's in need and come up with steps to make a difference. And while we're on the subject, is helping children your true passion?"

"I like kids," he said, wondering if he sounded defensive. "I want to help them."

"Fine, but what about old people? Or the planet? Or animals? Don't you care about animals?"

He didn't understand the question. "Helen, I'm not following you."

"I know. I'm sorry." She pressed her lips together. "Dylan, you have over twenty million dollars and your account is only growing. It's time to get serious. Put a percentage of your money away for yourself and your future, then come up with a way to help with the rest of it. Rather than piecemeal giving, why not figure out what matters the most to you and make a difference in that one area? Be strategic. If you want to help underprivileged kids in town, then team up with social services and local churches. If you want to help pay for braces, then talk to local dentists about who is really in need."

"You knew about that?" he blurted.

"I know nearly everything that happens in Wishing Tree and don't try to change the subject. It's time for you to start a foundation."

"A what?"

She smiled. "A foundation, or at the very least, a trust."

He wasn't sure of the difference, but understood what she was saying. So far he'd given away money randomly — finding someone in need and helping out. But the gifts were all relatively small and his winnings kept growing. He should be more strategic, as she'd said. Come up with a plan — causes he would most like to support.

Helen pointed at the building next to them. He glanced at it and realized they'd made their way to her lawyer's office.

"Don't make me meet with Gerald," he said, knowing he sounded like a twelve-year-old being told to eat broccoli.

"I'm not. We're merely using his conference room."

Helen glanced over his shoulder and waved. He turned and saw two very well-dressed women walking toward them. They had on thick wool coats and carried brief-cases. They were definitely not the tourist type.

"I took the liberty of inviting over some people I've worked with before," she told him. "They'll explain how a trust and a foundation work and which is best for you. They have people who can help you figure out what you most care about so you can give strategically while still protecting your future."

"Good to see you again, Helen," one of the women said as they joined Helen and him. "You look amazing, as always."

"I wish that were true, but you're kind to pretend." Helen smiled at Dylan. "All right, let's go inside and get started with the explanations. I promise to keep quiet while you take it in. Later, you can ask me any-thing you'd like."

Generous as always, he thought, bracing himself for a quick course in the intricacies of philanthropy and wondering how a kid like him had ended up with a problem like this.

River stood on the sidewalk, outside a brick building, not sure what was happening inside. She'd seen Dylan talking intently with Helen and had started to go over to them, only to stop when two other women joined them. They'd had a brief conversation before going into what were, according to the sign by the door, law offices.

She supposed this could be a client meeting, only why would it take place in a law office and why would Helen be there? Maybe the other women were friends of hers from out of town and they wanted to meet Dylan? Which made sense, except for the lawyer part. Any work contract would be with his employer, not with him.

River told herself it wasn't her business, turned away and continued walking toward her townhouse, doing her best to ignore a sense of unease.

Dylan wasn't up to anything, she told herself firmly. They were new in their relationship and she didn't need to know every detail of his life. If she had questions about the meeting, she should ask them later. He would tell her and then she would feel better.

Only she wasn't sure how to phrase the question and even if she figured that out, she wasn't sure she could ever let go of the suspicion that he was keeping secrets from her. Big ones that would change everything.

Jake hadn't been dress shopping with a

woman in a long time. It wasn't anything he'd ever done with Reggie, so he supposed the last time he'd waited patiently while the woman in his life tried on dress after dress would have been with Iona.

Not exactly a good comparison, he thought, remembering how she'd always been so critical of herself and had expected him to convince her she was beautiful. He'd never understood that particular game. Iona had been stunning and she'd been clear on her beauty and the power it gave her, so why had she made him tell her how great she'd looked over and over again? Worse, if he hadn't been enthusiastic enough, she'd refused to buy whatever the item was and had pouted for the rest of the evening.

He had a feeling that wasn't Camryn's style. So far she'd been intent on finding something for the twins to wear. Tall and more artsy Victoria had found a jade green dress with a layered skirt that came to just above her knees. The style was pretty without being too sophisticated and the softness suited her personality. Lily had gone for a white, sleeveless dress with slightly shorter full skirt. After twirling a few times, she pulled a chair in front of the big full-length mirror and sat down, then studied herself as she crossed and uncrossed her legs, then shifted in her seat.

"You're in orchestra, not trying out for a dance troupe," Victoria told her.

"I don't want to flash anyone," Lily said primly. "Or show too much thigh. A concert isn't the time to be sexy."

Victoria grinned. "We're fifteen. When are we sexy?"

Jake carefully kept his mouth shut, not wanting to get involved in that conversation. From what he could tell, the twins were happy being age appropriate. Camryn must be thrilled they weren't trying to grow up too fast.

As if thinking her name had conjured her, Camryn stepped out of the dressing room. Jake took in the body-hugging black fabric, the low-cut neckline and the way the modest, below-the-knee hemline belied the inherent sexiness of the style.

She walked past him to the mirror, giving him an excellent view of her hips and rear. Perfect curves, he thought, remembering touching her silky skin. On a perfect woman.

She met his gaze in the mirror and raised her brow slightly, silently asking what he thought.

"You're stunning."

She smiled. "Okay, that's a little strong, but I do like the dress. It's different for me."

"Now that's sexy," Victoria said, her tone approving. Her smile turned into a frown. "Isn't the Holiday Ball a, you know, *ball*? Shouldn't you be in something long and twirly?"

"I have one of those, too," she said, again looking at him in the mirror. "I'll show you that one next. I just thought this one was fun. For maybe a night out."

"I approve," he said, then chuckled. "Not that you need my approval."

"I want you to like what I wear."

"I do." And when she didn't wear anything at all.

Lily and Victoria joined her. The three Neff women stood side by side. The teens showed the promise of the mature, happy women they would be. Their red hair gleamed in the overhead light. They were strong, confident and achingly beautiful.

This, he thought longingly. This was what he wanted in his life. Those teenagers — shattered by tragedy yet showing their inner determination and love for each other. They'd found their way to living again. He wanted to watch them take the last few steps into adulthood, as they finished high school. He wanted to be the one standing on the porch when they brought their first boyfriends home. He knew what to ask and what to expect from the young men who would pursue them. He wanted to be there when they graduated and made final choices on their college. He wanted to load the car and help deliver them to their first dorm room.

His gaze shifted to Camryn. He wanted to be there for her, as well. She talked about wanting to leave Wishing Tree to resume her life in Chicago, but he couldn't help thinking she might have everything she wanted right here. She loved running Wrap Around the Clock. He had a feeling she would find it difficult to walk away from the business. He wanted to be around when she realized this was where she belonged. He wanted them together, finding their future.

But was he sure? Was he willing to let go of the past and trust himself not to be his father? Was he confident he wouldn't screw up, wouldn't break her heart the way his mother's heart had been broken? These women deserved the very best of him and he had to be sure he had that to offer. Otherwise, this was just a game of pretend and they would all end up with broken hearts.

# TWENTY-TWO

Several of the gingerbread houses were more like castles, with turrets and towers, melted hard candy filling in for stained glass. There were gingerbread mountains and gardens, a carnival ride. Under any other circumstances, River would have been inspired and in awe. As it was, she found it difficult to even pretend she was engaged by the competition.

Something was going on with Dylan. She knew it. She'd been unable to forget seeing him with those two women and Helen by the lawyer's office. She wasn't worried about an affair — she didn't think he was the type, there wouldn't be two of them and he wouldn't involve Helen. But there was something, and while she wanted an explanation, she was equally afraid of what it might be.

She did her best to return her attention to the detailed gingerbread constructions. The contestants had worked hard to create their amazing masterpieces and she owed it to them to do her job as Snow Queen.

"It's got to be the castle," Dylan said quietly, walking with her as she went from display to display. "Or the carnival ride." He glanced back at the landscape. "Or that one."

"They're all wonderful," she agreed. "But the castle has a nice blend of difficult construction techniques and lots of decorative detail."

He looked into her eyes and smiled. "You're the expert."

She held his gaze, reminding herself she liked this man. Being around him made her happy. She'd enjoyed taking their relationship to the next level, physically. If she trusted him with her body then shouldn't she be willing to trust him to tell her the truth?

They made one circuit of the entries, then agreed the castle was the winner, with the carnival ride coming in second. Geri made the announcement and handed out the ribbons. Family members gathered around to take pictures, and River hoped no one was too disappointed.

"Want to come over tonight?" Dylan asked, smiling at her. "I thought I'd cook something and we could practice our waltz."

Dinner sounded nice. If only she wasn't so uneasy about what she'd seen.

"You can cook?" she asked, mostly to distract herself.

"Sure. Helen made sure I knew the basics. I make a very impressive Spaghetti Carbonara and my Caesar salad is legendary. Pick you up at six?"

She opened her mouth to say yes, only to instead ask, "Who were those women?"

His confusion was genuine. "What women?"

"I saw you with Helen and two women outside of a lawyer's office. Are they potential clients?"

He stared at her, wide-eyed, the guilt on his face so clear, it was as if he'd audibly stated the emotion. He took a step back, cleared his throat and said, "Ah, yeah, clients. They, ah, want me to remodel something for them. A kitchen. They're thinking farm style, but they're not sure. Natural products the whole way."

She could practically hear him telling himself to stop talking. She supposed the good news was that Dylan was a lousy liar — she should take comfort in that. The bad news was he just lied to her.

She turned away, her heart sinking in her

chest. "They sound nice," she murmured, not sure what else to say. Confronting him about this wasn't her style. She was too disappointed and sad. She'd thought he was one of the good guys, but he wasn't. He'd lied and there was only one explanation for what was happening: there was something he didn't want her to know.

She wanted to tell him that she didn't have to know every little detail. That she could respect his privacy if only he would simply acknowledge the truth.

"I have to work," she said, accepting now she was the one not telling the truth. "Tonight. I'll be at the office until tomorrow morning."

He shifted so he could look at her. "River, are you all right?"

"I am. Just not looking forward to pulling an all-nighter. But it comes with the job, right?"

She met his gaze, kept her tone light and faintly regretful because unlike him, she knew exactly how to tell a lie and be believed.


Camryn, the twins and Jake arrived back in Wishing Tree well before noon. He offered to take her sisters to get Tinsel while she went to the store.

She arrived in time to help with a couple of rush wrapping requests from tourists who wanted to take home presents. The rest of the day flew by as she handled customers and ordered in more wrapping paper. Around four she realized she'd missed lunch and didn't have anything in the house for dinner. Nor had she thought to pull anything out of the freezer for a quick reheat.

"Takeout it is," she murmured to herself as she hurried to check on a wrapping party. Her sisters would enjoy the treat.

But when she texted them to find out what they'd like her to bring home, Lily informed her they had dinner waiting for her, compliments of Helen.

We spent the afternoon with her and she sent us home with fried chicken, mashed potatoes and roasted fall vegetables. I don't know which vegetables are fall ones, but she says they're really good.

I hope you told her thank you.

We did. We're good that way.

Camryn laughed. You are. I'll be home by six.

She tucked her phone away and hoped the

432

twins hadn't been too much of a bother for Helen. And that the older woman hadn't said or done anything Camryn and Jake might regret.

"Nothing to do about it now," she told herself.

It was dark and snowing by the time she made her way home, but as she pulled into the driveway she saw lights in nearly every window. Knowing her sisters were waiting for her made her happy. The holiday season was going so much better than she'd hoped. They had made so many good memories to mitigate the pain of the previous year. Healing wasn't easy but it was finally happening and she was grateful.

She walked inside to the delicious smell of chicken and the sound of music and laughter. Tinsel heard her first and came running.

"Hey, baby girl, I missed you." Camryn scooped up the little dog and held her close as Tinsel wiggled in delight and bathed her face with kisses.

Lily and Victoria joined her in the kitchen, each of them in jeans and holiday sweatshirts.

"We got the mail," Lily said, ticking off items on her fingers. "We collected the garbage and put out the cans, including the recycling. We fed Tinsel."

"Wow. That's a lot. Thank you."

"We're pretty amazing," Victoria told her. "The table is set and the fried chicken is reheating in the oven, along with the roasted vegetables. There's also an apple pie."

"That's a feast," Camryn said, setting down the dog and her bag, then stepping out of her boots and making a mental note to email Helen a thank-you.

"We called Jake to invite him over," Victoria added. "He has a meeting but he'll stop by for pie later. He's bringing ice cream."

"You're organizing my life for me," Camryn teased. "I like it."

They sat down to dinner. The teens brought her up-to-date on what they'd missed in the thirty-six hours they'd been gone.

"Helen wants to come see the dresses we bought," Lily said, serving herself mashed potatoes. "She says she's not going to the ball." Her mouth turned down. "She lost her husband a couple of years ago and it still makes her sad."

Victoria nodded. "She gets it about Mom. We talked about how loss is hard."

"It is," Camryn said, passing the vegetables. "But we're doing so much better this year."

"We are." Victoria speared a square of butternut squash. "Helen invited us over to Christmas dinner. She said it's going to only be family, so not as big as Thanksgiving. Lily and I talked about it and if you want to go, we do, too. We have fun with her."

Camryn hadn't thought that far ahead. "I think that would be nice," she agreed. "We hadn't really talked about Christmas dinner. I'd want us to take something with us."

"We could talk to River," Lily suggested. "She knows how to bake everything. Oh, Tinsel's invited, of course. Camryn, we have to get Tinsel her own stocking. I know we'll get her presents but she should have a stocking like Victoria and me."

"Hmm, it sounds like we need to go to the pet store very soon."

"Or we could find some things online," Victoria said. "I was looking today and there are some fun toys. I'm not sure what to get her for her big present. Maybe a dog bed."

"You mean aside from the five she already has?"

Victoria grinned. "She was lost in the cold. We need to spoil her." She took a bite of chicken. "When we go live in the big house on Grey Wolf Lake, we're going to need a lot more dog beds."

Camryn stared at her sister. "Excuse me?

When we what?"

The teens exchanged a look.

"Nothing," Victoria murmured, taking a big gulp of water.

"Why would you think we're moving into Helen's house?" she asked, terrified to hear the answer to her question.

"When you marry Jake," Lily said, avoiding her gaze. "You're dating and when people date they fall in love and get married. Helen said the house is too big for her anyway and she was thinking she could take over Jake's condo and the four of us —"

"Five with Tinsel," Victoria murmured.

"Right, the five of us could move in there. So the house stays in the family."

Camryn wished she'd thought to pour herself a glass of wine. Or twenty. Thoughts swirled and her head was spinning and she honestly had no idea where to even start.

"Jake and I aren't getting married," she said firmly. "We've just started going out and this is all way too much. Just no. No to the marriage, no to the house." And later Camryn was going to have a long talk with Helen about overstepping her bounds.

The twins exchanged a confused look.

"But you like Jake," Victoria said.

"I do. I like him very much. We get along. But that's not the same as falling in love.

Besides, he's staying here and in three years I'm leaving Wishing Tree so there's no way we —"

Two seconds too late Camryn realized what she'd said. Her sisters stared at her with identical expressions of horror and fear.

"You're leaving us?" Lily breathed.

Tears filled Victoria's eyes. "Where are you going? What's going to happen to us? You're our sister. You're supposed to take care of us. You can't leave."

"I'm not leaving you," Camryn said quickly. "I'm sorry. That came out wrong. I am taking care of you. I love you and that will never change."

They didn't look convinced.

"Then what?" Lily asked, brushing away her own tears. "Camryn, what are you saying?"

If only she could go back in time and never say the words. Of course she'd planned to have a conversation with the twins, but not like this and certainly not now.

She set down her fork. "There's nothing to worry about. It's no big deal. I've just been thinking that when you two go off to college there's nothing to keep me in town, so I might go back to Chicago and —"

"No!" Lily jumped to her feet. "What

about the house and Wrap Around the Clock?"

"Nothing's certain right now. Lily, please. I'm still in the thinking stage. Besides, you'll both be gone and you can visit me in —"

"Visit?" Victoria shrieked. "Visit? Because we're not going to live with you? We're not going to have a home. So we turn eighteen and suddenly you don't care? You didn't answer the question. What happens to the house? Are you going to sell it? We don't want the money. We want our *home* where we lived as a *family*. With our *mom.*"

"You can't do this," Lily told her, brushing her face. "You can't. I thought you loved us, but you don't. You just want to be done with us. You should go back to Chicago now if it's that important to you. I thought we mattered. I thought we were a family."

With that they both turned and ran upstairs. Tinsel quickly followed, her tail tucked, as if she sensed there was something wrong with her pack.

Camryn sat alone at the table, her stomach all twisted and a sense of dread settling on her shoulders. She had messed up in a thousand and one ways, she thought grimly. She'd hurt her sisters. Worse, she'd scared them. After all this time, they were finally happy and confident teens and now she'd set them back weeks or even months.

"I'm an idiot," she said aloud as if words would help. They didn't.

She went up to the second floor. Lily door stood open, but Victoria's was closed Camryn tried the knob but it was locked.

She tapped once. "It's me."

"Go away," Victoria said, her voice thick with tears. "Just go away."

"I'm sorry," Camryn told them. "I really messed up and I didn't mean to."

"We don't want to talk to you," Lily told her. "You're not even our sister anymore. You're just the person who got stuck taking care of us."

Camryn sank to the floor. "It's not like that," she said. "Come on, that's not fair. I love you. You know that."

"We're just a burden," Victoria shouted. "You never wanted to come back, did you? You never wanted to leave your other life. You hate everything about being here."

Camryn held in a sigh. "I'm sorry," she repeated. "I said everything wrong. Please let me in so we can talk."

"No," Lily told her. "Just go away. Leave us alone. You're going to anyway so you might as well start now."

She heard the pain in their voices and knew she'd done absolutely everything wrong. She knocked a few more times, but they ignored her. Finally, she went downstairs and curled up on the sofa.

An hour or so later Jake arrived. He took one look at her face and held out his arms.

"Tell me," he said. "We'll fix it together."

She rushed into his embrace. For a few seconds, with him holding her, she felt marginally better but then she stepped back and had to admit what had happened.

"I hurt the twins," she said, then explained how she'd accidentally mentioned leaving Wishing Tree.

"I was so focused on explaining that we weren't getting married and moving into your mother's house that I wasn't thinking about what I was saying."

He pulled her to the sofa and sat next to her. "You've never talked about wanting to move back to Chicago?"

"No. I knew they would get upset. I wanted to wait until they were older and wouldn't mind as much."

His steady gaze locked with hers. "They're always going to care about this house and the town. They feel like they're being abandoned all over again."

"I know," she said, trying not to wince as his words hit her heart. "But they'll be gone — away at college, living their lives. Am I

440

supposed to put everything on hold forever?"

"They didn't know anything was on hold. They thought you were happy."

There was something in his tone. She studied his handsome face, but couldn't tell what he was thinking.

"I'm not unhappy," she said slowly. "I enjoy my life here. I like the business and my friends."

He cleared his throat.

She managed a faint smile. "And you."

"Whew. I was afraid you were going to forget me."

"I wouldn't do that." She paused. "But I am still leaving, Jake."

"So you've made clear."

"I want to be honest with you."

"Has it occurred to you that I might be the only person in this house not mad at you and maybe you want to tread a little more carefully?"

She wasn't exactly sure what that meant, but thought maybe this was not the day for brutally honest conversation.

"I'm sick about the twins," she said. "I don't know how to fix things."

"That's because there's no solution. You're not going to promise to stay forever and they don't want to hear anything else." He put his arm around her. "They'll come around."

"I hurt them."

"Not on purpose and you apologized."

"Yes, but I don't think that's going to be enough."

River hadn't slept at all. She'd tossed and turned before finally making good on her lie to Dylan and heading to her office. She carefully turned off the store alarm, let herself in the building, then reconnected the system before heading up to her office. Once there, she booted her computer and sat staring at the screen.

Dylan had lied to her, which meant he was hiding something. What she didn't know was *what*. It could be something silly, something embarrassing but not significant. Or it could be really, really bad. While she knew she could ask him directly, she wasn't sure he would tell her the truth, which left her one other solution.

She put her hands on the keyboard, then pulled back. No, she thought. She wasn't going to investigate him. She wasn't that person. She knew better. Going behind someone's back was never the answer.

She wrestled with her options until she heard Camryn come in downstairs. River rose and went to talk to her friend. She walked into the store and called out a greeting. Camryn turned and River knew immediately that something was wrong.

"What happened?" she asked.

Camryn's face was pale and there were dark circles under her eyes. "The twins and I had a fight." She shook her head. "No, that's not fair. We didn't fight. I accidentally told them I wanted to leave Wishing Tree after they graduated from high school and they totally freaked. They're afraid I'm going to abandon them — emotionally and physically. They were happy and thriving and I totally messed up."

She covered her face with her hands. "If you could have seen the look on their faces. They've been through so much already. First their dad, then their mom. They were so happy in their lives and I screwed that up."

River didn't know what to say. "I'm sorry."

"Thanks." Camryn dropped her arms to her sides. "They locked themselves in Victoria's room. They only opened the door so I could take Tinsel out. I half expected them to be gone when I got up this morning."

"Where would they go?"

"I don't know. If they were just mad, I

could handle it, but they're shattered and that's on me."

Camryn sighed. "Sorry. I'm dragging you into something you have no part of. Let's change the subject. How are you?"

"Dylan lied to me and it's bad."

Camryn stared at her. "What? He lied? When? Are you sure? Dylan's a pretty good guy."

"That's what I thought," River admitted, then explained about the mystery meeting and how Dylan pretended the two women were clients.

"Has it occurred to you they were clients and he's just a dweeb?"

"They weren't. There was something about them, the way they were dressed. You don't wear a business suit to meet with your contractor — not after driving all the way from Seattle. Plus, Helen was there and they were at a lawyer's office."

"Maybe they're friends of hers."

"I don't think so." River took a step toward Camryn. "Do you know anything about Dylan you haven't told me? Is there some secret that everyone is —"

"Don't ask me that." Camryn looked away.

River's stomach dove for her toes and all the air rushed out of her. "There is a secret and you know what it is. Why didn't you tell me?"

Camryn faced her. "River, please do get upset. I can't take one more person b ing angry at me. I do know something abo Dylan but I promised not to tell. It's no bad, I swear. It's good and kind of unex- pected. He's not anything you need to worry about."

"Tell me."

"I said I wouldn't."

Which River respected . . . sort of.

"Talk to him," Camryn told her. "Tell him you're upset and concerned and scared. Explain about why you don't like people keeping secrets."

"He already knows that," River said. "I've told him dozens of times. So there *is* some- thing."

"Talk to him," Camryn repeated. "I'm sure he'll tell you everything."

River nodded slowly and returned to her office. If Camryn wasn't going to give her the information she wanted, she would find it another way.

It only took her a few minutes to break into the cabinet business's records. She quickly found the payroll information and from that, Dylan's social security number. After making a note to talk to the business over about his really lousy firewall, she reached out to associates with skills she no longer cultivated. Six hours and a couple of felonies later, she had a printout of a bank statement. The account was with a well-known investment bank, which wasn't the issue. Instead, it was the balance on the statement that took her breath away.

Twenty-two million dollars. Twenty-two million.

She tossed the paper onto her desk and told herself there was a perfectly logical explanation. There had to be. Not that ordinary people like Dylan often had accounts that big. So where had the money come from?

Her first thought was that he'd inherited it from Jake's father. Only the account was over ten years old and she knew the elder Mr. Crane had only been gone a couple of years. Nor had there been any deposits beyond interest, earnings and dividends. There also hadn't been many withdrawals. A few thousand every year and a couple for much larger amounts. Otherwise, the money just sat and grew.

But where had the initial three million come from? She knew Dylan hadn't been raised with money. He was a cabinetmaker, not a gambler or a drug dealer.

But she only had questions and no answers. All she knew for certain was Dylan had kept something very significant from her and that knowledge changed everything.

## TWENTY-THREE

Camryn couldn't remember ever seeing her sisters so upset with her. In the past two days the twins had barely spoken. The house was silent except for the occasional sound of their tears. She felt sick to her stomach and couldn't eat. Nor could she find the words to make the twins feel better. She'd tried several times, but they wouldn't listen. If she started trying to explain what she'd said, they simply left the room.

She knew she could force them to stay — threaten them with serious punishment — but where was the point in that? She wanted to get through to them, not have them ignore a lecture. But she didn't know how to make that happen.

At about four, Helen called the store.

"I thought you should know the girls are with me," Jake's mother said cautiously. "Apparently, they've run away. They asked if they could stay with me while they figure

448

out what to do with their lives. I told them they could and then immediately called you." Helen paused. "I didn't make this happen, Camryn. I know I meddle, but I swear I had nothing to do with this."

Camryn carried the phone into her office, then sank into her chair. The weight on her shoulders increased and her heart ached for the pain she'd caused.

"I know you didn't," she said softly. "This is all on me. I'm on my way over. Can the twins stay with you until then?"

"Of course. Or longer if that helps. What happened? Your sisters are such happy, delightful young women and now they seem, I don't know, broken somehow."

"I'll tell you when I get there. It's a long, stupid story and it's all my fault."

"You're being too hard on yourself."

"You don't know what happened."

"True," Helen said. "But I know you. I won't tell them you'll be here shortly."

"Thank you."

Camryn collected Tinsel and let her staff know she would be gone for a couple of hours, then drove out to the big house on Grey Wolf Lake. Helen met her at the door.

"They're upstairs in the media room," Helen said, ushering her inside, hugging her, then taking Tinsel. "We can go into my office and talk before you see them."

Camryn was about to say that she had to get to her sisters first, only to realize she had no idea what to say to them. She followed Helen down a long hallway and into a bright, pretty home office. They sat on an overstuffed sofa covered in a charming floral print. Tinsel curled up in a dog bed by the fireplace. Helen poured tea from a china pot and handed her a cup.

"Start at the beginning," Jake's mom said kindly.

"I messed up," Camryn admitted, tears filling her eyes. "I hurt them and I never wanted to do that."

She explained about how she'd accidentally blurted out that she was planning on moving back to Chicago after the twins graduated from high school.

"They were totally caught off guard," she said. "Now they feel like they can't trust me and that they don't have a home. They were just getting their lives back after we lost Mom. They were having such a good holiday season and now it's all ruined. Worse, they don't trust me and they don't feel safe."

Helen sipped her tea. "I didn't know you were planning on leaving Wishing Tree. We are a small town and not for everyone. Chicago is so vibrant. Your friends must be excited to know you're returning."

The change in subject was disconcerting but Camryn did her best to follow along.

"The couple I've kept in touch with are," she said slowly. "The others kind of drifted away. That's mostly on me. My mom was sick and I had my sisters and then we lost her and everything was so hard. I also had Wrap Around the Clock to run. Hanging on to them was just one more thing I didn't have time for."

"Long-distance relationships are challenging," Helen murmured. "You worked in finance before, didn't you?"

"Yes, for an investment company."

"Are they holding a job for you?"

"No. I'll have to find something when I get there."

"But you have contacts in the city."

"A few." Camryn tried to explain. "I didn't pick this. Any of it. The situation was thrust on me. I know that sounds dramatic—"

Helen's expression was kind as she interrupted. "Because it was. You lost your mother, your job, everything you knew. You were suddenly responsible for a business and your sisters, all the while mourning a great loss."

"Thanks for seeing that." Camryn hesitated. "I want to choose my future. I don't want to settle."

"That makes a world of sense." Helen put down her teacup. "Forgive me if this question is too blunt, because I do understand wanting to be in charge of your own destiny, but why do you want to move somewhere you don't know anyone, you don't have any connection to or have a job waiting? What exactly is so appealing about going back to Chicago?"

"It's where my life was when everything changed. It's where I can be who I was."

One second she'd been engaged, thriving at work and happy, and the next she'd been caring for her dying mother, knowing she was about to be the guardian of her fourteen-year-old sisters and running Wrap Around the Clock. She'd lost everything important to her and she wanted it back.

"You're not getting it back," Helen said gently, almost as if she could read Camryn's mind. "What you had before. My dear, that is long gone. You can have regrets and wonder how things could have been different, but you won't be able to re-create those circumstances. Life doesn't work that way. Imagine if I went out to find a man like my late husband and tried to have our same relationship again. It's not possible."

"I don't expect everything to be the same," Camryn said, only to wonder if maybe she did. Because Helen had a point about Chicago. If she was going to start over, why there? All that was waiting for her was a condo she could easily sell. Why not Seattle or Los Angeles? At least she would be closer to her sisters in one of those cities. There was nothing waiting for her anywhere but here.

"What will you do about Wrap Around the Clock?" Helen asked. "Sell?"

"I couldn't do that. It's a family business."

"With no family to run it."

Harsh but true. "I need to go talk to my sisters," she said as she put down her teacup and stood.

"Let me show you the way."

Camryn stood outside the media room. There was a movie playing — Disney's *Aladdin*. She listened to Robin Williams sing about being a friend, wishing she had a magic lamp that would solve all her problems. But she didn't and right now she was the only person who could make things right.

She walked into the room. Her sisters sat together on a large sectional, Lily's head on Victoria's shoulder. Camryn crossed to them, picked up the remote and turned off the TV, then sat on the coffee table in front of them.

Her sisters looked pale and more scared than defiant. She saw the pain in their eyes and knew she'd been the one to hurt them.

"I'm sorry," she said quietly. "I was so, so wrong to say what I did. I never meant to hurt you or upset you."

"But you did," Victoria told her.

"I know. You're angry and afraid and that's on me." She pressed her lips together. "You're my sisters and I love you. No matter what, I'm here for you. You'll always be welcome in my life. You'll always have a home with me."

Tears filled Lily's eyes. "But we don't want to live in Chicago. We want to live here. Even when we go away to college, this is our home." She sat up straight. "We'll be eighteen when we graduate from high school. Mom left the house to all three of us. You won't be able to sell it without us agreeing because there are two of us and only one of you. And we won't agree to it."

Camryn gave a strangled laugh as she realized they were right. The house, the business, were in trust, in all three of their names. No one of them had power over the other two.

"I always knew you were smart," she said.

454

"But whether or not I want to sell the house isn't the point, is it?"

Lily shook her head. "No. You don't want us anymore."

Now Camryn was the one fighting tears. "That's not true. You're my family and I need you so much. I could never let you go."

"Then why would you leave us?" Victoria asked.

"I wasn't leaving you. I was trying to find something I lost."

The twins looked at each other, then back at her.

"What does that mean?" Victoria asked.

"I don't know. I haven't figured it out myself. Not completely." Camryn thought about what she and Helen had discussed. "I had a whole future when Mom got sick."

"Plus, you were engaged," Lily said slowly. "We were talking about our bridesmaid dresses."

"I remember. I was happy and had plans and then everything changed. I love you guys and I want to be here with you, but I never had a choice in any of it and it happened so fast. Plus, losing Mom. I guess I've been thinking if I could just go back to where I'd been before I could reclaim some of what I had."

"Do you still want that life?" Victoria asked.

"That's a good question and one I've never asked myself. I assumed I did. I thought that was where I was going. Now I don't know anything except how much I love you both."

She drew in a breath. "Please come home. We'll figure this out. I'm not going anywhere without talking to you first. You're right — I can't sell the house without you agreeing, but that's not the point. I want you to know that we'll make these decisions together. About all of it."

"Will you stay until we're out of college?" Lily asked.

"You can't ask that," Victoria told her. "Camryn can't have her life on hold for seven years."

"She shouldn't have her life on hold now." Lily turned to her. "Why don't you like Wishing Tree?"

"I do. Very much."

"Then why aren't you happy here? Why isn't this enough?"

A really good question, Camryn thought. "I don't know. Sometimes it is." And sometimes she felt lost and alone.

"Stay through us graduating from high school," Victoria said. "No matter what."

"I was always going to do that."

The twins looked at each other again.

"We'll come home," Lily said.

Camryn's heavy heart lightened. "Thank you."

She stood. Both sisters threw themselves at her, wrapping their arms around her. She hung on tight.

"I love you," she said.

"We love you, too," Victoria told her.

"We do."

Which was what Camryn wanted to hear. She had her sisters back and they would work their way through this mess. But the damage had been done. She'd shattered their trust and while it could be rebuilt, there would always be scars and she had to learn to live with the guilt of that.

Dylan looked up at the staircase leading to River's office. He'd gone through all his options and as far as he could see, the only thing he could do was tell the truth.

He'd lied to her. He hadn't meant to but in that moment, when she'd asked about his meeting with the financial planners, he'd been caught off guard. After keeping his money a secret for so long he'd been unable to simply tell her what was going on, so he'd made something up. Feebly. He'd seen the disappointment in her eyes and that had haunted him.

"I'll tell her now," he muttered as he slowly climbed the stairs.

He walked to her office, knocked once and opened the door. River looked up from her computer. Any hope he'd had that he'd overstated the situation died when he saw her closed expression. She wasn't happy to see him.

"Hi," he said, stepping inside and closing the door behind him. "Do you have a second?"

She motioned to the chair in front of her desk, but didn't speak. He sat down and debated how to start. Social niceties seemed out of place, so probably better to just get to it.

"Those two women weren't clients," he told her. "I lied about that."

"I know. I could see it on your face. You're not a good liar."

Her green eyes were unreadable, but the stiffness in her body told him she wasn't happy with him.

"They're financial people who were talking about helping me set up a foundation. Or maybe a trust. I haven't decided." He shifted in his chair. "So I have some money put away. A lot of money."

She picked up a piece of paper and passed it to him. "You mean the twenty-two million dollars?"

Her words stunned him. "How did you know?" He took the paper and stared at a printout of his investment statement. "How did you get this?"

A really stupid question, he thought, considering what she did for a living. He stared at her. "You hacked into my account?"

"No. I don't do that anymore unless I'm under contract. But I have a friend who helped me out."

Outrage joined confusion. "You got someone to break into my account?"

"Obviously." She sounded more resigned than defensive.

"That's wrong and possibly illegal. You can't just do that."

"Isn't it a little late to be saying that?" She looked away, then back at him. "You need a new firewall for your laptop. What is it about this town that people don't feel the need to protect their cybersecurity? The whole world isn't nice. You can't know who you can trust."

"Yeah, I'm getting that," he said, his temper rising. "River, you had no right to do what you did. You can't just go hacking

459

into people's lives. It's wrong."

Her mouth twisted. "There's a news flash. Thanks for the share." She stood and glared at him. "You lied to me. Not just about the meeting but about who you are." She motioned to the statement. "Where did the money come from? What did you do to get it? Did you steal something? Or get involved with a cartel? If it wasn't really awful, you wouldn't be keeping it a secret. All the times we talked, you never said a word."

"You didn't need to know. Why do you care? It's only money."

"I don't care about the money. I care about the fact that you lied about it. I thought we were starting something. I thought we were sharing our pasts and talking about our lives." She looked away. "I thought I knew you."

"You do."

Her gaze returned to his. "No, I don't." She motioned to the paper he still held. "This is a huge deal. Now all your talk about money changing people makes sense. You weren't talking about Jake, you were talking about yourself." Her shoulders drooped. "I thought you understood who I was, but you don't. You were afraid knowing about the money would change how I acted. You don't know me at all."

460

He ignored the stab of pain her words caused and concentrated on his outrage.

"You shouldn't have investigated me," he repeated, stuffing the statement in his coat pocket. "I thought I could trust you."

"I could say the same thing about you. I guess we were both wrong."

Her statement hit him hard. Dylan absorbed the blow, knowing he had to hit back harder than her.

"What I choose to share with the world is my business. Not yours — mine. I'm sure your deal with the FBI has something about not breaking the law again. You might want to think about that the next time you hire some criminal to hack into someone's account. You wouldn't like prison."

He turned and walked out. He was half-way down the stairs when he heard the sound of something heavy hitting the wall. Her temper should have given him a sense of satisfaction, but all he could think was that whatever was broken was just the beginning of things going wrong.

Jake left the meeting and walked toward his office. He told himself he should be pleased — the resort was full, the guests were happy and the long-range forecast promised snow for Christmas. But even with his business life exactly where he wanted it to be, he couldn't shake a feeling of restlessness that had plagued him for a couple of days now.

He knew the cause. Ever since Camryn had told her sisters she was leaving Wishing Tree, he'd felt uneasy. He wasn't sure why he was bothered. The information wasn't new to him — she'd been up front since the beginning. But something in her saying it to her sisters had changed things and he didn't know why.

He turned the corner toward the executive suites. Margie, his assistant, was off this afternoon. He paused to see if there were any notes for him on her desk then walked into his office and immediately came to a stop when he saw the tall, slender, black-haired, blue-eyed beauty standing by the window.

"Iona."

She turned and smiled at him. "Hello, Jake. It's good to see you."

That wasn't exactly how he would have described the moment, he thought. Surprising. Possibly awkward. Definitely not happy.

"What are you doing here?"

She walked toward him and lightly kissed his cheek. "I was hoping for a warmer greeting than that. Aren't you pleased I'm here?"

Her perfume of choice — jasmine with

462

hints of vanilla — wafted around him. He'd heard once that scent memories were the most powerful but instead of immediately reliving their past, he found himself wanting to bolt for safety.

"Why are you here?" he asked again, stepping back.

Her full mouth settled into a sexy pout. "That's not very friendly. Jake, it's me. If you want to know why I'm here, you should ask your mother."

His mother. Why would she . . . He swore silently. "She put you on the list for Project: Jake's Bride?" he asked before he could stop himself. His mother had contacted Iona? What had she been thinking?

His ex smiled. "She did. I'd forgotten how charming she could be. I was a little surprised to hear from her. I didn't think she liked me all that much, but I guess I was wrong. I decided to take her up on her offer. So here I am. Ready to be a candidate."

She moved toward him and put a hand on his chest. "Tell me about the audition. You know I'm always up for anything. You want to get married and I'm open to the idea."

He removed her hand, telling himself not to share that the whole Project: Jake's Bride wasn't his idea. "We've failed at a relationship twice. No way either of us wants to try again. So once again, why are you here?"

"But I do want to try again," she told him. "You're a hard man to forget." She tilted her head. "Come on, Jake. We had some great times together. We're older now. More mature. I'm sure we could work through our problems and find our way to a very happy ending."

After two-plus years? Yes, his mother had given her a reason to show up, but why had she wanted one? They were beyond done. Iona didn't do anything without a reason, so what was it this time? A recent bad breakup? Annoyance that the second time he'd been the one to walk away? Then he wondered if the reason really mattered.

"I'm not buying it," he said. "I'm sorry you came all this way, but no. I'm not doing this."

She seemed to wilt. "Jake, don't say that. You're my destiny."

He held in a laugh. Her destiny? Seriously? "Not even close. We were done a long time ago. I should have listened when you left me. You were telling the truth when you said you couldn't love me. What you left out is the fact that you can't love anyone."

She turned away. "That's cruel."

"I don't mean it to be."

Her head came up. "You're making a

mistake if you let me walk away."

"I can live with that."

"I won't be back."

He could only hope that was true.

She waited a couple more seconds, then grabbed her coat and handbag from the sofa and stalked past him.

"You're going to regret this," she told him, her gaze filled with anger and scorn. "Women like me don't come around very often. You'll never forget me, Jake. Because I'm your destiny, too."

With that, she was gone. He walked to his desk and sank into his chair. Adrenaline washed through him, like he'd just witnessed a bad accident. Iona was trouble and he'd been lucky to escape her.

He couldn't believe she'd simply shown up in his office, expecting them to get back together. No way he wanted to have anything to do with her. He was looking for a different kind of woman — one who was calm and funny and easy to be with. One who made his heart beat faster and look forward to seeing her. Curly red hair was a must.

Camryn would never blow in and out of his life. She would be constant, because that was the kind of person she was. When he told her about Iona's showing up, she would be just as outraged and surprised as he had been. He would feel better that she knew.

Funny how they'd connected so quickly. What had started out as a holiday fling had quickly become something else — at least for him. He liked that she was in his life, that they were in a committed relationship. He wanted to —

Jake stood and crossed to the window. He stared unseeingly at the view as the truth slowly, painfully, settled on him.

He was in love with Camryn.

He didn't know when it had happened, or how, but it had and now he was in love with her. Totally and completely.

He wanted to keep seeing her and talking to her and touching her. He wanted mornings and nights and forever. He wanted to marry her and have the twins in his life. And Tinsel, because she was family, too. In a few years he wanted a couple of kids with her.

But before he could make any plans, a coldness swept through him. He might love her, but how could he plan a future when at any second, he could turn into his father? He didn't want to hurt Camryn the way his father had hurt his mother, but he didn't know how to not do that. He was his father's son after all.

He stared out the glass at the snow-covered mountains, as if the answer was out there, somewhere. He wanted . . . He wanted . . .

"No," he said out loud. "I'm not going to be like him."

And with those simple words came a realization that life was always about choices. He could choose to be like his father or he could choose to be someone else. A strong, devoted husband who did the right thing. He didn't have to cheat if he didn't want to. He could be the man Camryn deserved — if she would have him.

And if she wasn't leaving Wishing Tree.

Because her decision to stay or go wasn't about geography, he thought. It was about running away because she was afraid. If she wasn't willing to take a chance on herself, she sure wasn't going to take a chance on him. Not exactly a comforting revelation, but the truth all the same.

He'd gone and fallen in love with someone who couldn't, or wouldn't, accept that there was more to life than simply running away from her pain. But love her, he did. For always. And he had no idea what was going to happen next.

# TWENTY-FOUR

River huddled in the corner of the sofa, a box of tissues beside her. She knew that at some point she was going to run out of tears, but so far that hadn't happened.

How had things gotten so awful so fast? She liked Dylan — she assumed he liked her. But the secrets and the lies and what he'd said . . .

"He's not the one," she said, reaching for another tissue. "I was wrong about him."

"He was a jerk," Kelsey said calmly as she patted River's back. "He was thoughtless and stupid. Totally. This is on him. But you're getting a little ahead of yourself on the rest of it."

River blew her nose, then raised her head to stare at her sister. "You think he's the one?"

"I don't know. But it's one fight. A big one, but still just one. Why don't you see what happens before you end the relationship?" Kelsey's voice gentled. "Until this, you really liked him. That's a big deal."

"He lied to me. He's hiding twenty-two million dollars."

Her sister winced. "Yes, there's that. And maybe you should find out about it before you jump to conclusions. There's no way he's a drug dealer."

"Not now. But the money had to come from somewhere."

"He's not a drug dealer," Kelsey repeated.

River leaned back against the sofa. "You're right. Until this, I would have said he's a really good guy. He cares about people. He was so kind in the beginning, when I was scared about being the Snow Queen."

He'd protected her and laughed at her stupid jokes and he'd said she was beautiful.

"He doesn't trust me." She wiped her face. "He told me about being friends with Jake and how people treated Jake differently because he had money. He talked about how uncomfortable that made him when all the time he was hiding some big fortune."

She paused. "You know I don't care about the money — it's that I told him everything. About the hacking and the FBI." She looked at Kelsey. "I don't share that with just anyone."

"I know. You gave him a piece of yourself and he kept a really big part of himself from you."

River nodded. "It's like I was the only one in the relationship, which means there wasn't a relationship at all. He didn't trust me with the most important thing." The tears returned. "And while the money genuinely doesn't matter to me, it's significant because it matters to him. I thought we had something. I thought we were going somewhere with our relationship, but I was wrong — about that and about him. What else isn't he telling me?"

"I doubt he has anything that can top the twenty-two million."

"Probably not." River twisted the tissue in her hands. "I feel so stupid. I was excited about him and us. He taught me to waltz. I was thinking about how wonderful it was that I'd finally met a really great guy who cared about me."

"Why do you assume he doesn't care? I'm not saying he wasn't a jerk, but him getting mad doesn't mean he doesn't like you."

"Should I repeat myself and mention the trust thing?"

"You don't have to." Kelsey hugged her again. "But in case you really need to, let me ask you a question first. When was he supposed to tell you? The first time you met? 'Hello, I'm Dylan Tucker and I have twenty-two million dollars. The money obviously makes me uncomfortable because I don't talk about it and no one knows about it. How are you enjoying Wishing Tree?' "

River exhaled. "His voice doesn't sound like that."

"Not the point of the question. When would he have told you?"

"Maybe after sex?"

"That would be awkward."

"He should have said something. He shouldn't have lied!"

"Agreed. And he should have trusted you. I'm just saying, it's not as easy as you're making it sound. I haven't heard a word about Dylan being rich. You said the account was over ten years old, so this has been happening for a while and he hasn't talked about it. His keeping the information to himself isn't all about you."

"Which just proves the point that I'm not special and I was wrong to think we had something going on."

"River, no! That's not what it proves. Don't go to the worst-case scenario, please. You like this guy. I repeat myself because you liking someone is rare. You're so careful about who you let into your heart. You don't

471

trust easily."

"For good reason," she pointed out. "Look at what just happened."

"I know and I'm totally with you on his jerkishness. But you might think about the fact that until the last two days, he's been pretty amazing. Doesn't that make him worth hearing out?"

"When am I supposed to do that? It's not like he's been in touch with me. Obviously, he's as over me as I'm over him."

Kelsey shook her head. "Then you're both idiots."

River pressed a hand to her stomach. "I wouldn't mind being an idiot if only everything didn't hurt so much."

"That's your heart breaking."

"I know."

A broken heart meant she had cared more than she wanted to admit. A little voice whispered that if she'd been that involved with Dylan then maybe, just maybe, she should listen if he wanted to talk to her. That he just might be worth that second chance Kelsey had mentioned.

But that would require trusting him after all he'd done, and River wasn't sure she had that much faith left in her. Not anymore.

The sweet notes of Lily's flute solo filled

the auditorium. Camryn let herself get lost in the music, enjoying the possibly brief sense of things being back to normal. Almost normal, she thought, glancing at Victoria sitting next to her. Her sister glanced at her, smiled once, then returned her attention to her twin.

It was a start, Camryn told herself, knowing three weeks ago Victoria would have been clinging to her arm, humming along, whispering how great Lily was and didn't the white dress just totally make the moment.

Jake, sitting on her other side, next to his mother, squeezed her hand in silent communication. The man was oddly aware of the subtle nuances in her changed relationship with her sisters and was being incredibly supportive. If only this was a problem he could fix.

Lily finished her solo and the auditorium burst into applause. The loudest came from their row where several of Camryn's friends had claimed seats. River had texted to say she wasn't feeling well and couldn't make it, but Shaye and Lawson had joined them, along with Paisley, Reggie, Toby and Harrison.

Camryn appreciated the support. Only in Wishing Tree, she thought ruefully. Had this

473

been five years ago and in Chicago, she wasn't sure any of her friends would have come to her sister's concert. Not that they hadn't been great people, it was just different there.

"Lily is amazing," Helen said in a stage whisper, leaning over Jake to deliver the message. She held a huge bouquet of red roses she would deliver after the performance.

"She is."

Camryn returned her attention to the stage and the rest of the holiday concert. There were a few other solos, but none as good as Lily's. Of course that could be the big sister in her talking. When the overhead lights came on, they all stood and applauded, then fought their way to the stage where everyone hugged Lily, and Helen delivered her massive flower arrangement.

"You were spectacular," Helen announced. "I was so proud, even though I have no connection to your brilliance." She laughed. "You are a treasure, my dear." She touched Victoria's arm. "As are you."

The twins hugged her tight.

"We have a party to get to," Victoria said when they'd straightened. She turned to Camryn. "You're picking us up at eleven, right?"

"Eleven," Lily repeated. "You said we could stay out that late this one time because it's a special party."

And because she still felt guilty about what she'd put them through, Camryn thought. "Yes, I remember. I'll be there at eleven."

The holiday party was being sponsored by the orchestra members and held at the recreation building out by the ice-skating lake. Helen had offered to drop off the twins and Camryn was picking them up. There were chaperones, lots of food and soda, and no dark corners.

"You two run along and enjoy yourselves," Helen said, kissing Jake on the cheek. "I'll get the girls there safely."

Camryn took a second to speak to her friends, then took her coat from Jake and slipped it on.

"You know I could drive you," he said as they walked toward the exit.

"Don't be silly. There's no reason for us to both be out in the cold at eleven. I'll hang out with you at your place until it's time, then pick up the twins and head home." She stifled a yawn. "Maybe you could make me coffee."

"I can do better than that," he teased. "I can make you a latte."

"More hidden talents. You do know how to turn a girl's head."

"Stop! You're making me blush."

She was still laughing when they reached her car and he held open the driver's-side door. Once she was seated, he leaned in and kissed her.

"See you there," he said. "Watch out for black ice."

"You do the same."

She followed him to his condo and parked in the driveway before walking in through the garage. After slipping out of her heels, she left her coat and handbag by the door but carried her phone with her in case either of her sisters needed to reach her.

"Things seem better between you and the twins," he said, pulling milk out of the refrigerator.

"They're still dealing. You're right — emotions aren't as raw, but they're still holding back." She dropped an espresso pod into the machine. "I feel so awful about what happened."

"Hey." He moved in front of her and put his hands on her waist. "You need to stop beating yourself up."

"Why? I messed up so badly. Ugh. I know reliving the moment isn't helpful. I just don't know how to let it go."

He kissed her. "Let's make the lattes, then I'm going to tell you something that will make you momentarily forget your troubles."

"I doubt that."

"Have a little faith."

She smiled. "Now I'm intrigued. Tell me."

"You have to wait."

"Can I at least have a topic?"

He flashed her a grin. "Project: Jake's Bride."

"That is always fun to talk about."

They worked together and a few minutes later carried two lattes over to the sofa in his large family room. The window coverings were closed against the cold and dark. Jake picked up a remote, and seconds later the fireplace flared to life. Once she was settled, he sat next to her and put his arm around her. She snuggled close, liking the strength of him and the warmth. He was a good, steady guy.

"You've been a rock through all this," she told him. "I owe you."

"Happy to be around, but you were handling things."

"Badly."

"You're beating yourself up again. The only thing it accomplishes is making you feel terrible."

"Maybe I deserve to suffer."

He looked at her. "Isn't that a little dramatic?"

"Probably, but I wear it well."

He touched her cheek. "Iona came to see me."

Camryn needed a second for the words to sink in. She scrambled back on the sofa so she could stare at him.

"What? Iona? The one who got away and is so gorgeous you couldn't help yourself? That Iona?"

One eyebrow rose. "She didn't get away. I want to be clear about that. The second time around, I'm the one who left her. It's over."

She heard the words and mostly believed them but was surprised to feel a *ping* of jealousy deep in her chest.

"When did this happen?"

"A couple of days ago."

"And you're just telling me now?" Her voice came out a little more shrieky than usual. She cleared her throat. "I mean, you're just telling me now?"

"You've had a lot on your mind. I wanted to wait until we could have a real conversation about it, although the more I think about it, the less there is to say." He picked up her latte and handed it to her. "It's my mother's fault."

Once she heard those four words, everything made sense. "Project: Jake's Bride. Iona must have been on the list. But I thought she canceled all that until after the holidays."

"She did, but apparently, Iona had ideas of her own."

"She's always been the type of woman to go after what she wants," Camryn murmured, then sipped her latte.

He told her about finding the other woman in his office and how she wanted them to get back together. "I told her no. There's no way. I'm not interested in her. The first time could have happened to anyone. The second time is on me. I've learned from my mistakes and we're done."

"So no spark?" she asked, grateful her voice sounded normal.

"Nothing." He smiled at her. "You get all my sparkage these days."

"Sparkage? Did you really say that?"

"I did. You make me glitter." He frowned. "Wow, that came out wrong. Let's pretend I didn't say that."

She smiled, feeling her jealousy fade. "I don't know. *I make Jake glitter* seems like a bumper sticker to me."

"Glitter isn't even the right word."

"I'm not sure glow is better."

He shifted toward her and kissed her. "I have no interest in Iona or any other woman. That's the other thing I wanted to tell you. While I was dealing with the unexpected visit from girlfriends past, I had a revelation." His expression turned self-deprecating. "That sounds more grandiose than it is."

"I want to hear it anyway."

He looked into her eyes. "I'm not my father. I'm like him in a lot of ways, but I'm not the kind of man who cheats. I would never do that to someone I love."

His words made her happy. Finally, Jake had figured out who he was. "Told you so," she murmured, leaning in to kiss him. "You've had a busy couple of days."

"I have. There's one other thing."

"What?"

He straightened, putting a little distance between them, then met her gaze. "I'm in love with you."

Camryn stared at him, waiting for the punch line. Because there had to be something funny coming, something other than those words hanging out there like that.

But he didn't say anything else. He simply watched her, waiting for her to . . . . What? Say something back? There was nothing she could say. Nothing good.

"No," she said, scrambling to her feet and facing him. "Jake, don't say that. Please, don't. I like this. I like us. You're wonderful and we have fun and I don't want that to change."

His expression was carefully neutral. She had the horrible thought that she was hurting him, which she'd never wanted to do. She should say something nice, but all she could think about was making him take it back. If he didn't, she was going to have to run and get as far away from him as possible.

"Don't love me," she repeated, her hands twisting together. Panic settled low in her belly. "You can't. You shouldn't. We both knew this relationship came with an expiration date. That's better for me."

"Why? You don't know if you're leaving or not. You don't know anything at this point. What if everything you want is right here?" He rose, careful not to crowd her. "What if we can make this work? I love you, Camryn."

"No! Don't. Just don't. You think love makes it better? You think hearing this makes me happy? I just can't deal with it, not the feelings or the words." Tears burned in her eyes. "I liked what we had. Why did you have to go and change everything?"

He moved closer. "Don't run from me. We can figure this out. We have time."

She stared into his handsome face, knowing whatever they'd had was over. "I have to go."

"Camryn, please. We should talk about this."

She started for the garage door. "There's nothing to say," she told him, not bothering to turn around. She slipped on her shoes and her coat, then bolted for her car. Only halfway home, she had to pull over because she was crying too hard to see the road.

She didn't want his love, or him, she told herself. She wasn't interested in anything real. She hadn't wanted more. And now there was nothing but her broken, empty heart and the knowledge that yet again, she'd hurt someone she cared about.

Dylan threw himself on the sofa in Jake's office.

"I'm so pissed at her," he said.

Jake looked up from his computer. "By *her* you mean . . ."

"River. Things were going great between us. Better than great." The more time he spent with her, the more he liked her, or at least he had. These days he didn't know what to think.

Dylan sat up. "She hacked into my life. She got one of her friends to go digging around and she found out about the money."

"She can do that?"

"Probably but she doesn't anymore, so she had someone else do it. She knew about the account and how much was in it. Not how I started it, though. She asked if I was a drug dealer."

He still remembered his outrage. "She broke my trust. Things were good and she wrecked everything."

He couldn't believe it. After all this time he'd finally found someone who could matter to him. Someone he could see a future with and she'd totally messed up all they had.

Jake walked around his desk and sat in one of the chairs by his sofa. "I don't get it. River got a friend to pry into your financial situation? Why?"

Dylan looked away. "I ah, well, she saw me at the meeting your mom set up. To talk about the money and a foundation. When she asked me about it, I lied to her." He inched forward on the sofa. "But that's not the point."

Guilt bumped into him but he ignored it.

"She had no right to get into my business. She broke the law. I'm pretty sure of it."

"Going to have her arrested?" Jake asked drily.

"No. I'm just saying she's wrong."

His friend studied him. "Is it just me, or are you being stupider than usual?"

"Hey!"

"You're an idiot. Seriously, so dumbass as to embarrass your gender."

"You're supposed to take my side."

"Not this time." Jake leaned back in the chair. "So let's start at the beginning. You meet this woman. You're attracted to her and the more you get to know her, the more you like her."

"That doesn't have anything to do with this."

"It has everything to do with it," Jake told him. "You hang out together. You get along. You start to think she could be significant in your life. From what you've told me before, she's been pretty blunt about some bad stuff in her past and how she's different now. She's been up front and honest and was probably falling for you. So what do you do? Keep a twenty-two million dollar secret from her. Then when she found out, you said a bunch of stupid stuff you can't take back."

Dylan glared at him. "You don't know that."

"I know you. Sadly, you fight like a kid, saying things you shouldn't. You really need to up your game in the arguing department. There's a way to do it productively. I'm sure they have online classes."

"You're not helping."

"I am, which is more than you deserve. Come on, Dylan. You're in the wrong here. You knew the money was going to be an issue. I told you to tell her, but you wouldn't and now it's a thing and you don't want to accept responsibility so you're going to find a way to blame her, which means you're going to lose her and for the next five years, until you start this cycle again, I'm stuck listening to how lonely you are."

The harsh assessment surprised Dylan.

"That's not true."

Jake looked at him without speaking.

Dylan replayed his words in his head. "I don't keep doing this."

"Yeah, you do."

"There was no good time to tell her about the money. It's not the first thing you say and then I was in too deep."

Jake shook his head. "Idiot," he muttered. "This isn't about timing or even the money. It's about the fact that you won't trust people. You assume the worst with absolutely no reason to. Why else would you do all the crazy stuff you do so no one in town knows you have money? You're ridiculous about it. Would some people try to take advantage? Sure. But so what? Not the people who matter, and who cares about the rest?"

He leaned forward, his expression intense. "You set up River to fail, then acted shocked when it happened. You did this. It's on you. The worst part is I think you're crazy about her and you're going to regret losing her."

Dylan didn't want to think about that. "She broke into my accounts."

"It's what she does. She has skills and she used them."

"Not on me!"

Jake groaned. "You're the one she's falling in love with, so yes, on you."

Dylan froze. "She doesn't love me. Why did you say that? You can't know how she feels."

"She's quiet and socially awkward. You swept into her life and started hanging out with her. You know everyone in town and understand all the traditions. You're there for her. You go out, you laugh, you sleep together and it's all great. She trusts you enough to share everything about her life with you. Of course she's falling for you. Why wouldn't she be?"

"I . . ." Dylan closed his mouth and struggled for a reply. "She can't."

"Why? You won't let her?"

"No, it's just . . ."

Jake's stare was pointed. "If she's in love with you and you did all this, then you're even dumber than you thought? For what it's worth, I wouldn't worry too much. The odds of her still caring about you are shrinking by the day."

# TWENTY-FIVE

Camryn carefully trimmed the edge of the ribbon. With the store already closed for the day and all her employees gone, she could work in quiet and finish up the last of a dozen or so packages. She'd wrapped nearly eighty packages that day as the store entered the "less than ten days before Christmas" madness. She was starting to dream in wrapping paper prints, which normally she didn't mind. The busyness was good business and she enjoyed helping people take one more thing off their to-do list. It was just her heart wasn't in her work these days.

She alternated between devastated and pissed. Things with Jake had been so good and he'd gone and ruined it. She couldn't believe he'd told her he loved her. How could he? But every now and then she allowed herself to accept the fact that a wonderful man had told her he loved her and she'd been unwilling to even listen. If she'd had any doubts about not having worked through all her issues of the past year, knowing that made her flaws incredibly clear.

"Hey."

She looked up and saw River walking down the stairs into the store, her attention torn between the fact that River looked as bad as she felt and the bottle of tequila in her friend's hand.

"Hi." Camryn set down her scissors. "You okay?"

"No, you?"

"Not even close."

"That's what I figured. Where are the twins?"

"At home. They know I'm working late."

River held up the bottle. "Want to walk home? The alcohol should keep you warm."

"Sure. I just have a couple of packages to finish and then I'm happy to join you in whatever party you have going on."

River came over to help. She did the simple wrapping while Camryn took care of the decorations. When they were finished, they retreated to the break room. Camryn collected glasses, along with crackers and a can of nuts so they weren't drinking on empty stomachs.

River poured them each an inch or so of

tequila. They clinked glasses and took a sip. The liquor was smooth and burned all the way down. Now, if only it would help her forget.

"No offense," River said, "but you look terrible."

"I haven't been sleeping. You're not exactly perky yourself."

They looked at each other.

"Dylan?" Camryn asked.

River nodded. "Jake?"

"Yup."

They drank a little more.

"Want to go first?" Camryn asked.

River blinked away tears. "Sure. He lied to me. Stood looking me in the eye and lied. Oh, and I know about the money."

Camryn sighed. "I'm glad. I didn't like not telling you he's the town's Secret Santa, but I'd given my word."

River stared at her. "He's what?"

Camryn frowned. "The town's Secret Santa. I found out when he asked me to wrap seventeen hundred books. He's giving one to every elementary-aged kid in town. You didn't know?"

"No. He never said." The tears returned. "I asked him if he had any more secrets and he said no. But he does."

Camryn winced. "I'm sorry I said something."

"This isn't on you." River sniffed. "Although when compared to being a multimillionaire, the Secret Santa isn't a big deal."

"It's millions?" Camryn asked, slightly stunned. "Where did it come from?"

"I still don't know." She sipped her drink. "He started with three million dollars. It's grown to twenty-two million, which means he has a really great financial adviser."

She kept talking, but Camryn couldn't hear the words. "I'm sorry, what? Did you say twenty-two million dollars?"

"I thought you knew."

"That he was the Secret Santa. Not that he was uber rich." Camryn tried to process the information. "He drives a five-year-old truck and works a regular job, and he has twenty-two million dollars? I have no idea what to say to that."

She looked at River. "I get being upset about him lying to you, but why is the money bad? You can't believe he did something illegal to get it. Maybe Jake's dad left it to him."

"The timing doesn't work. I'm not saying I'm assuming the worst —"

"You kind of are. River, you know him. Dylan's a sweetie. He's not a criminal."

"I don't know that. I don't know anything except I shared all my past with him. All the bad, horrible stuff. I told the truth. I put myself out there. He had a thousand opportunities to tell me about the money and he didn't. And then he lied about it, which means it's a big deal to him. He didn't trust me with the information. He held back a significant element of his life. I thought we were falling in love, but I was the only one in the relationship."

Her lower lip began to tremble. "I slept with him. I trusted him and I was a fool."

Camryn circled the table to sit next to her friend. She hugged River. "You weren't a fool. Giving your heart is never foolish."

As she spoke, she silently wondered if Jake would agree with her on that.

"It is when the guy doesn't deserve it." She sniffed and straightened. "I'm okay."

Camryn returned to her seat. "I wish I could make things better."

"Me, too, but I'm stuck where I am. What's going on with you?"

Camryn didn't want to think about her own life. "I totally messed up my sisters."

"They're not still mad. I saw them at the holiday concert and they were fine."

"Oh, they pretend they're all right, but I can see the pain and worry in their eyes."

Camryn picked up her drink. "They were happy and strong and feeling safe and I destroyed that."

"You're being too hard on yourself."

"I'm not. I did that and I don't know how to make it right." She finished her tequila. "Jake told me he's in love with me."

"What?"

"Two nights ago. He just said it, like that's what people do. He told me he was in love with me."

She could still hear his voice in her head. Every now and then she almost got close to admitting she wanted him to love her, but then she reminded herself that there was no way she was ever getting involved. That she was leaving, that she had plans, that love was just too . . . too . . . terrifying.

"I don't want him to love me," she said as she poured more liquor in her glass. "No one should love me."

"Why?"

"I can handle being alone. I'm good at it. I got through losing my mom. I suck at parenting my sisters, but I'll learn from my mistake and never repeat it."

"You're scared," River said, watching her. "Of what? Losing one more person? Him breaking your heart? Of being happy and then having it all ripped away?"

"Any of the above," Camryn said lightly. "I can't love him."

"You're making a mistake," River told her flatly. "You're letting the fear win and that makes you small. You're not a small person. You're strong. Why can't you see that?"

"I'm not strong, I'm flawed and hanging on by a thread."

"Look at all you've done in the past year. You've gotten through the loss of your mom, you've learned how to take care of your sisters, you're running a successful business, you have friends and now a great guy. You're amazing."

Camryn wished that were true. "I can't love him back. I won't."

"You're going to regret losing him."

"Do you regret losing Dylan?"

River's eyes darkened. "No. I regret having him in the first place."

Jake couldn't figure out how to tell his mother what was happening without breaking her heart. They were in her office — the room of revelations and so many childhood memories. She was telling him about the Christmas dinner menu and asking if he thought anyone would enjoy a traditional plum pudding.

"Mom, I'm not seeing Camryn anymore."

His mother's eyes widened and the color bled from her face. "What? No. You broke up? What happened?"

A question Jake wasn't sure how to answer.

"You know we agreed to see each other exclusively," he began, knowing he wasn't going to mention the sex part of their relationship. Helen was, after all, his mother.

"Yes, you told me and the twins told me." Tears filled her eyes. "I thought it was going so well."

"So did I." He thought about taking her through the journey of Iona showing up, something they were going to have to talk about later, but decided fewer words were better. "I told her I was in love with her and she walked out."

"No!"

She seemed to crumple in her seat. Jake moved next to her and put his arm around her.

"Mom, you can't be upset with her. Camryn's finding her way through a lot of hurt and changes. She's still dealing with what happened to her, and she's scared."

"You're defending her?"

His mom's outrage made him smile. "Her rejecting me doesn't change how I feel. I'm not happy and it hurts to breathe every second, but I still love her."

His mother pulled a delicate lace hankie out of her pants pocket and lightly dabbed her nose. "Then you're a bigger person than I am. I'm furious and I want her punished. You fell in love with her. That has to matter. Does she think she can do better? She can't."

"I appreciate the support."

"I don't understand," she said mournfully. "You were so perfect together. Oh, the twins. What about them? We were all supposed to spend Christmas together and now it's ruined."

This time the sobs came in earnest. Jake pulled her close again, feeling the double blow of his pain and hers.

"Mom, I'm sorry."

"It's not your fault, and you're right. In a way, it's not hers, either. With her mother and everything she lost and having this life thrust on her — she doesn't feel like she's choosing." She raised her head. "Why can't she see how perfect you are?"

He managed a half smile. "I'm not perfect."

"Oh, I know that. I meant for each other. You're perfect together."

He'd thought they were, too. She was amazing and smart and sexy and those curls. Plus, the twins. For a brief moment in time he'd known he was the luckiest man alive. Until he'd realized that she couldn't accept what he had to offer.

"So you don't think it's personal," his mother said. "It's not that she doesn't love you, but she could love someone else."

He tried to not flinch at the thought of her with another man. "I'm fairly confident the problem is generic, not specific."

"Good. Then we just have to convince her to —"

"No," he said gently but firmly. "We're not going to convince her of anything." He shifted so he could look into her face.

"Mom, no. You're not to meddle. You're not going to casually visit Wrap Around the Clock or send messages through the twins. Camryn has to figure out what she wants herself. We can't tell her. Love doesn't work that way."

"But if I could . . ."

"No," he repeated. "You're going to have to give me your word."

She collapsed against him, the tears returning. He held her, trying not to notice how small she was. When she was directing the world and giving advice, his mother was larger than life, but in grief, she was defenseless and fragile.

"I wanted you to marry her," she said, her voice thick with emotion. "I wanted Lily and Victoria for my granddaughters and then more babies in a few years. I wanted you happy and new traditions in the house."

"I know," he murmured, stroking her back. "I wanted that, too."

More than she could know. He'd doubted himself for so long, been unsure he was capable of being the kind of man he aspired to be, terrified of turning into his father. He'd held back his emotions, his hopes, his dreams, in an effort to not make a mistake. With Camryn the relationship was meant to be temporary, so he'd been able to relax. To just enjoy himself. And then he'd found himself in love with her.

The irony of finally giving his heart to the one woman who wouldn't want it didn't escape him.

"How do we survive this?" his mother asked.

"We trust that we're going to heal. Every day gets a little bit easier." But trying again? Jake wasn't sure he had that in him. Not after losing Camryn. Not after coming so close to perfection and then having it ripped away.

Dylan stood outside River's front door. He

knew she was home — several lights were on in the townhouse. Plus, he'd already gone by her office and she hadn't answered there.

He'd been here nearly ten minutes, trying to figure out what to say when she opened the door. Assuming she did. For all he knew she had one of those remote cameras and was watching him right this second, thinking she never wanted to speak to him again.

Over the past couple of days he'd realized that maybe, just maybe, he'd jumped to one or two conclusions about what had happened the last time he'd talked to her. Had she been wrong to have a friend break into his accounts? Absolutely. Had he been a dick for lying and not telling her about the money in the first place? Probably. Were they doomed?

That, he didn't know.

He shoved his hands into his coat pockets, pulled them out, then took a step forward and rang the doorbell. Seconds later he was staring into River's wary eyes.

"Hi," he said, then paused, not sure what came next. "I thought maybe we could talk."

She hesitated long enough to make him think she was going to say no but at last she stepped back and motioned for him to enter.

They walked the short distance to her living room. He took a seat on the sofa while she stayed on her feet — arms folded across her chest. Neither her body language nor her expression were welcoming. He told himself to ignore that, and his own complaints, and just get on with explaining what had happened.

"When I was nineteen, I went on a camping trip with Jake and a few other friends. We all met in Montana and had a great time. On the way back, I stopped to get gas and ended up buying a few lottery tickets. Powerball, some others."

Her green gaze locked with his, but she still didn't speak, so he kept going.

"When I checked the tickets a few days later, I found out I'd won five million dollars." He paused, remembering how stunned he'd been. "I'd always been the kid who didn't have any money. Living with Jake and his family, I was surrounded by wealth, but it wasn't mine. I knew what it was like to patch up boots to make them last for the rest of the winter or pretend my shirts weren't too small because I was still growing. Five million dollars. I couldn't believe it."

She moved to one of the chairs and sat down. Possibly a good sign, he thought.

"I took the immediate cash option rather

than have it pay out over twenty years," he continued. "After taxes, that was about three million dollars. I talked to Helen about what to do. I figured I'd quit my job and live off the interest and never work for the rest of my life."

"You didn't do that," she said softly.

"No. I couldn't. I loved my work and I was too young to just sit around all day. I thought about moving somewhere, but Wishing Tree is my home. In the end I bought a nice leather jacket, paid off my used truck and gave the rest to an investment guy Helen recommended. Then I sort of forgot about it."

He rested his elbows on his knees and leaned toward her. "A few years later it had grown a lot. I took out some to buy the house I have now and started doing things around town. I paid for some old guy's fence and donated to the food bank. Every fall I buy backpacks and school supplies for kids who can't afford them. I do it all anonymously because I don't want anyone making a fuss."

"Because you've seen how people act when they know you have money."

"Yeah. That."

"You're the town's Secret Santa."

He grimaced. "I guess. I don't think of

myself that way. I'm just a guy who helps out. I didn't want to make a fuss and I didn't want to have to deal with the money. Dan, my investment guy, took care of things and every year the bottom line was bigger and bigger, which made me uncomfortable and made me want to ignore it more."

He shrugged out of his coat. "When I was about twenty-five, I met this woman. Bobbie. We fell in love and got engaged. I thought she was the one."

"Was she?"

"No. I didn't know how to tell her about the money so I didn't."

River's neutral facade cracked a little. "You were engaged to someone and didn't let them know you had over what, ten or twelve million dollars in the bank? How could you keep a secret like that from her? It's such a betrayal. You were going to marry her and have children with her, but you didn't tell her about the fortune you had?"

"When you put it like that," he said, hoping she would smile, but she didn't.

"I told her a couple of months before the wedding."

River looked at him like he was an idiot. "Why would you wait that long? She must have been so angry and felt so betrayed. All this time she thought you had a partnership, but you didn't."

"That's what she said and yes, she was angry."

He wasn't sure that small word described Bobbie's reaction. She'd been enraged and furious and hurt. She'd accused him of lying to her, of playing with her feelings, of not trusting her.

"Once she got over being pissed, she started talking about what she wanted to do with the money."

"But it's not community property," River said. "The lottery money is something you obtained before the marriage, so she has no part of it. As long as you keep it out of a joint account, she has no claim on it. Nor would anyone else."

"Bobbie didn't know that. She thought it would be half hers after the wedding."

River sighed. "So another way she was screwed," she said bluntly.

"That's how she saw it. She wanted us to move to Seattle and buy a house on the water, fancy cars. I told her I wasn't interested in that lifestyle and when she started to insist, I told her she had no legal right to the money. That's when things got ugly."

For the first time since he showed up, River's expression softened. "You broke the engagement."

"I did. She didn't take it well and threatened to tell everyone we knew that I was a secret millionaire."

River sighed. "That would have been hard to deal with. You had to pay her off?"

"I didn't have to, but it was easier. I gave her five hundred thousand dollars. She signed a confidentiality agreement and promised to never contact me again."

"That's a lot of money."

"She was really mad." He looked at her. "I handled the whole situation badly. With her and with you. I'm not good at this. I'm a regular guy living a normal life. I'm not meant to have that kind of money."

He drew in a breath. "That's why I was meeting with those two women. To figure out a plan. Helen's been on me to create a foundation or trust so I can give the money away sensibly. Not a roof here or books there. I'll put some aside for retirement and emergencies and the rest is to help people. I don't know how. I need to think about what I want to tackle. I've been reading and it seems better to focus on one thing rather than sending a little bit of money to a lot of places."

"Makes sense."

"I didn't know how to tell you," he admitted. "First, it was too soon and then it was too late and somehow I missed the day it was supposed to happen. Plus, I got scared that when I did tell you, it would go badly. I'm sorry about all of it. I never meant to hurt you."

Her eyes darkened. "You lied to me, Dylan, but that's not the worst of it. It's less about you not telling me than what you not telling me means. That matters because you were holding yourself back from what I thought was a relationship that was important to both of us."

She drew in a breath. "I remember you saying that you hated seeing people treat Jake and his family differently because they were rich, yet here you are, acting different because you're rich now, too. I told you everything. I was completely honest. I told you about the FBI and the hacking and the bad boyfriend. I didn't keep anything from you, even when it made me look stupid. But you kept who you are from me."

She was right, he thought grimly. "I'm sorry. That isn't what I meant to do. I don't want to lose you over this. River, I care about you. Other than this really big flaw, I'm an okay guy. Can't you see that? Can't you help me work through the money thing so we can find our way back to where we were? Please, can I have another chance?"

505

Her gaze locked with his. Hope flared only to die when he saw the resolution in her eyes. She stood and cleared her throat, as if she was having trouble speaking.

"I obviously have horrible taste in men," she said. "I need to accept that and stop trying to make a relationship work." She pressed her lips together. "Getting involved isn't easy for me. Trusting someone, sharing my feelings. I don't tell everyone what I told you. I gave you all I had, all I was. I thought that was where we were going. But the whole time you were hiding a defining part of yourself from me. I thought we were heading toward somewhere special, but you didn't. You were waiting for me to mess up."

Tears filled her eyes. "I was all in, Dylan, and you weren't. That's the bottom line. You didn't believe in me or us and I'm not interested in someone like that."

He wanted to tell her she was wrong about him only he was incapable of speech. It was as if she'd kicked him in the chest and he couldn't breathe. All the air rushed out and bone-chilling cold took its place. She sounded sad but determined. He knew there was no convincing her.

She walked to the front door and held it open. He struggled to get to his feet and walk outside. Before he could figure out what to say, she'd closed the door in his face.

He stood on her front porch, knowing he'd lost her. River was gone and he had no one to blame but himself.

# Twenty-Six

Camryn stumbled through the next few days doing her best to convince everyone she was fine. Fortunately, only a few people knew that she and Jake had started dating, so having their relationship end didn't require a lot of notification. River, on the other hand, had to deal with concerned looks and lots of worry. Dylan had graciously stepped back from his Snow King duties so the twins had gone with River to help judge the last Cookie Tuesday. The only event remaining was the Holiday Ball and no one had figured out how to handle that. The Snow Queen couldn't dance by herself.

"A problem for tomorrow," Camryn told herself as she drove home through the quiet, holiday-lit streets of her hometown. Nearly every house had lights across the rooflines. There were snowmen and Santas and trees sparkling in windows.

She ached all over — a deep physical pain that made it hard to sleep. She tried telling herself it was just the season — she was working longer hours than usual — but she knew there was another cause.

She missed Jake. Funny how he'd become such an important part of her life in such a short period of time. She missed seeing him and hanging out with him. She missed the sound of his voice and the way he always stepped in to handle whatever the problem was. He was dependable and strong, but more than that, he was sexy and funny and when he touched her, every part of her went up in flames.

He was also in love with her.

She was still grappling with that unexpected piece of news. She'd moved past being totally freaked to possibly accepting the truth of the words, but even if he meant them, she had no idea what to do with them. What did they even mean? He loved her. As in love-love? Which meant what? They went to the next stage of their relationship? If they were committed to each other now — or at least had been until her slightly unhinged bolting — then what was next? Marriage? Did he want to marry her?

She drove into her driveway and hit the button on the garage-door opener.

She thought she'd always seen herself getting married and having kids. A happy life with a man who loved her as much as she loved him. Safety. Security. Connection. They all mattered and if Jake was offering that, shouldn't she be jumping at the chance to make it happen? Because the problem certainly wasn't him or how she felt about him.

She pulled inside and turned off the engine. It had been her night to work late so it was nearly nine. She should be hungry but all she wanted was to take off her shoes, curl up on the couch and watch mindless TV for an hour before going to bed.

She walked inside and was immediately greeted by a happy, dancing Tinsel. The little Chihuahua whined and pranced until Camryn dropped her handbag and scooped up the dog and held her close.

"I missed you, too," she said, kissing the top of her head. "How was your day?"

"Camryn?" Lily called.

"It's me."

She picked up her bag and carried the dog into the living room. Her sisters were on the sofa, several photo albums spread out on the coffee table. They both stood and hurried over, hugging her extra tight. It was only then she realized they were crying.

Panic gripped her. "What's wrong?"

"Nothing." Victoria hung on to her. "We're fine. We were just looking at old pictures. You know of Mom and Dad and us when we were little."

"We're not sad," Lily told her, wiping her face. "Just remembering. Come see."

They all sat on the sofa, Tinsel on Victoria's lap. Lily flipped through the pages. Camryn saw the wedding photos when her mom had married their dad.

"You're so cute," Victoria said, pointing to eleven-year-old Camryn in a bright green dress.

"I was happy that day." Camryn traced the bouquet their mother held. "So was Mom. We all knew we were going to be a great family."

They studied pictures of their mom through her pregnancy with the twins.

"She was huge," Lily said, her voice thick with awe. "We had to hurt."

"She never complained." Camryn smiled. "I remember how excited I was to learn she was having twins."

There were pictures of the newborns, including several of Camryn holding each of them, and happy shots of unsteady toddlers. Pages and pages of wonderful memories, she thought, until there weren't any pictures for a couple of years.

"This is when Dad died," Victoria said, pressing her face to Tinsel's soft coat. "We were so sad."

Camryn nodded, remembering the shock and the sound of her mother crying. The twins had been young enough to not fully understand, but she'd known he was never coming back.

"Was it like when you lost your dad?" Lily asked her.

"No. I was only three when he took off. I don't remember much about it." Or him, she thought. One day he'd just been gone.

"Still." Her sister leaned into her. "You've lost two dads and your mom. It's hard."

It had been for all of them. Then they'd healed as a family and she'd graduated from high school and gone off to college, then her job in Chicago. But she'd lost that, too, and her fiancé and her friends. A whole series of broken hearts.

No, she thought, correcting herself. Her heart broken over and over. Just the one heart, shattered again and again.

She didn't know what that distinction meant, but she knew somehow it mattered. That what she'd been through was the reason she wanted to move on, to not have Jake love her. She couldn't rest, couldn't settle, couldn't believe, not anymore. Not with all those scars. It was like her heart was so damaged, the love couldn't get through.

Jake spent a hellish few days dealing with the fact that he might have lost Camryn. On the surface he was his regular self, doing his job, living his life. He'd even been there to help Dylan without letting on his own romantic life had been blown up, leaving him battered and bleeding. But on the inside, he was dealing with a heart that had been ground to dust.

He wanted to call her. He wanted to go by the store and see her. Just look at her, so he would know she was okay.

He groaned. Okay, so that was a lie — he didn't want to simply stare at her, he wanted to hold her and kiss her and have her tell him she realized she was strong enough to admit she was desperately in love with him and would he please give her one more chance? Which he would.

But he figured the odds of that happening were less than zero. Camryn had her own demons to fight and there wasn't anything he could do to make her see they belonged together. That was something she had to figure out on her own.

He returned his attention to his computer, telling himself going over the budget for the following year was usually one of his favorite things to do, as if that would help him pay attention more. Because missing Camryn, longing for her, was a difficult distraction to overcome.

He was deep into the first quarter projections for room service billings when he heard a knock on his open door. He looked up and was surprised to see Camryn standing there.

He instantly came to his feet and started toward her. She'd shown up. She was here.

But her wary expression and stiff body language told him she wasn't in his office to ask that they reconcile. If anything, she was here because there was a problem.

"Do you have a minute?" she asked.

"Of course. Are you and the twins all right?"

"We're fine. Why would you ask?"

"It seems like there's something wrong."

She walked toward his desk. He resumed his seat while she took a chair across from his.

She looked at him, then away. After a few seconds her gaze returned to his. "I need to ask you something. For River."

Not what he wanted to hear, he thought

grimly. "Go ahead."

She drew in a breath. "You know she and Dylan aren't seeing each other anymore and Dylan's withdrawn from his Snow King duties."

He swore silently. After what they'd talked about, after he'd told her he loved her and she'd bolted, she'd shown up to talk about Dylan not being the Snow King? Anger simmered, which he knew was only there because he didn't want to admit he was in pain. Had he meant so little to her? Had he been wrong about what was happening?

He started to tell her he didn't care about the Snow King or River, or Dylan, for that matter. Not right now. All he could see was the woman he loved, sitting so calmly in his office, apparently unconcerned about the fact that he'd offered her his heart and she'd rejected it and him.

But then he noticed the slight tremor in her fingers as she clutched her handbag. Her face was pale and there were dark shadows under her eyes. Her posture was stiff, her breathing uneven. All signs she was as affected by this meeting as he was.

"Are you asking me to be the substitute Snow King?" He spoke with a lightness he didn't feel. "I'm not sure I can carry off the crown."

One corner of her mouth lifted slightly. "You'd look good in the crown." She squared her shoulders. "There's still the Holiday Ball tomorrow. River's going to be there, along with half the town. I was wondering if you'd mind going."

She leaned toward him, her gaze locked on his. "Just for a bit, to be there for the first dance with her, so she's not left standing there, alone. You wouldn't have to dance with me or anything." Her gaze dropped to her hands. "Fifteen minutes. For River."

"You're a good friend."

"I know being Snow Queen has been hard on her. Standing there by herself, with no one to dance with, would be hard on anyone. But especially her."

"Like I said, you're a good friend."

He watched her as he spoke. Deep inside he felt a whisper of hope. Yes, she was here for River, but she could have made her case via text or even a phone call. She didn't have to come all this way. Maybe he was the biggest idiot on the planet but he couldn't help thinking she was really here for herself. And if he was right, then maybe she was having second thoughts about walking away from what he offered.

"I'll be there," he told her. "To dance with River. I'd also like a dance with you."

Her eyes widened. "Why?"

He smiled. "Because you're a beautiful woman and I enjoy your company. I also miss you."

Her gaze fell again. "I'm sorry about what happened between us."

"I know."

She looked at him. "You do?"

Jake mentally walked to the edge of the emotional cliff and stared at the abyss. He was going to jump — the only question was how bad the landing was going to be.

"You like me, Camryn. You might even be in love with me. Your inability to hear me out when I told you I loved you wasn't about me or what we have together. It's about all you're dealing with. You're scared." He paused. "No, you're terrified. I don't know if you're going to be able to love me back, but I'm pretty sure that decision isn't about me at all. It's about you."

He waited, not sure if she was going to laugh in his face, mock him for being a fool or simply walk out. Instead, she swallowed several times, then brushed away a tear.

"That might be true," she admitted. "I *am* afraid of a lot and I'm trying to figure out what I want and what's important. But it's hard."

He gripped the arms of the chair to keep

himself in place. While every cell in his body screamed at him to go to her, to hold her and never let her go, he knew that was the wrong move. She had to find her way herself. She couldn't be rushed or coaxed or prodded.

"I never wanted to hurt you," she whispered.

"I know."

"I'm lost."

"You'll find your way."

She gave a strangled laugh. "You can't know that."

"Look how strong you are. Look what you've been through."

She stared at him. "Are you going to wait for me?"

Hope grew but he did his best not to let it show. "Do you want me to?"

"I don't know," she admitted. "Sometimes. But the rest of the time I just don't think I can do it."

The hope balloon popped. He loosened his grip on the chair and rose, then circled his desk. Camryn came to her feet and reached for him. He wrapped his arms around her and held on.

They stood like that for a long time. He breathed in the scent of her, memorized how her body felt against his. When she drew back, he released her, despite knowing he might never be this close to her again.

"I need to get back to the store," she said, gathering her purse and coat.

He nodded. "I'll see you at the ball."

"Thanks, Jake."

"Sure."

She started for the door. He turned his attention to the windows, not wanting to watch her walk away again.

Halfway back to town, Camryn started shaking. She waited until there was a side street, then turned onto it and pulled to the curb. She sat there, telling herself to breathe, that she would be fine, that there was no reason to get emotional about anything. She'd asked Jake for a favor, he'd said yes, end of story.

Only she hadn't counted on how hard it would be to see him, to look into his hazel eyes and know that they weren't together anymore.

She'd liked being with Jake. He was so good to her and being around him made her feel . . . safe. No, she thought, staring out the windshield — not just safe. Loved. Which made sense, what with the man declaring that he loved her.

She leaned back against the headrest and

closed her eyes, ignoring the tears trickling down her cheeks. He loved her. Had she spent even a second thinking about what that meant? Jake, the man who had decided he would rather live alone than risk hurting someone he cared about, had offered his heart to her. Somewhere along the way he'd realized he wasn't his father — that he could trust himself enough to care again, to have the wife and family he'd always wanted.

She straightened and brushed away tears. "It's not like he proposed," she said aloud. Which he hadn't, but she knew deep down inside, that was where this had been going. That he'd decided she was the one. The *one*. And she'd walked away.

She'd left a wonderful, caring, sexy, handsome, smart, loving man whom she actually adored because she was afraid. Afraid of losing one more person she cared about. Afraid of the pain of loss, of getting one more emotional body blow. Afraid that the next time she was hit by something awful she would fall and never get up again.

"I can't do it," she whispered. She couldn't possibly take the chance. Better to . . .

"Better to what? Be alone and afraid for the rest of my life?"

It was a question she couldn't answer, so

she dug a tissue out of her bag, wiped her face and blew her nose. After taking a few deep breaths, she started the car and headed back for the main road.

When she reached Wishing Tree, she turned toward The Wreath. It was barely four in the afternoon the day before Christmas Eve. They were slammed at work with last-minute shoppers dropping off presents that had to be wrapped before noon tomorrow when all the stores closed.

As she drove along Celebration Pass toward Grand Avenue, she passed houses decorated for the holidays. Sunset was minutes away and all around her, lights came on. There were strings of them along roofs and trees in windows. One house had a stack of faux gifts on the porch. She recognized the coated paper she sold specifically for outdoor decorating. She'd come up with the idea over the summer, had found a vendor and had started selling it in early October. She'd sold out her first batch in two days.

There were other changes, she thought as she pulled into her parking space. The custom designs had only been a small part of the business when she'd taken over. Now they were thirty percent of sales. She'd hired a professional web person to expand their site and now she sold custom wrapping paper online. After the first of the year, she was going to look at gift-wrap packages, where she provided all the supplies, along with instructions, to create beautiful, elegant packages. She would sell the packages in the store and through the internet. Wrap Around the Clock had always been successful, but in the past year it had grown and that was because of her. Even more significant, she liked what she was doing. She enjoyed the work and the challenges and the people she worked with.

She hurried to the store, punching in the code to enter through the back door. After hanging her coat and putting her bag in her locker, she put on an apron and walked into the loud, busy retail area.

There were dozens of customers, picking out paper and ribbon or waiting to pick up packages. The door to one of the party rooms stood open and she could see the twins wrapping gifts with an ease and skill that came from a lot of practice. Holiday carols played through the speakers. Lights flashed on the Christmas tree in the corner. Tinsel, festive in a red-and-green holiday sweater, came running up in her little prancy way and circled around her, tail wagging in happy greeting.

picked her up and they all hugged again, the tiny dog between them.

After a few seconds they stepped back and wiped away happy tears.

"We have to get to work," Victoria said with a sniff. "These packages won't wrap themselves."

"But it would be cool if they did." Lily grinned. "Like in that super old movie — *The Sorcerer's Apprentice.* Only that was brooms, right? Or buckets of water? I can't remember. We'll look it up when we get home."

Camryn left them discussing their favorite animated movies and went to help waiting customers. Later, when she was alone in her room at home, she would think about what she'd learned about herself in the past hour and decide on a plan going forward. A plan worthy of the very special man she had fallen in love with.

# TWENTY-SEVEN

River got up early Christmas Eve morning to start baking. Her mom had arrived the previous afternoon and was staying with Kelsey and Brooklyn. They would all meet up for an early family dinner, then come back to River's place to help her get ready for the Holiday Ball that evening. After the ball she would rejoin them for midnight services.

She rinsed off the fresh cranberries she would use in her cranberry cookies with brown butter glaze then dried them. As she worked she wondered what she was going to do about tomorrow. Oh, she could fake her way through opening presents and the brunch that followed, pretending to enjoy herself and have a little Christmas spirit. Her mom and sister would know she was upset, but they wouldn't say anything. No, the big problem was Christmas dinner at Helen's house.

Jake's mother had invited everyone over and seeing how Elizabeth and Helen had become good friends, staying in touch when Elizabeth had gone back to Los Angeles, there had been no way to say no. But if River joined her family for the meal, she would see Dylan and she didn't know if she could handle that.

She'd expected to stay mad at him — to cut him out of her heart as much as she'd cut him out of her life. She thought the anger would help her heal and by the time she let it go, she would be totally over him. But that wasn't what had happened. Instead, she'd moved quickly from righteous indignation and fury to missing him.

Even as she told herself she could never trust him and that he hadn't been as invested in their relationship as she'd thought, she kept thinking that maybe she was being a little quick to judge him and even quicker to walk away. She was starting to wonder if maybe she'd been secretly looking for a reason to end things between them because she couldn't believe that their relationship would work out.

She'd never had a successful romantic relationship in her life. She'd always chosen the wrong guy and ended up being hurt. Even as she thought that, she knew Dylan wasn't like her other boyfriends. He was decent and caring — he followed through when he said he would. He bought braces for kids he didn't know and had decided not to change his life when he first won three million dollars. He'd taken such good care of her, he'd looked out for her. He'd been thoughtful and sweet and when she analyzed his actions, she thought maybe, just maybe, he cared more than she'd let herself believe. She just wasn't sure — of him or of herself.

But she knew for sure that she missed him more and more each day. And while she appreciated that Camryn had arranged for Jake to be at the Holiday Ball for the first dance, she couldn't help wishing Dylan was going to be there instead.

She dropped softened butter and sugar into the bowl of her stand mixer. As the machine swirled them together, she thought about texting him and asking him to come to the ball. Maybe after the dance they could talk and this time she would listen to what he said without already believing it could never work out. Maybe this time she could have a little faith. After all, Christmas was a time for miracles.

She glanced at her phone, then shook her head. No, she thought. She didn't want to text him. She wanted to see him in person. So she would gather her courage and go to the dinner tomorrow and see him. Depending on how he reacted, she would either take him aside to discuss what had happened or she would know they were finished forever. One way or the other, by the end of Christmas Day, she would have her answer.

"I'm so excited," Lily said, carefully carrying her white dress through the lobby of the hotel. "I can't believe we're going to the ball."

"Me, too." Victoria held her dress in one hand and a large tote bag filled with shoes in the other.

"We won't stay late," Camryn said. "We want to see the first dance and hang out with our friends for a bit."

Lily rolled her eyes. "You'll be dancing with Jake for hours. Just be done by eleven so we have time to get changed before we go to church. I don't think we should show up in our party clothes."

Camryn didn't say anything about the *dancing with Jake* comment. If everything went according to plan, she would be doing just that. But that wasn't a sure thing. She'd rejected him when he'd told her he loved her — there was no guarantee he was open to giving her a second chance. Still, she was going to tell him what she'd realized and how she felt about him. No matter what, she wanted him to know that she loved him and thought he was an amazing man. Whatever the outcome, he deserved to hear that from her.

They made their way to the bride's room. Paisley had offered it to all her friends, so they wouldn't have to drive over in their fancy dresses. Camryn opened the door and saw Shaye, Reggie and River were already there.

"You all look amazing," she said, ushering her sisters inside.

The twins hung their dresses on the rack by the wall, then rushed over to River and circled her, admiring her dress.

"I love the color," Victoria said. "We can't wear that shade of red, but it looks incredible on you."

Camryn walked over to her friend. "You are a beautiful Snow Queen."

River's smile didn't quite reach her eyes. "Thanks."

"You doing okay?"

"I think so."

Camryn lowered her voice. "Jake will be here. You're not going to be standing there by yourself."

as Snow Queen." The older woman's stern expression softened. "You've done well and we're all proud to have had you as part of our town holiday season." Her mouth thinned. "Unlike some other people who stepped down from their role, but let's not talk about that."

"Yes, we'll keep to happier topics," Paisley said, putting her arms around each twin. "Ladies, we're amazing. Let us go dazzle the ordinary mortals attending the ball."

They followed her out of the room and down the hall. Camryn told herself she could do this — she could tell Jake how she felt. She was stronger than she realized and she was in love with a wonderful man. All in all, she'd been very blessed and it was time for her to start acting like it.

River hadn't expected the ballroom to be so full. There were at least three hundred people there, all dressed for the occasion. There was a small orchestra and a huge dance floor where she would be expected to waltz with Jake in a few minutes. Just looking at the empty space made her heart pound and her mouth go dry. Honestly, she didn't think she could go through with it.

But there was no turning back. The second her steps faltered, Geri grabbed her arm and pulled her toward the small stage at the end of the room.

"There's no time for nerves," the other woman said firmly. "You'll do fine."

River was too busy trying to slow her breathing to actually speak.

Once they reached the stage, Geri released her arm. "I've decided against you wearing your crown. It's not exactly something that seems appropriate at a ball. Plus, with Dylan not being here, it would be odd for just you to have one."

"It also clashes with her dress."

At the sound of the familiar voice, River spun around. Dylan was standing right there, looking amazing in a black tux. When their eyes met, he gave her a slight smile.

"You look extraordinarily beautiful," he said. "I had a feeling you would. Plus, no Snow King should miss the first dance with his Snow Queen."

His smile faded. "Unless you'd rather dance with Jake."

She knew he was asking more than his six-word statement implied. Was she still angry with him? Was she willing to perhaps listen to him? Were they finished or was there a chance they could make it work? At least that was what she assumed he meant — she couldn't be sure without talking to him.

Geri glared at him. "You're back? Is that what you're saying? You expect to show up and dance the first dance with River, even after you resigned?"

He kept his gaze on River. "That's up to her."

"Can we have a second?" she asked Geri.

The older woman sighed. "The ball is due to start right at seven."

Dylan was already reaching for River's hand. "Five minutes," he promised.

"Fine." Geri's tone lacked graciousness.

Dylan pulled River behind the stage, then shifted so he was in front of her. He took both her hands in his.

"I'm sorry," he said quickly, meeting her gaze. "I realized a couple of days ago I never apologized for not telling you about the money and for handling the situation so badly. I'm sorry for what I said and how I behaved. I'm sorry I hurt you and that I lied. You were right. By not telling you about the money, I was holding back a big piece of myself. Those actions made you believe I didn't care about you, when I do. I hurt you and I hurt us. I regret that more than I can say. I was thinking about myself and how I was feeling instead of thinking about you."

She felt herself relax a little. "I was wrong,

535

too," she admitted. "I overreacted and then wouldn't listen. It was easier to be mad at you than admit I was scared of falling for you only to find out you didn't want me at all."

His gaze intensified. "I do want you, River. I want us." He gave her a self-deprecating smile. "I also happen to be someone who has about twenty-two million dollars, and having that much money scares me."

"Then you should probably start a foundation or something."

"Yeah, that's what I was thinking, too. I've been doing some reading and it turns out foundations have a board of directors. You'd be good at that."

His statement surprised her. "You'd want me to be a part of your philanthropy work?"

"I think you'd have a lot of great ideas." He glanced toward the stage. "We should probably get going on the dancing thing. That is if you want to dance with me. You never said if you'd prefer Jake."

Her heart was pounding so hard, but out of excitement and happiness, she thought.

"You're the one I want to dance with."

His smile momentarily blinded her, then he surprised her by saying, "I'll be right back."

He walked around the back of the stage.

536

She followed and saw him walking up to the microphone.

"Good evening, everyone," he said, his voice silencing the room.

Geri rushed over. "What's he doing?"

"I have no idea," River said, telling herself she had nothing to fear. Dylan would never deliberately hurt her.

He stood on the stage, gazing out at the crowd, then chuckled. "I'm the Secret Santa."

He explained about his lottery winnings and how he didn't want anyone to know because he thought it would change things, but that he was wrong. The only person it had changed was him.

"I ended up becoming exactly what I didn't want to be," he explained. "I was defined by money. So I'm telling you all now and I'll accept the consequences of that."

"We're not going to treat you differently," a man yelled.

"Trust us," a woman shouted.

Dylan grinned. "I'll do my best. I'll still be supporting projects in town, but I'm going to start a foundation. I'm not sure what I want to focus on, so feel free to give me your suggestions. Now, let's get this ball started. I have the privilege of dancing with the most beautiful Snow Queen ever."

He nodded at the orchestra and they started playing. Dylan stepped off the stage and walked to River. She moved toward him as he pulled her into his arms.

He leaned close and whispered, "Back, side, close, forward, side, close."

She smiled. "I remember."

They began to move. She felt everyone watching them. Nerves and fear struggled to take control, but instead of giving in, she let herself get lost in Dylan's gaze. He would keep her safe.

It took her a couple of minutes to relax into the waltz. Once she found her rhythm, she was able to steady her breathing and think about what had just happened.

"Now everyone knows your secret," she said.

He shook his head. "No more secrets. Not from you. Not ever. I mean that, River. I am sorry and I've learned my lesson." He hesitated. "I'm hoping you'll give us another chance. I think we're good together."

Her insides got all fluttery. "I think we are, too. I need to apologize, as well. I didn't listen and I was too quick to assume the worst. I should have pushed back when you didn't tell me about those women. I should have been more understanding when you told me why."

"So maybe we agree to forgive and start this thing over?"

She smiled. "How about we agree to forgive and talk the next time something goes wrong? Then we start in the middle, because I think that's where we are."

Just then the music shifted to another song and everyone joined them on the dance floor. Dylan guided her to the edge of the room. As the other dancers moved past them, he pulled her close and pressed his mouth to hers. River gave herself over to his kiss.

Later, she would invite him to join her and her family at church. After Christmas, she wanted to make sure they sat down and talked everything through, so they understood what had happened and agreed on how they would do better next time. But for now, for this glorious happy moment, there was only Dylan and how he made her feel.

He drew back and touched her cheek. "I know it's too soon to be saying how much I care about you, but I want you to know that I'm committed to you and to us."

"Me, too."

He smiled. "Merry Christmas, River."

"Merry Christmas, Dylan."

And then he kissed her again.

■ ■ ■ ■

Camryn searched through the crowd, hoping to spot Jake. As soon as she saw Dylan walk up to River, she'd wondered if Jake was here at all. Dylan would have mentioned his plan to show up and dance with River so there wasn't any reason for Jake to bother with the ball.

After ten minutes of looking, she was forced to admit he wasn't here. She tried to hide her disappointment as she watched River and Dylan take to the dance floor.

They looked good together, she told herself. And they were talking, which was good. Hopefully, everything would work out between them. She saw her sisters talking with Paisley and started in their direction. Maybe watching other people dance wouldn't be that interesting and they could leave early. The last thing she wanted to do was spend Christmas Eve in a crowd, while missing Jake.

"I believe you promised me a dance."

She looked up and saw Jake walking toward her. He was tall and handsome in his tailored tux and he'd come to the ball, even knowing he wasn't needed for the first dance.

For a second she thought about trying to act calm and unaffected, but then told herself there was no point in hiding her feelings when she planned to confess them to him. She picked up her full skirt and ran to close the distance between them. Jake caught her and hauled her against him. Before she could start speaking, his mouth settled on hers.

She wrapped her arms around him and sank into the kiss. Around them the other dancers moved on the dance floor, but she and Jake stayed where they were, hanging on as if they would never let go.

"I screwed up," she said when the kiss finally ended. "Jake, I'm sorry. I was so scared of loving and belonging. That's why I wanted to leave and that's why I couldn't listen when you told me you loved me. It was too much and I didn't trust myself to be okay. I acted like I was still broken from all the loss and maybe I am a little, but I'm strong, too."

She pressed her hands against his chest and stared into his eyes. "I want to stay here in Wishing Tree. I want to take care of my sisters and run Wrap Around the Clock and I want us to be together."

Fear nudged her, but she ignored it. She loved this man and she wanted him to know.

"I love you," she said proudly. "I love you so much. You are everything I've ever wanted and I can't believe you told me you loved me and I ran. I won't run again, I swear. I want us to be together — you, me, my sisters and Tinsel." She paused, thinking she might be taking things a little too far.

"What I mean is I'd like us to keep dating exclusively." She felt herself blush. "I wasn't pushing for anything more."

His smile was slow and sexy. "You can't push me, Camryn. I'm already there. I love you and I want all that you said. You, me, the twins and Tinsel. I want that forever. I want us."

Happiness made her giddy. "Me, too."

"Do the twins know you dumped me?"

"I didn't dump you," she protested. "I was finding my way."

"Uh-huh. Do they know?"

She shook her head. "I said we were both busy with work and holiday stuff. They think everything is fine."

"Interesting. So you weren't really letting me go."

She smiled. "I guess not."

"My mother will be relieved. She kept telling me you hadn't told her you weren't coming to dinner tomorrow and that I should take that as a good sign." He kissed her. "You were kind of cutting things close with that."

"I know, but once I realized I loved you and that you were going to be here at the dance, I thought we'd figure it out then."

He motioned to someone behind her. She turned and saw her sisters approaching.

"Jake!" Lily ran up and hugged him.

Victoria joined her. "We've missed you."

"I've missed you, too."

"You're coming to church with us, aren't you?" Lily asked. "Camryn said you were doing stuff with your mom, but we're all going to the same place, so we should definitely sit together."

"We should." He looked at them. "I want to marry your sister, but I want to make sure that's okay with both of you first."

Camryn nearly fainted. She'd hoped and maybe assumed, but she hadn't been totally sure he wanted that much of a future with her. The twins squealed and hugged him again.

"Yes!" Victoria shrieked. "Yes, yes, yes."

"Absolutely," Lily agreed. She turned to Camryn. "Victoria and I have already talked about this with Helen, so we're going to move into the big house on the lake and she'll take Jake's condo and then the three of us will rent out our house. Victoria and I will put our share away so that when we finish college, we'll both have a nest egg to help us get started. You can use your share however you want."

Jake shook his head. "I'm going to have to have another talk with my mother."

Camryn tried to take it all in. "Maybe we should wait on planning where we live."

The twins grinned at her. "Sure," Victoria said. "We'll talk about it in January." She looked at Jake. "Your mom said to tell you that she wants the whole place repainted. That gray you picked is too cold for her. She likes warmer colors. But the primary bath is perfect."

"My mother," he grumbled, but with a hint of affection in his tone. "Okay, I've been waiting all night to dance with your sister. Give us a half hour to enjoy ourselves, then I'll pick up my mom and we'll meet at your place so we can all go to church together."

The twins nodded.

Camryn and Jake joined the other dancers, their bodies moving together as he guided her around the floor.

"I'm clear on the fact that I haven't officially proposed," he said, smiling at her. "I was waiting for a little privacy and time."

She did her best not to giggle. "That's a

good idea."

"So not tomorrow."

"Probably not."

"Could you maybe leave work early on Monday?" he asked. "The twins and Tinsel could stay with my mom." His expression turned wry. "I have a feeling she'll happily change all her plans."

"Monday will be super quiet at the store," she told him. "So yes, I can get away."

"Then it's a date."

Her heart fluttered with happiness. "It is."

Despite not getting to bed until well after one in the morning, Camryn awakened a little after five. She should be exhausted, but she was too excited about the fact that it was Christmas and that she was spending the day with Jake and Helen and her sisters. She had a feeling that the twins, for all their talk about opening presents super early, wouldn't make an appearance until at least nine. Still plenty of time for gifts and blueberry waffles before Jake picked them up at noon.

She showered and dressed in jeans and a Christmas sweater. As she passed Lily's bedroom, she saw Tinsel curled up on the bed. The little dog raised her head, gave her a look that clearly said, "No way I'm getting

545

up this early," then closed her eyes and went back to sleep. Camryn chuckled as she quietly walked down the stairs.

Last night had been magical, she thought as she walked into the kitchen. She and Jake confessing their feelings, him asking the twins for their permission to marry her, the dance, then midnight services together. She couldn't remember being happier.

She started coffee and opened the refrigerator to pull out milk, only to jump when someone tapped on the back door. She spun toward the sound and saw Jake standing on their back porch. She rushed over and let him in.

"What are you doing here?" she asked. "It's five in the morning."

He leaned in and kissed her. "I've been lurking in your driveway for half an hour," he admitted. "I couldn't sleep and I wanted to see you, so I've been watching for lights to go on."

Warmth flooded her. "You could have called or texted."

"I wanted you to get your sleep. I didn't mind waiting." His hazel eyes softened with love. "I've been planning our future."

She grinned. "Have you? What did you decide?"

"Not decide so much as considered. Moving into the house on the lake isn't the worst idea in the world."

"It's big and gorgeous," she said. "Does it come with staff?"

She'd been teasing, but instead of laughing, Jake nodded. "No one lives in but there's a full-time gardener and a housekeeper, along with a twice weekly maid service."

Her mouth dropped open. "I totally forgot that you're rich."

"Yeah, I know." He sounded smug. "You're getting quite the package when you're with me."

She laughed. "I'll keep reminding myself of that."

"You should."

The coffeepot finished brewing. She poured them each a cup and they sat at the table.

"It's good Dylan and River are back together," he said. "They seemed happy when we saw them at church last night."

"I can't wait to hear what happened," she admitted. "Maybe I'll get some details this afternoon. They're a cute couple."

"Not as cute as us."

He put down his coffee, stood, then sat back in his seat. She couldn't read his expression, but she sensed something was wrong.

"Jake?"

He looked at her. "I don't want to wait. I couldn't sleep because I was planning tomorrow and it's going to be epic. I'm talking a big suite at the hotel and flowers and a fancy dinner served in our room. You're going to be dazzled."

She squeezed his hand. "I don't need any of that to be dazzled by you."

"When I picked up my mom before swinging by to get you and the twins, I told her what happened."

She was trying to follow the conversation. "I know. She was happy."

He stunned her by dropping to one knee. "Camryn, I love you. You're the most amazing woman I've ever known and I want to spend the rest of my life making you happy." He paused. "I'm doing this again, in the room, with the flowers and the dinner, but I also don't want to wait to know what your answer is going to be. Will you marry me?"

"Yes," she said, tugging him to his feet and throwing herself at him. "I love you, Jake, and of course I'll marry you."

He swung her around the kitchen, then lowered her to her feet and kissed her. Just when things were getting interesting, he drew back and reached into his pocket.

"The choice is yours," he told her, showing her a beautiful square-cut diamond ring created in an Art-Deco style. "This was my grandmother's but if you want something different, it's totally fine."

"It's beautiful," she whispered, blinking away tears. "I love it."

She held out her hand and he slid the ring in place. It fit perfectly. "The twins are going to be so excited." She kissed him. "I love you."

"I love you, too." He glanced at the ceiling. "So, um, how late do you think they're going to sleep?"

She took his hand in hers and tugged him toward the stairs. "We should have at least two hours, maybe three."

Once they reached her bedroom, he closed and locked the door, then turned to her.

"We'll give ourselves an hour," he said in a quiet voice. "Just to be sure we're dressed and downstairs before they're awake." His mouth settled on hers.

As she gave herself to the man who had claimed her heart, Camryn knew that today was going to be the perfect start for all the days they would have together. She felt certain about their future and their love . . . and all the Christmases to follow.

The employees of Thorndike Press hope you have enjoyed this Large Print book. All our Thorndike, Wheeler, and Kennebec Large Print titles are designed for easy reading, and all our books are made to last. Other Thorndike Press Large Print books are available at your library, through selected bookstores, or directly from us.

For information about titles, please call:
(800) 223-1244

or visit our website at:
gale.com/thorndike

To share your comments, please write:
Publisher
Thorndike Press
10 Water St., Suite 310
Waterville, ME 04901